PHARMAKON

FICTION BY DIRK WITTENBORN

Fierce People

Zoe

PHARMAKON

DIRK WITTENBORN

VIKING

VIKING
Published by the Penguin Group
Penguin Group (USA) Inc., 375 Hudson Street, New York, New York 10014, U.S.A.
Penguin Group (Canada), 90 Eglinton Avenue East, Suite 700, Toronto, Ontario, Canada M4P 2Y3 (a division of Pearson Penguin Canada Inc.)
Penguin Books Ltd, 80 Strand, London WC2R 0RL, England
Penguin Ireland, 25 St. Stephen's Green, Dublin 2, Ireland (a division of Penguin Books Ltd)
Penguin Books Australia Ltd, 250 Camberwell Road, Camberwell, Victoria 3124, Australia (a division of Pearson Australia Group Pty Ltd)
Penguin Books India Pvt Ltd, 11 Community Centre, Panchsheel Park, New Delhi—110 017, India
Penguin Grtoup (NZ), 67 Apollo Drive, Rosedale, North Shore 0632, New Zealand (a division of Pearson New Zealand Ltd)
Penguin Books (South Africa) (Pty) Ltd, 24 Sturdee Avenue, Rosebank, Johannesburg 2196, South Africa

Penguin Books Ltd, Registered Offices: 80 Strand, London WC2R 0RL, England

First Published in 2008 by Viking Penguin, a member of Penguin Group (USA) Inc.

PUBLISHER'S NOTE: This is a work of fiction. Names, characters, places, and incidents either are the product of the author's imagination or are used fictitiously, and any resemblance to actual persons, living or dead, business establishments, events, or locales is entirely coincidental.

ISBN-13: 978-1-60751-629-3

Printed in the United States of America

For Kirsten and Lilo

In memory of J. R. Wittenborn, PhD

PHARMAKON

PROLOGUE

I was born because a man came to kill my father. If he hadn't showed up with a gun in his pocket and bad thoughts in his head, I wouldn't exist, much less have a story to tell. This tragic footnote to my conception left me feeling as if I had three parents: a father, a mother, and a murderer.

My father suffered from strange and temporarily paralyzing attacks of catatonia that my family, with characteristic discretion, referred to as Dad's "Sock Moments." You would walk past my parents' bedroom door on the way to breakfast or the bathroom and glimpse Dad sitting on his side of the bed, fully dressed, legs crossed, one shoe on, sock in hand, about to put on his other shoe. Perfectly normal, right? Trouble was, sometimes ten or twenty minutes would pass, and you'd look in on him again, and he'd still be sitting there, sock in hand, staring at the other shoe he'd yet to fill.

Once my sister Lucy and I clocked him with the timer my mother used to make sure the roast beef was rare. Fifty-seven minutes passed before he got the other sock on. Frozen in time and space in his own thoughts, Dad would appear perfectly normal, except for the look he'd have in his eye. It wasn't a faraway, glassy-eyed stare; it was a perplexed squint, as if he were trying to see something he wasn't sure was there.

My father could have three episodes in a week, then there'd be a six-month reprieve. Usually, but not always, these becalmed fits of melancholic introspection would come over him in the morning as he readied himself to set off for work. But sometimes they'd ambush him in the evening, when he went upstairs just for a moment to put on a fresh shirt or wash his hands or get my mother her purse. Occasionally, according to my mom, they'd even bushwhack him after midnight, when a dry mouth or a bad dream would wake him, and he'd reach for his slippers with the thought of heading downstairs to make himself a cup of tea or a stiff drink. Only he'd never get there. Technically, those weren't Sock Moments, because my mother would wake up and find her husband cradling a slipper. But the question remained the same: What was going on in Dad's head?

Once, when I was eight, and Dad was lost in his bedroom with nothing but a sock to show him The Way Home, I snuck into the room, tiptoed past him, and slipped into his big closet. He used it as a dressing room. It was the grandest thing about the house we lived in then; it was a long, narrow, wondrous little right triangle of a room tucked under the stairs to the attic. It had a round window at one end that offered a view of nothing but sky, and it smelled of cedar and shoe polish and dust from parts of his life that were none of a small boy's business.

I knew I was trespassing. The closet was Dad's private space, to be entered only at his personal invitation and explored under his supervision. There were bone-handled pocketknives to be opened and closed, fly rods to be assembled, and a wooden crate that once held a dozen bottles of Château d'Yquem but now was home to the collection of Indian arrowheads and stone tomahawks he'd found in freshly plowed fields and unearthed in serpentine burial mounds during what had passed for a boyhood in his hardscrabble, Midwestern youth. But his hospitality had its limits. Even when I was a baby, if I crawled too far back in his closet and tried to open the old steamer trunk, latched, strapped closed, and too heavy to lift, visiting hour would be over. My father would pull me away from it as if it were radioactive, and in the grown-up voice he used with doctors who came to our house to talk to him, he'd announce, "Nothing in there pertains to you."

I remember asking him once, "Then why can't I look in it?"

"I've lost the key" was what he said, but I didn't believe it. I just figured that's where Dad kept his real treasure, and he didn't want anyone to know because he was afraid they'd steal it.

Back when I was invading Dad's private space at age eight I felt guilty on two counts: I was doing what I had been told not to do, and worse, I was taking unfair advantage of what seemed to be, until several decades later, my father's only weakness—his Sock Moments. Whether out of my own innate sense of fairness or fear of the great man paralyzed on the edge of the bed, I did not go directly to the trunk that loomed so large in my imagination. Instead, I contented myself with taking out the Indian artifacts. A noisy child by nature, prone to talking to myself out loud, I retold the stories he had shared with me about the Indian tribes that had lorded over the state of Illinois long before he was born; the Kaskaskia, the Cahokia, and the Peoria tribes, all decimated by their brethren, the Iroquois, in the Beaver Wars. But it wasn't the same. I wanted his voice; I wanted him to come back from wherever he was in his Sock Moment; I wanted him to hear me. Anything was preferable to the loneliness I felt knowing he could be so close and yet still so far away.

Suddenly desperate to break the spell that held him, I did the worst thing I could imagine, far more forbidden and dangerous and unforgivable than opening the trunk: I stood up on the overturned wine box, pulled out the squeaky top drawer of his head-high dresser, and took hold of the loaded .38 caliber long-barreled Smith & Wesson revolver he kept on top of his clean handkerchiefs.

He was so far gone even the sound of me opening the forbidden gun drawer did not wake him. Not even the click of me closing the cylinder snapped him out of whatever held him captive. *What if Dad never woke up? What if he never came back from this Sock Moment? What if he stayed petrified like that forever?*

Missing him, wanting him, needing him, and mad at him, I pulled back the hammer of the big pistol. My hands shook, my finger closed on the trigger. If I fired the gun, he'd have to wake up. No matter how severely I'd be punished, at least he'd be with me. An eighth of an ounce of trigger pressure away from bringing the hammer down on the Moment, the thought occurred to me: What if I pulled the trigger and he still didn't wake up?

Then I'd know there was no hope. I lowered the hammer and placed the handgun back onto tomorrow's handkerchief and closed the squeaky drawer.

I went back out into his bedroom and got down on my knees the way you do in church. Taking the argyle sock from his hand, I gently began to pull it onto his long, narrow, white foot.

I watched as my father's eyes focused down on me. They were gray, pearly, and wet, like the inside of a shell pulled up from the sea with something alive inside it.

"Daddy?" He had a scar shaped like a crescent on his forehead. His hair was gray and cut so short you could see the shape of his skull and the veins feeding his brain like the Visible Man model he had helped me put together.

"Yes?" He still sounded far away.

"What are you thinking?"

"I was thinking about . . ." The sock was on now. He was lacing up the shoe by himself. ". . . how I feel about things."

No question, my mother would have sent him to a good psychologist if Dad wasn't already a shrink himself, a semifamous shrink, in fact: Dr. William T. Friedrich. I failed Psych 1A myself, but I'm told if you made it to the second semester, your professor probably mentioned his name. He was what they used to call a neuropsychopharmacologist. If there's brain candy in your medicine cabinet, chances are my father's messed with your head, too.

BOOK I

DECEMBER 1951

That morning, Dr. Friedrich's first Sock Moment was years away. There was no scar on his forehead, and in place of the receding hairline, there was a thick cowlick of chestnut-colored hair. Back then Will, as he was called, was a thirty-three-year-old untenured, overworked, hollow-eyed ambitious associate professor of psychology at Yale with a wife, four children, a mortgage, and eighty-seven dollars in his bank account until payday.

It was the week before Christmas break. A skull-numbing arctic air mass had driven all things with feathers from the sky. The temperature had been in the single digits all week, and yesterday eleven inches of snow had fallen in as many hours. New Haven was frozen solid.

His car, which in fact wasn't a car but a monstrous old 1938 DeSoto ambulance that his wife had dubbed the "White Whale," wouldn't start. The streetcar he had to take into town was an hour late. When he finally got off at his stop near campus, it was snowing again.

The wind blew in fits. His eyes teared. As sharp flakes swirled up his pants legs, Will wished he'd listened to his wife when she had told him to put on long johns. Rock salt had turned the icy sidewalks to slush, and two blocks into this last leg of his morning's march to work, one of his galoshes began to leak. The week before Nora had told him to buy a new pair.

As ice water slowly filled his left boot, soaked through his shoes, and now squished between the numbness of his toes, he wondered why he had not listened to her. To save a buck making old galoshes last another winter, he had ruined his only pair of good shoes. Now, on top of having to buy a new pair of galoshes, he'd have to blow another five bucks on a pair of Oxfords.

Eager to get out of the cold and impatient for his future to begin, Will began to run. As his heartbeat rose, his mood improved. The cold was still making him cry, but he could at least smile at the memory of a time when snow equaled fun.

Friedrich felt more optimistic about the day he was facing when he stepped inside the building and was greeted by a brigade of buckets and wastepaper baskets collecting water as it dripped down from the ceiling. A janitor looked up from his mop. "Pipes burst. Classes canceled."

As Will happily sloshed down the hallway, he began to plan out a miniholiday for his family. He'd call Nora and tell her to start getting the kids into their snowsuits. They'd pull out the old Flexible Flyer from the garage and take the kids sledding. And afterward, they'd make hot chocolate, and he'd read aloud from *A Christmas Carol* or *Peter Pan* or perhaps . . .

Before Will could settle on which fairy tale to finish the day with, he realized that although the halls were empty of students, the offices were bustling with psychologists of every rank and persuasion—clinical, abnormal, behaviorists, neobehaviorists, humanists, psychoanalytic—all hard at work on research papers, projects, grants, and experiments while he was thinking about sleigh riding.

Yale was the Promised Land for psychologists in 1951. The brightest and the best battled and politicked to come to New Haven. Friedrich felt privileged, even blessed, when he was awarded the position of instructor just after the war. The head of the department, Dr. Hugo Cunningham, had welcomed him and the other newcomers with a faculty tea and the promise that "this department prides itself on being an open, eclectic, noncompetitive sanctuary, where all members of our staff, regardless of rank or tenure, are given a voice, as well as the opportunity to contribute, to work together, as we soldier on to disassemble, demystify, and deconstruct the magic that drives the clockwork of human nature."

Friedrich had later learned that Dr. Cunningham had worked in propaganda during the Second World War. The psychology department may have been a sanctuary for some; it had seemed that way at first, even for Friedrich. But now he saw it as a tweed tower with no way out.

When Friedrich first arrived, he, like everybody else in the building, had believed that if he kept his brain to the grindstone, his brilliance would outshine the brilliance of the guy in the office next door. But it was more complicated than that. With so many sharp minds being honed and wielded in such close quarters, you had to be guarded without seeming to be on your guard. What made the Yale psych department different, and in fact far more competitive, than your average above-average workplace was that everyone who worked there knew that they were being observed by people who had made a career out of judging who and what was and wasn't normal.

All were qualified for greatness, but only one, maybe two, per decade would extract something from their minds so novel and wondrous and inarguable that even their competitors would have to acknowledge the superiority of another's brain. If that happened, you became a full professor. Otherwise you had to wait until the senior colleague in your area of expertise either retired, died, or had a nervous breakdown.

By the time Friedrich had reached the stairway at the end of the hall, he'd put the Flexible Flyer back into the garage. He could smell the animal behaviorists in the basement lording over classrooms filled with mice. His friend Jens claimed to have taught rats to share. Will was just thinking about how much he liked the idea when a scream shocked out of a chimpanzee named Molly echoed up from below.

As he climbed up the stairwell he returned the nod of an elderly renowned therapist who never trimmed his nose hairs, deliberately wore two different colored socks, and encouraged the rumor that he had had an affair with Garbo while treating her for a mild case of agoraphobia. The right eccentricities were valued at Yale.

The third floor housed the head of the department and his favorites. He ran a program called "Communication and Persuasion." They'd all been in the same army unit during World War II, working on ways to tap into the collective subconscious to influence public opinion. Since then they'd formed a chamber music group that played on weekends.

Friedrich's office was on the fourth floor, with the other psychologists who had separated themselves from the pack by mastering the shadowy art of statistics. He and the other young psychometricians were hired guns, not just for the psychology department, but for the psychiatrists over at the med school as well. The ability to reduce the human condition to a set of numbers made them indispensable. They made up the rules and kept the score of the games that were being played among the headshrinkers. Will wanted to be more than a thought accountant.

Some of Friedrich's colleagues specialized in measuring IQ, memory, or senility. Yale had recruited Friedrich for a rating scale he had thought up at an Army Air Corps base in Illinois that was used to measure whether a mental patient was getting saner or crazier, happier or sadder, improving or deteriorating. Even those in the department who thought him brash, lacking in gentility, and possessing a farm boy's chip on his shoulder recognized that the Friedrich Psychiatric Rating Scale could give them the proof needed to convince the department they were on the right track.

On the day of its publication Friedrich felt a sense of pride he had not experienced since the age of twelve, when he'd earned enough money selling eggs from a roadside stand to buy back the family pony that his mother had insisted on selling to a neighbor in that first lean year of the Depression. He and Nora had gone out for chop suey to celebrate. There was just one problem. In the previous five years Friedrich's rating scale had proved only one thing: Ninety-five percent of the people psychologists and psychiatrists treated never got any better. In fact, most of them got worse after seeing a professional. Of course, Will Friedrich didn't talk about that in the psych building.

Last summer a neurologist had asked him to go down to Columbia and help him come up with the data that would prove lobotomies were both brutal and bad medicine. Friedrich administered his tests to patients before and after they received what was then called a "precision lobotomy." To get a clearer picture of the damage that was being done, Friedrich augmented the tests by asking patients who were under local anesthesia a series of simple, mathematical questions while the scalpel was cutting into their frontal lobe.

"What's one plus one? Two plus three? Count backward from a hundred." He could still see the face of the teenage girl with curly black hair who had been sentenced to neurosurgery by her parents. When Mom and Dad found out she had contracted syphilis at Wellesley, they had sent her to a state mental health facility. Shortly after her arrival, she had attempted suicide.

"Eighty-eight, 87, 86, 8 . . ." Will could still hear that girl counting down the last seconds she had to be herself, then gasping a sigh and mumbling, "What comes next?"

Friedrich's findings did not make him popular among those PhDs and MDs at Yale who were on the lobotomy bandwagon. Will knew it was just a matter of time before the numbers he and others came up with put the lobotomists out of business. But that didn't make him feel any less guilty for having interrogated a teenager on simple math while someone broke into her brain and stole her soul. Friedrich hadn't performed the operation, or ordered it, or put her in a loony bin. He hadn't cut into her head—it would have happened even if he hadn't been there. But he had watched it happen and done nothing to stop it. And that bothered him.

Throwing off his overcoat and kicking off his galoshes, Will slumped into his desk chair. There were a half dozen different research projects he could have started. He had toyed with the idea of doing studies on foster children, senility, and a half dozen other dark corners of health care that could have benefited from the spotlight of his mind, but Friedrich's ego couldn't shake the vain notion that somewhere in him was a big idea that could make the world a saner place.

As he reached for a yellow pad to make notes, a pencil fell off his desk. It was an early Christmas gift from the head of the department. Embossed on the pencil were the words "Publish or Perish." Friedrich snapped it in two, pulled on a leaky boot, and reached for his overcoat.

Will ran toward the exit. As he headed out the front door the janitor called out, "Where are you off to in such a hurry, Dr. Friedrich?"

"Christmas shopping for my kids."

"I'm glad somebody in here has some sense."

Feeling like an escapee from an institution, Friedrich whistled along to the Salvation Army band on Main Street and spun himself through the revolving doors of the first department store he came to. He had no trouble finding the children's department, and the robotic reindeer that pranced across the rooftops of a gingerbread palace worthy of the "Mad" King Ludwig was impressive. But the toys depressed him.

Gifts he could afford were either made of plastic or looked like they'd been sewn together by a sweatshop worker wearing mittens. There were big-ticket items he didn't have the money for but would have loved to find under his Christmas tree, even if he were a girl, like a chemistry set claiming to contain "everything needed to perform real scientific experiments at home": a crystal-radio kit, complete with its own soldering iron. But when he opened the box all he found was an assortment of chemicals available under your average kitchen sink, a nickel's worth of wire, some pegboard, and a soldering iron guaranteed to set off an electrical fire.

A saleswoman tapped him on the shoulder. "You opened the box."

"I'm sorry. I just wanted to see what was inside."

"It says what's inside right on the plastic wrapper."

"Yeah, but I wanted to see for myself."

"Well, you have, and that will be $8.54."

Will Friedrich was in the bar of the faculty club now, self-medicating with a beer, trying to think what his mother called "pleasant thoughts," i.e., trying to cheer himself up before he boarded the streetcar home. He felt contagious. Self-absorbed but not selfish, he did not want to infect his family with his mood.

If he couldn't buy what he wanted for his children, he would make them something they would never forget, create something that would give them memories he wished he had. He would go to the lumberyard, get wood, finishing nails, and little brass hinges and glue and construct a dollhouse. It would be for the girls, mostly, but his sons, ages three and almost two, were too young to think it so gender-specific that they would feel overlooked or emasculated. Yes, a wonderful dollhouse, three stories high, with windows big enough for little hands to reach inside, and floors that could be raised and lowered so that his progeny could get a sense of the three-dimensionality of the world and develop their spatial thinking.

But before the dollhouse was half built in his head, Friedrich began to pull it down. Imagining the girls fighting over it Christmas morning, Jack choking to death on one of the little plastic shrubs he was going to plant outside. Jack put everything in his mouth; last week he was nearly murdered by a cat's-eye marble.

Still thinking about the box he was in, Friedrich's mind moved out of the dollhouse and attempted to distract itself from his melancholy by constructing a whole new future for himself. He could leave Yale. Why not take his doctorate in psychology to where the money was: advertising.

For a brief, giddy moment on that bar stool he imagined himself working in a Madison Avenue ad agency. Living in a penthouse on Park Avenue, applying his insights to the frailties of the human mind, to creating subliminal ad campaigns, questionnaires that tricked the consumer into revealing what really made them willing to pay more for toilet paper.

Why not just pack it in and go for the gold . . . why not? I'm thirty-three, I have a wife, children, I'm too old to start a new career, and even if I wasn't, I'd have to begin at the bottom. I wouldn't even be able to afford to live in Manhattan. Besides, Friedrich didn't want to be an ad man any more than he wanted to sell his skill set to one of the foundations that funneled CIA money to clever young men at Yale.

Dr. Friedrich tried to remember why he had become a psychologist. If he'd had two more beers, or an audience, Will Friedrich would have answered that question with a glib and not entirely untrue "because it was the Depression and I didn't have the money to go to med school and become a real doctor."

Instead he thought of his mother and his older brother, Homer, and that other institution she packed her first-born off to the day after Will had left for his freshman year of college. He didn't discover what she'd done with Homer until he came home for Thanksgiving and found his mother holding a séance in Homer's bedroom. That was the fall she'd become a devotee of Madame Blavatsky and theosophy. It had taken him five days to hitchhike east to the New Jersey State Hospital at Trenton. He found Homer playing his harmonica in a caged room, while nearby a naked woman he could now diagnose as a classic schizophrenic finger-painted with her feces.

Homer didn't seem any worse for wear until he turned his head. The left side of his jaw was caved in. It looked like someone had taken a trowel to the inside of his mouth. Dr. Cotton, the director of Trenton, had pulled out a half-dozen of Homer's teeth based on his well-respected and much publicized theory that bacteria from tooth decay and the small bowel were the causes of dementia praecox.

Homer and his bowel had been scheduled to go under the doctor's knife the next day. Getting his big brother released before surgery cost Will the rest of his college money. He still didn't know why Homer couldn't always spell his own name and thought nothing of rocking for three or four hours at a time repeating the same phrase over and over again: "If it's not raining, you don't need an umbrella" was the one that was playing in Friedrich's head now. Will Friedrich wasn't sure if he'd become a psychologist to cure Homer or forgive his mother; all he knew was he hadn't succeeded at either.

What did occur to Friedrich at that moment was that one of the reasons he had lost faith in psychoanalysis—the unearthing of old wounds, the deconstruction of dreams, the dissection of fantasies and choices of words—was that after years of analyzing himself, he wasn't an iota happier. Exhausted, drained, and dissatisfied by a lifetime of picking his own scabs, he wanted to heal his patients, not listen to them bleed. He had enough of that in his own head.

Laughter erupted from the table behind him. A gang of Yale profs were holding court under a halo of cigarette smoke. He'd seen them at the club before. They always commandeered the same booth. Had they come in while he was building the dollhouse or thinking about Homer? Whatever, they were on their second round of cocktails and, as usual, were having a hell of a lot more fun than he was.

The five faculty members at the table belonged to a subset of academia Friedrich's wife called PWM—professors with money, either inherited or married into. Their vowels were polished by boarding school; they swam and played tennis at the New Haven Lawn Club; and they sent their children to a private school called Hamden Hall and "summered" in places Friedrich had never heard of much less wanted to be invited to until he had "come east." They prided themselves on knowing famous Negroes, having best friends who happened to be Jewish, signing anti-McCarthy petitions, and loving abstract art. All of which combined to make them feel superior to your average everyday garden variety snob, not to mention Friedrich and everybody else in the world.

The only member of the gang Friedrich recognized by name was Dr. Winton. Even if she hadn't been the first and only female instructor of psychiatry at Yale medical school, Bunny Winton would have stood out. She was over six feet tall, counting the long red braid she coiled on top of her head like a snake. Forty years old, she looked a decade younger. Her skin was pale, white, and translucent, like skimmed milk, and she was never seen outdoors without a hat. While her fellow profs had cocktails, she imbibed a cup of hot water—she'd brought her own tea. Plainly smart, in a tweed suit—just in case you didn't notice she was special even among the table full of men who had made careers out of being special—she wore a gold pre-Columbian frog on a leather thong around her neck.

"Best martini in the world," called out the man in the herringbone suit.

"21," boasted the guy who was cleaning his glasses with the end of an orange-and-black tie that he wore to let you know he went to Princeton.

"21's for tourists . . . Bath & Tennis, Newport."

"Harry's Bar." The only Harry's Bar Will Friedrich knew was in Evanston, Illinois. "San Marco, Venezia . . ."

Bunny Winton had the last word without looking up from the article she was reading in the *Lancet.* "It's the ten to one formula, gin to vermouth." Whereas the others smelled of money, she stank.

"How would you know, Bunny? You don't even drink."

"My father did. And besides, you don't have to have a weakness to appreciate it in others." She was bored with the game. She'd played along just to remind the old boys she could beat them at their own game.

A history professor he'd seen tooting around campus in a red sports car with the top down, even in the rain, sagely posed the next point of debate: "Happiest people in the world."

"You mean, besides us?" Everybody at the table laughed. Friedrich mouthed the words "horse's ass" and asked for his check.

"Firemen. They're heroes, everybody loves them, and they get to spend three weeks out of four away from their wives."

"Doesn't count, Fred," Bunny protested.

"What are you talking about?" Fred was the history professor.

"Women can't be firemen. You said 'happiest *people*.'" Dr. Winton held up her empty cup, signaling for more hot water.

"Women are people?" The group thought this was a scream.

Bunny laughed. Not at his joke but at the one she was about to make: "We're just like you boys, only smarter. Believe me, if there were a way to do without you, we would have thought it up a long time ago."

The prof with the beard thoughtfully stirred his drink with his forefinger. "I've got it. Happiest people are . . . soldiers, nurses, or doctors of either sex . . ." he lifted his drink in acknowledgment of Bunny, ". . . still in uniform, on the way home from a war they've won thinking about the sweetheart that's waiting for them at home who they don't know has been cheating on them."

"I thought we were talking about real people, not characters in one of your novels." Bunny had a nice way of making you feel stupid.

"Okay, Doc, what's the right answer?"

"The Bagadong."

"You're making that up."

"No, I'm quite serious. They're a tribe in New Guinea. We had a field hospital near their village during the war." She was Bunny Rutledge when she'd signed up straight out of medical school. When the U.S. Army refused to promise the woman doc a combat zone assignment at the start of the war, Bunny had taken the train to Canada and wangled a commission in the British Army.

"Are you talking about cannibals?"

"They are, among other things." Bunny smiled as she sipped her tea.

"You're telling us eating their enemies makes them happy?"

"I think it had more to do with fermented kwina leaves. The shamans call it '*gai kau dong*.' It means 'The Way Home.' They take it after bad things happen to them, after stressful events. Head-hunting trip gone wrong, child being eaten by a crocodile. And of course, they give it to girls after ritualized clitoral circumcision with a flint scalpel." Bunny Winton was having so much fun shocking the men that she didn't notice Friedrich taking notes on his cocktail napkin.

FEBRUARY 1952

Though they had never spoken or corresponded, Friedrich had learned all sorts of things about Dr. Bunny Winton over the previous two months. A trip to the library had told him that she had attended Radcliffe and Yale medical school, and worked out of Yale's pillared and domed Institute of Human Relations. He had dropped by IHR in the hopes of bumping into her. It didn't happen, but he did discover that the previously all-male department had decided she deserved office space commensurate with her first and only woman on the faculty status—her desk was wedged into a six-by-eight cubicle that before her arrival had been home to the janitor's mops, buckets, and brooms.

Behind her back they called her "Dr. Bunny." And scrawled above a urinal in the second-floor men's room, he had found a dirty limerick about Bunny that included her home phone number.

By coincidence, a graduate student at IHR named June, who came to him for therapy on Thursdays and whose husband wanted her to quit therapy and grad school to have babies, had brought up Dr. Winton's name in a session. She identified Winton as her role model, and worried that she didn't have the "intestinal fortitude" to put up with what Dr. Winton had to put up with.

All Friedrich had to say was "What do you think she puts up with?" and he was treated to an in-depth rehash of how Winton had written a paper about a study she had conducted entirely by herself on the use of hypnotics to bring out a patient's thought process. When she submitted it for publication, her name alone graced the title page, but when it appeared in print, the name of a male psychiatrist who was younger and less intelligent appeared on its cover first, even though her last-minute collaborator's surname started with the letter Y. Friedrich felt worse about what had happened to Winton than he did about milking one of his patients for information.

Will Friedrich couldn't remember where he'd overheard the gossip passing for gospel that Bunny had been hired solely because her uncle had already given Yale Rutledge Hall, and university elders were hoping Uncle would write another check. But nothing he learned changed his original opinion of Winton. He still thought she was spoiled and a snob, but he sensed that she had one quality he could both relate to and take advantage of: She was hungry.

What he didn't know was if he could trust her. But he would soon find that out, since at that moment Will was riding up the elevator to the office Dr. Winton retreated to when the broom closet became claustrophobic. She saw her private patients just off campus in the penthouse of a smart, professional building on Chapel Street. Will could have arranged a meeting in her broom closet at IHR, or at his office over in the psych building. But he did not want to run the risk of having other men's names attached to the idea he was carrying inside his head.

Friedrich knocked on the door. It buzzed open with an electric click. Bunny had a receptionist/secretary, but she was out to lunch. Her waiting room was decorated with Salvador Dalí drawings and a Corbusier leather couch. They shook hands. "I'm Dr. Winton."

"Will Friedrich."

She glanced at the small suitcase he was carrying and eyeballed him up and down as if she were trying to guess his height and weight. He had on his best suit, and yet her gaze made him feel shabby. That wasn't Dr. Winton's intention. It was just that he didn't look like an insurance executive who wore women's underwear, the patient she had never met but was expecting.

She gestured toward the room with a view of the green where she conducted her therapy sessions, taking note that he took the Danish modern recliner upholstered in pony fur and let her sit on the couch.

"So . . ." She smiled. "What brings you here, Mr. Friedrich?" She had a small notebook and a gold pen in her lap.

"Curiosity." Friedrich tried to sound casual, but there was an edge to his voice—he was nervous. She was looking at his hands. They were nicked with scars. He found himself wondering whether she read them as a sign of hard work or a propensity for violence. Friedrich knew he was projecting, and shook the thought out of his head.

"What specifically are you curious about?" She fingered the gold frog around her neck.

"Depression."

"What about it?"

"How to get rid of it."

"Your wife told me she's noticed a change in you."

"You've talked to my wife about me?"

"I thought you knew."

Realizing she thought he was a patient, Friedrich decided to make the most of it and play dumb. "Gosh, what'd she have to say?"

"Well, that she's disturbed and confused."

"About what?"

"You're not the first male patient I've had who's found it arousing to wear women's undergarments."

Her stare was unblinking, her voice professional. Giving her credit for that, he threw his head back and began to laugh. "I'm sorry, Dr. Winton, I think you have me mixed up with a patient. I'm a psychologist over at the psych department. I made an appointment with your secretary." Putting people on the defensive always made Friedrich feel more comfortable.

Friedrich smiled innocently as she checked her secretary's appointment book. He could tell she wasn't convinced that he wasn't suffering from delusions as well as erotic confusion.

"My mistake, Dr. Friedrich. I should have recognized your name." Had she heard of him, or was she just being the kind of phony rich people called being polite? "So, what brings you here?"

"I've been thinking about something I overheard you say at the faculty club a couple of months ago." Friedrich had his suitcase on his lap.

"I'm sorry, but for the life of me I don't recall having been introduced to you or ever having . . ."

Friedrich cut her short. "We didn't meet. I was eavesdropping on a conversation you were having about the happiest people on the planet; you mentioned something called The Way Home?"

"*Gai kau dong.*" As she slowly pronounced the words, Friedrich noticed that there were two photographs on her desk. He guessed the glamour shot of the guy on the yacht was her husband. He could tell the other one was taken during the war—it showed a younger Bunny, hair cut as short as a boy's, sitting in a dugout canoe wearing khaki shorts and mud-caked boots, an Enfield jungle carbine slung across her back.

"So what is it about The Way Home that interests you?"

"How do you know it's the plant your shamans brew up that's affecting behavior, and not superstition, the power of suggestion?"

Friedrich watched her smooth the wrinkles in her dress before she answered. "In the fall of 1944, I had a patient, a lieutenant in the Royal Engineers. In addition to suffering from malaria, dysentery, and the usual assortment of jungle parasites, he had been a Japanese prisoner for six months." She looked out the window. Her voice softened. "And in that camp, there was a Japanese sergeant, a textbook sadist, homosexual tendencies; he did things, unspeakable things, to my lieutenant . . ."

Friedrich took note of her use of the personal pronoun. Dr. Winton caught herself as soon as she said it: "I say 'my' because we were all such a long way from home, and the young men in those hospitals suffered so much, we were all possessive and protective of our patients." Friedrich wondered if the emaciated officer in the dugout canoe next to her was her lieutenant.

"I think the worst part for him was the things he was made to do to others in order to survive that left him feeling . . ." She turned back to Friedrich, ". . . less than good about being alive. He was severely depressed; he had attempted suicide twice. I had thirty patients under my care; it was just a matter of time before he succeeded, and so I gave him *gai kau dong*."

"Did you administer it, or the shaman?"

"I did."

"Was the lieutenant aware that it came from a witch doctor? Cognizant of any mystic connection or magical powers the natives attributed to what you were prescribing him?"

"None other than that we were fond of one another. Soldiers in the middle of nowhere have almost religious faith in doctors."

"Especially pretty doctors." Friedrich wasn't flirting; he was just being a good clinician.

"That, too. Anyway, a few hours after I administered the first dose, he experienced mild hallucinations. I had no idea of the strength of the stuff, so I followed the shaman's instructions; I gave it to him twice a day. Before the week was up he was able to talk openly about what had happened. He told me how they had to play soccer with a Dutch officer's head, and about sex acts he had to perform with the guards, horrible stuff. The interesting thing was, after a week or so, it didn't upset him in the slightest to discuss the degradation in detail. As a psychiatrist, all I can tell you is, he seemed totally at peace with the idea that he had done these things to stay alive. He spoke about them almost as if they had happened to someone else. Now that he was free, he was a different person, and there was no need to be ashamed."

Friedrich was so excited about the possibilities of what he was hearing, he didn't notice that Dr. Winton had tears in her eyes. "Have you ever thought about testing these kwina leaves, isolating the psychoactive ingredients, see if they work on patients here? I mean, a drug that could put people back together again emotionally after life has dismantled them. . . . A pill for depression, something that actually works?"

"Yes, I've thought about it." Dr. Winton had thought about her lieutenant, but not about what Friedrich was suggesting.

"Well, not to be blunt, but what are you waiting for?"

"The Institute of Human Relations is having enough trouble getting used to a female psychiatrist. I think it might be pushing them to accept a woman witch doctor."

"We could work on it together. You've worked with drugs. I read your paper on administering hypnotics. Sodium amytal. I did my dissertation on psychological testing. During the war, I worked for the Army. . . ."

She held up her hand. "To begin with, *gai kau dong* is made with kwina, and kwina only grows in New Guinea and we're in New Haven."

"I'm way ahead of you." Friedrich flipped opened his suitcase like a Fuller Brush man. It was filled with the waxy pale green serrated leaves of the kwina. Dr. Winton picked up one that had fallen to the floor. It smelled of rot.

"Where did you get this? The botany department doesn't even have . . ."

"I helped out a botanist at the University of Illinois who had a schizophrenic daughter. He knew someone who was doing field work in New Guinea."

"But how did you get it here?"

"Friends in low places. I did some testing of pilots at a flight school."

"What kind of testing?"

"Personality, aptitude, ability to perform under stress . . ." Friedrich didn't like her, but suddenly, he did trust her. "They were trying to figure out who were the best guys for suicide missions. I didn't know that until after the war."

"Would that have made a difference to you, Dr. Friedrich?"

"I probably would have failed a few more."

Friedrich thought about that for a few heartbeats, then pushed on. "Anyway, the chicken colonel in charge of the project owed me. He's stationed in the Philippines. Flies all over. I sent him a telegram about The Way Home. He checked it out, and now I have four two-bushel sacks of it in my garage. And best of all, I have one of these . . ." He handed her a small snapshot of a Bagadong shaman standing next to a hip-high wooden figure.

"You brought a shaman to New Haven?" Dr. Winton was looking at him as if he was wearing women's underwear again.

"No, but the colonel brought me one of the wooden jugs they ferment it in. We have to duplicate the procedure; this way we can get a yeast culture from the residue inside the jug. Of course, there's the possibility it's something in the local water, but I don't think so. At least it gets us started." Friedrich had the enthusiasm of a twelve-year-old farm boy entering his prize pig in a 4-H contest.

"Why me?" She looked at him like she suspected someone at IHR had put Friedrich up to this. "Surely you know other psychiatrists, more experienced and influential."

"Yes, but I came to you first because I couldn't think of anyone else with more to prove."

"You want to work with me because I'm a woman psychiatrist."

"That, and you gave me the idea. I just thought I should give you a chance to share in the credit."

"As optimistic and opportunistic as you are fair."

"I'm an old-fashioned guy. What do you say to my proposal?"

"I'm not quite sure I understand what you're proposing."

"Partnership. Want to see if it works?" Friedrich held out his hand. When she didn't shake it, it occurred to him to ask, "What happened to your friend, the English lieutenant you gave it to?"

"He died." She said it like she blamed the lieutenant for running out on her.

"Because of the stuff?"

"It was in a bombing."

"I'm sorry." Friedrich was anything but.

Bunny Winton had told Will Friedrich, "Let me think about it for a few days and get back to you." But as soon as he left the office, she knew her answer would be "no." She had struggled too long to be taken seriously at the med school to risk having her name linked to a study based on oceanic folk medicine, especially one inspired by anecdotal evidence culled from her efforts to save the life of a patient she had lost her virginity to.

Bunny did not want to think about The Way Home, and she resented Friedrich for barging in on her with the disappointments of her past, though she did recognize she felt a vaguely therapeutic release talking about it to someone other than her own analyst. After she saw the last of her patients that day, she sat down at her typewriter and wrote him a short note,

> Dear Dr. Friedrich,
>
> After careful consideration, I have decided not to take part in your research project. The story I told you about my experience with *gai kau dong* was relayed in confidence, and I trust it will remain so. I wish you the best of luck.
>
> Sincerely,
>
> Dr. T. L. Winton.

Her decision was signed and neatly folded. Her tongue was tasting the glue on the flap of the envelope when she suddenly stopped and thought about what she was doing. A moment later, she ripped up the letter and put the cover on her typewriter. No, on second thought, she realized it was better that she relay the above to Dr. Friedrich over the phone. She did not want any connection to *gai kau dong* in writing. An eavesdropping psychologist who shows up at your office in a cheap suit with a suitcase full of kwina leaves might be trustworthy, but he was definitely what her uncle called "a loose cannon." The more Bunny Winton thought about it, the angrier she was that Friedrich had intruded on her life.

Not wanting to put things off, she looked up his phone number and immediately called Friedrich's office. No answer.

That was Friday. It was Saturday now and Friedrich was out of her mind as she closed her eyes and listened to the last notes of Schubert's String Quartet in C Major at the recital given by a faculty chamber music group at Branford College. She was by herself. Her husband, Thayer, had stayed home to meet with a naval architect about a new racing yawl. He liked to sail, she liked to listen. The last two notes of the piece were what made it special, supertonic and tonic played forte. The effect they had on her eardrums prompted her to wonder if Schubert knew he was dying when he wrote them. A moment of silence, then applause—she considered the possibility that psychiatrists hear music differently.

Having forgotten to bring her own tea, Bunny had half a glass of sherry, asked after a neurologist's wife and children, and was putting on her gloves to leave when she realized that the second viola was also head of the psychology department.

Over a foul dip made of onion soup mix and sour cream, Bunny Winton made just enough small talk with Dr. Cunningham about his work so as not to make him curious when she inquired, "Someone at IHR was asking me about your Dr. Friedrich—any thoughts?"

"Unusual mix of things. He's the only person in the department who can do a standard deviational analysis in his head."

"So Friedrich's a numbers guy."

"He's more of a seat-of-the-pants kind of fellow. Intuitive. Surprises you with things."

"How so?"

"Well, it's really a matter of, you don't know how he comes to the conclusions he comes to, especially when he's right."

"Can you give me a for instance?"

"Well, a female instructor over in the Romance Languages department was receiving obscene phone calls, which were traced back to a pay phone at one of the dorms. The dean came to the psychology department to get our take on how it should be handled. Since there was no way of telling who was making the calls, there was nothing to be done, until a few months later Friedrich came into my office after having lunch with a bunch of students and gave me a name."

"How'd he get the student to tell him?"

"The student didn't tell him. It was just a notion Friedrich had, and since he couldn't back it up with anything, we took no action. A few months later a student was caught in the act, and sure enough, it was the boy Friedrich had told us to take a look at to talk to. And when I asked Friedrich how he figured it out, all the son of a gun said was . . ." Cunningham paused for effect and another glass of sherry, " 'he seemed like the kind of boy who'd need to resort to anonymous obscenity with a stranger to make intimate contact.' "

"What does that mean?"

"I have no idea."

When Bunny Winton got into bed that night and turned out the light, her answer was still "no." She and her husband had separate bedrooms but a shared bathroom was not the limit of their intimacy. They had tried to have a child, especially in the first year of their marriage. Theoretically it was possible she could still conceive.

But Bunny was not thinking about any of this as she lay in the darkness, her hair spread out across her pillow like a scarlet fan. She was thinking about how she had ended up in the bed she was unable to fall asleep in. When she married, right after the war, just out of uniform, it seemed a safe and sensible match to make. Not just because Thayer had so much money she wouldn't have to worry about his being after hers. At thirty-five, she was old for a bride. She thought she wanted to be safe, to live in a world that was clean and starched and ordered. She wanted to be as far from the jungles of New Guinea and memories of her lieutenant as she could get.

Bunny's eyes were open now. Still hoping for sleep, she tried to distract herself by thinking about the history of this bed she had inherited. It was made by an eighteenth-century master cabinetmaker by the name of Goddard, constructed of mahogany hauled out of the jungle by slaves. It featured four posters topped with finials shaped like pineapples and a carved scalloped shell on its headboard.

Her great-grandmother and her grandmother and her mother had died in that bed. And so, she guessed, would she. But before it was her turn, she wanted to do more than be the first woman on the staff of the medical school. It was at that moment Bunny Winton, née Rutledge, realized that she missed the jungle—in a way, even missed the war. Not the killing, but the sense that you were fighting for something. She longed to take a risk that would make her feel fully alive.

Without bothering to turn on the lamp on the bedside table, Bunny Winton got out of bed, sat at her desk, and by the light of a crescent moon picked up a fountain pen and wrote the following on a leaf of double-weight gray linen stationery:

> Dear Dr. Friedrich,
>
> After careful consideration, I have decided I am very much interested in researching The Way Home. As to how we might best coordinate our schedules . . .

APRIL 13, 1952

When Will Friedrich got in his car to go home after work that day, he felt better than fine. The Whale had started without his having to lift the hood, a rarity. The forsythia were in bloom, and he had been able to talk a promising tailback on the football team out of shock therapy. The kid had been arrested on his knees in the men's room of a Greenwich Village bar called the Lily Pad. Will had simply listened to the frightened football player's confession and said, "I don't regard homosexuality as a disease and I don't think shock cures anything."

Well-intentioned was Will Friedrich. Even though he knew he had risked his job by reassuring the boy that he wasn't sick, Will did not think of it as going out on a limb—he did not see himself as a beacon of enlightenment, just as a man doing his job. That afternoon he was as close to happy as a man who devotes his life to the study of unhappiness can be. Less than a mile into his journey home that day, Friedrich looked in the rearview mirror and saw a fine film of sweat collecting on his face. Suddenly, his throat tickled and his eyeballs felt like they needed to be scratched. Sneezing twice, rolling up the window, Will muttered to himself, "Christ, I'm getting a cold."

It was too beautiful a day for him or anyone else to be sick. The sky was the same shade of blue as a set of sheets he had liberated from an Army Air Corps hospital outside Chicago where he had worked during the war, when he and his wife were first married and the clouds on his horizon were as invitingly white as freshly fluffed pillows.

But when traffic stopped and he looked over at the big plateglass window of a department store over on the avenue, the promise of the day flew out the window, even though it was rolled up. It was a store he couldn't afford to shop in. Usually, the sight of the expensively dressed mannequins in its window would prompt superior thoughts such as, *ideas are important, not things*. Or, *shopping's the opiate of the people, not religion*. But that day, due to the clouds and the angle of the sunlight on the glass, the windows became a gigantic mirror, and all Dr. Friedrich could see was himself smiling inanely behind the wheel of a vehicle that belonged in the junkyard and he should have been embarrassed to drive. What did he have to be smiling about? He'd gone to college for eight years, and as his wife had reminded him that morning, their checking account was overdrawn . . . again.

Traffic began to move, but the reflection of himself stayed in his head. He turned on the radio, forgetting the tuner was broken and that the only station he could receive was the AM colored station out of New York. Usually the dark rhythms were all static, but today he heard them as clear as the bell that seemed to be going off inside his head. *Ain't no doctor in all the lan' can cure the fever of a convict man.* Leadbelly's wail didn't make Dr. Friedrich feel any better. But he did wonder why he identified with a Negro field hand who'd been sent to prison for murder. Though he'd given up on psychoanalysis—time and manpower prevented it from ever helping more than a handful of people—Friedrich never tired of psychoanalyzing himself.

Gunning the White Whale up the steep incline of the short driveway, Friedrich swerved just in time to avoid running over his six-year-old daughter Lucy's hand-me-down scooter. By the time he hit the brakes he'd flattened the new Schwinn bicycle he had just given Fiona for turning eight, the one he'd told her to put in the garage that morning.

"Why do I bother talking? No one ever listens to me," Friedrich muttered to himself. Of course, it was unrealistic to expect an eight-year-old, even his eight-year-old, to have the retentive abilities to comprehend the repercussions of her irresponsibility. If he'd had the money to buy her a new bicycle, he could have turned it into an object lesson by refusing to replace the bike she should have put away. But because he was unable to afford to replace the bike, his predicament was exacerbated by shame. Friedrich was well aware that he'd feel even more foolish for blaming his child and his wife, but knew he'd probably do both. He was embarrassed by his embarrassment.

Will Friedrich slammed the flat of his hand against his frontal lobe and was about to ask himself "What the fuck is happening to me?" when he looked up and saw a flock of hungry parrots dining al fresco in his mulberry tree.

If Dr. Friedrich had been a psychologist practicing on the citizens of Caracas, or Manila, or even Miami, the sight of eleven noisy parrots shrieking red, blue, green, turquoise, and tropical gold in his fruit tree would have been nothing out of the ordinary. Dr. Friedrich's mulberry tree being full of parrots in the front yard of a little two-story ersatz Cape Cod cottage in a housing development just outside of New Haven, Connecticut, this was an incident of greater magnitude. He was a thousand miles too far north to believe his eyes.

Having labored that morning in a poorly ventilated, jury-rigged chem lab taking the first of a series of tedious steps necessary to isolate the psychoactive ingredients of a drab little shrub native to the island of New Guinea, Friedrich's mind jumped to the logical conclusion: "I'm hallucinating." He said it out loud, like a miner who's just struck gold.

He climbed out of the White Whale without bothering to turn off the engine or close the car door. Hat on the back of his head, necktie blowing in the wind, he'd left the world of a broken bicycle behind. A spiderweb, woven between a climbing rose and a leafless apple tree that had died over the winter, broke across his face.

With the calm eye of a clinician, he reviewed the circumstances of the morning's fermentation in the basement lab over at the med school. He'd been there by himself, and was wearing rubber gloves. He was certain he'd not been so foolhardy as to touch his fingers to his lips. The active ingredient must have been absorbed into his bloodstream through his nasal passages. He put his finger to his nose. Yes, it was running. He tasted it. Slightly bitter, but not at all unpleasant.

Pulling a small black notebook and pencil out of his pocket, he checked his watch, jotted down the time, and made his initial observations. The first hallucinations he was aware of appeared around 5:00. Or was that reflection he saw in the store window a hallucination? Had that tailback really been arrested for sodomy in Greenwich Village? He'd call him up, see how he was doing, just to make sure.

Friedrich walked toward the shrieking, feathered apparitions with a smile on his face. In fact, he was grinning from ear to ear. This is why, at seventeen, after reluctantly leaving his brother in the care of a blind great-uncle who used Homer as a Seeing Eye dog, Will had climbed on top of a boxcar and headed west with $1.17 in his pocket. He had ridden the rails with bums, hobos, and men driven mad by lack of employment, and counted himself lucky that he ended up in California picking fruit for twelve hours a day, two bucks a week, and had told himself he had it good when he found a job in a cannery, all to save up enough money to go back to college.

This is why he had become a psychologist and taken a job at Yale at a salary that forced him to put off going to the dentist. Yes, this moment made even the indignity of having to teach Ivy League freshmen snobs statistics seem like time well spent. He, William T. Friedrich, had discovered something. Willy Friedrich, the farm boy from southern Illinois, had just stepped off the beaten track of what was on the pages of other men's textbooks into the untouched wilderness of the unknown.

Hofmann had accidentally discovered LSD in 1943. April 16, to be exact. Will noted that his hallucinations weren't like the distortions Hofmann had experienced. These parrots in his mulberry tree were goddamned perfect. There was a pair of macaws, one blue, one red, both with yellow eyes; a green-cheeked Amazonian; gold-headed parakeets with green wings and a tail feathered in turquoise; cockatoos that shouted obscenities and asked questions in Spanish and English; a threesome of lovebirds, and a drab but loquacious African gray. Friedrich recorded that he felt no confusion or disorientation in crisp penmanship; his handwriting was neater than usual.

His mind never felt sharper. It had been more than a year since he had read Hofmann's extract. And yet now, as he stood beneath these imaginary parrots, watching them bicker and squawk and flirt and fluff their feathers—Christ! Two of them were copulating—he could recall Hofmann's words verbatim: "I was seized by a peculiar sensation of vertigo and restlessness. Objects, as well as the shapes of my associates in the laboratory, appeared to undergo optical changes. I was unable to concentrate on my work."

Friedrich penciled, "No sense of vertigo—no fear." Friedrich stood on one foot, closed one eye, and slowly touched his forefinger to his nose, and then added, "No loss of motor skills."

Connecting the dots from the laboratory to what was happening in his mind, he wondered aloud, "Why parrots?" Was it because he had been bitten by one at age eleven at the Illinois State Fair in Urbana? Could it have something to do with the fact that parrots talk without understanding a word of what they are saying? Or was it simply that when his henna-haired mother reversed the charges on her late-night long-distance phone calls, warning him of train wrecks, car crashes, and fires that had not yet occurred, her voice had the same shrill, slightly hysterical shriek as that macaw who kept calling out, "Here they come, here they come."

There was no question Friedrich had stumbled onto something wondrous—until the African gray shit on the shoulder of his one good suit. Any hopes he had that the nausea of disappointment that gripped him might be a hallucination of humiliation stemming from his manifest self-doubt vanished when his wife, Nora, stepped out of their front door with their toddler, Jack, on one hip, and little Willy clinging to her leg like a limpet, bird book in hand.

"We've been watching them all afternoon." Will stared at his wife, then at the birds. That he hadn't even been the first to see the damned parrots iced his humiliation. The only positive emotion in his body was relief that he hadn't run inside and made an even bigger fool of himself by calling Bunny Winton. When he didn't respond, his wife called out, "Well, what do you think?"

The question was posed with a casual and cautious amusement. Nora was guarded with her opinions. Not because she didn't have them, but because she experienced them so strongly she felt betrayed and slightly carsick when they weren't shared by those she loved.

Looking up at the parrots, trying to think of something to say that would hide how ridiculous he felt, Dr. Friedrich didn't see the gravity with which her full-lipped smile dropped from her face when he turned away. Dr. Friedrich misdiagnosed his wife's wariness as fear of failure; he too wanted to see his own feelings reflected on those he loved.

They had met over the Bunsen burner in organic chemistry class. There was still heat, but after nine years of marriage it didn't warm him the way it used to. Her ability to laugh at life, once so seductive, had now begun to make him feel small. She thought it was amusing buying secondhand dresses at Nearly New, especially when the dean's wife recognized the flowered frock Nora had worn to the faculty tea as a dress she had donated. Friedrich was terrified by her ability to brag aloud at these same teas about saving twenty-five cents a week on shampoo by washing the family's hair in an emulsion of dishwashing detergent and lemon juice mixed in an Erlenmeyer flask. He loved her when she waylaid others with her intelligence, correcting a French professor on an irregular verb, or beating a physicist to the atomic weight of iodine when they did crosswords during the period breaks at the Harvard-Yale hockey game they had attended to please the dean, who placed great weight on school spirit. Friedrich was proud of her mind. Except, of course, when it ensnared him.

Nora was still waiting for her husband to reveal his feelings about the parrots. "They're wonderful, aren't they?" Lipstick being her one vanity and extravagance, Nora smiled a shade of Helena Rubenstein called Desire. Her cheeks were dimpled, her hand was on his shoulder, but all the time he knew she was thinking, *Hell's bells, if coming home to find parrots waiting for you doesn't make you happy, what in God's name will?*

The door slammed. His daughters were now dancing around him, laying claim to his attention and the parrots overhead. Fiona, the eldest, ebony-haired like her mother, stood on tiptoes to cast a bigger shadow. "The red macaw's mine. He's indigenous to South America. Did you know that, Daddy?" Fiona had an impressive vocabulary for an eight-year-old.

"It's not fair." Lucy—blond like Nora's aunt Minnie, had a predilection for troubling theological questions: If people go to heaven, why not dogs? And insects? And vegetables?—protested, "You just want that macaw because I called him first."

"I have to make pee-pee." That was Willy.

Friedrich wished his son didn't bear such a striking resemblance to his own older brother. It wasn't that Homer was unattractive or that Friedrich didn't like his sibling (Homer was handsome, in fact, and Friedrich loved him), it was just that Homer, now thirty-six, would have been hard-pressed to outscore Lucy on a Stanford-Binet intelligence test. "The word is 'urinate,' Willy."

"He's barely three, Will."

"It's less confusing if you teach a child the correct word first." Since Willy had already wet his pants, the point was moot. Will picked up his son and gave him a hug and a kiss to make up for Homer.

Nora was about to go inside for dry pants when Fiona began to shriek. "My bike!" Friedrich had forgotten about that.

"I warned you not to leave it in the driveway." He hadn't wanted to say that, but . . .

"We can fix it." Nora put Jack down on the lawn and extracted the twisted Schwinn from beneath the DeSoto.

"It's my fault. We'll buy you a new one tomorrow."

"Can I have a new bike, too?" Lucy, like most middle children, felt lost in the shuffle.

"We can't afford it," Nora protested.

"I can and I will." It was the mantra he lived by. Wiping the parrot shit from his shoulder, he handed Willy to his wife and tried to regain his dignity with a joke. "I think the gray one's depressed."

"How so?" Nora tried to straighten the twisted wheel.

"I see the same look in my eye every morning when I look in the mirror and shave."

Nora knew her husband defined depression as paralyzed rage. She laughed only because, as Fiona sobbed, Jack began to cry, and she didn't want to make it a trio. Her lip trembled, her eyes watered up, just the way they had when she misspelled "ennui" in the state spelling bee. As soon as the last letter was out of her mouth, she knew she'd made a mistake. It was too late to take it back. She didn't like to think about her marriage the same way: "Is that how you feel about your life?"

And then a smaller but genuine miracle happened: "Not when I look at you." That it was what she needed to hear didn't mean it wasn't true.

Dr. Friedrich's dreams of greatness began when he was nine and would sneak down to the root cellar where his mother made Homer sleep as punishment when he'd wet his bed in the summer. In the winter she was less cruel. In the cool, earthy dark, smelling of parsnips and potatoes, Will would put Homer to sleep with talk of all the wondrous things they'd accomplish together when he was grown up. Holding open a frayed atlas someone had purchased at the St. Louis World's Fair in 1903, running his fingers across maps where the hearts of continents were still marked "unexplored," Will would confide, "After we find the new tallest mountain in the world, President Calvin Coolidge himself will give us a medal and the money to build a rocket, like Buck Rogers, only better, because it will be real. And I, I mean, we'll . . ."

In 1952, the six inches between one's ears were the least explored territory on the planet. And the chemistry of feelings was thought by most to have as little to do with hard science as Kryptonite.

A thirty-three-year-old man who can't afford to replace a bicycle and thinks a flock of parrots in his tree is a sign he's on the right track is worse than lost; he's fallen. Feeling like he was sliding from the peak of a glacial mountain of narcissism, Friedrich reached out and grabbed hold of his wife like she was the last rung of a rope ladder dangling from the edge of the world.

"Why are you doing that?" Fiona had never seen her parents kiss on the mouth. Not like that, and never on the front lawn.

"Because we're happy." Nora giggled as her husband buried his face in the softness of her neck.

"Mama's Sleeping Beauty, and Daddy's waking her up." It was the other way around, but it was also Lucy's favorite fairy tale.

"That's stupid." Fiona watched jealously as Lucy threw her arms around her parents' hips, pressing them even closer.

Feeling left out, Willy pawed at his father. "Uppee me."

"Kiss." Jack wanted in too. Their embrace had more limbs than an octopus.

Friedrich was about to whisper in his wife's ear, "Let's get a babysitter and go to bed," when he felt a small hand on his penis. Lucy? Jack? Oh, God, please not Willy. He hoped it was his wife. "Was that you?"

"Was me what?" It had been more than a month since they had had sex. An erection flagpoled the front of his pants. Nora laughed.

Fiona was staring at his fly. Or was she just refusing to look her father in the eye? Will knew he was certifiable when he found himself imagining his daughter replaying the seminal moment of her sexual dysfunction to an analyst twenty years and a bout of nonorgasmic nymphomania later.

Will, hand in his pocket, was nonchalantly trying to girdle his erection behind his belt buckle when a foreign accent inquired, "Dr. Friedrich, in your professional opinion, do you think a tree full of parrots will have the same effect on my wife?"

It was Jens. The animal behaviorist lived across the street. Bristly, yellow hair, solid, and warm as a Dutch oven, so obviously a foreigner (shorts, sandals with socks), Jens had been the first person on the street to take notice of the parrots, which were still jabberwocking and squawking in the mulberry tree. His wife, Anka, and their twin girls were running across the street, blond and red-faced like figures from Brueghel dropped into suburbia. And a half block away, Fred Mettler, a physicist with a glass eye who had worked at Los Alamos, and his wife, the den mother of Fiona's Brownie troop, were being pulled toward the parrots by their three children, the youngest of whom, due to a fondness for running in front of cars, was kept on a leash.

After that, news of the parrots rolled through Hamden like ball lightning. It was spread via word-of-mouth, telephone, and children on roller skates. Buzz-cut boys with slingshots dangling from back pockets, girls in smock dresses tied in the back with bows, like presents waiting to be opened, shortcut through backyards, jumped fences, and rampaged through freshly planted gardens to glimpse the birds. Crabby old ladies and professional grouches, who waited on porches and sat behind draped windows, eager to report youthful trespass or misdemeanor, barked, "Johnny, Susie, Bill, Fred, Sam, Wendy, Gus: I'm calling your mother right now and . . ."

Mothers put dinner on hold to see for themselves. And husbands used to being greeted with a highball at the door found cryptic notes re: parrots in a mulberry tree on Hamelin Road.

And from their little starter house subdivision, the rumor of feathered fun moved up the hill, to the big old homes on the ridge, with maids' rooms, and views, and broad lawns landscaped with shade trees and boxwoods older than the century. Streets where PWMs lived next to bank presidents and businessmen who ran companies founded by their grandfathers. A world Friedrich drove through once or twice a week, sunk low in the White Whale so as not be recognized, just to see what life would be like once his name was in the textbooks.

An hour after he first saw the birds, Friedrich's threadbare patch of lawn was crowded not just with fellow academics connected to Yale, but with neighbors they never talked to and never knew they had—car salesmen, insurance brokers, bakers of bread mingled with headshrinkers and meteorologists, individuals who were richer and poorer for their ability to recite poetry in five languages or their intimate knowledge of the defenestration of Prague. As the parrots cackled and called out, "Hello! Shut up! Close the door!" and one tangerine-winged cockatoo wailed plaintively, "*¿Donde está Marjeta?*" over and over again, town and gown cracked witty, wise, and dumb about what had brought the birds to town.

"Ten bucks says somebody who owns a pet shop isn't very happy right now," opined the car salesman, who invited Friedrich to come down and test-drive a Nash.

"I called Creedmore's Pets and the University Zoo. Nobody's missing," said Sergeant Neutch, a Hamden cop who looked like a turtle who'd misplaced his shell.

A teaching assistant who'd written her doctoral thesis on *Don Quixote* volunteered, "The macaw speaks Spanish with a Madrilenian accent."

"They were unloading a freighter from Bolivia down at the harbor this morning. Maybe they got locked in the cargo hold." That was the policeman.

"Bolivia is landlocked," Jens interjected.

"Okay, Einstein, what's your explanation?"

"Commies." Jens winked at Friedrich.

"Are you telling me communists are using parrots to spy on us?" The cop was interested.

Jens put his finger to his lips. "Don't let them know we're onto them." Everyone who knew Jens and his wife were both card-carrying communists laughed.

"Maybe the hydrogen-bomb testing has affected migration patterns," suggested a botanist who had a toadstool named after him.

It was the physicist's wife's turn. "Fred says in twenty years we'll have atomic-powered vacuum cleaners."

"What's a vacuum cleaner?" Nora deadpanned.

Nora prided herself on her lack of homemaking skills.

"What if they have a disease?" A mother pulled her child away from the tree.

"You mean, like, parrot fever?"

"What if they're radioactive?"

"What about parrot-toe-nitus?"

"Is that like an ingrown toenail?"

Friedrich excused himself from what passed for wit to bring a chair out from the living room for a pregnant woman who looked like she was going to faint, directed several children to his downstairs bathroom, and heard the driver of a kosher butcher's truck, on listening to the cockatoo call for Marjeta, tell no one in particular, in a thick, consonant-heavy Mitteleuropean accent, "Marjeta was my sister's name."

Friedrich wondered but didn't want to ask what had happened to her. He cheered himself by giving Jack a hug and, at his wife's suggestion, headed toward the backyard to get the picnic benches.

Will was just lugging the benches around to the front of the house when he heard, "Portentous, don't you think, Doctor?" He didn't have to look up; he recognized Bunny Winton's voice. Her la-di-da accent no longer offended him; he found it amusing. It made it seem more like he was acting in a stage play about a research project rather than living it.

"What?" He hadn't expected her to come see the parrots, and he had no idea what she was talking about.

"The parrots; they're a good omen for the start of our project." She was surprisingly superstitious. She kept her keys on a rabbit's foot and a four-leaf clover in a crystal heart dangled from her charm bracelet.

"Let's hope."

"Sorry I wasn't at the lab this morning. Carol broke her arm at school and Thayer couldn't pick her up, so I had to play Mom." Carol was her twelve-year-old stepdaughter, and Mom was a game she had almost convinced herself she had no interest in playing.

"Dr. Petersen dropped in. I think he was disappointed you weren't there. He's keen on our work." Friedrich thought, but didn't say, *He's keen on you.*

No question, Bunny Winton knew both how things worked and how to make them work. Dr. Petersen was seventy-two years old. She had picked not only the most senior psychiatrist at the institute but the randiest to sponsor their research project. When she had laid out what they wanted to do, she sat cross-legged at the old goat's feet. Watching him watch her, she did everything but lick her paws and purr to close the deal.

Friedrich thought he had yet another reason to dislike his collaborator, until they walked out of Petersen's office and Winton whispered, "I'm sorry you had to witness that nauseating display of coquetry, but it was the quickest way to get him to say yes." Friedrich didn't like women who used their sexuality to fuel their ambitions. He was less certain how he felt about feminine wiles being used to further his own.

Thayer Winton was unloading two cases of beer from the trunk of his Cadillac. He was older than Bunny, tall, and had the kind of tan you got when you spent spring vacation winning the Bermuda race on your yacht. Friedrich had read about him in the Yale alumni bulletin left on the floor of the bathroom of a stall where he had once taken a shit. Dr. Winton had told Friedrich Thayer had married her because his first wife had died in childbirth and he wanted a mother for his daughter. "He got something else. Which I think he realized is what he wanted all along," was how she'd put it, as they'd chopped up the kwina leaves for their first fermentation.

"And what was that?" Friedrich had asked.

"A friend."

Widower, child to raise—Friedrich would have felt sorry for him if he weren't the heir to an insurance company up in Hartford.

"Thayer likes your wife." Bunny liked to say things that got men thinking. Friedrich looked over. Nora had her purse open and was insisting the millionaire take her money for the beer.

"I'm fond of her myself." Thayer wouldn't take the money. Nora had the last word by slipping it into his pocket.

It was about then that Jens came back from his house with a big pitcher of Manhattans and a stack of paper cups. And suddenly Dr. and Mrs. Friedrich, whose social skills were normally stretched by their annual baked ham and potatoes lyonnaise dinner for eight to suck up to the dean in hopes of tenure, were hosting the best cocktail party anyone in Hamden could remember.

No one noticed the tall, skinny, stoop-shouldered seventeen-year-old slowly pedaling up the hill toward the Friedrichs. A four-by-five Speed Graphic press camera hung from his neck, swinging back and forth like the pendulum of a ticking clock.

The camera was borrowed. The old fat-tired girl's bicycle, with the rusty chain and the seat too low, was his own. Each time he pushed down on one pedal, his opposite knee hit the end of the handlebar and the bike veered. Still, he had made the three-and-a-half-mile ride out from campus in less than an hour. His kneecaps were rubbed raw, and he had blisters on both his palms. Sweat dripping from the end of his nose, straining as he pushed down on the pedals, lips pursed tight as a sphincter, he was misery on wheels.

He had biked out to Hamden to photograph Dr. Friedrich and his parrots for a five-hundred-word human interest piece. It was his first assignment. Being a freshman, he wasn't even officially on the staff of Yale's venerable rag, the *Yale Daily News*. Being the kind of freshman he was—bearded with pimples and peach fuzz, too shy to look a person in the eye unless it was through the viewfinder of a camera, and, most un-Yale-like of all, saddled with the name Casper Gedsic, which everybody who wasn't of Russian/Lithuanian extraction mispronounced as Getsick, even if they weren't trying to make fun of him—Casper knew he was never going to be tapped for the masthead of his college paper. He knew it with the same unnerving intelligence that enabled him to give you the name and due date of the first comet to appear in the heavens of New Haven in the twenty-third century. No matter how many pots of coffee or cigarette runs he made for the upperclassmen, no matter how many hours he spent developing others' photographs of touchdowns scored and baskets missed, no matter how many misplaced modifiers he corrected rewriting lesser minds' copy, his gifts would remain untapped in this universe.

He did not think it any more unfair or fair than the fact he would not be alive to see the polar ice caps melt. It would happen, but not for him. Perhaps if he had gone to Choate or Hotchkiss, or grown up in Darien, or if there had been a brand of cough drops named Gedsic's, his lack of social skills, vegetarianism, even his old girl's bicycle might have been written off as eccentricities. But Casper was the only child of a widow from Vilnius who had survived the Nazis and the Russians and made it to the land of opportunity, only to end up picking cranberries in the bogs of southern New Jersey's Pine Barrens.

Tests with right or wrong answers, essays that asked him to compare and contrast, problems that involved numbers, unknowns that didn't breathe, that weren't flesh, were easy for Casper. People were difficult. So difficult that he had started doing grunt work for the school paper quite by accident. That first day of school, he had been looking for the astronomy club when he knocked on the door of the *Daily News*. Asked if he knew how to set up a darkroom, it was easier to say "yes" than to explain how he'd come to be lost.

As it turned out, Casper enjoyed standing in the corner of the paneled newsroom in a haze of cigarette smoke, as wannabe Edward R. Murrows and bogus Hemingways with butts parked in the corners of their mouths shouted orders and barked wisecracks, watching with wonderment and disdain at the ease with which other human beings could shoot the shit.

Casper was aware of the fact that he was the last choice for the parrot article. It was the Friday before the spring dance, already after four, when Whitney Bouchard, the features editor who had blown out his knee six months earlier in the Princeton game, heard about the parrots out in Hamden. He was rich, athletic, and as darkly handsome as Bruce Wayne, aka Batman. Whereas undergraduates who longed to be Whitney envied him, Casper regarded him as an exotic species of wasp and was content not to be stung. And since Whitney and everybody else at the paper (except for Casper) had dates coming in from Vassar and Wellesley and Bryn Mawr, coeds in camel-hair coats and saddle shoes to meet at the train station, corsages to pick up, and rubbers to slip into the backs of their wallets, Casper got his break.

Only Casper didn't think about it like that. He did what was asked at the paper under the not unreasonable assumption that if he kept his nose clean and to the grindstone, by the time he graduated, he would have enough strangers to introduce to his mother by their first names to give her the impression that he had made friends.

As Casper pedaled north through the campus that afternoon, light turning the spray from a garden hose into a rainbow made him think of the year 1666, the year Newton had reduced sunshine to wavelengths. Which made him think of gravity, which reminded him that a meteor shower would be visible an hour and half before the next dawn. Which in turn prompted him to consider the probability of Ted Williams's batting average. Thoughts ricocheted across the calm surface of his mind like a flat stone skipped across the water. Such was the random brilliance and potential of Casper Gedsic's brain, which would have continued its elliptical orbit of thought if it hadn't been for a sharp whistle.

Casper looked over his shoulder and saw a girl with the two fingers of her left hand making an instrument out of her smile. He had never seen a girl whistle like that. Blond, matching periwinkle-blue sweater set, she was waving now. Accepting of the fact that he didn't know girls like that and never would know them, he pedaled on, aware but indifferent.

"Hey you, on the bike."

Casper put on the brakes. "M-m-me?"

She was walking toward him. "Who else am I talking to?"

"R-R-Right . . . of course." Looking her in the eyes just long enough to see that they were a shade bluer than green, like the spots on the tail of a salamander, Casper turned his gaze downward to the pearls around her neck.

"I saw the press camera and thought you might be able to help me." The girl tilted her head to make eye contact. He worried that she thought he was looking at her breasts, which he was, and focused his eyes on the travel stickers that polka-dotted her suitcase: Lake Placid, Palm Beach, Val d'Isère.

While she talked to the top of his head, he briefly considered and dismissed the idea of volunteering the fact that Val d'Isère was where Hannibal was deserted by his Saracen mercenaries. "How?"

She was already looking over his shoulder for someone less obscure to help her. "I mean, when I saw the camera, I thought you might be on the staff of the paper."

"I'm a freshman." It wasn't a non sequitur to Casper.

"Are you a foreigner?"

"F-f-f-freshmen aren't tapped for the paper unt-t-til the end of their sophomore year."

"So you do work at the paper?"

"Yes."

"Do you know Whit Bouchard?"

"Yes."

"Well, do you know where he is?" He could hear the impatience in her voice.

"No."

"Are we playing twenty questions?" It was her laughter that made him look up.

"No . . . I mean, I could look for him."

"That's sweet, but you don't have to do that." She lit a cigarette. "I told his sister, Nina—she's my roommate—to call Whit and tell him I'd be taking the earlier train. But you know Nina: in one ear and out the other."

"I d-d-don't know Nina."

"You'd like each other. She's insanely smart, but dumb when it comes to dumb stuff. I'm Alice Wilkerson, by the way."

Casper was sure he hadn't heard her right. "I'm Casper."

They shook hands. He was glad she was wearing gloves. His hands sweat even when he wasn't nervous; he suffered from hyperhidrosis, abnormal and chronic perspiration. His body sweat even when he wasn't exerting himself. His mother told him it was because he thought too much.

"Hey, stop trying to steal my girl and get out there and interview those parrots." He was relieved Whit didn't call him Getsick. He watched Alice turn and run toward Whit with open arms. Just before she kissed him, she looked over her shoulder. "See you at the dance, Casper."

Casper got back on his bike knowing he wouldn't be seeing her at the dance. He didn't have a tux, much less a date. Having never gone out on a date his whole life, dating, like melting of the polar ice caps, wasn't an experience he worried about missing.

But there was something about the way she said it—"see you at the dance"—that shifted the idea into the realm of possibility. And as the afternoon sunlight mottled the path beneath his wheels with shadow, he felt a sensation that fate and nature had insulated him from—hope.

What if his photograph and five hundred words were so dazzling, so rich with metaphor and insight, that Whit was impressed? What if Whit liked them so much that when he got to the last line, he lit a smoke and announced to everybody in the newsroom, "This dog'll hunt." Which is what Whit would always say when he really liked something. And following the progression of impossibility as if he were calculating pi, Casper was bold enough to imagine Whitney's calling up his sister Nina, "I've got this buddy named Casper. He's got a funny last name, but you'd really like him. And . . ."

For the first mile after Alice, he played variations of his pipe dreams. He imagined Whit's sister was first a brunette, then a redhead. Blue eyes, brown eyes, green, he worked her up in his imagination until she burned with the incandescence of white phosphorous. Hot as Rita Hayworth, but with the wit of Katharine Hepburn. And the intellectual rigor of Shelley's wife—*Frankenstein* was Casper's favorite novel.

But daydreaming was one of the few disciplines that didn't come naturally to Casper. "What if" was a game he didn't know how to play. Hope was so new to him that it almost felt toxic. And though the sun was still shining and the air was scented with lilacs, a cloud passed over him as he pedaled down the streets of New Haven. Five hundred words and a snapshot of a shrink and his parrots weren't going to impress Whitney, much less prompt him to introduce his sister, especially if she had the body of Rita Hayworth and the brain of Marie Curie.

By mile two of his journey the bicycle seat was just beginning to raise a blister on his buttocks. What had seemed like an opportunity to change the trajectory of his life now felt more and more like a cruel joke. *The bastard gave me the assignment because he thinks I am a joke.* Suddenly, the thoughts he was throwing across the still waters of his mind were weighted with an anger and resentment Casper hadn't felt since eighth-grade graduation, when he'd become so lost in his recitation of "Hiawatha" that he'd wet his pants on stage.

Fuck you, Whitney. I didn't get into Yale because of my last name. I won the Edison National Science Prize. I had to take a test to get into this hellhole. I got a hundred percent correct—perfect.

Casper was riding down a street that wasn't familiar. Horns blared. Someone shouted, "Watch where you're going, buddy." But Casper didn't hear them. For by now it had occurred to him that his journey felt like a joke because it was a joke. There weren't any parrots. No shrink. They'd made it all up to see if he was gullible enough to do it. He'd seen them play jokes like that on other maggots. That's what frosh were called. And worse, he could see Whitney and that blond bitch Alice shacked up at the Taft Hotel, laughing.

Paranoia flamed his anger into a state of mind that melted logic. And even now, as he pedaled up to Friedrich's and saw the parrots, he was still outraged. And though no one noticed his arrival, his mind was shouting, *What are you looking at?*

Dropping his bike, not bothering to put down the kickstand, Casper opened his mouth to scream *Stop it!* And would have if the strap that held the camera to his neck had not caught on the handle of the bike. He fell, chin first. His jaw hit the sidewalk. His glasses fell onto the lawn. The impact of real pain, the salty taste of blood in his mouth, the sight of it dripping onto his hands, brought him relief, soothed him so quickly and completely that Casper felt like he'd woken up from someone else's nightmare. What was he so angry about? Why did he ever think Whitney was going to introduce him to his sister?

"Are you all right?" Fiona Friedrich handed him his glasses.

"I-I-I-I'm not sure."

A drop of blood dripped from his chin onto Fiona's white Mary Janes. "You better put iodine on it."

"I don't think I'm going to die."

"Dogs pee on the sidewalk where you cut your chin. It could get infected. You could get . . . I forget what they call it, but my daddy says if you catch it, you can't open your mouth. Not to eat or to drink and you die."

"Lockjaw. I've had a tetanus shot." Casper was surprised how much easier it was talking to children. Not that he could remember talking to any since he was a child. He told himself he should do it more often.

Nora Friedrich was there now. "Let's get you inside and wash that off." Fiona took his hand and led him toward the house.

Nora carried his camera. "You must be from the paper."

"How did you know?"

"Your friend Whitney called from the paper to say you'd be coming. Pretty amazing, isn't it?" She was pointing at the parrots. Casper was thinking of something else.

Chin bandaged and orange with Mercurochrome, Casper posed Friedrich with his arms raised beneath the mulberry tree as though Friedrich had conjured the parrots out of thin air. After pointing out the different species, the pair he'd seen mating, the one that called out for Marjeta, Friedrich introduced Casper to now slightly tipsy instructors and assistant professors who glibly volunteered theories about the parrots' unexpected arrival in Hamden. These ran from UFOs to weather changes brought on by nuclear testing.

Friedrich gave Casper more than enough for his five hundred words. But there was something about this freshman that made Friedrich want to give him more than that. Perhaps it was simply that Friedrich had had two beers, and the way the big press camera hung around Casper's neck reminded him of the time his mother had tied a dead hen around the throat of Homer's dog, Lilly, to teach the poor hound not to chase chickens. It took two weeks for Lilly to paw the rotting hen carcass from around her neck. She never chased chickens again, but it didn't make her overly fond of humans—she bit anyone who tried to pet her, except Homer.

Perhaps it was the sweater with the big Y on it that the kid was wearing. Whoever had spent weeks knitting it by hand for him had picked the wrong color yarn. Casper's sweater was navy, while Yale's shade of blue was the color of a box from Tiffany's. It was the kind of thing Friedrich's mother's would have done on purpose, the kind of mistake that announced to anyone connected with the university that not only was Casper on scholarship, but was infected with a strain of geekiness so acute even the other scholarship students would steer clear of him for fear of being contaminated.

It was 7:30 now. All the neighbors had left. The sun had set. The parrots had quieted down, and Friedrich was trying to think of where he had heard Casper's unfortunate last name. As Casper used up the last of his film, taking blinding, flashbulb-popping snapshots of Nora and the children catching the first fireflies of the season, Friedrich studied the awkward boy the same way he watched the patients through the one-way mirror in the mental ward of the hospital. It was how he looked at people when he cared about them. Friedrich focused on all that was slightly off. The twitch in the Orbicularis oculi muscles above Casper's right eye; his forefinger's nervous habit of rubbing small, concentric circles in his hair above his left temple when he was asked a question. And now, as he heard Lucy ask Casper, "Where are you from?" he heard a slight stutter.

"S-S-Seabury, New Jersey." Casper stepped on one of his spent flashbulbs as he walked over to Friedrich to say good-bye. "Oh my God. I'm sorry."

"It's okay."

"No, no it's not." Friedrich watched as Casper fell to his knees and began picking the tiny shards of glass from the earth. "One of the ch-ch-children could step here and cut themselves."

"Don't worry about it, Casper." Friedrich pulled the awkward boy to his feet.

It was unusual for Casper to be touched. It felt almost like a hug. "Thank you for sharing your family with me. Really, Professor Friedrich, it's been a privilege."

"It was our pleasure, son." Friedrich had already forgotten Gedsic's first name.

"Come on, children, time to say good night to Casper." Nora held Jack in her arms.

"If you'd like, I can make you prints of the photographs." Still trying to remember why Casper seemed so familiar, Friedrich didn't respond. "Don't worry, it wouldn't cost you anything," Casper added nervously.

Friedrich let go of the boy's hand. The idea that this kid thought he couldn't afford to pay for pictures of his wife and children, that somebody called Gedsic felt sorry for him, made Friedrich's mood plummet. The residue of the day's earlier humiliations were still in him: the white whale of a DeSoto he couldn't afford to fix; the bicycle he ran over but didn't have the money to replace; the drug he hadn't discovered. Friedrich's cheeks flushed, his heart rate rose. He was studying himself now. Shocked by the visceral jolt of the same mix of anxiety and depression that one of Jens's lab rats registered when they pressed on the food bar and got a hot shot of electricity instead of the kibble of dog food they'd been expecting, Friedrich snapped, "I can pay for my own photographs."

Casper heard the edge in the doctor's voice. "I . . . I . . . I d-d-d-didn't mean it that way." The stutter was back. His fingers worried circles on the side of his head like he was trying to scratch a hole in his temple.

Nora didn't hear what had been said but sensed the joy suddenly bleeding out of the end of what had been a wonderful day. Friedrich's jacket was off, his shirttails were out. She slid her free hand up his back. The warmth of her hand, the touch of her fingertips reminded Friedrich of all the good that had happened and the promise that there would be more of it tomorrow. He felt his heartbeat slow down. His anxiety dipped and his mood elevated. If only he could prescribe Nora's touch, the gentle pressure of a hand on one's back, life would be different for the Caspers of this world.

"What I mean to say, Casper, is 'thank you.' I'd appreciate that. Sorry if I sounded gruff. I get that way when I'm hungry."

Nora had removed her hand, but the warmth lingered. "Would you like to stay for dinner?"

"I d-d-don't want to cause you any trouble."

"It's no trouble. I'm afraid it's just going to be bacon and eggs."

"I can't have bacon. I'm a vegetarian."

Nora volunteered, "We'll have potatoes and string beans."

The children were asleep and the Friedrichs were in bed. They'd made love twice, something they hadn't done since before the Korean War. Nora was just drifting off when Friedrich suddenly sat up. "He's the A-bomb kid."

"What?"

"I heard some guys in the physics department talking about him. I thought they were kidding, but . . ."

"What are you talking about?"

"They said there was this sad-sack kid in the freshman class who had submitted a design for an atomic bomb in a high school science contest."

"How do you know it's Casper?"

"They said he was from New Jersey."

"It's a wonder he didn't get arrested." The Friedrichs would later find out that the FBI had interviewed both Casper and his mother when the judges of the Edison National Science Contest informed them that one of their contestants had submitted a model for a thermonuclear device that as far as they could tell would work. National security prevented Casper from being declared the official winner, but it got him into Yale.

Will scratched the back of his head. "It's almost as if he lacks joy receptors."

"Where are they located in the brain?"

"I don't know; I just made them up."

"Geniuses are always lonely." Nora turned off the light.

"I don't know if he's a genius." Friedrich was jealous. "Anyway, why do you say that?"

"Because I live with one." He knew it wasn't true, but he liked hearing it.

Friedrich's black-and-white photo of the Bagadong fermenting vessel did not do justice to the presence of the object among the Bunsen burners and test-tube racks of the old chem lab in the basement of Sterling Hall. Fashioned from the trunk of a belian ironwood tree, nearly three feet tall, weighing nearly two hundred pounds, it held just shy of four gallons. Cut with stone axes and hollowed out with hot coals, it was carved to look like a squatting man on one side, a woman on the other. The male figure had a phallus, as long and stout as a billy club. The head of the penis was sheathed in beaten brass that had been cannibalized from an artillery shell. The female figure featured breasts nippled with iron nails stolen from a missionary, and a vagina fashioned from the jawbones of a primate (Dr. Winton, after much debate, had decided that its teeth had once belonged to an orangutan). Friedrich was more interested in the ethnopsychological implications of the fact that the male and the female shared the same head—which was also the lid of the fermenting vessel.

Perched on the slate countertop next to the lab sink, the periodic table bannered behind it, the figure seemed to cast a shadow on them, even when it didn't. Hands, sweat, use had smoothed its surface and given the wood a darkly damp patina, as if it were perspiring. The eyes of the shared face were wide open; the whites were inlays of bone, with huge dilated pupils of red coral. The mouth was lipped in cowry shells, the man/woman was neither smiling nor angry; the expression was one of superior calm.

As Friedrich had hoped, the residue of dried *gai kau dong* in the bottom of the vessel provided the yeast culture necessary to ferment the kwina leaves into a crude beer. By day seven they had 3.78 liters of The Way Home as it would have been prescribed by the Bagadong shaman to ameliorate the grief and fears and depressions of a bereaved widow, an orphaned child, a spurned lover, or a warrior who had lost his hand, or his courage. To make administering this drug easier and more scientific re: dosage, as well as to ascertain in what form, if any, kwina was psychoactive, Friedrich and Winton distilled off the alcohol, then dried the remaining liquid in a vacuum.

By day ten The Way Home was reduced to a saltshaker's worth of faintly chartreuse crystals. *Gai kau dong* was referred to by its initials, GKD. Doctors Friedrich and Winton had not quite become friends but were relaxed enough in one another's company to borrow cigarettes from each other's packs without feeling the need to ask.

It was day eleven. The crystals had been diluted in sterile water at a ratio of a hundred to one. Colorless and odorless, The Way Home now resided in 1,000 milliliter glass-stoppered Erlenmeyer flasks. Friedrich and Winton sat on stools, admiring the purified fruits of their labor. Will's shirtsleeves were rolled up, tie loosened; he wore a black rubber apron tied around his waist. She wore a freshly laundered lab coat and sensible shoes cobbled out of alligator. "What do you think we should call it?"

"Nothing, until we find out if it works." Will wasn't a pessimist. It was just that he had learned the hard way that you won't be disappointed if you expect the worst. They both reached for the pack of cigarettes on the counter at the same time. There was only one Lucky left. "You can have it." Will handed her the smoke.

"We'll share. We're partners, after all, Dr. Friedrich." They never used first names. Winton lit it off the Bunsen burner, took a drag, and passed it to Friedrich. He had sworn to his wife he hadn't started smoking again. When she smelled the stink of cigarettes on his clothes, he blamed it on Winton. He didn't feel guilty about the lie until he tasted Bunny's pink lipstick on the end of that shared cigarette.

"When this is all over . . ." Winton took back her cigarette, ". . . I think I'm going to turn Jack and Jill into a planter." They were her nicknames for the figures on the vessel.

"Please correct me if I'm wrong, but did I ever tell you or imply that you could have the fermenting vessel?"

"No . . ." Bunny stubbed out the shared cigarette. "I apologize for being presumptuous."

"I already promised it to my wife." He hadn't, but Winton's sense of entitlement annoyed him a little more each day.

"Is Nora fond of primitive art?"

"Why do you think she likes me?"

"That is not a question I've ever thought about." She picked a bit of tobacco off the tip of her tongue and jotted down something in her notebook.

Friedrich wondered why he'd brought Nora into the conversation, and changed the subject. "We're gonna need thirty-six rats for our initial tests."

"I should think one or two would be enough to determine if it's toxic. The only way we'll know the psychological effects of GKD is to test it on humans." Winton had put a tea kettle on the Bunsen burner.

"I'm not comfortable letting anyone take this until I've seen hard evidence it has a beneficial effect."

"You're implying I imagined its effect on Lieutenant Higgins?"

"I just don't think you were objective."

"On what grounds?" She looked at him like a dog who'd growled at her.

"Because I think you were in love with your patient and probably had slept with him. All of which I understand and am in no way judging you for. But . . ."

"Point taken." The kettle was whistling. "Well, Doctor, how do you propose to determine whether GKD makes a rat less depressed? Or more to the point, how do you intend to depress the rats that are taking part in your tests? Give them unhappy childhoods? Dead-end jobs?"

"I'll have the rats in a controlled situation that provokes a general sense of hopelessness." He said it like he was ordering a burger at a lunch stand.

"Such as?"

Friedrich winced as his mind tried to chase down a thought that had just poked its head into his consciousness. "You could think of depression as a way of pretending you're dead, like an animal showing its throat. And if we think about this like one of the cannibals who thought this stuff up, to be a good cannibal, you can't be defensive. What makes them function well in their society is the same thing that makes us function well—focused aggression in the face of chronic, inescapable adversity. So we depress the rats by putting them in a situation all their instincts tell them they can never escape from."

"How are we going to do that?"

"Drowning . . . in a pool with no exit, and you can't touch bottom. Put them up against a hopelessness they can feel and taste, and see how long it takes them to give up and stop swimming. That would approximate the emotions that bring on depression in modern-day life."

"Clever, simple, and bleak." Winton looked at Friedrich as if she felt sorry for him.

"That's me." Friedrich scratched his head and looked wistfully out a basement window that offered a view of feet hurrying to places he'd never been.

"What's wrong?" Winton enquired with uncharacteristic softness as she sipped her tea.

"I was just thinking what sort of tank we'll need to build to test all the rats at once."

"I've already got one."

Will didn't really begin to understand who Dr. Winton was until they began testing. The effect of GKD on rats was ascertained in an indoor swimming pool housed in a redbrick Georgian folly on the grounds of her uncle's estate overlooking the Connecticut River. The pool was Olympian in more than length. The roof above it was a giant stained-glass skylight designed by Tiffany to transform overcast afternoons into blue-sky days. There were headless Roman statues, potted palms that touched the ceiling, and a steam heating system that rendered the temperature equatorial.

Friedrich and Winton worked in eight-hour shifts. A butler delivered a hamper of sandwiches and a fresh thermos of coffee twice a day. The groundskeeper had lowered the water level in the pool and removed the ladder, so the drowning rats couldn't claw their way out. They tested male and female pairs and marked them with nickel-sized dots of Easter egg dye on the tops of their heads for easy identification. The rats with the red dot on their head had been fed twenty grams of raw kwina leaves mixed with peanut butter; Friedrich suspected that if the psychoactive properties of the kwina leaves were absorbable in their raw state, the Bagadong shaman would have had his patients chew the leaves or brew them in hot water, like tea, instead of going through the effort of fermentation.

The two rats with blue Easter egg dye on their heads had been fed a hundred milliliters of the alcohol that had been distilled off the fermented *gai kau dong.* (Friedrich thought it unlikely that the psychoactive properties were distilled off into the alcohol, but he was taking no chances with his big chance.)

The pair of rats with the green dot on their head had been fed one ounce of the same form of fermented *gai kau dong* that had had such a healing effect on Dr. Winton's lieutenant.

The rats crowned with purple were the ones Friedrich and Winton were placing their bets on. They had consumed two ounces of the dissolved crystals. Friedrich had pointed out that this would have been the equivalent of a human being imbibing a gallon of The Way Home. Winton had argued that since they were interested in seeing a clear demonstration of its effects, they should not be too concerned with the fate of the rats. The pair she had fed three ounces of crystals went into convulsions and stopped breathing before they got around to deciding whether to dot them with pink or black.

The control group, those that had had nothing but kibble for breakfast, were marked with a spot of yellow.

Friedrich had worked with rats before—they bit. Their incisors vibrated, cut you to the bone. Under the fluorescent lights of a psych lab, it was easy to be detached while watching a rat drown or shock himself to death. And if they had just bitten you, it was acceptable, even natural, to take some adolescent pleasure in having a hand in their demise. But Friedrich found the idea of watching the rats struggle, panic, give up, and sink to the bottom of a pool decorated with a mosaic likeness of a robber baron wearing a toga and holding a trident both ironic and depressing. He was flushed with enough adrenaline that the thought that he identified with the rat made him smile as he lorded over the drowning pool.

The realization that he had partnered up with a woman connected by blood to the kind of money and power that built indoor pools that weren't used because the owner preferred to spend the spring tarpon fishing in the Gulf of Mexico not only awed Will Friedrich, but made him feel at the very bottom of the primal cortex of his brain that he had stepped into a trap of his own making, that something was now being tested on him.

Some of the rats treaded water, face to the wall of the pool, until their noses bled. Others swam back and forth across the pool at odd angles, hour after hour, in the hopes that a different trajectory would lead them out of the exitless hell their rat lives had become.

Just after lunch on day three, the rats began to die. The first pair to go were the two that had been fed the alcohol. Friedrich was not surprised. Of course, a hundred milliliters of alcohol in an eight-ounce animal was the equivalent of a human drinking a dozen martinis and swimming the English Channel. Five hours and eleven minutes later, the first of the two rats who had ingested the kwina leaves turned on his back and drowned. The female gave up eleven minutes later. A few minutes before ten o'clock, the control pair began to show signs of giving in to the madness of their plight.

Friedrich was getting tired of waiting for rats to drown. His efforts to turn off the heat in the pool house had been unsuccessful. He had taken off his trousers and was sitting in his boxer shorts when Dr. Winton showed up early for her 12:00 to 8:00 A.M. shift. The temperature was nearly a hundred. Friedrich was too hot and tired to be embarrassed. "Sorry, I didn't expect you for another half hour . . ."

"I understand completely. Sensible. I should have worn shorts myself." She watched him as he pulled on his trousers and reached for his shirt. She was as neat and clean as a printed page. She stayed in a guest room up at her uncle's big house; it was easy for her to stay fresh. As always, her hair was braided into a serpentine bun. For an instant it looked like the male of the control pair was going to give in to the inevitable. But at the last second, he followed the female as she headed yet again for the opposite side of the pool.

Friedrich's mouth tasted like an ashtray. He was looking forward to a shower and a few hours' sleep next to his wife. Winton had a sticky bun in one hand and a cup of tea in the other. Her eyes were fixed on the pair of rats marked with purple dye. They had decided that if those two, the ones that had been given The Way Home, survived eight hours longer than any of the other rats, they would know they were onto something. "You know, there's no real need for you to drive back in the morning. I'll call you and let you know how it turns out."

"I think I'll stay through the night and see for myself."

"Does that mean that you don't trust me to take accurate notes?"

"It means I'm curious." The butler knocked. Instead of the usual hamper, he wheeled in a tea cart.

Winton explained, "I thought you deserved a decent meal." There were lamb chops with paper socks on the end of the bone and asparagus and scalloped potatoes under a silver chafing dish.

Friedrich hoped food would wake him up. He waited for her to join him. "Please, don't stand on ceremony. Start without me." She was peering down at the control rats now. "Hey, you, Butch." She was talking to the male control rat. "That's cheating." Winton's nicknames and one-sided conversations with lab animals was getting on Friedrich's nerves. He looked over just in time to see the male rat climb up on the female's back. "The brute's drowning her to stay alive."

Friedrich helped himself to the potatoes. "They're copulating." His mouth was full.

"That's how my uncle says he wants to go." The rats continued to mate as they sunk to the bottom of the pool.

At 6:00 A.M. the following morning, the rats who had been fed the same fermented Way Home that the shamans prescribed and that Winton's lieutenant had imbibed began to tire. Snapping at one another midpool, it almost seemed as if they argued briefly about when to give up. They drowned almost simultaneously. But the two who had consumed GKD in its purest form, two ounces of diluted crystals each, were still swimming laps.

Winton handed Friedrich a cup of coffee that tasted like it had been brewed in a sock. Together they watched the rats swim back and forth, back and forth, rodent eyes glowing red in the first light of the day; undaunted and unfazed by their predicament, they endured, certain they would prevail. Dr. Winton flicked her cigarette into the pool and clapped her hands. "We've done it."

Friedrich yawned and smiled at the same time. "It would appear so, Dr. Winton." Friedrich was thinking how he'd surprise Nora with the news. Flowers? Candy? Or would he trick her, pretend the test was a bust, get her to feel sorry for him, and then pull her into bed with his triumph. If he waited another fifteen minutes, the big kids would be at school.

Winton stared at one of the strawberries that were left over on the dinner tray, then slowly, deliberately, she popped one in her mouth and walked over to the bar at the far end of the pool and produced a bottle of Veuve Clicquot.

"What's that?"

"Breakfast." She handed him the champagne to open and stuffed three more strawberries into her mouth.

It had been twenty-seven hours since Friedrich had slept. He was punchy with fatigue. The thought of champagne on top of the bad coffee was making him feel queasy. He popped the cork anyway. The rats on The Way Home were still swimming. On the way home was where he should be.

They drank the champagne from coffee cups. Friedrich watched the drugged rats swim on. "Think we can reproduce this synthetically?"

"If our initial pilot study with humans pans out, we'll get the organic chemistry department to spectrum it out in a column chromatography." Winton was looking at her reflection in the glassy surface of the pool. "One thing's for certain: It's some kind of antihistamine."

"How can you say that?"

Winton was looking at her watch. "I'm allergic to strawberries. I love them, but whenever I eat them, I break out in hives in a matter of minutes . . . antihistamine's the only thing that takes care of it. It was just a hunch."

It took Friedrich a minute to put it together. "You took The Way Home?"

"If I didn't believe in it enough to test it on myself, I couldn't very well give it to my patients, could I?" Her smile was Mona Lisa lazy. Her pupils were dilated. And her voice and manner were softer and more inviting than he could ever remember.

Friedrich was furious. It was unscientific, it was unprofessional; she could have had a toxic reaction, she could have had an epileptic seizure and stopped breathing, like the two rats they put in the garbage.

"How long ago?" Friedrich's voice was calm, but he was angry.

"About when you had that cup of coffee." She smiled.

"How the hell much did you take?"

"About as much as you would give a fifty-pound rat." She wasn't trying to be funny.

"How do you feel?" Friedrich began to make notes.

"Like celebrating."

Friedrich took her pulse. It was fast, but within the normal range. "Any paranoia?"

"No." She closed her eyes. "Just a strong desire to . . . celebrate."

"What does that mean to you?"

"Well, the night I graduated from medical school, I celebrated by taking off my clothes and skinny-dipping. Swam all the way across the river to the other side."

"Is that what you want to do now?" Friedrich was speaking to her like a patient.

"No. At the moment, I feel the urge for physical release. You know, that tingling sensation you feel before you realize you're feeling lust."

"How do you feel about that?"

"It's a nice feeling. Don't you like it when you feel strong sexual desire for someone?"

Friedrich felt himself getting an erection. In his mind she had already taken off her clothes, and he wanted to get out of there before she actually did. "I'm uncomfortable with you making sexual overtures toward me."

"I wasn't thinking about having sex with you or anyone in particular, Dr. Friedrich."

He might have believed her if it hadn't been for the smile on her face. "We'll talk about this tomorrow. I think I should go home now."

"What's wrong with you?"

"I didn't agree to this. We're not part of the experiment." His voice echoed over the water.

"Then why are you taking notes?"

Friedrich put down his pen and began to pack up his briefcase.

"You're a psychologist. You asked me a question, I gave you a candid answer, which you misinterpreted. It happens to me with my patients."

"You are not my patient." Friedrich was walking, but he felt like running.

"Drive carefully."

Friedrich paused at the far end of the pool, reached into water, and grabbed hold of the last two rats by the fur on the back of their necks, then walked out the door. As he gently set them down into the grass and watched them disappear into the garden, he felt like he was dreaming.

Even though he told himself he had done nothing wrong, Friedrich could not shake that *what have I just done to my life* feeling as he drove home that morning. The test was an unqualified success. There was no question the rats had survived because they had been given The Way Home. But did that mean they were happier? Certainly, the happiness Friedrich thought these results would bring him was not forthcoming.

He was angry at Winton for dosing herself with the drug without telling him. By not giving him the chance to be the first guinea pig, she had deprived him the opportunity to join that heroic tradition of doctors who dared greatness by testing their miracle cures on themselves.

Hartford dentist Horace Wells became the father of anaesthesiology, proving in 1844 the pain-killing capabilities of nitrous oxide, aka laughing gas, by inhaling a large quantity of the same, and ordering a fellow dentist to pull out a perfectly good tooth from his jaw, reporting he "didn't feel as much as the prick of a pin." Wells ended up a chloroform addict who committed suicide in jail. More disturbing to Friedrich was remembering something about Wells's partner and former apprentice ending up rich and famous off of Wells's discovery.

Friedrich searched his mind for a medical first with a happier ending and thought of Dr. Werner Forssmann, who proved it was safe to catheterize the human heart by slicing open his arm and feeding a catheter into the right atrium of his own heart. Johns Hopkins had fired him for the stunt, but Forssmann was a shoo-in for the Nobel Prize one of these years. Friedrich knew Madame Curie's husband had done a first to himself, but at that moment was too infuriated to recall it.

Winton could blame her sexual overture, whether she was conscious of it or not, on the drug, dismiss it as a side effect. But he had no easy excuse, no chemical scapegoat, for the jumble of primitive impulses he felt as he ran from the drowning pool.

Should he tell Nora what had happened? Confess everything and thereby convince himself, if not her, that it was nothing? His work with Winton was just beginning. They would be alone together for hours on end in the months to come. Years to come, if they were truly successful. If Nora got jealous this early in the game, life would be hell. If he told her the truth, i.e., that he ran away with an erection, it'd be almost as bad as if he'd stayed there and . . .

Driving slowly, letting others pass, he wondered, *If I've done nothing, why do I feel guilty?* He knew the answer to that when he began wondering if he would have been more successful sooner if he had married someone as rich and powerful, and as accomplished, as Bunny. And if Nora knew he had such thoughts, what was to keep his wife from thinking likewise? She could cheat on him in her imagination and he would never know. She could be cheating on him right now. Friedrich shook the thought from his mind and decided to say nothing.

By the time he'd gotten to Hamden, Friedrich's paranoia, his doubts about himself, his motives, and his questions about the path he was on had evaporated. He deserved to be a success. Friedrich was lost in the warmth of his newfound entitlement and self-appreciation. His needs, his predicament, were unique. They had to be protected. It was clear to him: Without him as himself the world would be a dimmer place.

Friedrich stepped on the gas and made it to Hamelin Road in record time. He was neither embarrassed nor chagrined when he turned the key and the White Whale backfired and refused to stop rumbling. The brown spots on his lawn and the peeling paint on his front porch didn't depress him. He picked up his daughters' bicycles and Will's skates with a smile on his face.

The three oldest were in school, Jack was napping, he heard Nora in the shower. He stepped in with her without bothering to take off his clothes.

"Have you lost your mind?" Nora laughed, as she pushed her hair out of her face and looked up at him.

"On the contrary, I have finally found it." His hands were on her, he was pleased to find her breasts were rounder and fuller than those of Dr. Winton.

"Come on, Will, what's going on?"

"I'm happy."

"So I see."

He kissed her on the mouth. "I need you."

He turned her around to face the wall. They had never done it that way before.

After they were done, they went into the bedroom, closed their eyes, and began to whisper. In the past, whenever she had asked him to touch her in a certain way, tried to instruct him in the likes and dislikes and curiosities of her body, Friedrich would balk, freeze up, and take her suggestions as criticism. But for the next hour her husband listened to her, took in what she wanted to share with him as he had never done before, or in fact, would ever be able to again for the rest of their marriage.

Afterward, they lay in bed and he told her, "This is going to change everything."

Friedrich had no idea that the reason his coffee had tasted so bitter that morning was due to the fact that Dr. Winton had sweetened it with The Way Home without telling him.

As planned, Dr. Friedrich and Dr. Winton met in the lab at four to type up their notes. They were clinically courteous with one another. After they had finished collating their observations re: the effects of The Way Home on the rats, Friedrich broached its effect on Dr. Winton.

"I don't mean to cause you any embarrassment, Dr. Winton, but I think it would be of value to discuss some of what you said when you were under the influence of GKD."

"I quite agree." She watched him as she sipped her tea. She wondered if it was her imagination, or did he in fact seem bolder, more aggressive, since she had given him the drug in his coffee. She had intended to tell Dr. Friedrich the truth the night before, but his reaction had been so emotional, she did not want to risk upsetting him. Winton had already decided it would be more informative to watch for any lingering effect on him without his knowing that he was a subject in her private study.

"Do you think GKD's a sexual stimulant?"

"If you mean, did it arouse me or heighten the sense of arousal I felt at that moment, I would have to say 'no.' But it did make me feel on a conscious level that I would like to feel that way. And I felt none of the shame or inhibition that would have, under normal circumstances, prevented me from revealing that to a man. I felt free to be myself, and to make the most of myself." Dr. Friedrich made note of what she was saying in a black composition book. "You don't think that's a good thing, Dr. Friedrich?"

"I don't see it as good or bad. It's just anecdotal evidence worth noting."

"There's one other thing that might be worth noting." Winton was washing her teacup now. "I didn't worry in the least about what I had said to you, or have the slightest concern about having put you in what was so obviously an uncomfortable position, until a few hours ago."

Casper hitchhiked north that Saturday morning, passing the time between rides calculating perfect numbers, those whose proper positive divisors (excluding itself) add up to the number: 1 + 2 + 3 = 6; 1 + 2 + 4 + 7 + 14 = 28; 1 + 2 + 4 + 8 + 16 + 31 + 62 + 124 + 248 = 496; 1, 2, 4, 8, 16, 32, 64, 127, 254, 508, 1016, 2032, 4064 = 8128 . . . While he begged a lift with his right thumb, he held his left hand aloft, and with his bony, nail-bitten forefinger, traced and erased an endless stream of invisible numbers across the ether as if the whole universe were his blackboard.

They had taught Casper that all the perfect numbers that had ever been calculated were even, but Casper pushed on, sure there was an odd one waiting for him out there somewhere. Numbers bubbled up within him with the carbonated fizz of a shaken-up bottle of pop, igniting inside his head with a silent flash, like fireworks exploding underwater as he worked the progression over and over again as effortlessly as anyone else would hum a tune.

Casper didn't just have a feel for numbers, he *felt* them. As such, each digit had a separate personality: 1 was a bright light; 5 was loud, like a clap of thunder; 6 was the most modest of integers; 9 the grandest. They were friends he had known since the crib, played with since before he could speak.

He was juggling the divisors of $2^{88}(2^{90} - 1)$ when the driver of a Mayflower moving van coming out of the Esso station across the road pulled over and gave him a ride all the way up Route 1 to Providence. When he got out there, Casper was thirty-seven digits further down the road to nowhere, his numerical joyride was interrupted by a lift from a Presbyterian minister and his wife on their way to see a ballgame at Fenway Park. The wife gave him a cheese sandwich wrapped in wax paper, which he ate even though the bread was stale and he wasn't hungry.

When the minister asked him if he thought God was a Red Sox or a Yankees fan, Casper stopped chasing the perfect number long enough to stutter, "G-G-G-God loves the g-g-game more than those who play it." And though Casper didn't mean it the way the minister thought, after moments of silence, the reverend announced he was going to use the line in his next sermon, and went two and a half miles out of his way to drop Casper off at Harvard Square.

From the bounce in his step, the way he paused to smell the just opened blossoms of a cherry tree, you would have thought Casper had just found an odd perfect number. In a way, he had done something almost as incredible: He had hitchhiked to Boston to see a girl. Only he didn't think of it that way; to Casper, this outing into the larger world was an experiment with/on himself.

As he walked across the square in the direction of the Radcliffe dormitory where she resided, he could still not quite believe he had set out on this journey, and even more amazing, that he hadn't turned back on this wildly optimistic, decidedly un-Casper-like adventure. Not only was this the first time he had ever hitchhiked, it was the first time he had ever dared to go see any girl anywhere, ever. Most reckless of all, the girl had no idea he was coming or that he even existed. He didn't want his past to contaminate the chemical reaction he hoped to experience within himself.

The girl he had come to see was the sister of the same Whitney who had sent him to report on the parrots, roommate of Whitney's girlfriend, Alice Wilkerson, the girl with salamander eyes who had described Nina Bouchard as "insanely smart, but dumb about dumb stuff." And most important of all, Alice Wilkerson had said out loud, "You'd like each other." And since the parrots had turned out to be real rather than the practical joke he had suspected, and the Friedrichs had not just been polite but actually seemed to like him, i.e., had invited him to dinner, and Mrs. Friedrich, who was smart and a looker (not that she made a big thing about it) had told him to call her Nora and come back and see them soon and kissed him on he cheek instead of just shaking hands good-bye . . . it seemed not unreasonable in the calculus of Casper's mind that perhaps someone "insanely smart" might be crazy enough to, if not like him, at least not dismiss him as pond slime.

As he pedaled back from Friedrich and the parrots that night, Casper had recalculated the trajectory of his life, and after two weeks of figuring in every unknown variable into the unknown equation of his life, had come to the conclusion that the long shot that he might know what it was like to be kissed by a female other than his mother and a professor's wife who felt sorry for him was worth the probability of humiliation.

To limit the downside of this experiment he was conducting on his life, Casper had not told Whitney he was going to drop in on his sister unannounced. He had not given the features editor of the *Yale Daily News* the slightest indication of his interest or intentions other than casually inquiring as he worked the mimeograph machine, "What do you think Alice meant when she s-s-she said your s-s-sister was 'insanely smart'?"

"What?" Whitney was standing on *Webster's* dictionary, raising and lowering his heels to the floor, stretching out his Achilles tendon in the hopes of playing football next fall. "I'm not quite sure I follow you."

"Did she mean she was c-c-crazy and smart or u-u-uniquely intelligent in a way that others p-p-perceived odd?"

"Odd."

"How odd?"

"She writes her English papers backward to make it more challenging."

Casper showed no emotion as he took in the information that day. But now that Nina's dormitory was in sight, Casper's pace slowed and his heartbeat rose. No question, his body chemistry was affected by proximity. His forefinger began to work that spot on his temple. His confident stride turned into a shuffle.

Though he was entirely sexually inexperienced save for the daughter of the cranberry picker who lived in the upper half of their two-family company shack back in Seabury, New Jersey, one Molly Klinger who ate roots and showed her vagina to him and every other child of either sex who lived in the neighborhood, he had heard his classmates at Yale who had dates on weekends talk about girls and how to make them do stupid things like actually like you. He had listened to the boasts and lies and exaggerations of the young men destined to lead America, and had distilled that there was some truth to the maxim "When women are concerned, honesty is not the best policy."

In fact, to Casper, the whole courtship ritual, putting your best foot forward, being polite, courteous, etc., was at best deceptive and ultimately dishonest. He had seen the way Yalies who delighted in being able to belch the longest and loudest took pride in mustering up farts that smelled like a dead animal left in an unplugged icebox, deceived the girls, blind dates, and sweethearts they squired about on weekends. Noses were not picked, farts were not released, belches were swallowed, and guys who would rather have a root canal than take a class on art history jumped at the suggestion of spending the afternoon at the museum. And even though the guys said they did it to make it to first base or get a hand job, when Casper analyzed their fun rather than envied it, the scientist in him saw that the real reason they pretended to be someone else was that if they didn't, they would be alone.

Casper had always felt superior in his loneliness. Yet the events of the previous few weeks had made him wonder how the push and pull he observed other bodies exerting on one another might affect his own gravity.

As he stood before Nina's dormitory on the Radcliffe quad, it was hard for him to imagine the women of the Seven Sisters schools in their saddle shoes, cashmere sweaters, and camel-hair coats burping and farting and picking their noses, but logic told him that they were both as desperately phony and lonely as guys were.

The rub that paralyzed Casper was that if everybody who walked on their hind legs was lonely, why didn't they just accept the feeling as a fact of life? Why the compulsion to pretend to always feel different than how you really feel? And though he did not want to be part of the deception, he felt himself being pulled by a force as real as gravity into a strange place in search of a girl he had never met who did not know he was coming.

The first floor of Nina's dorm was a lounge: sofas and armchairs upholstered in couples and threesomes, warming themselves around a fireplace that was not lit and did not work. There was a girl with red-rimmed eyeglasses that made her look like a surprised insect seated at the reception desk. Casper felt himself disassociate as he watched the Casper reflected by the mirror behind the desk approach the insect girl.

"Can I help you?" Casper had never felt so humiliated to be a human being.

"Is A-Alice Wilkerson here?" Casper was sure she was counting the blackheads on his nose.

"You know Alice?" The insect girl squinted up her face in disbelief.

"Y-y-yes. Yes. In a way." Casper was not going to stoop to a lie.

"Well, you're out of luck. She's visiting her boyfriend at Yale."

"Well, a-a-actually, I've come to see her roommate."

"I get it." The girl at the desk smiled at him like she actually thought he might be okay. "Nina just left for the library. If you hurry, you can catch her." She came out from behind the reception desk. "She drives a two-tone Buick, red and black, can't miss it."

"Students are allowed to have cars?"

"Nina's father fixed it." A father that fixes things, special privileges, the "insanely smart" Nina was suddenly sounding like an "insanely spoiled" rich girl. He told himself the journey was an enlightening disappointment, a mistake he would never make again.

He left the dormitory, ready to hitchhike home. Then he saw Nina opening the door to a Buick that matched the description. Her eyes were wide set, her mouth generous and bowed, her hair was the golden brown of a wild silk moth. She was beautiful—too beautiful.

He was ready to call off the experiment. It would never work out with someone this lovely. Then he saw she had two canes and her legs were encased in steel braces. Casper was transfixed as he watched her struggle to open the car door. She reached down to release the lock in her braces at the knee, and slid gracefully behind the wheel. Whereas Nina's being crippled by polio would not have been a plus to 99.99 percent of Yale freshmen, to Casper Gedsic it meant that he had a chance.

Casper was so overwhelmed by the way in which the improbable had morphed into the possible before his eyes that he did not think to call out her name until the Buick had pulled away.

Casper began to run. It was difficult to keep up the pace and ask directions to the library at the same time. Getting lost twice, nearly hit by a laundry truck once, an hour later he was still two blocks from the library. Bent over double to catch his breath, he saw the rear end of Nina's two-tone Buick halfway up a one-way street.

A man in a leather jacket and jackboots was leaning up against the driver's window. His hair was duck-assed over his collar and his cheeks were cratered with acne. Leather Jacket looked up and down the street and opened Nina's car door. When a police car passed, he closed it, stepped away from the car, and lit a cigarette. Casper was disappointed that Nina would have a friend like this. It was a heartbeat or two before he realized that this juvenile delinquent was about to steal Nina's car.

Casper was on the passenger side of the Buick now. He saw the custom hand controls mounted on her steering wheel for the brakes and gas. More important, he saw the keys dangling in the ignition.

The face on the duck's ass swiveled in his direction. "Get lost."

"J-j-j-just give me a minute t-t-t-to . . ." Casper smiled as he opened the passenger door. He had been beaten up enough in his life to know that a grin confuses a bully before it enrages him. Casper was hoping that would give him enough time to . . .

"What the fuck are you doing?"

"I f-f-forgot my keys." Casper had them in hand now. He pushed the driver's side door lock down before Leather Jacket could open the door and throw him out of the car.

"Why didn't you say it was your car?"

Casper locked the door now. "I didn't know you were trying to steal it."

Leather Jacket laughed. No question, the trajectory of Casper's life had changed.

He found Nina between HA and HL in the library's card catalog room. He passed her slowly, goggle-eyed, like a fish in a neighboring aquarium. It was too good to be true. She was writing down the Dewey decimal numbers of the works of Heidegger. She had just jotted down the title of Heidegger's *Being and Time*. Her nostrils flared and she tickled her cheek with a tendril of her hair as she flipped through the card catalog. All wasn't just right in the world; it was perfect. He had pushed his luck enough for one day.

Wanting to savor the possibilities of the future, not wanting to risk a setback, he borrowed an envelope from an assistant librarian, and on the outside wrote Nina's name and the following: "For the time being, being and time does not permit more than this thank you for giving me the opportunity to prevent your car from being stolen. Do you think Heidegger was really a Nazi? Yours respectfully, Casper G."

Putting the keys inside, he licked the envelope and handed it to the assistant librarian. "Could you give this to the girl with the cane over by the card catalog?"

As she read the note, Casper admitted, "It's d-d-d-difficult to be funny about Heidegger." When the assistant librarian laughed out loud, Casper shushed her and headed home to replan the rest of his life.

WANTED
VOLUNTEERS FOR PSYCHOLOGICAL STUDY

Dr. Winton and Dr. Friedrich are interested in individuals who have experienced loss, grief, disappointment, and/or depression and would like to see an improvement in the quality of their lives. Participants must be available to meet on campus one hour every week from May 15th to September 15th and keep a brief journal of their reactions to the medication they will be taking. Those selected will receive five dollars per week for their participation, payable at the conclusion of the study.

CONTACT
Dr. William T. Friedrich, rm 307, Psych Building
Dr. B. Winton, rm 211, Inst. Human Relations.

Winton had typed up the above while Casper was on his way home from Radcliffe. It was Monday now. Friedrich was in the lab fermenting the second batch of GKD. They were equally impatient to get started. Though the doctors would have said they had nothing in common save for a scientific interest in the chemistry of unhappiness, both had the same chip on their shoulders. Doctors Winton and Friedrich felt equally gypped by life. Curiously, each felt that the other had an unfair advantage. Winton made no secret of the fact that she believed that if she had been born a man, not only would the world have been her oyster, but she would already have devoured it.

Likewise, as he watched her brew her tea over his Bunsen burner, Friedrich was not above stewing. *If I had one tenth your fucking money and connections, I'd . . .* But if things were fair, neither of them would have been blessed with an IQ that put them in the ninety-ninth percentile.

Their plan was to have forty people take part in the test: twenty men, twenty women. Half would be given a placebo, the others a daily dose of The Way Home eyedroppered onto a sugar cube—roughly a quarter of what had saved the life of the two test rats that Friedrich had liberated into the garden. All human participants would be led to believe they were given something that would make them feel different, i.e., better. Friedrich and Winton would have liked to have a larger test sample and a longer test period, but they barely had enough kwina leaves for four months.

Friedrich read what Winton had typed up. "When did you decide we should pay our test subjects?"

"If we pay them at the end, they'll be less likely to drop out of the study. It's summer. The volunteers we're looking for are unhappy, and unhappy people are unreliable people."

"Where are we going to get the money?" At five dollars a week, Friedrich's half would be sixteen hundred dollars. He only made sixty-eight hundred dollars a year. "I don't want to wait around for a grant, and besides, we'll be in a much stronger position to get real funding for this if we have data."

"I wasn't thinking of a grant."

"Really?" He pronounced the word as Bunny did, like a slow slap in the face.

She took it and answered back in kind, "I'll contribute the funds."

"I'm not comfortable with that."

"I'll loan you your share. You can pay me back. The important thing is maintaining our momentum and not having them quit on us."

"It puts me in an awkward position."

"Okay, let's not test it on civilians. It'll be easier if we test it on long-term mental patients. I guarantee you you'll get more dramatic results." It was what she had wanted from the start.

"I'm interested in seeing if GKD can keep people out of mental hospitals, help them function while they're still functional." In his daydreams Friedrich imagined a world five years from now where a synthesized substitute for GKD would be prescribed like penicillin. He knew the survival of a few rats was no guarantee of the fame or fortune he longed for. But it was possible the drug and other drugs it could lead them to might just be able to alter the chemical reactions within the brain so that depression, schizophrenia, anxiety, compulsive behavior, and all the rest of what ails our brains might be treatable with a prescription, filled at your corner drugstore.

That very morning, halfway through shaving his upper lip, he had so given in to the dream he found himself fantasizing about who they would get to play him if they made a movie about his contribution to the betterment of mankind. It wasn't so far-fetched. They made a movie about the guy who cured syphilis, *Dr. Ehrlich's Magic Bullet,* starring Edward G. Robinson. Friedrich considered the possibilities as he scraped off the night's whiskers. Jimmy Stewart? Gary Cooper? He cut himself as his mind auditioned Gregory Peck for the role Friedrich hoped to live.

"Without impressive test results, we won't get that far. Look, we're both after the same thing." More or less, that was true. "My money can make it happen faster. For all we know, someone else could be doing the same research with kwina that we are now."

"I can guarantee you that they're not."

How could Friedrich be so sure? He had grown more confident, determined. She wondered if the dose of *gai kau dong* she'd given him had anything to do with the change. It had been three days since she had dosed them both with The Way Home. Friedrich was still in the dark about that, but she still felt the tingle of empowerment.

"I don't care about the money. But if you're too proud to accept it, we can put it in writing. All monies I invest in research will come out of first profits." It was the first either had mentioned that there might be money in this. "I'll keep receipts, I'll charge you interest. You can even dictate the agreement. Happy?" She pulled a pen out of her purse and took a sheet of blue carbon paper from the drawer to make them both a copy.

Will cleared his throat. "Doctors Friedrich and Winton agree that they are equal partners in all research concerning the medicinal applications of kwina leaves and the indigenous fermented beverage *gai kau dong*. Any and all scientific publications regarding this search will bear both their names, and any profits stemming from their research will be split fifty-fifty after Dr. Winton has been repaid one thousand six hundred dollars."

"You don't trust me, do you?"

"I trust human nature." Friedrich pocketed his copy in his wallet. Winton put hers in her purse.

That afternoon their advertisement for test subjects appeared on the bulletin boards of Yale, thumbtacked next to offers of summer jobs, tutoring French in Nantucket, math on the Cape, and employment as counselors and waterskiing instructors at lakeside sleepaway camps in the Adirondacks. In the hopes of recruiting twenty female guinea pigs, Dr. Winton posted the same offer in the nurses' locker room at New Haven Hospital and the student lounge of a nearby girl's junior college.

Friedrich had stayed up all night grading quizzes so that he and Winton could get an early start in the lab the next morning. She was late. He was struggling to drain the fermenting vessel by himself. Full, it weighed over two hundred pounds. One hand gripping its ironwood penis, the other clutching its nail-tipped breast, Friedrich was embracing the dark figures that decorated its facade as if in a ménage-à-trois when Winton finally slammed through the door. "You're late. Give me a hand before I drop this goddamn thing."

"Drop it . . . Our lab privileges have been revoked. We can't do the test. I found this in my mailbox this morning." She shoved a tersely worded handwritten note from Winton's no longer kindly old mentor, Dr. Petersen, in Friedrich's face as he muscled the fermenting vessel back onto the countertop.

It read as follows: "Dr. Winton, you have betrayed my trust. This is not the research project you outlined when you obtained my permission to use the facilities of this school. I want you and Friedrich in my office at ten o'clock to discuss disciplinary action."

Friedrich felt like he was being flushed. His endorphins swirled him downward. "Disciplinary action." In an instant the future he had built on the promise of The Way Home crashed down on him. The drug worked. He didn't yet have the statistics to prove it, but he was sure of it. More important, he felt it. He could not, would not, let a fucking old Freudian fossil like Petersen flush not just his idea, but his new, improved idea of himself. Friedrich closed his eyes and imagined taking Petersen's head in his hands and pounding it against the wall. When the fantasy had drawn imaginary blood, Friedrich blinked and shook the image from his head as if it were an insect crawling into his ear. Winton was saying something but he didn't hear her.

"Disciplinary action." No tenure, no full professorship at Yale, no movie.

He wondered how he would break the news to Nora as he put on his jacket and straightened his tie. "What's the bastard's problem? We proceeded exactly as we told him we were going to."

Winton waited until they were halfway up the cool, dark staircase to Petersen's floor to ask, "There wasn't anything that could be construed as unethical or illegal in the way you obtained the kwina and the fermenting vessel, was there?"

Friedrich stopped climbing the stairs. "The answer is no, but it might be construed as unethical or professionally irresponsible that you didn't ask that question before you got involved."

"Rest assured I'll be more careful about my conduct in the future."

To get to Dr. Petersen's office they had to walk down a long, dimly lit corridor lined on both sides with metal shelves that sagged under the weight of more than a hundred gallon-sized glass jars, each containing a human brain floating in a formaldehyde bath. Each brain was carefully labeled in a spidery hand: Carmen Silva, poetess Queen of Rumania; John McCormick, inventor (steel plow); Ephraim Rosenbaum, pyromaniac; Thomas Mangan, alcoholic; Donnata De la Rosa, opera singer; Jim J. Jefferson, Negro tanner; Reginald Chapelle, homosexual; Ian Wainwright, murderer (poisoned twelve women); John J. Seward, Secretary of State; and on and on and on.

Some brains were as dark as coal, others as pink and delectable as a baby's bottom. The one belonging to Dr. Herbert K. Glenway, the nineteenth-century phrenologist who had begged, borrowed, and stolen the collection his whole life and willed it to Yale, looked like it had been used as a football. Because it had.

Dr. Petersen barked, "Enter," before they even knocked. The white-haired shrink who had made a career out of one lunch with Freud didn't bother to stand or shake hands or invite them to sit down. He was combing his beard with a fine-tooth silver comb, a nervous display that accompanied anger. His face was pink, wizened, and ticked with age spots. He looked like a skull inside an udder. "How could you ever think I would allow this?" He crumpled the notice they had posted on the bulletin board and tossed it into a wastepaper basket that bore the college seal.

"The psychology department didn't have a problem with—"

Dr. Petersen cut him off. "Shame on them, shame on you. Have you two been taking this stuff yourselves?"

"Dr. Petersen, I won't dignify that with an answer. But I think it's fair for you to know that if you cancel our lab privileges, I will appeal your decision directly to the board of trustees." Bunny's uncle was on the Board.

Friedrich was stupefied. He had had no idea the study was that important to her.

"I think the board of trustees would share my rather old-fashioned belief that the law means something." Winton looked at Friedrich.

"What law are you under the misperception we have broken?" Friedrich chose his words carefully to offend.

"It is you that is misperceiving the gravity of this situation." The udder shook at his impudence. "You have embarrassed the university and disregarded the welfare of the student body. You may think I am senile, but I am not. And since you insist on making matters worse for yourselves by feigning innocence, I will spell it out: The students you plan to recruit for this test are under twenty-one, are they not?"

"Some of them."

"Fermenting produces alcohol, and it's against the law for individuals under the age of twenty-one to consume alcoholic beverages. It's also against the law for an adult to supply underage individuals with alcohol." Friedrich smiled. "I fail to see the humor in this situation, Dr. Friedrich."

"We evaporated off the alcohol. Sir."

"What?" Petersen looked around the room as if he had woken up from his recurring nightmare and found himself lecturing naked.

The old man didn't know how to back down from his rage. Friedrich helped him. "I apologize, Dr. Petersen, for not making that clear to you."

"Apology accepted." He wanted to forget this had ever happened.

But Winton wasn't finished. "Just in case anyone else has a problem with our research, could you perhaps just give us a short note indicating you have an awareness of what we're doing, and that we have adhered to your guidelines?" Friedrich waited as she got their asses covered in writing.

As they walked down the corridor of bottled brains, Doctors Winton and Friedrich began to giggle like schoolchildren who had gotten away with putting a frog in the teacher's desk.

They worked together until the end of the day. Friedrich went home, Winton was five minutes late to the psychologist she saw twice a week. As usual, she spent most of her remaining fifty minutes ruminating about all the little things she didn't like about Dr. Will Friedrich. What she liked about him was harder to put into words. Her therapist theorized that what attracted her to

Friedrich was that she didn't know much about him. Familiarity breeds contempt wasn't how it was put, but that was the idea.

"Do fish have feelings?" Lucy was worried about the hook. The Friedrichs were going fishing that Sunday, if Dr. Friedrich ever came out of the psych building.

"Not like people do." Nora had been sitting in the White Whale with her four children waiting for her husband to come down for thirty—no, thirty-three—minutes; every time she looked at her watch she felt more trapped by time and motherhood and . . .

Fiona looked up from Nancy Drew. She felt a different kind of trapped—the hot car, the annoying sweetness of her little sister, and Willy picking his nose and wiping his boogers on the pant leg that brushed against her knee as he struggled to assemble the fishing rod her mother had already told him twice not to play with. "That's because fish are cold-blooded," Fiona announced. Reminding her siblings she was the smartest made Fiona feel like she was less trapped. Nora wondered what might have the same effect on herself and still make her feel needed. That was her hook.

"So are some people we know." When her husband and Winton had first advertised for test subjects, they were worried that they wouldn't find forty people willing to volunteer their sadness for a study (so far they had fifty-seven prospective guinea pigs). He and Winton had worked late on Friday and all day Saturday interviewing subjects. Will had promised her that he only had four students to talk to on Sunday morning. He had sworn to her as he ran out of the house that morning to Bunny Winton in her Cadillac that he would be outside waiting for the Whale at 11:30. It was after twelve now. She knew all about The Way Home and how goddamn important it was, and what it was going to mean to them (which, of course, meant him). And even though the rat experiment didn't prove anything to her, she believed him when he told her, "This is going to change our world." But thirty minutes is a hell of a long time for someone who's tired of feeling taken for granted to wait.

Dr. Friedrich had no idea his wife had purchased an open steamship ticket to France on the Holland America line when she was seven months pregnant with Fiona. It was a one-way ticket, passage for one, good for any crossing, bought with the two hundred dollars Nora had never told Friedrich her great and maiden aunt Minnie had given her the morning of their wedding. "Just so you can always change your mind," was what Minnie had said. Nora Elizabeth Friedrich, née Hughes, knew how to keep things hidden. The ticket lay buried in her underwear drawer beneath a negligee her mother had given her for her wedding night, and that she had been too impatient to put on.

Jack lay sprawled across the front seat, head on her lap, sleeping. The fountain pen she hadn't noticed him take out of her purse was clutched in his hand, cap off. She knew the blue ink that had leaked out onto the white of her Mexican skirt wouldn't come out. Will had given her that dress when they were still in college. It had red flowers embroidered around the hem. It made her feel like someone else, someone exotic, someone like that Mexican painter she'd read about in the paper with the one eyebrow. It took her a moment to remember the name. But she wasn't a Mexican painter, she was a mother, and mothers have to learn to leave some things in the drawer. Willy was poking her in the back of the head with the fishing rod she was getting tired of reminding him not to play with. "Willy, stop that." She forgot about the bleeding pen.

For the third time, Willy inquired, "Who's cold-budded?"

"It's cold-blooded, Willy, and nobody we know is that way; we only know nice people." Nora wasn't feeling nice. Why not tell them how it really is? Nice is the exception. Less than nice is the rule. Why make them learn the hard way?

Fiona waited until she had caught her mother's eye in the rear-view mirror to confide conspiratorially, "Dr. Winton's not nice."

"Why do you say that?" Nora tried to make her query sound more casual than it was.

"She called me precocious."

"From Dr. Winton, that's a compliment."

"The fish in *The Fisherman and His Wife* had feelings." Lucy was still worried. "That fish could talk. He gave the fisherman three wishes because he didn't want to stay caught, so he had to have feelings."

Fiona gave Lucy a withering look. "That's a fairy tale for babies, baby."

"Lucy's a baby, Lucy's a baby." Willy teased Lucy because he was scared to do it to Fiona.

"I'm older than you, baby."

"If I catched a talking fish, I'd sell it for lots and lots of money to the zoo and buy a boat and catch more fish." Willy had already announced he wanted a toy cash register for his birthday.

"I wouldn't let you," Lucy told him flatly.

"It's my talking fish, I can do whatever I want . . . baby."

"You're the baby. You still wet the bed, baby." Lucy smiled triumphantly. She enjoyed being mean in defense of the helpless and magical.

"Lucy, we don't tease about things like that. Your brother had an accident. Everybody has them."

"I don't have accidents. Fiona doesn't have accidents. Mommy and Daddy don't have accidents. Only babies have accidents."

Willy swung the fishing rod at his sister. Lucy pushed it away. The rod tip whipped across the side of Nora's face. She felt like she was being mugged by life, punished for something she hadn't done.

Willy wailed. Fiona had just slammed her book down on his knee. "I told you to stay on your side of the seat."

"Quiet, all of you!" Nora was shouting.

"He got his boogers on me."

"Wipe them off. It's not going to kill you."

Nora reached around to grab the fishing rod. Jack rolled off her lap, his head hit the steering wheel, he woke up crying, "I'm hungry."

"Stop it!" If anyone had been listening, they would have

thought she was being attacked. Nora scrambled out of the car. She slammed the door without thinking of little fingers.

"Mommy, what are you doing?" Lucy called out. But Nora didn't answer. She didn't know what she was doing.

Jack was reaching out the window, "Hungry . . ."

Fiona started to get out of the car. "I'm coming."

"Nobody's coming with me. Everybody: Stay in the car." She ran from the vehicle like it was going to explode.

"Mommy, don't leave!" Willy was getting scared. So was Nora. "What's wrong?"

Nora took the stairs to her husband's office two at a time. By the time she'd reached the second floor, she was muttering, "I've had it." She stormed down the green linoleum hallway, her Mexican dress billowing around her. The least depressed of the four lonely undergraduates who were waiting to tell Dr. Friedrich their problems looked up at Nora and thought to himself, "Hot stuff."

Nora opened the door without knocking. She didn't care if she embarrassed her husband or one of his goddamn spoiled Yale brats. She didn't expect to find her husband talking to a pretty forty-three-year-old woman whose skin was the color of orange marmalade. Blue straw hat, flowered dress, polished shoes, she looked like she was going to church. Nora had seen the colored woman cleaning the toilets in the ladies' room at Branford College. She did not say what she'd been planning to say to her husband out of respect for the cleaning woman, not Will. "Excuse me for interrupting." Nora shook the woman's hand. "I'm Nora Friedrich."

"Betty Stackhouse."

Nora's head swiveled to her husband. "You promised."

"Miss Stackhouse, I apologize for this intrusion." His voice was infuriatingly flat and emotionless. Inside, he was raging, *How dare you?* He saw Nora's invasion as symptomatic of a growing lack of respect for him, his work. Things were going so well, something, someone had to sabotage him. Why not his wife? Not that Nora would do it on purpose. But he had female patients who had done that to keep or gain a hold on their husbands. No, Nora would do it out of love, because when you love someone, you overlook their weaknesses, and in doing so, unintentionally encourage those weaknesses until you are taking turns being cripple and caretaker. Between heartbeats, this thought came and sank inside him like a stone. "As you can see, there are people who need to see me."

"Your children need to see you. Your wife needs to see you."

"I hear that." Miss Stackhouse looked at Friedrich as if he were a comb dropped in a urinal.

"Is there anything you have to say before I leave?" Nora gave him one last chance.

"Drive carefully."

"It was a pleasure meeting you, Betty."

Miss Stackhouse eyeballed Friedrich sternly. "You just gonna let her leave?"

"She's just going fishing."

"Yeah, but for what?"

"Where were we, Miss Stackhouse?"

"You asked me why I thinks I de-pressed."

"And?"

"How you feel, all you got to look forward to in this life is cleaning up other people's messes?" The truth was, that was just how Friedrich often felt.

When Nora got back to the car and told the children "Daddy has to work" each displayed their disappointment differently. Fiona sulked and said she wanted to go home. Lucy began to draw a picture to give to Daddy to make up for all the fun he was missing. Willy waited until after they had stopped for gas and everyone had used the bathroom to wet his pants, and Jack sang the only line of the only showtune he knew, "Oh, What a Beautiful Morning" over and over and over again. After they pulled over and put on the extra pair of dungarees Nora had brought in case Willy fell into the river, they all sang along with Jack: "I've got a beautiful feeling . . . everything's going my way."

They were meeting Jens, the animal behaviorist's wife, and

their two girls on a sandy stretch of brook called the Mill River that ran through a forest of ash and maple and dogwood just below a two-mile-long scenic rise of traprock called Sleeping Giant, picnic spot by day, lover's lane at night. She and Will had talked about attempting the latter but never made it. As she drove down the muddy, rutted road to the stream, the Whale's muffler scraping dirt and rocks, Nora wondered if they would make it.

Jens, barely five feet, Anka, over six, and their pale, blue-veined daughters had been there for over an hour. The Dutch contingent had built a fire, rounded it with river rocks, and laid out blankets. His wife knitted as their twin girls solemnly played "Twinkle, Twinkle, Little Star" on a pair of midget violins. Jens was trying to teach their poodle, who could already sit, lie down, roll over, and play dead, to walk on a beach ball.

What was their secret? Being Dutch? Communists? Did getting bombed in World War II make it easier for this mismatched couple to make peace with the disappointments of life? Nora didn't knit, her children couldn't play musical instruments, they didn't have a dog, and her husband's only hobby was ambition. Being an only child, Nora had an ideal of family life that only seemed to be realized in other families.

Nora watched her children tumble out of the Whale and wreak havoc with the sylvan setting. Willy kicked the beach ball out from under the poodle, Fiona bullied away one of the violins and promptly broke a string, Lucy hooked her foot in Anka's yarn as she skipped toward the river, making a snarl of a morning's worth of knitting. And Jack was naked. "I'm sorry . . . Willy, stop it! Fiona, don't. Lucy, say you're sorry . . . Oh, Jack . . ." Her youngest had just thrown his diaper into the campfire.

"What happened to your husband?" Jens nibbled on one of the dog biscuits he had brought to train the poodle.

"Work."

"Your husband is such an American."

"That's one word for him."

Jens, in his short shorts, sandals, and socks, wife and daughters with their clogs and long, blond braids, Dutch beer cooled by the river . . . their foreignness made Nora think of the unused steamship ticket in her underwear drawer and all the steamships that had set sail without her. At that moment she felt like a prisoner to her husband and her children and, most of all, to love. The thought made her feel guilty, less than maternal. Jack reached up to her, "Uppeee!" Nora pulled the youngest up into her arms and began to cry.

"I'm sorry, I don't know what's wrong with me." It was the eighth time she'd apologized since arriving.

"Being loved is exhausting. Go for a walk, you'll feel better, we'll look after the children."

Nora wiped away her tears. As she headed up the path that ran along the brook she heard Jens call out, "Which ungrateful child wants to catch the first fish?"

When she looked back and saw her children clambering around the beer-bellied Dutchman shouting, "Me . . . me . . . me," Nora started to cry again, for just the opposite reason she had burst into tears in the first place. To have life pull on her was maddening. But not to feel that pull was worse. She wondered if it was the same for a man, specifically for her husband.

A half mile later she was feeling better. She'd crossed the stream on moss-covered rocks without falling in. A trout rose and swallowed a dragonfly whole, and a monarch butterfly up from Mexico mistook the red rose on the hem of her skirt for the real thing.

As she turned to go back to the life she had made for herself, Nora looked up at Sleeping Giant. Its feet pointed east, head west, its chin reached for the sky. She hadn't realized she had wandered so close to the slumbering Spirit Monster—that's what her husband had told the children the Mattabeseck Indians believed the sandstone and green traprock to hold. She had been sure Will would give them nightmares with the stories he told them about Sleeping Giant. But Will had a gift for casting a gentle light on scary things.

"According to the Indians, the first thing that Giant's going to do when he wakes up and shakes off his dirt blanket is drink up all the java in the world. Then he's going to eat all the ice cream. And then . . ." She missed her husband when she thought of him like that. Craning her neck back, shielding her eyes from the glare of the sun, she followed the flight of a pair of red-tailed hawks. As she watched them ride the thermals her eye caught hold of a small figure pushing a bicycle across the side of the Giant's nose a hundred feet above her.

What with distance, angle, and glare, it was hard to be sure, but it looked like a child. Stepping back to get a better look, Nora scanned the precipice for a parent. There had to be someone up there with him? It was crazy to let a child drag a bicycle up there.

She had been gone close to forty-five minutes; it was time to get back to her own children. But the reproachful father or mother she expected to appear and pull the child away from the edge didn't. And there was something about the way the boy (she was sure it was a boy now, one wearing a striped T-shirt) kept looking over his shoulder. It reminded her of Willy when she spied him doing something he knew was forbidden—playing in the street, about to light a match—but didn't think anyone but God was watching.

She cupped her hands to her mouth to shout a warning, "Get back . . . Stay where you are . . . are you lost? . . . where are your parents?" But what if he heard her and looked down and got scared and slipped, or fell? Feeling foolish and yet as sure as only a mother can be that something terrible was on its way to happening, Nora began to run.

The path up to the Giant's head was steeper than she remembered. She slipped on loose rock. The boy was no longer visible by the time she got to the top. She was breathing hard, her face was beaded with sweat, and her dress was torn. The sky was dizzyingly blue. You could see all the way to the Long Island Sound. But Nora wasn't looking at the view. As soon as she saw the rusted old girl's fat-tired bicycle, she knew the child that needed her help was Casper.

She found him sitting on the edge of the cliff face that formed the Giant's chin. His legs dangled in the wind. It was a hundred-and-fifty-foot free fall from his perch. Nora didn't know that the black, imitation leather case next to him contained his dissection kit. Or that he had sterilized all the instruments it contained, even though he only needed the scalpel to sever his antecubital vein. He could have cut himself in his dorm room, but he did not want to risk rescue.

His plan was to make an incision at "the faucet," the crook of the arm where blood was taken. Too much of a coward to talk to a crippled girl in a college library, he knew he didn't have it in him to jump. But he could bleed. Once he'd lost enough blood, gravity would pull him over the edge. And even if the sight of his own blood made him nauseous just the way pig blood did in biology class, the dizziness that accompanied his squeamishness would only make it easier to fall.

Casper had chosen this spot for its view of the sea. He wanted to end life looking out at where life began. Perhaps as he fell he'd find a pattern to the irrational numbers that added up to disappointment.

Nora was standing behind him now. Yesterday's newspaper was folded in his lap. Nora didn't recognize the photo of the college girl. But she could read the headline: CAR CRASH KILLS COED. It was Nina Bouchard.

Nora looked down at the picture of the two-toned Buick speared by a telephone pole. The hand accelerator on the steering wheel had gotten stuck.

The wind rustled the pages of the paper. She could see an ant crawling up the back of Casper's neck. He did not bother to brush it away. "Was she a friend?"

"S-s-s-she would have been."

"You didn't know her?" Casper shook his head no. "Then why are you . . . ?"

"It's my f-f-fault." Casper had calculated his culpability. If he had stayed home, if he had let the crater-faced hood steal the car, if he hadn't longed to be her hero, if he had had enough heroism to ask her out on a date, they would have kissed, instead of the Buick and the telephone pole. Casper looked up. He could tell Mrs. Friedrich didn't have a clue. "You'd have to be me to understand."

"Casper, please come back down with me. You're not responsible."

"W-w-we're all responsible. M-m-most of us just don't like to t-t-think about it."

"What I mean is, you're not God."

"W-w-w-we're all God."

"You need to talk to my husband."

"He can't change how I f-f-f-feel."

"He can, I promise." She reached out her hand. She knew she was making a promise her husband couldn't keep. Like Casper said, we're all responsible.

Casper didn't say a word as Nora walked him down off the Giant. Nora told him to put his bike in the back of the Whale. Jens and his wife agreed to bring the children home with them. As she explained to the kids, "Casper doesn't feel well . . . I know he doesn't look sick, but he is."

Casper soothed himself, calculating the number of leaves on the branch of the elm tree that swayed overhead, then the number of limbs on the tree, the number of trees in the woods, in the county, in the state, in the country, in the hemisphere . . .

Nora pulled over at the first phone booth she saw. She hadn't considered the possibility that Will might not be in his office until she started to dial his number. Should she take him to Student Health? To the hospital? Call his mother? She couldn't leave him alone. But she had her own children to look after. And Jack was crying as she drove off.

Casper wasn't her problem, Casper wasn't even her husband's problem. As she listened to the phone go unanswered in her husband's office, she remembered how her aunt Minnie used to say "There's only so much a body can do."

Friedrich was down the hall, about to descend the stairs. He figured the ringing phone was Nora; no one else would call him at the office on a Sunday. He was still seething about the way she had invaded his domain. He ran back down the hall, fumbled with his keys, reached for the receiver, intent on letting his wife know just how pissed off he was—*Does she think I like working on weekends? Enjoy disappointing my children? If she could just stop thinking of herself, stop being the victim,* he *could be the goddamn victim for a change.*

"Thank God you're there."

As soon as he heard the panic in her voice, his anger distilled into worry. "Are you all right?"

"Yes . . . no." She gave him the broad strokes—Casper, cliff, suicide. "No, he didn't jump, but he was about to."

"Bring him here."

It was what she wanted him to say. "I love you . . . I'm sorry about barging in."

"It's all right, I love you, too." Will started to put down the phone, worst-case scenarios began to bubble up inside his head, like Casper's numbers. "Wait, Nora, hold on: Does he seem agitated?"

She looked out the glass of the phone booth. Casper was worrying thin air with his forefinger. "No . . . I mean, I'm not sure."

"Have him lie down in the back while you drive him in."

"Why?"

"He might try to do it again while you're driving."

"What do you mean?'

"You know, jump out of the car, grab the steering wheel, hurt you while trying to hurt himself. Look, I'm probably just being paranoid, but just in case."

"Right, I get it."

Nora approached the Whale cautiously. "Casper, I want you to lie down in the back."

"W-w-w-why?"

"My husband says it will make you feel better."

Casper did as he was told. The Whale, having been an ambulance before Friedrich resurrected it into a station wagon, provided plenty of room for the boy to stretch out. "C-c-convenient of D-D-D-Dr. Friedrich and you having an ambulance."

Will was sitting on the steps of the Psych building waiting when she pulled up. His tie flapped in the wind as he stood up; he stretched and yawned and pushed his cowlick out of his eyes. When things were good, her husband unraveled. But when there was a problem, he was unnaturally calm, eerily at ease. There was a warmth to his detachment.

"You made it." Friedrich opened the back of the Whale and helped Casper out. "I'll call you after Casper and I finish dinner." He held up a grease-stained paper bag.

As Casper pulled his bike out of the back, he stuttered, "I'm a v-v-v-vegetarian."

"And that's why I got you an egg sandwich." Will had his hand on Casper's shoulder as he quietly guided the boy across the lawn. "It's such a gentle evening, I thought it'd be nice to talk outside."

Nora marveled at the lightness of her husband's touch, infinitely kinder to a stranger suffering than he was to himself, or to his wife. He let her know she should leave with a wave of his hand.

They sat on a bench in the courtyard of Sterling Library, fifteen stories of Gothic Revival. Millions of books separated them from the outside world. The lights were on but the library was deserted. Friedrich assessed the potential danger Casper posed to himself by studying the way the boy ate his egg sandwich. He took small, methodical bites, one after another, back and forth across the bread, as if he were eating corn or typing.

Compulsive, but hungry. Though Dr. Friedrich had no data to support it, in his experience, patients who are about to attempt suicide are uninterested in food. After Casper wolfed the egg on rye, Friedrich split a Hershey bar with him. Blood sugar up, doctor and patient began.

"Was today the first time you climbed up on the Giant?"

Casper looked at his feet and nodded yes.

"Any special reason?"

"D-d-didn't your wife tell you?" Before Friedrich could say "I'd rather hear it in your own words," Casper added casually, "I was going to k-kill myself."

"Is that something you think about often?"

"There wasn't a need before." Friedrich had a way of leaning into someone in a conversation that made them feel as if they'd asked a question, even if they hadn't. "I did the math," Casper explained. His eyes followed the vapor trail left by a lonely jet fighter skirting the lower depths of the stratosphere.

"What kind of math?"

"Algorithms. Are you familiar with Claude Shannon's information theory?"

Friedrich nodded. "Vaguely." He had no idea what Casper was talking about.

"He's at MIT." The boy hugged himself and rocked back and forth the way Homer did when he was trying to make himself understood. Each limited by the way their brains worked. Was that the link that connected him to this strange boy? "He developed an equation to calculate coincidence, chance, predicting the unpredictable."

When Friedrich was talking to a patient who claimed to have had lunch with Napoleon or the president of the United States or Satan, he could be reasonably confident the individual had lost touch with reality. But with Casper's brain, he had no idea whether the boy was talking sense or nonsense.

"He's the father of cybernetics." Friedrich, like most people, had not yet heard the word "cybernetics."

"How's all this tie in to the girl, Casper?"

"You haven't read Shannon's work, have you?"

"I told you, I'm familiar with it."

"Well, there's this guy named Kelly who took Shannon's equations and put them to use to make bets."

"Bets on what?"

"On anything in life where chance is involved." Casper wrote the following on the egg bag:

$$\mathbf{E}\log K_t = \log K_0 + \sum_{i=1}^{t} H_i$$

"You take the probabilities in whatever game or wager you're making, plus the insider information, and you have the best strategy for winning. It's derived from information theory, where you have probabilities which are introduced by noise in the system, the information you're trying to convey. You follow me?"

Friedrich nodded dumbly.

"*H* is your edge, insider information, known, random factoids. Me. I stutter when I get nervous or excited." He wasn't stuttering now. "I forget to brush my teeth. I suffer from hyperhidrosis. The only girl I've ever been able to imagine being with who might want to be with me was a cripple, and she's dead. K_t is the outcome of the bets you make, the chances of winning after so many encounters. Getting the girl, the other human element."

"So what does this equation tell you?"

"Put it this way, Dr. Friedrich: I-I-I-I'd have a better chance of playing s-s-shortstop for the Yankees than I do of m-m-meeting another girl like N-Nina."

"And how does that make you feel?"

"Well, mathematically, there's a certain probability of ultimate ruin."

"I'm not talking about the math. I mean you."

"If l-losing someone I never m-met, s-s-someone who is just an idea, hurts this much, what w-would it be like to lose someone I'd actually touched? What p-p-power would the p-p-pain be raised to then? I thought it'd be b-better to start fresh."

"As what?"

"Oxygen, carbon, hydogen, nitrogen, calcium, phosphorus, potassium, sulfur, sodium, chlorine, magnesium, iodine, iron, chromium, cobalt, copper, fluorine, manganese, molybdenum, selenium, tin, vanadium, and zinc."

"So why didn't you take the leap back to the periodic table?"

"I w-w-wasn't going to jump."

"But I thought . . ."

Casper popped open his dissection kit. Friedrich looked at the scalpel, startled. He'd never considered that Casper was carrying a weapon; he should never have let his wife drive him into town.

"Do you hurt now, Casper?"

"N-no."

"Why do you suppose that is?"

"Your wife t-told me you could c-cure me." Will knew Nora hadn't used those words.

"Of what?"

"Of being me." It was at that moment Friedrich realized it was not Homer he related to when he looked at Casper, it was himself. His empathy was genuine, but his interest was selfish.

As the sun set mauve and the stars unfurled on the night, Friedrich and Casper talked about what it meant to be Casper. Dr. Friedrich had listened to many lonely and disturbed souls describing their unhappiness with the human condition over the years, and he had spent many lonely nights himself reading case histories and scientific accounts of every kind of soul sickness, but Casper was the first subject he'd ever encountered who compared his feelings of alienation to the paradoxical observations a physicist by the name of Dr. Fritz Zwicky had made about the gravitational pull of cluster galaxies.

"When you m-m-measure their g-g-gravity, they should be ten times larger than they are. There's a m-m-missing mass. You can't see it, but you know it's there, 'cause you can m-m-measure its pull. Your light's trapped before it reaches another human's eye." Casper licked the tip of the lead of his pencil and began to write more equations on the paper bag.

It was after nine. They'd talked for almost three hours. Friedrich was relieved he didn't feel professionally obliged to check Casper into a psychiatric ward. If he had to write a diagnosis for Casper at that moment, he would have called him a highly functional obsessive compulsive with marginal schizophrenic tendencies. But there were times in his life when he would have diagnosed himself similarly.

If Yale found out a student had attempted suicide, he'd be suspended. And if Yale forced Casper to go back to his mother the cranberry picker (who Casper hadn't mentioned once), he'd be even more depressed about the light that struggled to escape his missing mass, and hence more likely to climb back up the cliff face of Sleeping Giant and "start fresh." Friedrich found himself rooting for Casper's mind.

Dr. Friedrich tilted his head to catch Casper's eye. "We're going to keep what happened today between ourselves. But under one condition: We're going to meet right here next week, same time, same place, on this bench in front of Sterling, and you're going to promise me that until then you will not do anything to hurt yourself." Friedrich held out his hand.

"A-a-agreed." Casper and the psychologist shook on it.

Friedrich wasn't finished with him; he held onto Casper's hand. "And if you think you're not going to be able to keep that promise, you're going to call me. No matter what time it is. Middle of the night, first thing in the morning, dinnertime, doesn't matter. You're gonna call me first." Friedrich was gripping his hand hard.

Casper nodded yes. Friedrich let go and wrote down his home and office phone numbers. Casper said thanks, and they shook again.

Friedrich was halfway to the trolley stop when Casper called out, "When do I get the drug?"

"Did my wife tell you?"

"I-I-I saw the notice on the bulletin board."

Over the course of three days in mid-May 1952, Friedrich and Winton handed out small brown glass bottles, each containing seven sugar cubes, some laced with GKD, some not, to forty individuals between the ages of eighteen and fifty-nine. They were instructed to take one each morning after breakfast and to store the rest in a cool dark place.

Though Friedrich and Winton had interviewed the prospective subjects independently, at the start of the study, when the first week's worth of sugar cubes were handed out in brown pill bottles, both doctors were present. All the volunteers were assured their participation would remain confidential, as would any and all details about their personal lives revealed during the interview process and during their weekly sessions with the doctors over the subsequent four months.

Friedrich and Winton agreed it would have been ideal if they both could have been present for each participant's weekly session. But both had to teach summer school; they'd be hard-pressed to schedule twenty additional private sessions into their workweeks. Recognizing that test subjects might be more forthcoming in answering questions concerning perceived behavioral change for members of their own sex, they decided that Friedrich would handle the follow-ups on the Yale undergrads and Winton would monitor the nurses and the junior college coeds they'd recruited plus Betty, the cleaning woman who was tired of cleaning up other people's shit.

Doctors Winton and Friedrich requested that all subjects refrain from discussing their participation in the drug study with their family and/or friends. They were wary; a change in treatment by the outside world would color their experiences under the influence of The Way Home. It was Winton's idea not to schedule back-to-back meetings with the participants. She wanted them to do everything in their power to make sure participants had no contact with or knowledge of the others who were taking GKD. Neither one of them wanted their test results skewed by subjects comparing their reactions to the drug. They wanted the feelings reported to be the participants' own.

Casper was the only subject who hadn't gotten his medication. Winton had asked him to wait outside the lab.

Winton lowered her voice. "Look, I know I said yes to Gedsic, but I've changed my mind, I don't want him in the study. I think we're asking for trouble having a student who's attempted suicide."

"He didn't attempt it, he thought about it." Friedrich had already lit one of her cigarettes before he remembered he'd quit.

"He did more than think about it. You told me he brought his dissection kit."

"But he didn't use it." Curiously, Friedrich had never mentioned the fact that Casper was the kid who'd designed an A-bomb for a high school science fair.

"What if, God forbid, he ended up in the group that's getting the drug and he made another attempt?" Winton lit one for herself. Her therapist had suggested that she stop sharing smokes with Friedrich.

"What if we don't give him GKD and he kills himself?"

"We're running a double-blind placebo. There'll be a fifty percent chance he'll be getting nothing but pure glucose. Why endanger the study when you don't even know . . ."

"I checked the logbook. This one's the real thing." Friedrich held up the bottle of sugar cubes and gave it a rattle.

"That's cheating."

"This kid can make a difference in the world. If we can make a difference in him . . ."

"No."

"Didn't you tell me your lieutenant had tried to kill himself before you gave it to him?"

A moment later Friedrich called Casper into the room, and Winton handed the boy his first week's worth of GKD. Casper waited until his cube was half-dissolved in his mouth to ask, "W-w-what's it derived from?" The volunteers had all been told the medication in the sugar cubes was an organic compound.

Friedrich smiled at him. "It's a plant, Casper."

"What s-s-species of plant?"

"I'm afraid we can't tell you that, Casper."

"W-w-why?"

"Because it's one of the rules of our study." Winton gave Friedrich a glance.

"Why?" Casper was starting to sound like Jack.

"Because you would go to the library and look it up, and you might read something about it that might influence your reaction to it." Friedrich had helped Casper get a summer job at the library.

Winton waited until Casper had left the room to say, "He's going to be a problem."

"Wouldn't you want to know what you're taking?"

"I wouldn't want me in my study, either."

Casper came back through the door without knocking. "I-I-In the journal you want me to keep, how long do you want my daily entries to be?"

"A line or two will be fine." Winton forced a smile.

"S-s-sometimes f-f-feelings are more c-c-complicated than that."

"It's not a test, Casper."

"Yes, it is."

"Yes, you're right, it is a drug test. What I meant is, it's about your feelings; just write whatever you feel; it can be as long or as short as you like; there's no right or wrong."

"Of course there is, Dr. Friedrich."

Casper wanted to feel different. He waited all day and into the night to feel a chemical hand pull him away from the edge. He had come down off the Giant, but he refused to live with the pain. The waiting and the hope that was tied to it rubbed salt in the hurt and exhausted him.

His first entry in the diary of feelings he was keeping for Dr. Friedrich read, "May 17th, 1:30 PM. No Change. Hopelessness^2 = pointlessness^3. Being alive feels like a punishment." When he crossed the last "t" he turned out the light and crawled under the covers, longing for dreamless sleep.

A dog barked, a siren raced to another crime in progress, and the thought of Nina lying next to him, touching him with her nakedness, her metal braces chucked on the floor next to the rest of her clothes simultaneously gave him an erection and made him cry.

Casper tried to distract himself by looking out the window in the direction of galaxy clusters not visible to his human eye. He thought about the question of missing mass, not as a personal problem but as a riddle to take his mind off the sadness that pulled at him.

There was a physicist at Princeton who was calling it "dark matter." The words made him think of whole stars and the worlds that orbited them being sucked farther and farther into invisible and inescapable darkness. Then he began to imagine there was dark matter in him, pulling him ever inward, smaller and smaller and smaller, until his existence could only be measured by loss.

Casper turned on a light, picked up his pen, and added these words to his first entry: "Bad thoughts." The next day his entry read, "no improvement." The same two words synopsized the sugar cube's failure to sweeten life over the course of the next seventy-two hours.

By day five Casper so dreaded the depression that had collapsed in on him with consciousness that, as soon as his eyes winked open, he jumped out of bed and ran as if chased by the darkness out of his room to the bathroom at the end of the hall. He stood under the shower a good ten minutes before he realized he was singing along to a song he'd never heard before: Dry those tear drops, don't be so sad . . . Some brand-new baby can be had . . ." The music wafted down from the radio, balanced on the windowsill of the triple on the floor above him.

How miserable could he be if he was singing in the shower, much less a song called "Anytime, Anyplace, Anywhere"? He thought of Nina, saw the photo of the crash inside his head, and thought of how different things could have turned out if he had let her car be stolen. Or perhaps just had the courage to talk, to speak to the girl who had captured his heart. It was still sad. And if he kept thinking about it, he would undoubtedly begin to weep. But . . . why?

Something had shifted inside him overnight. It was no longer so personal. It had happened to him, but the drug moved him just far enough away from his feelings so that it was more like watching a natural disaster on a newsreel than the main feature, something that had happened to him.

Casper dried himself carefully, brushed his teeth gingerly. He didn't want whatever had moved inside his head to shift back into its old position and darken the day. Back in his room, Casper wrote in his diary, "No reason to feel better, but do." The feeling that he was safe, i.e., that it was safe to think about Nina without feeling responsible, hatched and mated and multiplied in him like sea monkeys as the day progressed.

His job at the library had started the day before. As he pushed his trolley of books through the stacks, returning volume after volume to their proper places in the Dewey decimal scheme of things, Casper found himself able to painlessly reorder sentiments and thoughts and feelings that just the day before had made his mind flinch—it was as if Casper had stepped into the skin of someone just like him, only different.

At lunch, when he ate his egg sandwich, it tasted different, crunchy and salty, so much better than yesterday's egg on rye. When the librarian told him he'd gotten the wrong sandwich and he discovered he'd just eaten bacon, he didn't gag or feel queasy. No, the thought that an animal had been slaughtered to satisfy his appetite only made him muse, *What else have I been missing?*

That afternoon he dallied reading the first sentence of books he'd thought beneath him, never bothered with, never heard of: Melville's *Typee,* Proust's *Cities of the Plain,* Llewellyn's *How Green Was My Valley,* Grahame's *Wind in the Willows.* The vastness of what was unknown ceased to make his universe feel like an empty room. Over a solitary dinner of cheddar cheese, saltines, and an apple, Casper shocked himself by writing in his diary, "Feel surprisingly okay . . . happy?" Casper was just learning what that word meant to others.

The next morning he reached for his sugar cube before he got out of bed. He could taste it on his tongue as he stepped into the shower. It tasted like the wrapper on a stick of licorice. When the radio didn't come on, he sang the Yale fight song as if he were getting ready to take the field.

Casper only had one worry—the possibility that the darkness would come back. That was the worm in this otherwise delicious apple. Was he really safe, or was he just kidding himself? Casper, still being someone not unlike Casper, devised a test.

He waited until it was dark before he climbed aboard his rusted bicycle and began to pedal. It was a hot and windless night. The telephone wires sizzled. As the katydids sang, moths orbited the street lamps on velvet wings.

The Egyptian gates to Grove Street cemetery were locked. Casper hid his bicycle in some bushes on High Street and jumped the wall. What better place to test his emotional state, his ability to resist the pull of the gravity within him, than the grave of his loss? If he could face what could not be fixed, perhaps he had a chance.

A back copy of the *New Haven Chronicle* told him a graveside service for the Bouchard family had been conducted two days earlier. The cemetery was larger than he had expected, long rows of headstones in gray-and-pink granite, chiseled dates of birth and death, sometimes followed by beloved wife, husband, daughter, son. There were old-fashioned names like Jebediah and Lieselotte, and thirteen Townsends planted tight as tulips, families closer in death than in life.

Casper had already begun to weep when he saw the marbled angel on a plinth that bore no name, just "Son," and under it "Born January 21st 1823, died the same."

He wandered the stately marble orchard for more than an hour before he found Nina Bouchard. Her headstone was carved in the shape of an open book. Her epitaph was from Byron: "Sorrow is knowledge, those that know the most/must mourn the deepest o'er the fatal truth,/The Tree of Knowledge is not that of life."

Casper started to read it aloud but could not finish. Braced for the worst, he waited for the realization that he had missed his one chance for happiness to sweep him back into his depression. But instead of the tidal wave of recrimination and self-loathing he expected, Casper was flooded with a comforting melancholia that bordered on ennui: *It's tragic she died, but everyone here has died. What about the kid that only lived a day? Everybody dies; it's a fact of life; it's out of your hands, my hands.*

What now made Casper sad and worried as he brushed away his tears at Nina Bouchard's graveside was how close he had come to dying for her, dying for a girl he'd never said a word to. In the darkness of that graveyard Casper could now see clearly that she wasn't the only girl in the world who read Heidegger. There were other "crazy smart people" in this world besides her and himself, and Casper's only responsibility at that moment was to worry about himself. He'd never thought of life as a job, like putting books on library shelves, but that's what it was. He began to think what Dr. Friedrich referred to as "healthy thoughts"—to stay alive, to make the most of things, to take advantage of good fortune when it befalls you, to change what you can and forget what you can't. Like Dr. Friedrich said, "The past doesn't exist."

When Casper found himself wondering whether they buried Nina with or without her braces on, he felt a hiccup of guilt, which he quickly soothed by deciding that the next time he came to visit, he would bring her a bouquet of flowers. Ready to return to the world, Casper was looking for the shortest way out when he heard a match being struck behind him.

Whitney Bouchard had a cigarette in one hand and a pint of Old Crow in the other. He had on the same suit he'd worn to her funeral two days ago.

"Nina was the best, wasn't she?" Whitney staggered slightly but did not slur his words.

The truth, as Casper had so recently realized, was that Nina was a complete stranger. The correct response to Whitney's statement would have been "I didn't know her." But Casper had come to realize that it's the living who are important. Casper nodded yes.

"Sorry I didn't invite you to her funeral."

"I didn't expect it." Casper was no longer stuttering.

"Should have invited you." He took a pull off the Old Crow before he confessed, "She read me the note you gave her the night before. . . ." He spilled some bourbon on his lapel as he wiped a tear from his eye. "It meant a lot to her. Hell of a lot."

"It did?"

"Stuff like that means the world to a girl. Especially a girl like Nina."

"I'm glad." He was.

"You're the first guy who ever tried to pick her up. Braces, polio . . . most guys, shits like me, couldn't see past that."

"She was beautiful." Casper smiled at the thought of her looking over her shoulder as she got into her Buick.

"You're lucky, you're smart enough to see what really matters, what's inside." Whitney took another pull of Old Crow and offered it to Casper. Casper shook his head no. He already felt intoxicated by the strangeness of their intimacy.

Casper only then noticed tears were streaming down Whitney's face.

"God, I'm ashamed." The sight of Whitney Bouchard, football hero, faux Hemingway editor of the paper, undergraduate Batman, weeping as helplessly as Casper had, elicited a joyous empathy in Casper. Though it was dark, Casper could see he wasn't so different after all.

"There's nothing to be ashamed of."

Whitney dropped his head on Casper's shoulder. His breath smelled of vomit and sour mash. "I was embarrassed of her being a cripple, didn't want her near me; I always made up excuses to leave her behind. She was alone so much."

"She had Heidegger."

"That's something."

"That's a lot."

"You're okay, Casper." He didn't call him "Getsick."

They walked back through the graveyard in silence, then helped each other up over the wall. Whitney insisted on giving him a ride back to the dorm as he got behind the wheel of his Packard. The bottle of Old Crow shattered on the pavement just before he slurred, "Maybe you'd better take the wheel." Whitney passed out before Casper could tell him he had never driven a car . . . Of course, he'd seen people do it.

Key in the ignition, clutch, gas, brake . . . like so many things in life, it wasn't as complicated as Casper thought. As the clutch popped and the car lurched down High Street, Casper caught his reflection smiling back at him in the rearview mirror. Incredible, but true—he was okay, Whitney was his friend, and he was driving a Packard into a parallel universe.

Friedrich had a different kind of journey ahead of him that evening, but it, too, was a kind of test. Dr. Winton had listened to her shrink and decided to begin demystifying her attraction for her collaborator by inviting Friedrich and his wife to a party she was giving that night. The invitation was for seven. It was five 'til. The babysitter they had never used before was late, and Nora was not only not ready to go out the door, she hadn't even come out of the bathroom.

Freshly ironed shirt, new tie, blue suit just back from the cleaners, Friedrich loitered at the foot of the stairs, glaring at his watch and bellowing, "Nora, for crissake, we're gonna be late."

No answer.

It had already occurred to him that she was paying him back for making her wait in the faculty parking lot in the White Whale with the kids and a fishing pole the Sunday before, and then sending her off to Sleeping Giant on her own.

It was a fifteen-minute drive to the Wintons'. Though he had never physically crossed the threshold of this or any of the other big houses (at Winton's uncle's, he had only been privy to the pool house), in his mind Friedrich had been inside. He had imagined what it would be like to have a spare four or five thousand square feet, a half dozen working fireplaces to sit by while you looked out leaded windows and watched your children play on two acres of lawn mowed by somebody else.

At that moment his own freshly bathed and pajama'd *kinder* were in the kitchen eating wieners and ignoring their broccoli. He didn't need to go to a party at Bunny's to know her house wouldn't stink of boiled tube steaks and a bunch of dandelions rotting in the jelly jar Lucy had placed on the windowsill a week earlier. There'd be fresh-cut flowers in crystal (if not cloisonné) vases at Winton's house; the jumble of life would be ordered in closets, cupboards, and drawers, not strewn across the living room rug.

In fairness to Nora's admittedly lackluster housekeeping skills, the Friedrichs' house at that moment was comparatively neat. It wasn't the bouquet of weeds in the jelly jar that reeked; it was the two-day-old dirty diaper Jack had hidden under the couch that was ripe. And yes, the typewriter on the card table didn't make for an elegant living room. But it was set up there so he could close the door on them and work into the night. Those were *his* papers and dirty coffee cups and unemptied ashtrays. And, in fact, he had been the one who'd forgotten to put away the *Little Red Hen* and the bowl of popcorn and the chalk that he had just stepped on. But Dr. Friedrich didn't see it that way. It was their mess, not his, that was drowning him.

Blindly dumping the coffee cups, the popcorn bowl, the jelly jar, and the *Little Red Hen* into the kitchen sink, then cursing as he pulled his children's favorite book from the dishwater, he began opening cabinets looking for a dustbin. The garbage was not in the liquor cabinet, but once it was opened he was confronted by more mess. Why save an empty bourbon bottle? And the gin had fruit flies floating in it. He didn't even drink gin. And yet he was infuriated. It was the waste that galled him.

The knock on the kitchen door was the babysitter. He shouted, "Come in." She was fifteen years old, and wore a poodle skirt and a look of horror. Standing there with a bottle of bourbon in one hand and a fifth of gin in the other, he could just imagine what she'd tell her parents.

In Hamden or anywhere else in 1952 America, babysitters were the suburban equivalent of the KGB. They were the secret police, reporting the slightest variations of the norm to the neighborhood, using their youth, tickle rubs, and the promise of candy to elicit innocent confessions from children about their parents. At least, that's how Friedrich saw it.

One of the liquor bottles broke as he dropped it into the trash. The kitchen was hot. He was sweating through his shirt. Apologizing for the heat, he opened the window. "I don't know how it got so warm in here."

The babysitter pointed to the stove, the burners were on full blast. "God, I'm losing my mind."

Lucy piped in, "When he's hot, my dad takes his pants off." The babysitter backed toward the door.

"She's joking."

"No, she's not." That was Fiona. "You like to get naked." Fiona and Lucy squealed with delight. There was much talk of nakedness in the Friedrich household. Fiona added, her cheeks flushed, "Especially at night." The babysitter looked out the window nervously. The sun was about to set.

Friedrich began to back out of the kitchen. "I'm just going to check and see what's holding up my wife."

"Do you have a television?"

"No . . . ah, shit!" Will had just gotten ketchup on his clean suit.

"Daddy said 'shit.' "

"And he deeply regrets it." Wiping the ketchup off the sleeve of his no longer clean suit, Friedrich turned to the babysitter in the hopes of sympathy. "You know how it is sometimes."

She shook her head no.

Friedrich retreated to the stairs, shouting, "If we don't leave now, there's no point in going . . . honey?" He added the "honey" for the benefit of the babysitter.

No answer. "If you don't want to go, you should have just said so and we could have made up an excuse." He was running up the stairs now.

Nora called out from the bathroom, "Don't project. I want to go to this party." Friedrich tried to open the bathroom door; it was locked. He hated it when Nora used psych lingo on him.

"You must have some ambivalence about it or you wouldn't make us late."

"We don't want to be the first ones there." She made no move to unlock the door. "And the sooner you quit rattling the doorknob, the sooner I'll be ready to go."

"If you know the party's at seven and it takes fifteen minutes to drive there, why wait 'til seven to take your shower?"

"Because I had to iron *your* shirt and bathe *your* children."

"Why not let the goddamn babysitter give them a bath?"

The bathroom door opened a crack: "Wanda Flowers." Wanda was a pyromaniac Friedrich had tested at the Illinois Institute for the Criminally Insane who had been masturbated with a bar of Ivory Soap every time her babysitter gave her a bath. The Friedrichs took turns being paranoid.

"You don't even have your dress on." Nora had the last word by slamming the door.

When Nora finally emerged from the bathroom, clothed and ready to go, she was wearing a new shade of lipstick called Red Sands and, not owning any eyeliner, she'd used a charcoal pencil from Fiona's drawing kit. She admired herself in the mirror.

Friedrich's head swirled like a gun turret and his jaw dropped.

"That good?" Nora turned to give him a kiss on the cheek.

"Why aren't you wearing a dress?" Professors' wives didn't wear pants to dinner parties, not if they wanted to be asked again.

"I wanted to do something different. I made them myself. Fabric, thread, cost me less than two dollars." They were made of velvet and each pant leg was as full as a skirt.

"You can't wear pants to Dr. Winton's."

"They're fashionable, Will."

"Says who?"

"*Vogue* magazine. Saw a picture of a pair just like it. In Dr. Mueller's office." Dr. Mueller was her gynecologist.

"You're pregnant?"

"No . . . but if you could see the look on your face." She had spent too much time on her makeup to cry.

"That look was about the pants, not about you being pregnant." The look was panic, spiked with anger.

Friedrich herded his wife down the stairs, knowing that Nora would make him pay for the exchange that had just taken place between them. Tonight? Tomorrow? Next year? He guessed there was an emotional commerce between all couples. His wife, thrifty by nature, stoically banked her disappointments. He sometimes wondered what she was saving them up for.

As they headed for the front door collecting hugs and kisses from the children, the babysitter announced, "Everybody gets one bedtime story, then we say our prayers."

"We don't pray." Fiona said it with an air of superiority. The babysitter fingered the cross around her neck and stepped away from the Friedrichs.

Nora wasn't aware that her husband had greeted the girl armed with liquor bottles, or that he'd said "shit." But realizing that she had forgotten to warn her husband that this new babysitter's father was the Unitarian minister, she was correct in thinking the girl was about to quit. "Are you communists?"

Friedrich laughed nervously. "No, of course not."

"What Fiona meant is, we don't say our prayers out loud. Prayer is a private thing in our house."

"Why?"

Nora looked over at her husband for help.

"We're Druids." He couldn't help it.

"Is that like Church of England?"

"Sort of."

As soon as the front door closed behind them, Nora exploded in laughter that wouldn't stop. Tears streamed down her face, her makeup ran, and her stomach hurt. When they got into the car and the joke seemed to have passed, she had her compact out to repair the damage. But then she looked over at Friedrich seriously, said the word "Druids," and convulsed all over again. She was hungry for laughter. And by the time they had pulled up in front of the Wintons', the joke had erased the look her husband had assaulted her with when he thought of having another child.

The truth was, Nora liked being an outsider, or rather, she liked being on the outside looking in with Will. Their neighbors had nothing they wanted. They were immune to the fifties epidemic of keeping up with the Joneses. Will and Nora Friedrich were alike in that they believed that what they wanted could not be bought, but they were hopelessly mismatched in one regard. Though it didn't always make her happy, Nora had what she wanted; Will believed it was waiting to be won. The prize in hand was never enough for him. What he had in hand was devalued by his own touch, and this, from time to time, broke his wife's heart.

Winton lived in the biggest house on the best street in Hamden. The style was mock Tudor, but it was a serious house. It wasn't a mansion like her uncle's place on the Connecticut River where they had tested the rats. But it boasted a garage that was larger than Friedrich's whole house, and its lawn was umbrellaed by elm trees that had sprouted during the War of 1812. There was a second-floor sleeping porch off what he guessed was the second-floor master bedroom, and a crescent moon cut in a wooden gate that offered a glimpse of the only backyard in Hamden that boasted a swimming pool.

Friedrich knew it was childish, but it cheered him up to note that the elm was blighted and the windows too small to offer much of a view; what Winton had inherited could be improved upon by him.

The front door opened before they had a chance to knock. It was Dr. Winton. The first words out of her mouth were, "You're wearing trousers!" Friedrich had already given Nora an I-told-you-so look when he realized that Bunny was also wearing pants.

If a photographer had snapped a picture of Friedrich following Bunny and Nora into the living room, you would have sworn that this was a portrait of a man who was relaxed, at ease, comfortable. In fact, he felt like a blister getting ready to pop. Everything rubbed him the wrong way. He didn't like being wrong about Nora's trousers, or discovering they weren't the last guests to arrive. It even bothered him that Winton introduced him as the "brilliant Dr. Friedrich I've told you all so much about."

What was Winton buttering him up for, what was she after? And it doubly irked him that after giving him the big buildup, all

Nora got was "and his extremely fashionable, lovely young wife." He could already hear Nora on the way home: "You're brilliant, and I'm the wee little wife. If I'd finished my own dissertation instead of typing yours, I'd have a goddamn doctorate, too." Friedrich was so busy being annoyed at Winton for her condescension and Nora for the outrage she'd voice on the way home, that he completely failed to notice his wife was entirely enjoying herself.

Friedrich downed his drink in a gulp, musing that the only thing worse than getting no attention was getting all of it. A pregnant woman put down her gin and tonic and lit a cigarette and inquired, "Do you ever psychoanalyze small children?"

"Well, since there's no such thing as a grownup . . ." Friedrich made everybody laugh and didn't have to pretend he believed in psychoanalysis. Dr. Petersen, the Freudian, was lurking. And he had a new hearing aid, "But this afternoon, I was thinking, it might be interesting to do a study of the sexuality of preschoolers." The delight his daughters had taken in telling the babysitter about his habit of taking his trousers off when he got hot had given Friedrich the idea. "Prepubescent girls are charged with sexuality. By ignoring it and pretending it doesn't exist, we're damaging their potential for a full and rewarding sex life."

As he hoped, the pregnant woman was shocked. More surprisingly, Petersen seemed interested. If *gai kau dong* worked out, he'd be able to get money to research all sorts of things. Drugs were just a window into the mind.

"Very interesting. Could you repeat that?" Petersen was trying to get his new hearing aid to work.

Friedrich repeated himself, slowly and loudly. "I said, I'd like to do a study on . . ." He put his arm around Nora's shoulder, thinking well of himself for including her in his glow.

Nora appeared to be gazing at a picture of a naked woman, all breasts and teeth on a field that looked like a melted rainbow. "That's a beautiful De Kooning."

Winton stopped listening to Friedrich. In 1952 there wasn't another person within a mile who had heard of De Kooning, much less recognized one of his paintings. "You like modern art?"

"When it's good."

"You wear pants and you like De Kooning." She pulled Nora out of Friedrich's grasp and called out to her husband, who was at the other end of the room talking to an art dealer from New York who wore a turtleneck instead of a necktie and was spending the weekend, "Thayer, we've got a kindred spirit."

Friedrich watched as Winton and his wife walked away from what he had to say about their daughters' innate sexuality. The pregnant smoker followed them. Dr. Petersen put his hand on Friedrich's shoulder. "Your idea reminds me of something Freud mentioned in passing one afternoon . . ." Most of all, Friedrich didn't like worrying about his wife being included only to have her hijack the conversation. He escaped Petersen by asking directions for the bathroom, and beelined it to the bar.

The liquor was free, the people were friendly, and he had finally made it into one of the big houses on the hill. And yet, the blister under his skin was so raw it began to weep. He tried to shake the feeling by admiring the antiques that littered the room. He liked old things. But sitting in a Chippendale chair just made him think of all the people who had to die for him to now have the pleasure of sitting on it.

Nothing soothed it until he caught sight of a small, dark man in a black suit sitting alone on the patio outside, staring in at the party as if he were watching a game show on TV. His eyes were large and pale and watery. He was younger than Friedrich, twenty-eight at most. And though he was smiling to himself, smirking, actually, at the goings-on inside, there was something in his pale, blue eyes, a dampness to his stare, that made him look as if he was about to cry but wasn't ever going to.

Bunny Winton was waving to him to come over and join her and her husband and Nora and the art dealer and a man who gave away money for the Rockefeller Foundation. If Friedrich had been himself, he would have been happy, eager to meet the grant giver. The success Friedrich longed for required deep pockets. The Rockefeller guy could give him money for research on GKD, or the sexuality of prepubescent children . . . Will Friedrich knew what he should do, but he wasn't even tempted. He got up and turned his back on it all and joined the little man on the terrace, for Friedrich's first loyalty was to unhappiness. Though he worked on a drug to ameliorate it, in his heart Friedrich felt it was a human being's natural state.

The stranger introduced himself by offering a cigarette from his pack. "Exhausting, being polite." His voice was hoarse and his accent Eastern European.

"It takes less energy than being rude."

"That's true." The little man found that funny. "What do you do?" Perhaps because his English was limited, he did not waste words.

"I'm a psychologist." There was something about him that was familiar to Friedrich, besides the sadness.

"Is that a good job?"

"It's hard work."

The stranger held up his hand like a guard at a crosswalk. "I'm sorry, but digging a ditch, this is hard work. Helping people . . ." he shrugged, ". . . is easy. Killing them is harder." He said it with a smile on his face and introduced himself as Lazlo. "If your job is so hard, why do you do it?"

"For my kids." It was what he told Nora.

"You want to give them what you didn't have."

"Basically."

"Easy. When they are sixteen, give them the key to your house and don't come back. Let them drink and fuck on the kitchen table." People didn't say "fuck" out loud in Hamden.

Friedrich didn't like thinking about his daughters playing doctor under the table, much less imagining them fornicating on top of it. "Is that what you wish your parents had done?"

"No wish. It happened. Prague, summer of forty-one to summer of forty-two, happiest year of my life. Not so great for the rest of the world."

"Your parents just gave you the keys to their house and left?"

"Not voluntarily. Nazis."

"Why'd the Germans let you stay?"

"I worked for them. I helped the families pack up and get ready to go to the camp. It was clever having a teenage boy get them ready. Made it seem less frightening. That's how I met my first girlfriend." Lazlo reached up and clapped a mosquito to death. There was a spot of blood on his palm. "I was his last supper." When Friedrich saw the numbers tattooed on Lazlo's wrist, he knew where he'd seen him before.

"You were at my house." Friedrich couldn't fathom how the driver of a kosher butcher truck had ended up at Bunny Winton's.

"If your parrots have heard from my sister Marjeta, let me know."

"Where is your sister?"

"With my parents."

Friedrich waited for Lazlo to say more. When he didn't Friedrich felt obliged to change the subject. "What are you doing these days?"

Lazlo pointed at a girl in her mid twenties at the party. She was tall and sallow and looked like a Modigliani that had been to the optician. "Her father has an art gallery in New York City." She was standing next to her father; behind her he could see Winton's husband leaning over Nora. He was showing her something in a book. He would have suspected Thayer of looking down the front of Nora's blouse if Bunny hadn't been there turning the pages.

The art dealer's daughter waved to Lazlo. He smiled back with boyish sincerity, tossing his hair, waving back as if he were on a departing train. He elbowed Friedrich and whispered, "She . . . very hard work."

"Aren't we all?"

Friedrich stood at the lectern, back to the blackboard, and tried not to sound bored. "Statistics is the mathematics of collection, organization, and interpretation of numerical data." It was the first day of summer classes. He liked statistics. His ability to gather, collate, reduce facts to numbers that could not be argued with separated him from the psychoanalysts. So far he had only succeeded in using statistics to prove those who were being doctored weren't getting well. But soon he would use them to bulwark his triumph.

Back then statistics was a new hammer in the toolbox, and no one manipulated it as elegantly as Friedrich. For a man who could do a standard deviational analysis in his head to have to teach the ABCs of Statistics 101 was, well . . . mostly what Friedrich didn't like was being told by the dean that if he wanted to make a much needed six hundred bucks teaching summer school, he had to teach statistics.

"Specifically, in this course we are going to focus on the use of statistics and the analysis of population characteristics and social phenomena by inference from sampling. You will learn the difference between the logic of correlation and that of causation." Friedrich had fifty-five minutes left and he was already looking at the clock and fighting a yawn. His own words seemed to suck the air out of the lecture hall.

There was a lethal grimness to the undergrads who attended summer school in '52. Every seat was filled. The students who looked too old to be college boys were men who had spent their undergraduate years in the army or navy or air force and were now racing through Yale on the GI Bill. The eager young ones, ramrod straight in the front row, were ROTC, cramming four years of college into three so they could get out of Yale in time to be killed in Korea.

The back row was football players who had already flunked the course once and were hoping Friedrich was enough of a gridiron fan to give them the C-minus they needed to play ball in the fall. Everyone wanted to get on with it, had bigger fish to fry, and none more than Friedrich.

The hall was hot, the fan was broken, their eyes glazed. A tackle, red-faced, beefy, and thick as a rump roast, was already starting to snore. Friedrich would have hit him with a piece of chalk but he didn't have the energy.

"And though all I'm saying to you about statistics may sound boring to you this afternoon, by the time you finish this course, you are going to look at statistics as something wondrous, a veritable sorcerer's stone." Friedrich was trying to make it interesting for himself, if for no one else. It wasn't working. "Can anyone tell me why I say that?"

Blank faces stared back at him. No one raised their hand. The buzz of a lone housefly made the silence that greeted him more deafening. "Well . . . it's because statistics allow us to measure change and predict the future. Which makes statistics the future." Friedrich wasn't necessarily sure that was a very pleasant thought. He dropped it before pursuing it any further and threw his chalk at the snoring lineman. He missed. The students snickered. At him or the lineman?

Irritated by that uncertainty, Friedrich digressed. "For instance, based on the grades each of you have received in other courses at this university, and the looks on your faces, I can predict right now who's going to fail this course." They weren't laughing now. "Of course, some of you might want to prove me wrong." Friedrich hated professors who threw things and made pompous threats.

Friedrich cleared his throat and deviated altogether from the syllabus he had submitted to the dean. "Those of you interested in extra credit to increase your chances of passing are invited to collect data in your free time for a statistical analysis we will be conducting over the summer semester on the relative promiscuity of Vassar girls, Wellesley girls, Radcliffe girls, and chorus girls."

After a brief pause, whoops and hurrahs breathed life back into the dead space of the lecture hall. The students who didn't applaud pounded on their desktops. Friedrich felt like a goddamn Mr. Chips.

Thirty minutes later the double doors in the back of the hall swung open. It was the head of the department's secretary, five feet tall and seventy pounds overweight. She didn't leave her chair, much less the psych building, except to get lunch or deliver bad news. Nora? The kids? The dean couldn't have found out about the extra-credit project unless that freckle-faced ROTC kid who'd raised his hand to go to the bathroom had . . .

The secretary was breathing hard by the time she reached the lectern. Friedrich lowered his voice, "What's wrong?"

"Will you kindly tell your patients not to leave messages for you at the psychology office? We're not an answering service."

"What patient?"

"He wouldn't give his name, but he said it was an emergency and that you'd know who he was and to tell you he needs help. He insisted you'd know where to find him."

"How did he sound?"

"I didn't take the call myself; I was at lunch. But the TA who took the call said he was crying."

"When did he call?"

"Lunchtime. I didn't see the note on my desk 'til just now." It was almost five o'clock.

Friedrich leaped from the stage, feeling like an assassin. As he ran to the exit he shouted, "Read chapters one and two tonight. Gentlemen, there will be a quiz."

It was a half mile to the bench in the courtyard of Sterling. Friedrich hadn't run that far that fast since railroad bulls wielding ax handles had chased him across a freight yard in Salt Lake. He had escaped their wrath by hiding in the bottom of a boxcar crowded with veal calves on their way to slaughter.

The bench where they'd met the last two weeks was empty. It had been more than three hours since Casper had made his call for help. Had he gone back to the Giant? Taken the scalpel from his dissection kit? Bent over, hands on his knees, Friedrich tried to catch his breath and think. There was a pay phone in the basement of the library. He'd call the police from there, have them send a car to Sleeping Giant. Friedrich took a knee to tie his shoe. A robin was pulling a worm from the ground, Casper's note was written in chalk on the slate walk:

Dr. Friedrich, waited as long as I could. You can find me hanging in my room, 303 Vanderbilt Hall.—CG.

Friedrich ran, even though the race was lost. He took the dormitory stairs three at a time, fell, scrambled to his feet, and pressed on. Casper's floor was deserted. His door was ajar. Friedrich silently pushed it open. His shades were drawn and the lights were off. Casper's body lay motionless on the bed. Faceup, eyes closed, his left arm dangled off the bed. Darkness pooled on the floor beneath his fingertips. Friedrich saw the dissection kit on the desk next to the bottle that had held his sugar cubes. The study was over. The selfishness of the thought made Friedrich feel like something dirty stuck to the bottom of a shoe, but he couldn't resist. Friedrich hadn't just failed; he had had a hand in this sad boy's demise.

He fought the urge to run for help. He made himself take it all in: the Spartan neatness of the desk; a photograph of Friedrich and his family and the parrots thumbtacked to the wall, below an overexposed snapshot of Casper's mother that made her face look like a solar flare; underpants washed in the sink, hung to dry; the black composition book that held the diary Friedrich had asked him to keep. Friedrich reached for the light switch. He had to see it all. It was the least he could do.

"What's wrong, Dr. Friedrich?"

Casper sat up. Friedrich's head spun around. He felt like God had just yanked his chain. It took him a moment to shift emotional gears. Relief was followed by an ebb tide of profound annoyance. He tried not to let it show.

"How are you doing, Casper?"

"Good." His voice was drifty.

"Then why did you call me?"

"I need help."

"The person who took your message said you were crying."

"I was excited." Casper didn't want to worry Friedrich any more than he already had.

"Why are you lying in the dark?"

"I don't like to waste energy. We could turn on the light, if you'd like."

"That's okay. So, were you thinking of hurting yourself again?"

"No."

"Well, then, why did you write that I could find you hanging in your room? Given your history, you know I'd be concerned."

"I didn't think of it that way." Casper laughed. "It's an expression I heard from Whitney Bouchard, Nina's brother, hang, as in 'hanging out.' It's slang."

"Whitney Bouchard?" Newspaper editor, football star who broke his leg keeping Princeton from crossing the goal line, handsome, blond, rich, golden: He wasn't a god, but in the pantheon of Yale undergraduates, he was as close to Achilles as you could get.

"He's my new friend."

Friedrich took note of the fact that Casper had turned an acquaintance into a friendship. "Is there something about this friendship that bothers you?"

"No, he's a great guy. My problem is I got another job."

"I already got you a job at the library."

"But this is a better position for me."

"What sort of job?"

"Bartending at the Wainscot Yacht Club." Friedrich had never been to the Wainscot Yacht Cub, but he had heard Winton and Thayer belonged. Even snobs thought it was a snobby place. Friedrich found it hard to believe that the Bouchards or the club would extend themselves to Casper. "Whitney got me the job. He wants me to spend the summer with him."

"He told you that?"

Casper nodded yes.

Friedrich considered the possibility that Casper had misinterpreted an offhand remark of Whitney's, was taking the rich boy literally when he was merely to trying to be polite—things like that had happened to Friedrich when he first came to Yale. "What else did Whitney have to say?"

"He thinks he's a shit, but I see what really matters." Casper smiled proudly.

"He used the word 'shit'?"

"Yes."

Friedrich wondered if it was a side effect of GKD. Not an irreversible setback for the study. He'd talk to Winton about lowering Casper's dosage. "How did this friendship with Whitney and the job offer and the invitation to spend the summer all come to pass?"

Friedrich sat in the dark and listened to Casper's excited recap of his trip to the graveyard, Whitney's guilt about how he had treated his crippled sister, the bottle of Old Crow, Whitney passing out, driving Whitney home, staying up all night with Whitney's mother talking about Nina.

Casper took a deep breath, then added, "Mrs. Bouchard told me I was a gift from God." The improbable was turning into the delusional.

The only question for Friedrich was, did Casper's relaxed grip on reality merit calling Winton and having her put the boy into a psychiatric hospital for observation? Friedrich didn't want to do it. He genuinely wanted to do what was good for Casper, not what was going to make GKD look good. But he was also not unaware that even if Casper survived the next suicide attempt, the fact that he was on the drug when he tried it would kill their drug. The only way to protect The Way Home and Casper was to play it safe.

Friedrich was trying to think of a way to lure Casper someplace where there was a phone—maybe he was being overcautious, but he couldn't shake the idea that it wasn't safe to leave the boy alone like this. He'd call Winton. He'd rather hear "I told you so" than make a mistake. She'd probably want to pull some strings and get him into a private mental hospital. He wasn't crazy about that idea, but . . . remembering that Casper had developed a taste for flesh, Friedrich was about to suggest a burger at a diner called Louie's that made the preposterous claim that it had invented the hamburger, when a voice echoed up from the quad below, "Hey, Casper, you need help with your suitcase?"

Friedrich snapped open the shade. Either it was Whitney or Friedrich was delusional, too. Casper jumped off the bed, opened the window, stuck his head out, and shouted, "We'll be down in a few minutes, Whit."

Friedrich turned on the light to get a better look at his patient.

More unbelievable and far more disconcerting to Friedrich than Casper's Dickensian graveyard fantasy and subsequent embrace by the Bouchards was the fact that Casper was changing into a navy blue blazer with a Wainscot Yacht Club crest.

Casper saw Friedrich staring at his costume. "Whitney loaned them to me. After he vomited on my clothes." Casper didn't have to reveal that Whitney had also offered him a bathroom equipped with fresh toothbrush, scented soap, dental floss, shampoo, grooming aids that were completely foreign but not at all unpleasant. Yes, Casper looked different. "Whit said I could keep them. It's what you have to wear when you bartend at the club."

Casper opened his suitcase and put a patent-leather-brimmed captain's hat on his head. There was something about the way he smiled and the rakish tilt of the cap that was so un-Casper-like—feline, almost predatory—that made Friedrich think of Marlene Dietrich. The oddness of this association distracted Friedrich from the anger that roiled up in him at the thought that after all he'd done for Casper, the costumed ingrate was going to screw up his research.

Friedrich picked up the empty bottle from the desk. "Casper, you've made a commitment to the research."

"I wouldn't give that up, Dr. Friedrich. You just have to look at me to know it works."

"What do you mean by that?"

"I'm not sure, but it doesn't worry me that I'm not sure. That's good, isn't it?"

"Yes."

"Why don't you look happy, then?"

"I don't like going out of my way to get jobs for people who quit them the next day. And how the hell are you going to meet me once a week if you're living at the Wainscot Yacht Club?"

"You're mad at me."

"No." He was, but it didn't seem to bother Casper.

"I won't be living there. Whit asked me to bunk in the guesthouse with him behind their cottage. Why do they call a thirty-eight-room house a cottage?"

"It's not my area of expertise."

"Gotcha. Anyway, I checked the schedule. I could take the train in Mondays, my day off. I was hoping we could switch my appointment. That's why I called. The job starts tomorrow. We're driving down tonight. I was also hoping you could give me next week's medication now. Because of you, because of it, I have an opportunity I never even thought about wanting. But now that it's there, I want to make the most of it."

"What do you see this as an opportunity for making the most of?"

"Being me."

Whitney drove Friedrich and Casper to the psych building and waited in the car while Friedrich took him upstairs to give him another week's course of GKD. Casper assured him he would not tell Whitney he was participating in the drug test and would remember to take his sugar cubes every morning.

The fermenting vessel was in the corner. When Casper asked what it was, Friedrich said, "Nothing."

"Who wants ice cream?" Friedrich called out of the window of the Whale as he pulled into the driveway. Nora was lying on the grass, reading a first edition volume of T. S. Eliot that Thayer Winton had given her at the party. The kids were playing on the swings she had guilted Friedrich into constructing out of two-by-fours in the side yard.

Strawberry, chocolate, and vanilla, he had splurged and bought a quart of each on the way home from work. His children, leaping off the swings he had built with his own hands, his wife throwing aside T. S. Eliot's *The Waste Land* and running toward him with the kids, all at once on a summer's evening sweetened with honeysuckle and hand-packed ice cream—the moment was as good as it gets until Friedrich saw the arc of the empty swing seat Fiona had just leaped off of peaking ten feet in the air and then coming back down toward earth with a cruel twist of its chains toward the back of Jack's head.

No time to shout a warning, all he could do was watch and exhale as Jack suddenly stooped to pick a dandelion and the swing seat sailed harmlessly past. Frozen to the spot, visions of his youngest being lobotomized by a homemade swing flashing before him, he didn't move his right hand from the door frame of the car as Willy grabbed the ice cream bag and slammed the car door closed.

Friedrich's legs buckled. He felt the bones in at least two fingers snap and his palm tear open. Strangely, opening the car door with his fingers in it hurt even more. He was proud of himself for not blaming Willy. The ice cream was eaten in the Whale as Nora drove to the hospital.

Two fingers in a splint, his right hand swollen as tight and purple as an unripe plum, it was two months before he could write or take notes. Winton insisted they trade offices; the Aalto-designed desk she had in her private office had a tape recorder and hidden microphone built in. It was activated by a foot pedal under the rug. He had twenty subjects a week to interview and report on. If he met them there, she argued, he could dictate his notes after each session onto the tape recorder.

Friedrich said no. What he really felt was that he didn't want to be any more in debt to his collaborator than he already was. He already owed her the money they were paying the subjects. On Saturday Winton had treated Nora to a trip to New York and taken her to an art gallery to see a show by some guy called Pollock. From the way Nora described the show, it sounded to Friedrich like a cross between a Rorschach test and a cocktail party. Nora had paid for her own train ticket, but still . . . what he really wasn't comfortable with was his wife's newfound friendship with Winton—Nora called her "Bunny."

Realizing that holding a pen or pencil in his broken hand was even more uncomfortable than being further in Winton's debt, Friedrich grudgingly accepted the offer of her penthouse office. And so, on that next Monday and every Monday thereafter that summer, instead of meeting Casper on the hard bench of Sterling courtyard, Friedrich and the atomic-kid-turned-bartender met in Winton's office to discuss how GKD and the Wainscot Yacht Club had been treating him over the previous week.

The temptation of the tape recorder had been too great; Friedrich decided to record the interviews as well as his notes after Casper and the other subjects left. He did not mention the fact that a hidden tape recorder was running—the boy was doing so well, why make Casper self-conscious?

A graduate student transcribed the tapes in duplicate. The transcription of that first session in Winton's office was twenty-seven pages long, plus three quarters of a page of single-spaced notes. Friedrich circled the following passage in red pen:

F: So, how do you like being a bartender?

C: At first, I was nervous. I mean, I don't drink and I'd never even been to a bar. I read a mixologist's handbook, but that's not the same. Anyway, so when I felt myself getting anxious, I thought of you, how you know how to make people like you, trust you, open up. It's part of your job.

F: How do I do that?

C: Like you're doing now, you smile and lean toward them, but you're careful not to get too close. Oh yeah, and very important, you keep still so they maintain eye contact. You make people feel like they're the only person in the world. Did you learn that from your father?

F: Maybe subconsciously; he knew how to tell a story people liked to hear.

C: It's funny, talking to the people out there, how you can get them to overlook your name's Gedsic, your mother picks cranberries, that you don't belong. People's lack of intelligence, their limitations, are like gravity. It's a force you have to reckon with if you want to make forward progress.

F: What's progress?

C: To be accepted, make them like you.

F: How do you make people do that?

C: It's like racing dragons.

F: What?

C: They're a class of sailboat they race out there. Whitney's going to the Olympics. He teaches sailing.

F: How's making people like you like a sailboat race?

C: Sometimes you see them sail a mile in the wrong direction to catch a breeze that will put them across the finish line first.

F: I'm not sure I understand what you're . . .

C: Well, if you're honest . . . no, straightforward's a better word, and tell someone, "I don't know anybody here and I'd like to be your friend," you're a jerk, a desperate creep. But if I start out by saying, "It's amazing how much Wainscot's changed."

F: Have you ever been to Wainscot before, Casper?

C: No, but it was obvious from the old photographs that are hanging around the place that it's changed. And everyone at the club is always going on about how it's not what it used to be and how many new members there are and, so, I let us have a shared point of view.

F: Anything else you do to make people like you?

C: I don't correct them when they're wrong, and flattery will get you everywhere.

F: How can you be sure these people you think like you aren't just pretending to like you?

C: Because they invite me over to their houses for dinner even when they know Whitney's out on a date with Alice and can't come. Her family lives in the cottage next door.

After the session was over, Friedrich dictated his notes on Casper Gedsic, which began as follows:

> CG now makes more direct eye contact and has improved personal appearance, better posture, complexion

has cleared, improvement in overall hygiene. No longer stuttering, seems distinctly calmer and less anxious. When I shook his hand, it was dry. Check medical records to see if in fact CG was diagnosed as having hyperhidrosis. Subject is tan and appears to be more physically fit.

Two sessions later Friedrich circled the following portion of the transcript, this time in blue ink:

F: So, how's it going, Casper?
C: I met a girl.
F: Great.
C: No, what's great is, she likes me. Her name's Eloise. She's a birder.
F: What?
C: A birdwatcher. She's interested in ornithology.

Three pages later, also circled:

F: So what do you and Eloise do besides watch the ospreys?
C: There's an awful lot of swimming. At night after work, the gang gets together on the beach.
F: You don't sound too excited about that.
C: I don't know how to swim.
F: How do you go swimming, then?
C: I wade out until water's up to my chin, and pretend.
F: Why don't you learn how to swim?
C: I've tried, believe me. I just can't get the hang of it. I understand the buoyancy of saltwater, the physics of the flutter kick and the crawl. I mean, intellectually, I know I'm going to float. But . . .
F: But what?

C: I just can't shake the feeling, if I can't touch bottom, I'll be sucked under by the water.
F: Don't you think it's kind of dangerous to go swimming when you can't swim, especially at night?
C: I guess I figure, if I put myself in deep enough, eventually I'll learn.

The following Monday Friedrich's hand had healed enough for him to scrawl the word "interesting" in number two pencil across the first page of that afternoon's transcript:

F: How's your girl?
C: Eloise is not my girl.
F: What happened?
C: There was a beach party. I went up to Whitney's to get more beer, and when I came back, Eloise and Whitney were gone. And when I went looking for them, she was bobbing for apples out by the jetty.
F: What?
C: Eloise had Whitney's penis in her mouth.
F: What did you do then?
C: I watched until they were finished. I'd never had a blow job, so at least I learned how it's done.
F: How did you feel about this?
C: I was upset. But I wasn't going to kill myself or anything.
F: That's good. Did you confront Whitney?
C: The next day.
F: What did he say?
C: He said he was drunk and he didn't know what he was doing, and how sorry he was, and it didn't mean a thing. Which was really the most insulting thing he could have said, if you think about it.

F: What did you say to him?

C: I told him that according to the American Medical Association, he was already an alcoholic. Whitney drinks in the morning.

F: Did that worry him?

C: Mostly he was worried about Alice finding out about him and Eloise.

F: Who's Alice again?

C: At the time we had the conversation about his nascent alcoholism, Alice was still Whitney's girlfriend.

F: And did Alice find out?

C: Yes.

F: How?

C: She asked me if it was true and I told her it was. Then we went for a walk and talked about what we should do about Whitney's drinking problem. We decided to wait and see if he sobers up by the start of the school year. He and I are rooming together, so I'll know.

F: You don't sound very upset by all this.

C: Good things came out of it.

F: What sort of good things?

C: Well, Alice and I realized that we had other things in common besides our fondness for Whitney. We're dating now.

F: You're dating Whitney's ex-girlfriend while you're living in Whitney's guest house? What does Whitney have to say about that?

C: He says he got what he deserved, and it's his own fault, and Alice is a great girl. Which is all true. He's drinking more than ever.

F: Do you feel in any way you betrayed your friendship?

C: I didn't put his penis in Eloise's mouth (laughter). I meant that as a joke. What can I say, Dr. Friedrich? I'm sorry, but I'm not sorry. Whitney's loss is my gain. Sex with Alice is great, much better than with Eloise, more satisfying . . .

and I don't have to pretend to be interested in ornithology.

F: That sounds awfully mercenary.

C: People screw their friends' wives and girlfriends all the time.

F: Not in my experience.

C: That's because you've never been to the Wainscot Yacht Club. There's this guy at the club with a Concordia yawl. Each weekend he pulls in with somebody else's . . .

The graduate student included the following note in the transcription of the session: "Dr. Friedrich, I think you must have accidentally pressed 'erase.' There's two minutes and forty-one seconds of static on the tape."

That part of their session had not been erased by accident. The man with the Concordia yawl who dropped anchor every weekend with someone else's wife was Thayer Winton. Casper rowed out a bottle of champagne to him on one occasion; the yawl was fitted with a queen-sized bed. The most disconcerting detail of all was, as Casper put it, "A guy at the bar told me Winton uses the same trick with every one of the wives. His opening move is a first edition of T. S. Eliot's *The Waste Land*."

SEPTEMBER 1952

The parrots had been in Friedrich's mulberry tree for almost six months now. They no longer drew crowds or inspired articles in student newspapers. Except for the occasional stranger who'd double take, pull over, knock on the door, and inquire, "Do you know what's in your tree?" they had ceased to be a thing of wonder in the neighborhood. As it is with all things that don't belong, familiarity had devalued their splendor.

Neighbors complained that the parrots nipped fingers, helped themselves to vegetable gardens, and in one case, strafed a house cat named Fluffy. At a town meeting someone even suggested they be shot (they did that with starlings one year), and if not that, trapped and rereleased in someone else's neighborhood.

Lucy didn't know that, but she was right to think no one loved the parrots anymore except Dad and her.

Fiona, after three weeks of second grade, had come to see the birds as one more hurdle to acceptance. Having a psychologist for a father (her new best friend's dad called him "the headshrinker") made her odd. Having a father who still drove around town in a broken-down ambulance instead of a car meant he was an embarrassment. And a mother who persisted in buying secondhand clothes and washed her daughter's hair in dishwater detergent added humiliation to her stew. Parrots that shit on her friends whenever they came over was one more awkwardness than she could bear.

Willy, who could now not only say "urinate" but impress his dad by peeing standing up, only paid attention to the parrots when his father was around. Throwing things at them, better yet hitting them, was a sure way to get the professor's attention. Willy, being a clever three-and-a-half-year-old, already knew that a psychologist's idea of punishment was a cozy sit on the lap and a calm, nonthreatening talk about being kind to animals, followed by an insightful, "Willy, are you mad at the parrots or at Daddy?" The part of Friedrich's disciplinary lap time Willy loved most was "You know that if Daddy didn't have to work, he'd love nothing more than to stay home and play with you all day."

Even Nora, who had proclaimed the parrots a miracle when they first arrived, had now grown impatient with the birds, particularly with the African gray who mimicked her husband's voice so perfectly and sweetly when he called her name, "Nora . . ." she never failed to come running. Being at the beck and call of a husband was unsatisfying enough. But a parrot . . .

And though their pediatrician couldn't say for certain an allergic reaction to the birds was the cause of the rash that blotched Jack's neck and armpits, the possibility made her wish they would fly away and things would go back to the way they had been. Lucy had been at the pediatrician's office with her mother when the doctor examined Jack for the second time. "Why not get rid of the parrots and see if the rash disappears?"

"I couldn't do that."

"Why not?" Lucy noticed her mother blush the same color as Jack's rash.

"They make my husband laugh." Lucy didn't know that the sound of her father's laughter, the way he threw back his head, relaxed and easy, his arrogance transformed into contagious confidence, was what had seduced her mother. But the synapses of her now seven-year-old brain did connect the idea of sacrifice with love.

"I love you, Gray," Lucy whispered through the screen of the kitchen window to the African gray that was perched on the front porch railing as the rain poured off the eaves. Initially she had been smitten with the red macaw, but after Fiona claimed it as her own, Gray had charmed her with his black tongue. While the other parrots hung out in the mulberry tree, Gray alone ventured up onto the porch. It had been raining hard all morning. She loved him so much, she kept the fact from her mother that the same rash Jack had had turned her own bottom red as a baboon's.

"You can't love a bird." Fiona was playing doctor with her younger brothers. Jack was the patient, Willy was the nurse. The operating table was a large white chafing dish normally used to cut up turkey on Thanksgiving and Christmas, now placed under the kitchen table for impromptu invasive surgery on Jack.

"I love Gray, too." Jack loved everything.

"Jack, lie still, you're dying." Fiona pushed Jack down on his stomach lengthwise on the platter.

"Does dying hurt?"

"Not once you're dead. Nurse, take his temperature." Willy pulled down Jack's shorts.

"I'm gonna marry Gray." Lucy was blowing kisses through the screen.

"Marrying a parrot's even dumber than loving one." Fiona was washing her hands, preparing to operate.

"Gray's not a parrot. He's an African prince who's been turned into a bird by an evil witch."

"You can't marry an African prince."

"Why not?"

"Because he'd be a Negro. And then you'd have Negro babies, and people wouldn't be nice to them."

"I don't like being a patient." What Jack didn't like was having his temperature taken rectally with a ruler.

"If we don't take your temperature, you'll die," Willy announced in his most grown-up voice.

Jack scrambled to his feet, pulling the white tablecloth down over his head. "I'm a ghostie." Jack held out his hands like a zombie.

Willy liked pretending he was scared. "He's a ghost, run away!"

"Get back here, Nurse!" Jack and Willy ran, hoping Fiona would chase them.

"I'm going to count to ten . . . one, two . . ."

"What are they doing in the car?" Lucy looked beyond her feathered Prince Charming to the White Whale parked in the drive. Her parents had been in the backseat for almost forty-five minutes. It had stopped raining, but the car windows were too fogged up for Lucy to see what was going on.

"They're making babies."

Though Lucy was barely seven and Fiona was not yet nine, they knew all about how babies were made. In fact, they knew more about copulation than most Hamden High School girls did in 1952. Friedrich had answered any and all questions about reproduction gracefully and matter-of-factly. Determined not to shame, confuse, or titillate his daughters, he spoke about the facts of life with the same bored deliberateness he would have conveyed if he were reading the instructions to a Mixmaster: "The man puts his penis in the woman's vagina."

Shame, confusion, and titillation? Friedrich's mother had provided toxic doses of all three. Every Sunday morning before church his mother would make him and Homer hug her before she and his father returned to the bedroom to engage in that domestic tussle that passed for connubial bliss in the Friedrich household. "Come, children," she would call out to her boys and demand a hug. "Come warm me up, Daddy's going to hide his tail in me!"

Knowing the correct words for the body parts involved in reproduction wasn't half as exciting to Lucy as knowing it was happening at that very moment in the backseat of the ambulance parked in their front yard. Since her mother had said making babies was a beautiful thing, Lucy reasoned, *Why shouldn't I watch?*

Fiona was back to playing doctor. Using a butter knife for a scalpel and ketchup to simulate blood, she removed Jack's imaginary tumor. Lucy slipped out the front door. Gray ruffled his feathers and tracked her with his yellow eye as she tiptoed across the soggy lawn to see how love was made.

"Just tell the truth." Her father was talking loudly inside the car. He had not told Lucy people talked while they made babies.

"Will, I am running out of patience." It was funny to hear her mother use the same tone of voice on her father that she heard when Lucy tried to give Gray a bath, or wore her best and only party shoes to walk in puddles. "I have told you the truth, and quite frankly, I find it sad and infuriating that when I tell you I am happy and in love with you and I am not sleeping with anyone else and I don't want to sleep with anyone other than you . . . you refuse to believe me." Since Lucy woke her parents up each morning and never found anyone besides her parents in the bed, she was nearly as perplexed as her mother was about her father's suspicions.

"Nora, admit it and you'll feel better." Her dad used that trick to get Lucy to admit she was lying.

"Speak for yourself; I feel fine."

"All right, *I'll* feel better if you tell me his name. I swear to you I will not be angry if you just tell me who he is."

"You really would feel better if I give you a name?"

"Absolutely."

A circle appeared on the inside of the backseat window. Her mother was drawing a happy face with her forefinger, two dots for eyes, a line for a nose, and a half circle for a smile. Then Gray called out nervously as a plane flew low over the yard. Lucy didn't hear the name her mother gave, just her father yelling, "How could you? Him, of all people."

"I didn't." Her mother was giggling. "But you said a name would make you feel better, so I gave you a name. You're being ridiculous." Nora looked past the outline of the smile she had drawn and saw Lucy staring at them.

"Ye gads, Lucy's outside listening to this." That and "hell's bells," were the closest Lucy had ever heard her mother come to swearing.

"How much did she hear?"

"Enough to know her father's . . . never mind." Nora opened the car door. "Lucy! I was just coming to see if you'd like to help me bake cookies." Nora did a convincing job of pretending she was happy. She wondered which was worse, lying to a child or burdening them with the disappointments of adulthood.

"Why were you fighting?" Nora took Lucy by the hands and swung her around, trying to distract her.

"We weren't fighting, we were playing a game. Your father says silly things, and I tease him."

Lucy looked up at her father. "Who is Mommy sleeping with?"

Friedrich's answer was to glare at his wife and pull Lucy's right hand free from her mother's grasp.

"Happy?" Nora asked. Lucy was. Her father holding one hand, her mother the other, Lucy liked being in the middle of things.

Lucy had her parents on the front porch now. Fiona was scurrying around the kitchen, frantically dismantling the operating room. Jack came out the kitchen door, shirtless, smeared with ketchup. "I have cancer!"

"Fiona cut out his tumor. I told her you'd be mad." Willy was a natural-born squealer. "And I told her I didn't want to tell on her but you'd be mad at me if I didn't."

"You did not. Willy's lying; it was his idea to play doctor."

Before any grains of truth could be separated from the day's chaff of doubt, a brand-new glistening green Chrysler woody convertible slithered up to the curb in front of the house. Doris Day was singing "Bewitched, Bothered, and Bewildered."

The man at the wheel was young and tan and perfectly dressed—blue blazer with a silk handkerchief peeking out of a crested breast pocket over a creamy white turtleneck Irish fisherman's sweater (the sort that wouldn't be sold in America for fifteen years). More rugged and outdoorsy than he appeared, he was as unnaturally masculine as a mannequin. Lucy would still rather marry an African prince who had been turned into a parrot, even if their babies would be Negro. But if the curse on Gray couldn't be broken, the young man now getting out of the Town & Country convertible would do.

It wasn't until Gray squawked "hello" that Lucy realized that the young man who was now walking up the walk toward them was holding hands with an older girl. This unknown female quantity that approached had Snow White's face, Cinderella's hair, and a gold charm bracelet just like the one Dr. Winton jingled when she pretended to like children. The sight of this perfect couple conjured up a disorienting mix of desire and resentment that made her wrap her arm around her father's waist and bury her face in his darned vest.

"Hello Lucy, hello Fiona." Neither of the girls had any idea who they were talking to.

Lucy peeked out from behind her father, who was oddly silent. "How do you know my name?" For a brief instant she considered if he was one of the frogs Willy had captured and she had set free in the creek behind her house.

"We met last spring. I took photographs of your father and the parrots."

"You look different." That was Fiona.

"That's because I feel different." Casper looked over at the girl whose hand he was holding, as if she had turned his frog self handsome with a kiss.

"Casper, what a wonderful surprise." Nora was too startled by the transformation to notice that her husband did not share her surprise.

"Doctor Friedrich, Mrs. Friedrich, I'd like you to meet Alice Wilkerson." Alice shook their hands.

"Would you two like some coffee, or, tea, or . . . ?"

"No, thank you, we don't want to impose. I just came by to give you a present."

"That's not necessary, Casper." Lucy noticed her father eyeing Casper the same way he would study her before asking, "Do you have a temperature?"

"It's for all of you, the children, too."

As Nora Friedrich continued to protest, Casper ran back to the Chrysler. Something big and wrapped in brown paper was lying lengthwise across the backseat. It had a big red bow on it, and it was round and taller than Casper. "This is too much, we can't accept," Nora called out.

"It's our present too, Mommy," Lucy protested.

Casper wrapped his arm around the gift and dragged it across the lawn like there was a body inside.

"Will, help him." Friedrich took one end of it. It was more awkward than heavy; even he was curious to see what was in it.

"Can we open it? Can we open it? Can we, please, please?" Lucy, Willy, and Jack shouted and jumped up and down as Friedrich and Casper carried it up onto the front porch. Fiona, feeling too old to do the same, felt left out and pretended she wasn't excited.

"It looks more impressive than it is," Casper told them apologetically.

Alice volunteered, "We saw it yesterday in the window of an antique shop on the way up to my grandfather's." (It would be thirty minutes before Dr. and Mrs. Friedrich would be able to put together that Alice's grandfather was a former governor of

Connecticut.) Lucy, Will, and Jack ripped away the brown paper, revealing a towering Victorian birdcage big enough to imprison a man.

"It's beautiful, Casper." Nora liked it so much, she kissed him on the cheek.

"I saw it and thought of you, Dr. Friedrich." The remark puzzled Friedrich, but the cage was indeed beautiful. Its bars were woven out of brass and zinc wire hammered and trompe-l'oeiled to look like bamboo entwined with vines.

Casper and Alice stayed for tea. Nora and Lucy baked cookies after all. Alice helped in the kitchen, insisted on washing the dishes, and relaxed enough to confide, "I've never met anyone like Casper."

"Yes, he's unusual."

"We've been talking about marriage."

Nora said, "That's wonderful." But at that moment, that wasn't how she felt.

Over tea Fiona showed off her vocabulary, telling Willy he was "simian," and Lucy sang "Petit Poisson," only to burst into tears when she couldn't remember the final verse.

Friedrich said she was overtired; Casper said the same thing had happened to him once, only he made it worse by wetting his pants. Everyone laughed.

As Casper drove off with Alice into the sunset, Friedrich put his arm around his wife. "He seems to be doing okay."

"He seems like a whole different person. I saw him last month. He seemed more relaxed and confident, but nothing like this."

"You didn't tell me you saw him."

"Yes, I did. I told you I ran into him downtown. We had a very funny conversation."

"What about?"

"*The Waste Land.*"

"I would have remembered that." His eyes narrowed as he imagined his wife bobbing for apples with Casper. In his head he'd already seen her do it with Thayer. He was just beginning to make himself miserable.

"He loaned me a nickel to call you." Nora pushed her hair behind her ear. "It's funny, I kind of miss the old Casper."

"What's that supposed to mean?"

"Just that your drug works."

"How do you know he's on the drug?"

"He is, though, isn't he?"

"It's a double-blind placebo test. I don't even know."

"But you'd tell me if you did know, right?"

"That would be unethical."

At 6:15 A.M. the next morning Friedrich was awakened from a dead sleep by a child's scream, sharp as a knife cutting glass. It was Lucy. Before he was awake he was running toward the sound, his brain caffeinated with parent paranoia. It was coming from downstairs. Was there a fire? Had she fallen, cut herself? Was an intruder dragging her out of the house?

He found her on the front porch. She was pointing at the parrot cage, Casper's gift. Friedrich did not know if they had come over one by one or migrated into captivity all at once. But every single parrot had left the mulberry tree and crammed themselves into the cage except for the gray.

"Daddy, you've got to set them free."

Friedrich was sure he had closed the door to the cage the night before. "How the hell . . . ?" Grey sat on the railing and ruffled his wings. His eyes twinkled manically as he threw his head back and mimicked a laugh.

Will opened the cage door with his good hand and tried to shoo out the birds. The cockatoo bit him on the thumb and wailed, "*Donde está Marjeta?*" Friedrich left the cage door open all that day and through the night. But the parrots didn't, wouldn't, couldn't budge. The idea that the birds preferred Casper's cage to the freedom of the mulberry tree in his front yard depressed and annoyed Friedrich more than he'd admit. The next day he tried to lure them out with special treats, pumpkin seeds and corncobs. All the parrots stayed behind bars except for Gray, who feasted.

Friedrich gave them five days to fly free. He didn't want to believe they had come to him in the hopes of finding a cage. In the end he had to call the ASPCA. The man who took them away promised they'd be well cared for.

They kept Gray. Lucy continued to believe he was an African prince. But Friedrich's feelings toward Gray changed. Looking into the glare of Gray's eye, past his own reflection into the heart of the family beast who would not be tricked by the cage, Friedrich could not help but think that Gray had been the culprit who had lured his brothers and sisters into the cage and then locked the door with his beak. Of course, none of it would have happened if Casper hadn't come to take the damn picture.

Friedrich had what turned out to be his last session with Casper on a Monday in late September. Casper had called and asked to meet Friedrich on the bench at Sterling. "Let's finish where we started, for old time's sake." When Friedrich had first heard his voice, he thought it was Thayer. More than Casper's appearance had changed. His high-pitched, nasal, South Jersey accent had been refined over the course of his summer behind the zinc-topped mahogany bar at the Wainscot Yacht Club into a substantial and intoxicating tenor, fruity with a touch of sweetness, like a well-mixed Manhattan.

Friedrich arrived at their old meeting place early. There'd be follow-ups with Casper and the other test subjects over the next few months. Since Dr. Winton had reported seeing no withdrawal or addiction problems either in her lieutenant or among the Bagadong, they saw no need to taper off the drug.

The sky was a pale shade of blue that made Friedrich think of a blank check. The campus was crowded with freshmen. Friedrich watched as loafered lost boys in tweed jackets unknowingly made decisions that would add up to the man they would be stuck with when they graduated. He had a strange urge to warn them. But of what?

Friedrich's hand was finally out of the cast. The study was done, the summer of sugar cubes over. After this last meeting Friedrich would go back to his office and evaluate Casper using the same rating scale he and Winton had employed to evaluate Casper and his thirty-nine fellow test subjects every week since the start of the study, the Friedrich Psychiatric Rating Scale.

Friedrich's Rating Scale was nine pages long, seventy-two different areas of behavior, qualities of personality and behavior to be observed and judged. It contained questions to be rated 0 (no pathology) through 3 (extreme pathology):

Question 27:
Makes no attempt to influence or control others.
Attempts to influence others indirectly, e.g., by comments, allusions, flattery, etc.
Attempts to control others by direct comments or requests.
Insists on controlling others by any means at his/her disposal.

Question 46:
Does not try to attract the sexual interest of others.
Dresses, behaves, or speaks in a manner that may attract the sexual interest of others.
Dress, behavior, or speech is explicitly provocative or exhibitionistic.
Makes direct and unmistakable physical approaches of a sexual nature.

Question 62:
Shows no unusual inclination to smile or laugh.
Smiles or laughs readily.

Smiles or laughs at things that are not humorous or amusing for most people.
Smiles or laughs at things that are decidedly unpleasant for most people.

Grouped in symptom clusters, tabulated, and scored via factor analysis, it measured change. People and their lives and the feelings they felt and the thoughts in their heads were broken down into a series of numbers that when tallied would determine whether or not GKD altered behavior in ways that were desirable, and ultimately marketable, to both the scientific community and the world at large.

Friedrich and Winton knew it worked. Over the course of the last four months, one of Winton's nurses had gone back to college. Another reported being less irritable, i.e., she'd stopped giving the toddler the back of her hand. Another had lost twenty-six pounds. The cleaning woman had become the first female deacon in the history of the Christ Is Lord Baptist Church. One of Friedrich's boys, who suffered from a mild case of acrophobia, had not only climbed into the cockpit of a plane, he'd gotten his pilot's license. Self-improvement equals self-fulfillment. Friedrich believed that. But did the symptom clusters factor out to happiness?

Of the twenty subjects who weren't on placebo, only two reported no improvement in the quality of their lives. One complained of intestinal side effects, but since he had a previous history of chronic colitis, it was inconclusive whether or not diarrhea was an occasional side effect of GKD. Of course, no one's improvement was as meteoric as Casper's. But as Friedrich had told Winton from the start, "Casper's special."

Friedrich had brought a yellow legal pad and pen to take notes, but he already knew how he would have to answer the questions posed by the Friedrich Rating Scale. The trouble was, the Friedrich Rating Scale did not cover all the changes he had observed in Casper Gedsic. Friedrich's test would reduce Casper to a number that would make him a victory. But that was not an accurate way to describe how he felt about Casper. The purloined accent, the borrowed clothes, the stolen girlfriend—all could be considered "self-improvement" in a sense. Casper had made real progress. But there was something phony about it, something that Friedrich didn't trust.

The success of his rating scale depended on his objective observations, but he couldn't shake the feeling that Casper had given him the cage knowing that it would lure the parrots back inside.

Casper arrived in a pinstripe suit, his shirt was French-cuffed, and the links at his wrists were amethysts set in gold. He had taken his last sugar cube that morning. "Sorry I'm late, Professor Friedrich." Friedrich noticed but did not note that Casper had ceased to call him "Doctor." "I got held up having lunch with Alice's father."

"How'd that go?"

"Did you know he was given a seat on the New York City Stock Exchange for his twenty-first birthday?"

"You don't say. What did you and Alice's father talk about?"

"Gold. Specifically, how you can predict fluctuation in its price based on market history, current events, threat of war. I came up with a mathematical formula. It's pretty simple, but it seems to work."

"You've been buying and selling gold?"

"It began as a joke. Well, a challenge. Made over the bar at the yacht club. He and I both started out with a hundred thousand dollars in imaginary capital and speculated, bought futures, sold, short, that sort of thing. When Labor Day came and I'd doubled my money, he got interested how I did it, and . . . here, I'll show you." Casper took out an alligator agenda with a silver pencil attached and neatly began to write out a series of cosines.

Friedrich focused on the smile on Casper's face as the elegant young man handed him the formula written out on gilt-edged paper with a silver pencil. "Try it out, see for yourself. We've made over forty-seven K in the last two weeks."

"You made forty-seven thousand dollars?" Friedrich struggled to keep his jaw from dropping.

"No, not me personally. Alice's dad did. He gave me ten percent. Which was very fair of him, considering he was the one who risked the capital. It's based on an extrapolation of the work of the philosopher Laplace. You know, Laplace's demon—know everything about the past and you can predict the future."

"The future's not firm ground, Casper. Say, just supposing, what if someone discovered a huge deposit of gold? The price would drop."

"It's possible. But . . . basic human nature, self-interest, would seem to suggest, if not guarantee, that your discoverer would keep his discovery a secret so as not to flood the market and lower the price of gold and devalue what he had worked so hard to dig up."

"What if someone discovered how to manufacture gold synthetically?"

"Alchemists have been trying to do that for a long time. Besides, if it happened, someone would pay the fellow who discovered it enough to forgo being famous in return for being rich. He'd destroy the formula."

Friedrich stared at him. "You're not taking notes, Professor Friedrich. Something wrong?"

"No." There was, of course. "I'm taking it all in."

"I'm not giving up physics, if that's what you're worried about."

"I'm not worried if you're not, and you seem to be doing well."

"I'm happy. It's not quite the right word for how I feel. But whatever it is, I like it, and it's thanks to you." Casper adjusted his French cuffs and admired his amethyst links.

"You're the one who changed your life, not me."

"I wish I could say Whitney was happy. Alice and I talked to Whitney's mother about the drinking."

"How'd Whitney feel about that?"

"Drinks more than ever, blames everything on me; he says terrible things about me. He has this idea he can get me kicked out of Yale. He'll probably call you."

"To say terrible things about you?"

"That, and his mother's ordered him to see a psychologist. I recommended you."

When the hour was up, Casper shook Dr. Friedrich's hand. The ten-bell carillon of Harkness Tower was ringing out the hymn "All Things Bright and Beautiful."

"Now can you tell me the name of the organic substance I've been taking?" Casper hadn't let go of Friedrich's hand yet.

"No."

"I knew you'd say that." Casper let go, turned, and started to walk away, then looked back with a smile. "Will you ever tell me?"

"When we publish the results of the study you can read about it. I'll see you in two weeks."

"Maybe we can get together before that." Casper called out.

"Maybe." Friedrich wanted to be done with his day, and with Casper Gedsic. Packing up his briefcase, he decided to put off filling in the blanks on Casper until tomorrow, and headed home early.

Friedrich drove home slowly, but not carefully. He drifted through yellow lights, crossed the line, and strayed over into the wrong side of the road without realizing it. A cigarette waited in his mouth for ten minutes before he remembered to light it. Reaching into his pocket for a match, he pulled out Casper's formula for gold. He balled it into garbage. The window was already down. He was about to throw it away, then stopped . . . what if it worked? The math was beyond him.

Was he simply envious of Casper's brain? Or the way he was using it? Friedrich was ambitious, he wanted more: a house on the hill, private school for his children, an alligator agenda. Was it simply that Casper was getting more faster, that the student was better than the teacher? Or was it that Casper showed no shame or guilt, was unconflicted about his reinvention? Quaint as it seems, social climbing was bad manners in 1952.

When he got home Friedrich's brain downshifted to the here and now. There was a silver Jaguar sedan parked at the curb. Foreign cars were a rarity in Hamden back then. Thayer drove a black Cadillac; he thought he remembered Whitney driving a Packard. Casper had said Whitney was going to call. It'd be like a rich, spoiled, aspiring alcoholic to come to his home unannounced. Casper said he had a motorcycle now. Maybe he'd bought a Jag to go with it. Anything was possible.

Friedrich had told Nora he was going to work late. She wasn't expecting him for several hours, and he wasn't expecting to get out of the Whale and hear his wife's laughter bubbling down from their bedroom window, carefree and girlish as a daisy chain. She laughed like that after she had an orgasm.

What if . . . who knows . . . anything? Silence now. Where were the children? What was she doing up there? The image of his wife bobbing for a stranger's apple flashed inside his head.

Friedrich entered his home as silently as a thief. It was a game. He didn't really believe Nora was up there with . . . but if he didn't believe it, why was he walking on tiptoes? He climbed the stairs, careful to avoid the squeaky step. The bedroom door was ajar. Nora didn't see him. She stood in front of the mirror, wearing a pink slip he had never seen before. In the bathroom, the water was running. He heard a man's voice.

He pushed the door open slowly. It was more sordid than the fantasy in his head. A man was sitting on the toilet in his underwear. There was a long moment of rage before he realized it was the Czech he had met at Winton's. It took Friedrich a moment to even remember his name, to focus on the fact that—Lazlo, that was his name—was holding a copy of *Little Red Hen,* and that the laughter was coming from his boys who were at that moment splashing in the tub. *Why is this stranger sitting in my bathroom in his underwear reading to my naked sons in the bathtub?*

"Your fish were getting me wet and there wasn't room for me in the tub." His suit was hung from a coat hanger on the bathroom door.

Normally, Friedrich's mind would have gone straight to

"pervert." But he was so relieved not to have walked in on his wife having sex, he greeted Lazlo like a long-lost friend: "Great to see you, Lazlo." Then, in spite of his relief, added, "What are you doing here?" He tried not to sound suspicious. All psychologists know they're crazy. They just try not to advertise it.

"The butcher that I used to work for when I first came here had to have his thumb amputated. Osteomyelitis. Pinkie, the cheap bastard, he deserves to lose, but without this . . ."—he held up his thumb like he was hitchhiking—". . . we would have lost our grip when we tried to climb down from the trees. I visited him in the hospital."

"I'm sorry. I mean, I'm glad to see you, but . . ." He was still suspicious.

Nora appeared in the doorway and kissed him. She was wearing a dress now. "I missed you."

Willy announced, "Jack spilled chocolate sauce on Mom's dress."

"I was changing. I didn't hear you come in." Nora wrapped her arms around her husband's neck and kissed him twice more.

Friedrich was still trying to get his bearings. "Your Jaguar, Lazlo?"

The Czech nodded. "You know what they call them in England? Jews' Bentley." Lazlo laughed.

Nora glared at him as she dried off the boys. "That's a horrible thing to say, Lazlo."

"To me, what is horrible is the *Little Red Hen*. Not sharing the bread. Capitalist propaganda. And very un-Christian. If a Jew had written this book, the hen would at least have had the decency to offer to sell the pig some bread."

"Why do you talk like an anti-Semite?" Nora didn't find it funny.

"I'm anti-everything." Lazlo thought that was very funny.

Friedrich laughed, too. "Where are the girls?"

"At Jenses'."

"Lazlo gave us a ride in his new car." That was Willy.

Lazlo put his pants on in front of them. Lazlo made anything seem natural. "New suit, too. Very expensive. Silk mohair. Had to get, because of the Jag. Also, had to get new hi-fi, new apartment. Jaguar is a very expensive car."

"Things seem to be going well."

Lazlo shrugged. "My fiancée's mother's brother is in scrap steel. You are looking at the new vice president."

"Only in America." Friedrich suddenly felt like everybody had found a shortcut to the good life but him.

"This is how the whole world runs. Here you just pretend you do it like the *Little Red Hen*."

As they headed downstairs, Lazlo announced, "I needed an excuse to visit you, so I bought you a present." In fact, he was curious; Friedrich looked all-American, but he seemed as displaced as Lazlo. Lazlo wanted a family, but he knew he could never make one.

They followed him outside and he opened the trunk of the Jaguar. There were three large burlap sacks filled with tulip bulbs.

"Lazlo, you shouldn't have."

"All right, I'll sell them to you."

Friedrich wasn't sure why he thought that was funny. Perhaps he just needed to laugh.

"My florist gave them to me. I buy a lot of flowers for my girlfriends."

"I thought you had a fiancée."

"Do you eat the same dinner every night? Roast beef, roast beef, roast beef. Even if it's filet mignon, boring, not to mention unhealthy."

"That's horrible."

"No, is kind . . . if I have a girlfriend, I am nicer to my fiancée when I am with her. If I have two girlfriends, I am twice as nice. It would be cruel to her and to them to be faithful."

"Makes sense to me." Friedrich was suddenly having a good time.

"It better not." Even Nora thought it was funny.

"So do you want me to give them to you or do you want to pay me for them?" Lazlo was carrying one of the bags of tulip bulbs up to the house.

"Don't you want some tulips for yourself, Lazlo?" Friedrich picked up the other bag.

"I hate tulips. Filthy flowers, especially the bulbs, disgust me."

"How could anyone hate tulips?"

"Try eating them for a year."

The next two nights Friedrich was woken by the same dream: Nora was bobbing for apples inside his head. The imaginary room where this betrayal was taking place was dark. He could not see who she was fellating. Each time he woke up before he could say or do anything. The third night he had the same apple-bobbing nightmare, only this time he stayed asleep long enough to pick up a fire tool and put a dent in the forehead of his wife's phantom lover. There was blood everywhere. When Nora turned on the light in his dream to clean up the mess he'd made, Friedrich saw the face of the man she had betrayed him for—Friedrich woke up with a gasp when he realized he had just murdered himself.

Dr. Friedrich had told his patients on more than one occasion, "When you dream, you are talking to yourself." For the rest of that night he lay awake, listening to Nora breathe, analyzing what he was trying to tell himself. Scared to close his eyes, frightened of his dreams, he wanted to feel different but didn't know how. For the first time since he had heard about The Way Home, he was tempted to take it himself.

Winton was between classes. She was in her broom closet of an office, feet up on her desk, halfway through what she vowed would be her last cigarette for the rest of her life, trying to decide the best way to approach getting the molecular structure of GKD analyzed. Going through official university department channels would mean putting in a request to the psychiatry department, and in turn having them put in a request to the chemistry department, who would in turn have to . . . what with politics and protocol, it might be six months or a year before Yale's mass spectrometer gave them GKD's chemical composition, which then they'd have to begin work on synthesizing.

Winton was onto her second last cigarette she would ever smoke for the rest of her life when someone knocked loudly on her door.

"Come on in." She wasn't expecting Friedrich. He looked tired and had cut himself shaving, and had stopped it with a bit of toilet paper.

"You're done already?"

"No, it's actually going slower than I'd like."

"There's no rush. Well, there is, but . . . you're still bleeding."

A drop of blood trickled down his neck. She handed him a Kleenex.

"Thanks." He dabbed it just before it reached his collar.

"So what brought you all the way over here?"

Friedrich closed the door behind him. "Do you have time for a new patient?"

"Man or woman?"

"Man."

"Has he been to a psychiatrist before?"

"No."

"Is he a close friend?"

"Friend is the wrong word. I have mixed feelings about him. He's paranoid, delusions of grandeur, insecure narcissist."

"Sure. What's his name?" She opened her calendar.

"Friedrich."

She jerked her head back as if Friedrich had just swung a bat at her. "You want to talk to me in a professional capacity?"

"Yes." Friedrich was as amazed as she was. He'd never been on the other side of the couch.

"You're not concerned our professional relationship, as well as our friendship, might . . ."—she hadn't thought of him as a friend, not truly, until this moment—". . . might interfere with the process?"

"You're the only psychiatrist I trust."

"I am flattered, but . . ." It was unprofessional of her to even consider. "Is there something specific?" Friedrich was standing; but she was already talking to him like a patient.

"Yeah . . . I'm making myself miserable." He fought the urge to tell her about his dream. Sharing it would make it less of a fantasy.

"How does Monday at five o'clock sound?"

"Fine." Friedrich opened the door.

"I know it wasn't easy for you to ask for help."

"I say that to my patients, too."

"I'll waive my fee."

"I'd prefer you didn't. Paying's part of the process."

"Just for the record, you know we're doing something wrong here."

"I've known that for a long time, Dr. Winton."

As he drove back across campus, Friedrich looked at himself in the rearview mirror: "It's official now, you're crazy." Strange but true, just making the appointment, admitting he had a problem, made him feel better. Wondering if that was all he needed, he was debating whether or not to cancel his appointment with her this afternoon, or just wait until . . . that thought was blindsided by a blur in the corner of his eye. His cerebrum rocketed a message to his right foot. Suddenly, he was standing on the brakes, wheels locked, tires screeching; all Friedrich's brain was thinking about was stopping the Whale before it flattened the motorcycle that had stalled in the midst of pulling out into traffic a few feet before him.

It was Whitney, just out of the liquor store, a case of Old Crow strapped to the back of his motorcycle. Friedrich could tell by the difficulty Whitney had restarting the motorcycle he'd already had a few. An open bottle of beer fell from his jacket pocket as the Triumph sputtered to life, and Whitney wobbled at high speed down the street.

Clearly, Casper wasn't exaggerating about Whitney's turning into a drunk. And if he wasn't exaggerating about that . . . Friedrich tried to remember what he'd done with the formula for gold.

The Friedrich family was planting tulips. It was Sunday morning, October was a week old, and Indian summer had kept the leaves from showing their colors. The bulbs Lazlo had given them had such wonderful names: Queen of Marvels, Red Sun, Sweet Love, Flaming Springgreen, Kingsblood, Mon Amour, and Friedrich's favorite, Marjolein, "large, tapered petals of rich, salmon scarlet touched with yellow and the edges of the blossoms shaded salmon pink."

The descriptions wired to the bags inspired Friedrich to dig whole new flower beds for them. He drew them out on a paper napkin over breakfast. It was Jack's idea to make one of them in the shape of a full moon. "Tulip moon" was how the three-year-old verbalized it. The older children didn't think it fair that Jack had a tulip bed of his very own.

"You always do what Jack wants." Fiona voiced the consensus.

"Daddy, why do you like Jack more than us?" Willy, like his father, felt shortchanged at birth.

"I love all my children equally." Friedrich knew that wasn't true.

"Then why don't you treat us the same?" Lucy didn't care about tulip bulbs, but she planted great stock in love.

"That's because each of you is different. I treat you as individuals."

"Tulip moon for me!" Jack shouted out triumphantly. Friedrich wondered what it was that made him love his youngest the most. Did he see too much of himself in the faces of his others? Jack looked like Nora. He hoped it was that simple.

When they started digging, the sky was overcast. But a cool breeze, courtesy of an arctic air mass circling the Great Lakes, blew the grayness out to sea. The sky dilated into blue with great, long swirls of cloud high overhead that Friedrich told the children were called mare's tails when he was a boy.

Friedrich turned the earth over with a rusty spade. Nora worked next to him with a hoe, breaking up the clumps of earth, then leavening in handfuls of lime and manure. The children helped—that is, they got in the way, but in a charming way. Growing up on a farm, Friedrich had watched his own parents work like that, shoulder to shoulder. As the first blister of the day rose in his palm, he remembered how his father would tell stories to make it seem less like hard labor.

Stories of neighbors and childhood friends who had fallen out of love and run off with railroad brakemen and got girls in the choir pregnant or had been born with webbed toes or harelips or clubfeet; those who had died of influenza and tetanus and heartbreak—stories Friedrich's mother, Ida, would interrupt with, "The way you gossip, you'd think you'd been born a woman."

To which his father would always reply, "I'm not gossiping; I'm contemplating the human condition." What Friedrich liked to remember best were those moments when his father would drop his shovel, hoe, scythe, whatever, reach down, and pull a flint arrowhead or stone tomahawk out of the ground, spit on it, rub it clean on his shirttail before handing it over to him. "Things only stay buried so long."

Friedrich also remembered the day after his ninth birthday when he and Homer were on a train platform waving good-bye to his father as he left for Chicago to talk to a man about opening up a John Deere tractor dealership in the county seat. Ida didn't like the farm.

Two weeks later he and Homer were feeding the chickens. His mother came outside with a letter in her hand. She told them, "Your father died in a hotel fire with a woman."

He recalled after a long cry hugging his mother. She smelled of tuberoses. What he liked remembering least was when he finally came up with a thought that would make them all feel better, and said, "At least Daddy wasn't alone." His mother slapped him.

After she said she was sorry and didn't mean it, she asked him and Homer nicely to go kill the rooster for Sunday dinner.

The tulip moon was ten feet across, concentric circles of Red Suns and mauve Sweet Loves and Kingsblood followed by Mon Amour planted in holes twelve inches deep with broken oyster shells in the bottoms to keep the voles and moles from dining on the bulbs over the winter.

"Did your dad teach you to put oyster shells in the bottom of holes?" That was Willy. He would have different memories of his father than Friedrich had of his.

"No, we couldn't afford tulips." Friedrich had thought about his father enough for one day.

"Why do you know how to do it?"

"I read it in a book."

"Is that how you learned everything you know?" Fiona smiled.

"Mostly. But not everything."

"Will you teach me something you didn't learn from a book?" Reading wasn't coming easily for Lucy. Dyslexia?

"Something I didn't learn in a book . . ." Friedrich repeated the question slowly, baffled by the fact that at that moment he couldn't think of one goddamn thing that he hadn't learned from a book. "A snake can bite you after you cut off its head." Friedrich lifted his sleeve, and showed Willy a scar on his wrist where a blacksnake had bitten him.

"Wow." Willy was impressed. "Why'd it bite you?"

"I put my hand where it didn't belong."

"Jack's planting the tulips upside down." That was Fiona.

"Maybe they'll bloom in China."

"Don't be silly, Daddy." Lucy laughed.

"It's good for Daddy to be silly." That was Nora. It had been Nora's idea to roll out the old concrete birdbath that the previous owners of their house had left in the garage and place it in the very center of Jack's tulip moon. Friedrich filled its heavy scallop-shaped cement bowl with a hose and a blue jay promptly flew in for a bath.

Friedrich's spade was now turning up a new flowerbed along the path in front of the house that made a sloppy S between the driveway and the front door. He was sweating, blisters had risen and popped, and his hands hurt. Nora offered him her gloves, but he resisted. "Getting soft, time to toughen up" was what he said to her.

The first time the phone rang, Nora ran, but she missed it. A few minutes later, it rang again. Friedrich sprinted. He was out of breath when he picked it up. "Yeah?"

"Professor Friedrich?"

"Yes, who's this?"

"It's Whitney Bouchard. Is this a bad time?"

Friedrich lied. "No . . . what's on your mind, Whitney?" Casper had told Friedrich Whitney was going to call.

"I'm not calling about me, sir." He slurred the "sir."

"Whitney, have you been drinking?"

"Casper's the one you should be worrying about."

"Right now, I'm worried about you."

"For your information, he's made a list."

"Daddy, come back." Jack banged on the glass of the kitchen door.

"A what?" As Jack's fists pounded on the window panes, he imagined the glass shattering, shards slashing his wrists.

"A list."

"What sort of list?" Nora pulled Jack away from the window and her husband's fantasies of doom.

"People he blames." He could hear the ice rattling in Whitney's glass. He remembered Casper's saying Whitney was going to say terrible things about him, how he wanted to get him kicked out of Yale.

"Whitney, you're drunk."

"That doesn't change the fact you're on his list. I didn't make the cut."

"Does that bother you? Do you think he should blame you, Whitney?" Without thinking about it, Friedrich had shifted into the doctor-patient mode.

"I didn't do anything to him."

"But he did something to you."

"He turned into a jerk. You should see the way he brown-nosed everybody at the club. Did he honestly think people weren't going to see him for what he is?"

"What is he?"

"The worst kind of social climber, Doc. The kind who thinks he's superior to the people he's sucking up to." Friedrich felt the small hairs on the back of his neck rise. It was as if Whitney were talking about him, not Casper.

"Who else is on Casper's list?"

"Alfred Griswold."

"You called the president of Yale?" If Whitney talked to Griswold, Casper would be kicked out of Yale. Maybe even if it wasn't true.

"No, you think I should?"

"Not unless you want the president of Yale to expel you for being a drunk. Whitney, if you need to talk to me, call me during office hours."

"Casper is the one that needs talking to. He stole my girl, stole my clothes, God knows what else. He rummaged through all my drawers."

"As I recall, you loaned him the clothes, Whitney. And you stole his girl first."

"What girl?"

"The bird-watcher."

"Well, if I loaned him the clothes, he should have given them back. And none of that makes it alright that he stole my motorcycle."

"Did you see him steal it?"

"Well, the keys are gone, he's gone, and it's not where I parked it last night."

"Maybe you were too drunk to remember where you left it. Be careful of what you accuse people of, Whitney."

"Don't say I didn't warn you, Doc."

Friedrich hung up the phone, thought of calling Whitney's

mother, but decided he'd better talk to Casper first. He dialed the pay phone in Casper's dorm. The line was busy.

He didn't like the sound of a list. He tried to imagine what reason Casper could possibly have to make one. What could he be unhappy about? What could he blame me for? Paranoids make lists. That wasn't Casper's problem, that was Friedrich's problem. The world was Casper's oyster that fall, not his enemy. Friedrich went back to his family and the tulips.

They were almost done. There were just six bulbs left, one for each of the Friedrichs to plant. Nora and the children were on their knees, dropping the bulbs into the last of the holes they had dug—small hands burying spring's promise. Friedrich's back was starting to hurt. He'd used muscles he'd forgotten he had. He stood behind them, leaning on a spade, smiling down on his family. *If it all turns to shit, we can always become farmers,* was what he was thinking but didn't say.

Wanting to build on the day, not undercut it, he kept his doubts to himself and decided to kiss the mole on the back of his wife's neck instead. He was just about to drop the spade when the slow thump of a single-cylinder engine caught his ear.

When he turned his head he saw Whitney's black Triumph motorcycle heading their way. Helmet on, goggles in place, the biker was careening up the wrong side of the street. The motorcycle wobbled, the driver in danger of losing his balance. Friedrich guessed Whitney'd been too loaded to remember that Friedrich had told him to call him at the office for an appointment.

Friedrich didn't want to talk to him. He was relieved when the motorcycle passed him by. He let the shovel fall and went back to the idea of kissing Nora's neck. But the motorcycle turned around. Whitney had seen them. The motorcycle rolled to a stop two houses down, opposite side of the street. He got off the motorcycle, put down the kickstand, then took off his helmet and goggles and reached into his pocket. Friedrich realized it was Casper at the same time he saw the boy was holding a gun. Casper was on their side of the street. It was too late to run.

Friedrich took a knee next to his wife. But instead of putting his lips to the beauty mark on the nape of her neck, he whispered, "Don't look up and don't say a word."

"What are you playing at?" Nora thought he was trying to sound sexy.

"It's Casper."

"So . . ." She started to turn her head.

"Don't look. He has a gun." Friedrich whispered, but Casper seemed to hear him. Keeping his finger on the trigger, he shoved his revolver into his jacket pocket. It was still pointing at the Friedrichs.

"What? Why would he . . . ?"

"I'm serious, just do what I say."

"Whispering's not polite."

"You're right, Fiona, it's not." Friedrich pretended he didn't see Casper. "Come on, everybody, let's go inside."

"I don't want to go inside. It's boring inside."

"What is going on?" Nora was scared and angry.

"Whitney called. Says Casper has a list of people he blames." Friedrich looked up and, in the glass of the picture window in front of his house, he saw Casper's reflection staring at their backs. He was walking toward them now, mouth open, his lips pulled back like Homer's dog when it was ready to bite.

Nora put her arms around the children. "It's time to go in the house now."

Lucy stood and turned around before Friedrich could stop her. "Hi, Casper. Want to plant tulips with us?" Casper was on their lawn now. His right hand still gripped the pistol in his pocket. Friedrich could only assume he wanted to get so close he couldn't miss. Friedrich armed himself with the shovel and waited for Casper's response.

His clothes were wrinkled, and there was a grass stain on one of his knees. His hair hadn't seen soap or a comb in days. The finger of his left hand clawed at the side of his head; he looked like his old self.

Lucy took two steps toward him. "Is that your motorcycle?"

Casper stopped walking.

"Can I go for a ride?"

Casper slowly shook his head no.

Friedrich forced himself not to glare at the boy or look him directly in the eye. He focused his gaze on Casper's chest, slowly moved his hands to the end of the shovel handle. He'd only have one chance to break his neck with a blow to the head. That's what he intended to do. "Lucy, don't bother Casper now."

The seven of them stood frozen in misunderstanding until Jack suddenly stood up, made his fingers into claws, screwed on his scariest face, and growled. Casper turned and walked back to his motorcycle. Helmet and goggles on, he kick-started the engine, clicked it into gear, and pulled away from the curb. He ignored the children as they waved and shouted, "Bye."

"What's wrong with him?" Fiona inquired.

"I'm not sure." Nora roughly yanked the children through the front door.

Friedrich stood on the lawn, shovel in hand, hyperventilating fear even after Casper and Whitney's motorcycle disappeared down the street.

"Lock the doors and the windows, and take the children upstairs." Friedrich's voice was calm as he dialed the operator.

"Is a storm coming?" Willy shouted.

"No . . . maybe . . . yes. Operator, get me the police."

"How could you let us be out there if you knew . . . ?" Nora was crying.

"I didn't know."

"Yes, you did." Nora slammed the window so hard the pane cracked. The police were on the line now.

"This is Dr. Friedrich. I live at Ninety-two Hamelin Road. I want to report a boy on a motorcycle. He was just here. His name's Casper Gedsic."

"What'd he do?"

"He stole a motorcycle and he's got a gun."

"He stole your motorcycle?"

"No, the motorcycle belongs to his roommate. Look, none of that's important. The point is . . ."

"Whose gun?"

"I don't know."

"Did he point it at you?"

"The point is, I'm a psychologist, he's a patient of mine. I think he's having a psychotic episode and is a threat to himself and others."

"Did he threaten you?"

"I've been told he has a list of people he blames."

"For what?" The cop was taking notes.

"He's not happy with the treatment he received. Look, I know the president's on the list. . . ."

"The president of the United States?"

"No, Yale. His name's Griswold. And I think Dr. Winton might be on it. I tried to call her, but it's busy. She lives up on Ridge."

"We'll send a car to Winton's." Friedrich hung up the phone and dialed Winton. The line was busy.

An hour later the doorbell rang. Nora was reading to the children from *Charlotte's Web*. The spider had just begun to speak. Friedrich peered through the drawn curtains before going downstairs to answer the door. Two black-and-white patrol cars were parked at the curb.

Nora held Jack in her arms as she looked down through the curtains and watched Friedrich talk to the cop who stood on the front step. After a very few words, a complex sentence at most, Friedrich hit his forehead with the palm of his hand, staggered, then grabbed hold of the railing to keep himself from falling and slowly lowered himself down onto the stoop.

Her husband came up the stairs slowly and grabbed a sport coat. "I'll be home as soon as I can."

"Are we safe?"

"No." One of the patrol cars stayed parked in front of the house while Friedrich drove off with Sergeant Neutch.

She was still holding Jack. He was getting heavier. Jack yawned and nestled his face into her neck. Nora told the others she was going to go down and make Jack a peanut butter sandwich before she put him down for bed.

Fiona picked up *Charlotte's Web* where she left off, reading aloud to Willy and Lucy in her most grown-up voice.

By the time she got to the kitchen Nora was feeling a kind of exhausted that scared her and made her dizzy. The weight of Jack suddenly seemed unbearable. It took all her strength to open the refrigerator door. She felt impossibly tired, as if life were a weight pressing in on her on all sides. She forgot why she'd come there, how she'd gotten to this point in time and place. She put Jack down and leaned back against the stove. The pressure increased. Breathing seemed scary. She wished she didn't have lungs. There was no safety from anything, not even this. She imagined that this was what it felt like if she were a diver on the bottom of the ocean who was getting ready to drown, who had already given up.

It was the same feeling Nora had had the other time, when she'd felt so overwhelmed by the inevitability of disappointment, the pointlessness of enduring, that she could not lift her hands or open her mouth to stop Jack from reaching into the frosting and upending the five-pound bag of sugar onto the floor. She watched him turn and move toward the door. Her eyes were open, but her brain would not tell her what she saw.

As Friedrich and Sergeant Neutch turned up the hill, an ambulance wailed by, lights flashing, sirens on. Three state police cars and a second ambulance were parked haphazardly on the cobblestone circle in front of Winton's house. Car doors were open. A police radio crackled.

The stepdaughter was in the back of one of the cruisers. Friedrich and Sergeant Neutch heard her scream as they walked beneath the rustle of the blighted elms. The girl kicked and flailed at the doctor who held the hypodermic aloft like a knife.

Neutch filled Friedrich in. The stepdaughter had come home from a tennis lesson and found her father in the front hall, crumpled facedown at the foot of the stairs. She thought he'd fallen, knocked himself unconscious, until she rolled him over.

Thayer's face was covered with blood. A .22 caliber bullet had entered his head just to the left of his nose and exited through his jaw—Thayer had been in the ambulance that had screamed past them.

"Sorry to see you again under these circumstances." Neutch was talking, Friedrich wasn't listening.

"We've met?"

"I was there when the parrots showed up." They shook hands again. Friedrich didn't know what to say.

A flashbulb exploded in Friedrich's face as he followed Neutch into the house he once envied. A police photographer was taking pics of the crime scene. Chalk outlined the spot where Thayer had nearly drowned in his own blood. A state cop with a cauliflower ear told Friedrich more than he wanted to know. "He was still here when the daughter came home."

"Who?" Flashbulbs, blood, and fear disoriented Friedrich.

"Casper Gedsic. The kid on the motorcycle you called about."

"Oh yeah, right."

"You think someone else was involved?"

Friedrich stared into the library. The crime photographer was taking pictures of Winton now. She was sprawled back in her chair behind her desk. Her head was tilted to the side, inquisitively. The desk drawers had been rifled. Rating scales were scattered across the floor. One of the state cops was standing on a piece of graph paper that illustrated their success. Winton's eyes were wide open. She returned Friedrich's stare. She looked . . . surprised. They didn't see this coming. There was a bullet hole in her throat.

"Dr. Friedrich, I asked you a question." The cop with the cauliflower ear was still waiting for an answer.

"What?"

"Do you think someone else had a hand in this?"

"I don't know what to think."

The state cop who'd been on the car radio came in and announced, "They just found the motorcycle behind the bus terminal."

"You have any idea where he might be going, Dr. Friedrich?"

Friedrich shook his head no.

"We talked to the Bouchard kid whose motorcycle he stole. He said Gedsic had a death list. You were number one, Winton was number two. Any idea why he didn't do this to you first?"

Friedrich was still shaking his head no.

"Well, you're lucky." Friedrich did not feel that way.

Neutch drove him home. Gray called out hello as he and the cop walked across the freshly planted tulip beds. The other cop who'd been left watching over the family was in the kitchen, eating canned spaghetti with the kids. Willy was asking to see his gun. Fiona was pestering the officer with questions. "Have you ever killed anyone? Would you kill anyone? What if you shot an innocent bystander?"

Lucy was drawing a picture of the tulip bed in full bloom to cheer Daddy up. Nora had told them their father had gone to help someone who was sick.

As soon as Friedrich made eye contact with his wife he began to weep. Willy burst into tears and ran to him, clutching his leg. Fiona had her arms around his waist. Lucy sat in place, tears streaming down her face, trying to draw a picture that would make everyone stop crying.

Nora's lower lip trembled. A tear careened down her cheek as she wrapped them all in her embrace. "We're going to get through this." Neutch and the other cop averted their eyes from the intimacy of this resolve.

Lucy stared out the window. "There's a man in our garden."

Neutch ran to the window. "Where? I don't see anything."

"I only saw his shadow behind the pricker bushes."

Friedrich's world swirled around him. "Where's Jack?"

Fiona looked under the table, Lucy checked the bathroom, Nora ran into the backyard. Friedrich was right behind her. He was still calling his son's name when Nora wailed, "No!"

The birdbath in the heart of the tulip moon had been pulled off its pedestal. It had fallen at a puzzlingly oblique angle. Jack's face was lifeless in two inches of water. The bruise on his forehead continued to swell and darken even after Jack was pronounced dead.

BOOK II

My first distinct memory is looking for myself in the family photo album. It was 1958 and I was four and a half. The album was as thick as a Bible, bound in leather; its leaves were stiff with snapshots pasted on imitation parchment, oversized pages in a fairy tale illustrated by Kodak, waiting for a text.

My hands could barely grasp it. Homer, my father's older brother, was sitting next to me on the couch. My brother Willy, then nine years old, had twice the vocabulary of Homer, who was forty-two and had a beard that was worthy of a nineteenth-century statesman. Silky and black, it hid the cave in his jaw where the mad doctor had tried to cure him of his simplicity by pulling teeth.

Homer gave himself a one-armed hug as he rocked back and forth, repeating the same phrase over and over again. With his free hand he helped me flip the pages without ripping them: "Careful. If we tear the page, the page will be torn."

That day I was wearing my favorite shirt—cowboy. It had pearly plastic snaps instead of buttons and Roy Rogers embroidered on the breast pocket, tossing a lasso over my heart. Homer sported a tie and suspenders, his pants coming almost to his armpits. Fiona was thirteen going on fourteen then. The night before, while drying the dishes, she was reprimanded by my father for calling Homer retarded. My father said he was "special." Back then that word wasn't thrown around the way it is today.

As it is with all memories, some of this I did not remember but learned later; I embellished it, colored it in with information garnered from undigestible tales regurgitated over family dinners, from conversations and arguments that helped pass the miles on family car trips, and from looking at the snapshots my father was taking of that day as I sat with Homer and Lucy on the couch. The future ferments the past, some memories become more intoxicating with time, others evaporate. It's hard to separate what you think happened from what you know happened. Especially in our family.

All I know at this first moment of recall is that the couch smells like Homer, scents I will later come to identify as Old Spice and baby powder. A double hernia forced Homer to wear a truss that looked scary and chafed. Lucy sat on the other side of Homer. She looked older than twelve and had told me she had just gotten her first bra. She couldn't decide whether it was tragic or beautiful that Homer would never know how handsome he was. Homer, at that point in time, did in fact bear an uncanny resemblance to Montgomery Clift in the part of Sigmund Freud released four years later as *Freud: The Secret Passion*.

Homer and my grandmother were visiting from Illinois. It was the first time they had ever been east. Ida, as my grandmother liked to be called, had hennaed hair, a copy of Kahlil Gibran's *The Prophet* in her purse, and a Ouija board in her suitcase. She called my father "Sonny Boy." And though Ida talked not unlike the farmers who rode wagon trains west on *Million Dollar Movie* (we had a TV now), my grandmother had a homespun, haughty elegance and a habit of holding your face between her thumb and her forefinger to make sure you were looking her in the eye, all the while chain-smoking Pall Malls through a red Bakelite cigarette holder.

As Homer and I flipped through the pages of the photo album, Fiona showed off at our new baby grand piano, Beethoven, "Für Elise." My mother passed a tray of iced tea. A pair of big liver-and-white ticked pointers stood guard just inside the front door and began to bark as the boy next door approached our door. His name might have been Bud; I definitely remember he wanted Willy to come out and play catch.

Homer laughed when Gray, the parrot who lived on our front porch, called out the dogs' names in my mother's voice, "Thistle, Spot: Hush." The dogs minded the parrot better than my mother. Homer was still helping me flip the pages. They're crowded with tiny black and white snapshots with crimped edges. There were pictures of everyone but who I was looking for—me.

Homer seemed to sense my anxiety, or perhaps he just got tired of warning me about tearing the page. Whatever, his serious baritone reassured me: "We'll find you. You're here, so you're here."

Sure enough, when he turned the page there was a photograph bigger than all the rest in the album. I recognized the cowboy shirt I was wearing. Homer tapped the picture with his long, white finger. "There's Zach." That was my name: Zachariah Wood Friedrich.

"Look," I shouted to the room. "There's me!" Sometimes, when I dial up this first moment of self-awareness, I hear my father's voice telling me, "That's not you; that's your brother Jack." Other times it's my mother who gives me my first hint about how much I don't know about what I think I know. They must have mentioned Jack's name before, but this was the first time I heard he was my brother.

Homer clasped his head in his hands and wailed, "Sorry!" Even Homer knew more about Jack than I did. I remember being profoundly confused.

"If he's my brother, why doesn't he live with us?" Lucy reached over and tried to snatch the album out of my hands, but I wouldn't let go of it. "Where is Jack?" I asked.

"Sorry, sorry, sorry . . ." Homer wailed the same word over and over again like he was a phonograph record and the needle was stuck in his groove.

My father put his hand on Homer's shoulder. "It's not your fault, Homer." Whose fault was it? I wondered.

Lucy was still tugging on the album, trying to get me to turn the page on Jack. "Look, Zach, here's a picture of you and me sleigh riding in the snow."

"Where is Jack?" I demanded, as Willy slipped out the door to play catch—his least favorite activity next to playing with me.

Ida announced, "Jack is in the celestial kingdom on the other side." Ida was a theosophist—she reached out her hand to make me see eye to eye with her, but my father pushed her away before she could get me in her clutches.

"Stay out of this, Ida." Even my dad called her Ida.

"Jack!" Gray took up the call from his perch on the front porch. My father slammed the window. It didn't stop the parrot from calling out the name of the lost son. "Jaaack."

My own mother, suddenly unable to put down the tray of iced tea, stared through me. "Jack . . ." She wanted to say more but that was the only word that came out of her mouth. Even though he wasn't in the room, it sounded to me as if she was talking to him, not me.

The dogs began to bark. Fiona hit false notes on the piano as she tried to drown us out. Lucy was still trying to show me a picture of happier times. We struggled over the album. Homer was the only one who heard the page rip. "Once you rip the page, it stays ripped." My memory of what was said was corroborated decades later by Lucy. She has total recall when it comes to sadness.

My father knelt down next to me and spoke to me in a voice I would later discover he used on patients; as smooth and flat as an oil spill, it could make anything sound bearable. "Jack had an accident." Officially, that's what Jack's death was. According to the state of Connecticut, only Dr. Winton was murdered, but I was years away from finding out about that.

"What happened to him?" I asked. My mother stared through my father now as she and the rest of us waited for his answer. How much do you tell a four-and-a-half-year-old? How much was he willing to admit to himself—then, now, ever? As a psychologist, he believed the worst thing a parent can do is lie. But when the psychologist is the parent . . . like everyone says, you do the best you can.

"Jack drowned." That's what the autopsy said.

"Is he going to come home when he gets better?" My mother put down the tray and left the room. Lucy had tears in her eyes. Fiona closed the lid on the piano keys.

"Jack can't get better. He's dead."

"Is he in the ground?"

"Yes, he was buried before you were born."

"Is he still there?"

"His body's there, Zach."

"What else is there?"

Ida couldn't resist. "His spirit is with us. Right here in this room . . ." The idea wasn't nearly as scary as my grandmother.

"Shut up, Ida."

"Was he nice?"

"Very nice."

"Nicer than me?"

I don't know how Jack would have looked if he'd had a chance to grow up. Perhaps there would have been no resemblance. As an adult I've been told I have a profile nearly identical to that of my great-uncle Clyde, a tall, hollow-eyed Scotsman who suffered from curvature of the spine, came to America to build bridges, and had a weakness for laudanum. Whether you believe it all comes down to DNA or bad luck, the fact is, as a child I was a dead ringer for Jack. Ida wasn't wrong about my dead brother being in the room. Whenever my parents looked at me, they saw Jack. Sometimes Dad saw Dr. Winton, too. And, oh yes, let's not forget Casper. Ghosts, living and dead. They were all in the room.

Casper had told his attorney he did not want his mother to come to court, explaining obliquely, "I'm not who she knows." The attorney relayed these wishes to Mrs. Gedsic by phone. She came to

New Haven anyway. Sat next to him in court. The newspapers described her as "small and foreign" and gave her age as forty-three. She wept softly as evidence was presented and whispered to Casper in Latvian. He looked away and did not answer. The photograph of her arriving in the courthouse that appeared in the paper showed her to be missing two teeth and in need of an overcoat. She had the look of a sparrow caught in a blizzard.

When the judge gave his ruling, she gasped, "It's not true" in Latvian. Casper said nothing, and did not return her embrace when she kissed him. All he had to say vis-à-vis good-bye was, "Don't come and see me, please."

"You know what's best for you." She had never understood how his brain worked. "If you change your mind, I am always your mother."

Casper spent that night in the New Haven jail. The next morning he was transferred by ambulance to the Connecticut State Hospital for the Criminally Insane in the town of Townsend. His ankles and wrists were shackled. Which was hardly necessary, due to the 2 ccs of amobarbital that had been injected into his right arm shortly before he left the city jail.

The ambulance ride took a little more than an hour. He had driven by the mental hospital once on Whitney's motorcycle, considered for a few hundred feet of pavement what it would be like to be locked inside.

When it was founded in 1868, it was called a lunatic asylum. Then and now it was a prison without the privacy of cells. It had grown by virtue of state money and bequests from families happy to have a place to warehouse embarrassing relatives; locals and those in the insanity business referred to it simply as Townsend.

When Casper arrived, there were seven buildings. Red brick, overlooking a New England college town and the valley beyond, it was a deceptively pretty place—rolling lawns, curving drives, stately elms. The grounds were surrounded by an iron fence. Those like Casper, the criminally insane, were housed in the original building, which was separated from the rest of the mental facility by eight feet of chain-link fence.

Casper was a limp and groggy chemical drunk when he was removed from the ambulance by a trio of beefy orderlies he would come to know as the Pep Boys. They were called that because their names were Manny, Moe, and Jack, just like the guys that advertised the auto parts stores on the radio. The shackles were not removed until he was inside and the steel doors were locked behind him. Stripped naked, head shaved, he was showered with a hose, dressed in vomit-green pajamas, and taken to Ward B.

Dr. Herbert Shanley, a thirty-seven-year-old staff psychiatrist prone to outbreaks of eczema and garish neckties, examined Casper. Having never gotten over the fact that he had not been accepted to Yale, he took a certain pleasure in processing the ex-undergraduate. He was familiar with Casper's case, besides what he had read in the paper and the gossip and idle talk among his fellow mental health practitioners. Dr. Friedrich had written him a seven-page typed single-spaced letter about Casper Gedsic, his IQ of 173, his death list, the threat he posed to the living. Shanley took all this into account and decided to play it safe and start Casper off with the first of what would be his daily dose of 100 mg of chlorpromazine, aka Thorazine.

With Thorazine on top of the amobarbital that he had been given that morning, by the time Casper was strapped in his bed that night, he was the living dead. The meds clamped a chemical governor on the magnificent engine of his mind. His brain slowed until there were no longer thoughts, just pictures. As he closed his eyes he saw himself as an insect trapped in amber. He could not remember how he knew of or where he had seen such a thing. It was just there, inside his head.

On his second night in Ward B, after the lights were dimmed—they were never turned off entirely—a patient from the next bed crawled in next to him. His name was Socrates. Casper would later learn he was a Greek short-order cook, former Greco-Roman wrestler, and ex-YMCA boy rapist. The restraints made it easy for the wrestler to manhandle Casper's genitalia and rectum. Casper was so medicated that he could not even muster the thought *I'm being raped.* The concept of outrage, injustice, was beyond his comprehension. He did not understand where the image of someone bobbing for apples came from, or what it meant. It was just there inside his head, flickering like a broken neon sign.

Compared to other hospitals for the criminally insane, Townsend was considered a beacon of enlightenment. Patients were not left to fester in their own feces. There were no Dr. Cottons roaming the ward, extracting teeth and lengths of bowel. Occasionally there were beatings, but never prescribed by a physician. And though the Pep Boys could have and should have kept a closer eye on Socrates at night, in comparison to the orderlies Casper would have encountered at other mental institutions for the criminally insane, they were positively benign.

Penologists and psychiatrists would have concurred: Casper was not being punished, he was being treated. There was no arguing that 100 mg of a tranquilizer like Thorazine made a patient who had killed a woman and crippled a man in a homicidal rage, a patient who had a history of violence, less likely to become violent. In his years at Townsend Casper never, not once, inflicted bodily harm on anyone. But the commonly held belief that tranquilizing the criminally insane reduces their anxiety and therefore makes them more receptive to the benefits of psychiatric therapies was at best dubious. As Homer would have put it, If you can't think straight, how are you gonna learn to think straight?

Perhaps because Casper's brain was such a finely tuned instrument, such a complex mechanism of wonder, it was acutely affected by the changes Thorazine inflicted on its chemistry. In the right dose chlorpromazine will kill you. Perhaps his mind shut down to keep the poison from spreading any farther than it already had. Whatever, in the months that followed, Casper shuffled through the routine of life in Ward B—like a somnambulist.

He could remember to urinate, empty his bowels, eat when food was placed in front of him; he could even answer questions. But he had no understanding of the words that were coming out of his mouth.

"How are you today, Casper?" There was a soft rasp to Dr. Shanley's voice, like the nap on a flannel sheet.

"Okay, I guess." Casper had gained fifteen pounds. His gait was hobbled to a slow shuffle, and he had a tendency to drool. But that was to be expected with Thorazine.

"You don't sound sure of that."

"I know."

"Why do you think that?"

"I can't think."

"Do you know where you are?"

"Can I go home?"

"Where's home?"

"I'm not sure."

"Well, that's something we'll have to work on."

Dr. Shanley noted after this early interview: "Gedsic's breakdown due to his inability to accept what he's done. Fitting in well—acceptance of ward routine, ability to follow instructions—meds seem to be helping, continue 100 mg Thorazine daily."

As spring heated up into summer, Casper's mind stayed in hibernation. Only he didn't think of it that way. He knew he wasn't asleep, and yet he was sure he wasn't awake. His brain had shut itself so far down, he could not make the connection between the meds and the slug he had become.

He could recall going to Dr. Winton's house, the gun, the blood, but he couldn't recall them as a chain of events. They were petrified out of time like the insect trapped in amber (it was in fact a moth) that floated in his imagination. His mind refused to send the messages necessary for him to comprehend how they belonged to him. His past was a series of hieroglyphs he did not know how to decipher.

There were glimmers that someone else was lurking beneath the chemical permafrost. That next summer, on the afternoon of June 18, 1953, the Pep Boys brought in a radio so they could listen to the Red Sox play the Tigers. In the seventh inning, the Sox scored seventeen runs. And when Gene Stephens, the Sox's left fielder, got his third hit of the inning, the announcer said, "You're listening to the first time in the history of the great game of baseball a player has had three hits in one inning. Somebody, tell me, what are the chances of that happening?"

"One in one hundred sixty-three thousand four hundred and fifty-two." Casper said it matter-of-factly, as he slowly worried the spot on his temple with his forefinger.

"How do you figure that, Casper?" Moe laughed.

"I don't know."

Casper remembered that he had once been smart. He just no longer knew what that meant. Irrational numbers still bubbled up and exploded inside his skull. But they no longer added up.

In August of that summer the Pep Boys rolled in a trolley loaded with old books and magazines, library cast-offs carefully screened not to include reading material that would titillate or inspire antisocial behavior: a Hardy Boys adventure titled *The Missing Chums, A Life of Howard Taft, The Story of Plymouth Rock,* old copies of *National Geographic* (minus the pages that featured native titties and bare-assed tribesmen). Casper made no requests, even though the sight of books brought a smile to his face. The Pep Boy named Jack thought he was being funny when he said, "This is a good one for you, Casper," and handed him an impressive volume titled *Lawn Care Made Easy.*

It took all of Casper's energy just to lift the cover, not because it was heavy, rather because he sensed he was no longer interested in knowing what was inside. By chance. he opened to a chapter titled "Weeds." Slowly, struggling with each word, he read aloud inside his head: "As every gardener knows, weeds are the enemy . . ." Why? It was a question that hadn't occurred to him to ask in a very long time.

Dandelions, finger grass, fonio, umbrella grass, Arizona cottontop, silky umbrella grass, pigeon grass, and the crabgrasses: Queensland blue couch, pangola grass, slender crabgrass, longleaf crabgrass, Jamaican crabgrass, Indian crabgrass, Madagascar crabgrass, twospike crabgrass, dwarf crabgrass, velvet crabgrass, shaggy crabgrass, violet crabgrass, naked crabgrass . . . the names were just words; the photographs of undesirable shoots of life did not mean anything to Casper.

He was ready to close the book. He turned the page out of habit. In bold-faced letters he saw the words "jimson weed." The photograph was black and white. He saw it in color, its forking purple stems erect, its irregular-teethed leaves the color of maple, its flowers trumpet-shaped, purple and white, opening and closing at irregular intervals during the night, hence the nickname, "moon flower."

He had seen it before, not in his old world that he couldn't remember, but in this one. It grew in the wasteland he now inhabited. The book of lawn care told him it also had another name: locoweed. It was then that his mind told him it was time to wake up.

The next day, as his fellow inmates shuffled about outside in a caged square of macadam known as the exercise yard, Casper found *Datura stramonium* growing up through the cracks in the blacktop along the edge of the chain-link fence. A sentinel of stalks the grounds crew had missed grew almost two feet tall, their egg-shaped fruit spined and large and as heavy as walnuts. He did not know if the seeds had been sown by the wind or excreted from one of the starlings that perched on the top of his chain-link cage.

The Pep Boys were arguing about the pennant race. Socrates was picking his nose, the air was being kicked out of a basketball. No one saw Casper reach down and harvest the leaves with the swipe of his hand and put them in his mouth. It didn't seem like it, but Casper was thinking clearly now.

Ten minutes after ingesting the handful of foul-tasting locoweed leaves, Casper's pupils ratcheted down to pencil points. His mouth was dry, his tongue a desert. His body told him to vomit, his mind overruled the command. His intelligence had been dormant, silent for so long, that now that it was back in force it seemed like a separate entity. It felt like a reunion with a much-missed old friend. Only . . . Casper corrected himself. He didn't have any friends. The embrace was more intimate than that, more like a long-lost lover. Casper didn't have any lovers either. (Socrates did not count.)

Having taken enough locoweed to make a twelve-hundred-pound steer hallucinate, he could imagine all sorts of things. In that afternoon's session with Dr. Shanley, as he watched the shrink reach into a bowl piled high with sugar cubes and drop one into his coffee, the other cubes sprouted arms and legs and crawled out of the bowl and began to dance across the desk in a conga line that brought back memories of a sweeter time.

When his fifty minutes with Dr. Shanley were up, Casper stood up and tried to walk. His arms and legs seemed to belong to someone else. His gait was jerky, exaggerated. He moved down the hall like a marionette. Only Casper was pulling his own strings now.

Dr. Shanley's notes on that day's session concluded with "choreoathetosis not observed previously: watch." By the time Casper sat down to dinner that evening he had to grip the seat of his chair with both hands to keep from falling off the roller-coaster ride he was on. The Pep Boys and his fellow inmates morphed into what they were, primates. Socrates appeared as a baboon. The Pep Boys were gorillas. And he was finally himself.

His breathing grew shallow, his heart raced, his face felt flushed. And yet, his body felt chilled. Sweat trickled down the sides of his face. Casper knew the dosage of jimson weed he had in his system was poisonous. But it was too late to worry about that. Besides, it wasn't the first time he had been prescribed poison.

The first seizure hit him just as he was remembering that the early American settlers in Jamestown had used a salad of moon flowers to defeat a garrison of British soldiers who had infringed on their liberties: Bacon's Rebellion, 1676. Casper, a new hybrid of rebellious American, felt vaguely patriotic as his arms and legs jerked spasmodically and his head fell forward into his tin plate of pork and beans. Casper wondered if the Pep Boys were smart enough to keep him from swallowing his tongue.

He woke up the next morning in the infirmary. Aside from a jackhammer headache and a sore throat, he felt better than he had in years. The headache was a chemical hangover. His throat hurt because a tube had been inserted down his esophagus when they pumped his stomach. Spinach having been on the menu the previous day, the half-digested tangle of jimson leaves did not raise any suspicions.

The onset of choreoathetosis, noted in the afternoon session, followed by his collapse at dinner—shallow breathing, rapid heartbeat, the seizures—were all classic symptoms of a toxic reaction to medication. Casper had been doing so well on Thorazine, his sudden allergic reaction caught Dr. Shanley off guard. It was unusual, but not unheard of. His body temperature had reached a hundred and four—at a hundred and five, brain damage begins.

Shanley was greatly relieved when Casper pulled through. Besides the paperwork involved in losing a patient to untoward side effects, there was something about Casper that Shanley liked. Dr. Shanley's response to the entire incident was prudent and appropriate. He immediately took Casper off the Thorazine and substituted a comparatively light dosage of the recently synthesized experimental indole alkaloid, reserpine.

Thorazine had been a chemical hammer. Reserpine was a gentler weapon in the psychiatric arsenal. Derived from Indian snakeroot and long chewed in its country of origin by the likes of Gandhi to enhance philosophical detachment during meditation, it was a serendipitous choice of antipsychotic for Casper. Reserpine left him feeling light-headed and often faint, but his brain had been abused for so long, it had developed an ability to take a punch. Casper's mind was still on a leash, but it was just long enough for his thoughts to roam in a new direction.

Casper didn't know if the whole plan had been in him from the start. But now that he was reunited with not all but at least part of himself, he knew what he had to do next. Reserpine did not make it easy to think, but with a mind as agile as Casper's, even at half speed, he was leaps and bounds ahead of Shanley.

In his first therapy session after Casper was on his new meds, Shanley began by asking, "How are you feeling, Casper?"

"I'm much better."

"Why do you think that?"

"Well, after the way you saved my life, I think I owe you the truth. I've got to trust somebody."

"I'm your doctor, Casper, you can trust me."

"I want . . . I need to talk about what happened in Hamden; it's time I faced up to why I'm here."

"That's a good sign."

"Dr. Winton's dead."

"That's true."

"I know who's responsible. I can't hide from that anymore. I'd be sick to do that, and I don't want to be sick."

"In your mind, who's responsible?"

"Not just in my mind, it's fact, truth, undeniable. Punishment fits the crime. If a person won't accept blame, they're crazy. I don't want to be crazy anymore."

"Crazy's not a word I use, but you could say they're in denial."

"Right."

"Who is responsible for what happened, for your being here?"

Casper thought of Dr. Friedrich, saw him upside down, the way he looked through the viewfinder of the press camera that first day, parrots squawking in his mulberry tree, wife and children beside him happy and smiling and free. Dr. Shanley thought he was making real headway when he leaned forward in his chair and urged Casper down the path of enlightenment by softly repeating the key question: "And who is responsible, Casper?"

Casper began to cry. "Me, of course." Casper wept not out of remorse, but at the beauty of his plan.

I was fourteen years old when I finally discovered I was born two years to the day after that Sunday of tulip planting and death. My father, being a psychologist, was careful to protect me from the tragedy my birth commemorated. My mother's intelligence kept her grief at bay most of the year. She willed it away, kept it hidden with that unused steamship ticket in her underwear drawer. Her disappointment only leaked out enough so I noticed it on my birthday. Nothing was ever said. I guess there was a kindness to their silence. But when you have to connect the dots yourself, you're bound to make mistakes.

My father worked hard to make sure my birthdays were so full of pin the tail on the donkey and sack races and piñata-bashing that he would be too distracted to think about Jack or Winton or any of the rest of Casper's dark matter that bound us as a family. Ice cream cakes and a hired clown who was really a doctoral student who couldn't finish his thesis, and presents my father never could have afforded back in the days when he was living on an assistant professor's salary at Yale, only succeeded in making my siblings envious and reminded my parents just how powerless they were to escape the shadow of our secret history.

My mother always cried as I blew out my candles—then apologized to no one and everyone. As she'd help me cut the cake, her fingers entwined with mine on the handle of a silver cake knife, she'd act like it was over—wait until I'd opened the last of my gifts before excusing herself to bed. They slept in separate rooms when I was a small child. She said my father snored. But on my birthday, when she went to her bed, my mother didn't get in it. She just lay on top of the covers and stared at the ceiling, afraid to close her eyes for fear the roof would fall in.

Whereas my mother couldn't make it through my birthday without tears, my father never stopped smiling. The rest of the year his mood was unpredictable. But on my birthdays his good cheer was relentless. His grin was relaxed, but the effort to keep it on his face made him sweat. Even when we had my party outside, the perspiration beaded on his forehead. When he took his jacket off his shirt was soaked through. I remember Lazlo's looking at my father and announcing, "Now I know why I like being miserable—happiness is too much like hard work." Unlike my father, when Lazlo said sad things, he smiled to let you know he didn't begrudge you your joy.

Even though my father's friend Lazlo, who referred to himself as a "bounced Czech," told me on numerous occasions, "The only thing I hate more than children is tulips," he never missed my birthday. He was the only friend my father kept from New Haven. Much engaged, but never married, the little man from Prague who Rolfed syntax and inflection had gotten rich selling scrap. "I am garbage man to the world," was how he put it.

It didn't matter where Lazlo was in the world, Tokyo, Texas, Tehran, he'd show up on October 7 with outlandish presents: a BB gun with a telescopic sight for my fifth birthday; a set of razor-sharp ninja throwing knives for turning six. Before I had mastered a two-wheeler, Lazlo had given me a minibike with a 6-horsepower Briggs & Stratton gas engine, all taken away by my parents before I could hurt myself.

Greedier than most children, I loved Lazlo for the presents. But what I liked about him was that it was easier to feel you were normal with someone as peculiar as Lazlo around. He always came early to help my father hang the crepe paper and stayed late to keep my father company after my mother had retired to her bed with her tears.

Lazlo would walk beside us as my father carried me up to bed. And when he tucked me in with Lazlo watching, my father would say, "Good night, my friend." Not "Zach" or "my son," but always "my friend." Which I guess is what he tried to be to me. And Lazlo could be counted on to make the same joke, which never failed to make my father laugh. "As your Jewish godfather, I must caution you about associating with friends like your father."

"Why's that?"

"Because your father is not a Christian."

"What are you, Dad?" I asked.

"My friend, I'll let you know when I figure that out."

Casper Gedsic remained at large for two full days after the murder of Dr. Winton. The killing and subsequent manhunt drove the Korean War off the headlines of the New England papers for more than a week. The fact that Casper was a Yale student dating the granddaughter of a governor, and that Winton was *Social Register* rich, and that there was lots of blood made it fodder for the New York tabloids as well. When Casper was finally apprehended, he was found sleeping in the forward cabin of a fifty-foot schooner that was in dry dock at the Wainscot Yacht Club.

Perhaps he thought he was at sea and had made good his escape. The death list with my father's name on it was found folded neatly in his wallet.

The evidence against him was incontrovertible. The stepdaughter gave an eyewitness account of seeing Casper standing over her stepmother's body with a pistol in his hand. His fingerprints were on a .22 caliber eight-shot Harrington & Richardson revolver found next to a rosebush a quarter mile away; the ballistics matched. My father was not called to testify and did not volunteer. A jury was never assembled to pass judgment.

A trio of eminent psychiatrists examined Casper. Two pronounced him a paranoid schizophrenic; the third judged him a sociopath with schizoid tendencies. Casper's state-appointed attorney pleaded insanity. Casper remained mute. The judge sentenced him to life in the Connecticut State Hospital for the Criminally Insane. According to newspaper accounts, Casper refused to give any explanation for his actions other than to say, "They made me."

Among psychologists and psychiatrists in the academic community, the case was well-known but little discussed. They categorized Dr. Winton's death the way my father dealt with Jack's—a tragic accident. But then, isn't that what all murders are?

A crazed, delusional patient kills the brilliant young physician trying to help him—it was an occupational hazard, remote, but real. Dr. Winton wasn't the first mental hygienist who suffered at the hands of a paranoid. My father's research on *gai kau dong*, his study of its effect on depression, its uncanny ability to produce that subtle electrochemical state commonly called happiness, was never completed, much less published.

My father and Dr. Winton had kept their research to themselves. Desperate to be the first, they ended up, well, CRAZED YALIE KILLS LADY SHRINK was not the headline they'd hoped to garner. Their adviser on the study, Dr. Petersen, was the only person at Yale privy to their preliminary test results. They were in the bottom drawer of his desk when a blood clot formed in his carotid artery and turned out the lights in the left hemisphere of his brain. Stroke, coma, he died the day after Casper's capture. Perhaps he would have added something to the inquest.

In spite of the fact that Yale became the first Ivy League college to expel a student for murder, there was no scandal. The Yale community was more isolated then, a fortress of greatness more than an ivory tower, immune to any and every thing but success. Alfred W. Griswold, the president of Yale, was number three on Casper's list. Winton was number two. My father was number one. My father had his theories as to why Casper, the Angel of Death, had passed him over that Sunday and gone straight to Winton's. But he never shared them.

By the time the tulips had flowered the following spring, Winton's husband was out of the hospital. All Thayer remembered was the doorbell ringing. The bullet Casper fired into his face damaged his tear duct. His right eye wept constantly. No one was sure whether it was the way Thayer fell against the stone floor in the hall or the beating Casper inflicted with the help of a field hockey stick that fractured his spinal column at the T8 vertebra. When not in his wheelchair, he walked with canes. There was a picture of him in the paper the following summer at the helm of his sailboat, winning the regatta. He stayed in Hamden and endowed a scholarship in his wife's name.

My father left Yale at the end of that academic year. Yale wanted him to stay. He had promise, he was on the right track. He could do a standard deviational analysis in his head, he was alive. The head of the department took Dad out to lunch and tried to talk him out of leaving. My father always said he left because they didn't make him a full professor. It was more complicated than that.

In June of '53, he traded in the White Whale for a brand-new robin's-egg blue Plymouth station wagon with automatic transmission and a V-8 engine, and drove what was left of himself and his family south.

Rutgers, the state university of New Jersey in New Brunswick, not only made my father a full professor at double the salary, he only had to teach one semester per annum of doctoral candidates in the final year of their PhD program—the rest of the time, he was free to do research.

Rutgers wasn't Yale. Except for the old Queens College, a handful of dark brown nineteenth-century stone buildings, and an impressive iron gate, the campus was a dreary, sprawling hodgepodge of clapboard and stucco. Happy homes for the skilled laborers who used to work in the factories that lined the banks of the Raritan, fouling its waters blue green with chemicals, had been hastily coopted by the university as its ambitions grew and the factories closed and the workers moved on to places not yet poisoned.

We lived across the river in Greenwood in a pre–World War I housing development that had seen better days. Now that my father could afford it, there was no High Lane Club to join, no polite private school to send his children to, i.e., nothing to offer proof positive that all he had compromised he had compromised for them.

Our house in Greenwood was three stories of gingerbread bric-a-brac with a curving porch curtained by a tangle of unpruned rhododendrons and old maple trees that provided too much shade for grass to grow green. It was clear from photographs that our house was twice as big as the box they had lived in back in Hamden. But I never once heard my father say something nice about our home in Greenwood. My mother would occasionally well up the energy to talk about fixing it up, tearing down walls to enlarge rooms, adding a terrace, a fireplace, bigger windows in the hopes of making it more cozy and less claustrophobic. But my father would always say, "What's the point? It'll never be right."

Other more renowned and scenic universities courted my father. He had offers to go to Boston, Philadelphia, San Francisco. His rating scale and tests were being used all across the country. He knew the questions to ask, the statistical formulas to tell America just how crazy it was getting.

New Jersey was a strategic retreat. My father picked Rutgers because New Jersey, the Garden State, was where the drug companies were. Hoffmann–La Roche, Merck, Sandoz, Johnson & Johnson, Ciba all lay between the Delaware to the west and the Passaic to the east, the Tigris and Euphrates of prescribed modernity. The sixty-mile crescent that lay between those rivers was the cornucopia of pharmacology.

I was not yet one year old when Miltown hit our local pharmacy: $C_9H_{18}N_2O_4$. It was named after a town in New Jersey. A pink pill that put your blues to sleep, it made everything feel okay, even when you knew it wasn't. Newspapers called it the "happy pill." Wildly addictive and incredibly popular with middle-class housewives, it was sometimes referred to as "mother's little helper." Family doctors all around the world gave it to brides-to-be nervous about their wedding nights, and to wives diagnosed frigid by their husbands. By the time I was three, one in twenty Americans was on Miltown.

For a few years, it swept anxiety, what the ladies' magazines called "emotional problems," under the carpet. By that time people had begun to notice that if you upped your dosage, you felt a buzz. If you took a little more, side effects included stomach upset, blurred vision, headache, impaired coordination, nausea, vomiting. Try to stop? Convulsive seizures. Take too many, your body forgets how to breathe. By then a prescription for Miltown was being written out every second of every day.

No longer just a psychologist, Dad was now a neuropsychopharmacologist. He didn't come up with the drugs that made the world feel better about itself; he just picked the ones that had promise, designed the tests, came up with the numbers that brought them to market. Dad stayed out of the lab after Hamden.

Officially he was a consultant to the drug companies. Over the years he worked for almost all of them. He wrote books and articles with titles I still don't understand. He worked hard and lived frugally. He still lived the dream of the magic bullet. Ambition and salvation were one and the same to Dr. Friedrich.

Bunny Winton's name had never been mentioned in our house, not once. Fiona was eight when Dr. Winton was murdered. Lucy was seven. They remembered the day the tulips were buried. They met Sergeant Neutch at our house in Hamden. They heard my mother wail, "No!" They saw Jack facedown in the birdbath.

My parents hid the newspapers in the days after the killing. Fiona was a precocious reader. Her friend showed the headlines to her. Lucy remembered. They filled Willy in on it. They had met Casper, they knew the bogeyman was real.

It must have been hard for them to resist telling the secret to me when I was little. But to their credit, they did. Dad had told them there was only one thing they could do that would be more unforgivable than telling me about the shadow in the pricker bushes: playing with the big, blue-black revolver my father kept loaded in his bedside table.

Our neighbors in Greenwood weren't academics; they were professional people, small-business owners, midlevel management. A sales executive named Lutz who worked for a paint company lived directly across the street from us with his wife, June, and their five children. Over the hedge to the east were the Murphys. The father was a plant manager for Squibb. They had three boys.

Behind us was a pediatrician, Dr. Goodman, who had daughters the same age as Fiona and Lucy and a cherry tree that hung low over our back fence, pink with blossoms in the spring, heavy with fruit in the summer. I was sixteen months away from being born when we moved to Greenwood. But I imagine our neighbors were pleased when they heard a youngish professor with a wife, two girls, and a boy had bought the old Conklin house on the corner. They looked forward to meeting us, had every reason to believe we'd fit right in. And when they looked out their window in the summer of '53, and they saw us arrive with the moving van, they must have liked what they saw. My family looked neat, clean, reasonably attractive, white, had a brand-new Plymouth station wagon, and all their fingers and toes. They couldn't see what was missing from our family. Not at first, at least.

My father blamed my mother for getting us off on the wrong foot in Greenwood. June Lutz, head of the PTA, den mother, Girl Scout leader, piano teacher, and everything else a mom was supposed to be in 1953, waited until the movers had gotten all our furniture into the house before coming over to welcome us into the neighborhood with a freshly baked plate of brownies.

My mother was upstairs when Mrs. Lutz knocked. As she hurried down the stairs, she saw the smiling neighbor holding the baked offering through the glass of the front door. My mother made herself smile and wave. My father had told her she was obviously clinically depressed and had tried to talk her into going into therapy. "I'll go when you go" was what she had said. Even though she felt as if her life had miscarried, she was prepared to pretend she was happy, to open the door and ask Mrs. Lutz in, offer her coffee, introduce her to the children, say all the things that are expected: "How sweet, you shouldn't have, you have to give me the recipe."

If only the mover hadn't chosen that exact moment to ask, "What do you want us to do with the crib?" It was Jack's crib. Back in Hamden she had told the movers to throw it away. Her husband had insisted they bring it. It was the smell of the mattress that got her, Jack's smell. My mother was so rattled by loss, all she could do was point to the cellar door. Mrs. Lutz watched incredulously as my mother suddenly turned her back and retreated back up the stairs to the dark, narrow room she had reserved as her bedroom. My mother forgot all about the brownies until Willy found them on the doormat the next morning.

My mother wanted to go across the street, knock on the door, and explain. But she knew she could not tell Mrs. Lutz about why a crib sent her running without telling her about Jack, which meant telling her about Casper, which meant she could remain silent, but she would not lie about what had killed her youngest. When Willy broke the plate, my mother gave up. She could explain herself or the dish, but not both.

When my father learned of the brownie incident he went out and bought a hand-painted platter from Portugal to replace the broken plate, had it gift wrapped at the store, and delivered it to the Lutzes himself. He had come to Greenwood wanting things to go well.

At first, it seemed like he could make it right. Mr. Lutz answered the door, told my dad to call him Chuck, and invited him in for a drink. Mrs. Lutz loved the plate. My father was so eager to make a fresh start, he made small talk with Lutz about the pros and cons of rotary versus reel-blade grass motors. It was all going well until Chuck asked him, "Where in Connecticut did you say you were from?"

Friedrich hadn't said he was from Connecticut. He guessed the realtor had mentioned it. "Outside of New Haven."

"Fall must be beautiful in Connecticut." Mrs. Lutz was putting the plate on their mantle.

"I bet it's pretty nice here, too. I noticed your sugar maples."

"You want to rake the leaves, you can have 'em."

Friedrich laughed at Lutz's joke.

"You're the first psychologist we've ever met." Mrs. Lutz was throwing away the gift wrapping now.

"We're just like anyone."

"Didn't I read something about a psychologist being murdered in New Haven by some student who went off his rocker?"

Friedrich studied them. *Did they know about him and Casper? How much did they know? Who told them? Fiona, Lucy . . . who else knew? Did everybody know?* "It was a psychiatrist."

"They're real doctors, right?"

Friedrich was so worried about what they might know about him, he didn't even take offense. "Psychiatrists are MDs; I'm a PhD."

My father put down his drink and stood up. "Anyway, we have a lot of unpacking to do. I just wanted to explain about my wife."

"Oh, there's no need to explain."

"I just wanted you to know Nora's . . . shy."

"We're having a Kiwanis picnic down by the park this Saturday."

"Maybe another time. Sorry about the plate, and sorry she couldn't come to the door."

"Don't worry about it." That wasn't what my father was worried about. "We understand." They didn't, of course.

That night my father sat my mother and siblings down at the dinner table and told them there were several items that wouldn't be unpacked in Greenwood. Casper, the Wintons, and Jack. They were not to discuss those subjects with any of their new friends.

"Why not?" Fiona asked. She missed Hamden already.

"You want us to lie." Lucy liked making up stories.

"No. I don't want you to lie. I just don't want you to bring it up." Friedrich looked over. Nora was staring down at her dinner plate as if she were reading a map.

"Why? We didn't do anything." That was Willy.

"What your father means is, it's no one's business but ours." My mother was talking to her coleslaw.

"We're making a fresh start. There is no need to let anyone know what happened in Hamden."

"You mean they wouldn't like us if they knew?" Willy was good at pinning my father down.

"They might have second thoughts."

"About what?"

"Christ, don't be obtuse. People gossip. When they gossip, they get things wrong. I'm telling you, it'll go better if you don't talk about it with outsiders." That included me, once I was born.

People did gossip. The Lutzes talked to the Murphys, who told the Goodmans. The Friedrichs were an "unusual" couple, which meant odd, which in a matter of weeks translated as "weird."

According to Fiona and Lucy, my father doomed them to geekiness when he removed the street number from the front steps. If he had told the neighbors a psychopath had come to his house once and he didn't want it to happen again, they would have understood his desire to make his house difficult for anyone outside the neighborhood to locate. As it was, the neighborhood first just thought he was peculiar for removing it, and then decided he was crazy for blaming the post office for not delivering his mail. Our family's secret and my father's paranoia cut the family off as surely as if he had relocated to an island or constructed a drawbridge. When someone in the community who hadn't yet heard we were weird sent my parents or sisters or brother an invitation to a wedding, a christening, a bar mitzvah, a dance, by the time it finally arrived, the event had occurred, and it was assumed we had deemed them unworthy of even a response. The Friedrichs were thought to be snobs, people with better places to go and people to meet. In truth, we were in quarantine.

My siblings never mentioned Casper, the Wintons, or Jack. But they talked about Hamden all the time. For them it was a place where my parents had friends, cocktail parties, neighbors they liked, and a backyard where other children wanted to play. And though they made it clear our family was never normal, they enchanted that time and place into a magical kingdom where laughter came easier and parrots flew in from nowhere. All I knew was the weirdness of living in a house with no address and having a mother who wept when you blew out your candles. It's strange, feeling you'd already missed the boat at age six.

Greenwood affected each of my siblings differently. Lucy, in an effort to give our neighbors an explanation for our peculiarities and distance herself from the weirdness, told the Lutzes we were adopted. And to this day Dr. Goodman believes my father's oddities were due to a brain tumor. Willy watched TV and ate Oreos. A lot of Oreos. So many Oreos, in fact, he was now twenty pounds overweight. A seven-year-old with breasts is not the first one chosen for fun and games. The public school system of Greenwood had infuriated my father and Willy, who was born in December, by insisting my brother wait a year to start kindergarten. He was the oldest, biggest, smartest, and saddest boy in his class.

Fiona believed she could avoid contamination by being perfect. She got straight As, won piano recitals, and made friends with the least attractive people in high school so that she would seem even more perfect.

The secret was safe, or rather, I was safe from it. I knew Jack was in the room. But the other ghosts stayed away . . . until I learned how to swim.

I was seven and everybody in my family could swim but me. It wasn't that I didn't like getting wet. I could play in the bathtub for hours. And I was all for wading in lakes, rivers, ponds—even the ocean. I wasn't afraid to go in the water. What terrified me was losing touch with the bottom. Even with a life preserver on I could never bring myself to push off, to let go of what I knew and float free.

My father tried every motivational approach a psychologist could imagine. Praise, bribery, positive thinking, scientific explanation, accompanied by my mother in her modest, black-skirted swimsuit, my father in his plaid trunks would demonstrate over and over again that the body floats as long as there is air in your lungs. Nothing he said could convince me that I wasn't the exception to his rules, that I wouldn't sink like a stone. In frustration he once resorted to good old-fashioned shame and humiliation: "A dog can swim, a cat can swim, Christ, even a hydrocephalic can swim."

My mother told him, "That's cruel, Will." And once she explained what a hydrocephalic was, I agreed.

"I just don't want the boy to drown." My mother said nothing, and thought of Jack. Which is exactly what I was thinking of. If

Jack had drowned in a birdbath, what was to keep me alive if I dared venture out of my depth?

I wanted to swim almost as much as I wanted to please my father. I'd stand chest deep in cold water until my lips turned blue and my fingertips were as wrinkled as white raisins, waiting for the courage that kept the rest of my family afloat. Then, just when I'd finally be ready to do it, Willy would cluck like a hen and shout, "Chicken!"

"He does it to get attention. You should really send him to a child psychologist that specializes in phobias." That was Fiona.

"Don't worry, Zach; I took junior lifesaving." Lucy was, if nothing else, well-intentioned.

Then my father would say, "Trust me, Zach. Nothing bad is going to happen to you."

Thinking but not saying, *That's what you told Jack,* I'd wade out of the water, turn my back on them, and try to comfort myself with the warmth of a damp towel.

Embarrassed that I could not swim, ashamed that I did not trust my own father, and knowing that if I tried to explain, mentioned Jack's name, I'd make them all sad, I resorted to deception.

When my family went to a lake or a river or the sea, I'd forget my bathing suit, feign I was coming down with a cold, swear to God I had a stomachache.

"If that's how you want to be," my mother would say. I did not want to be afraid. I was.

In the first week of the July of my seventh year, my father announced we would spend the upcoming Saturday picnicking on a then unspoiled white dune stretch of New Jersey shore called Island Beach State Park. I, of course, didn't want to go. Panic was followed by delirious and unexpected relief when Fiona at the last minute volunteered to stay home with me. "I really should practice for my piano recital." Fiona was seventeen.

"I don't feel comfortable, you two being alone."

"It's a duet. Gayle's coming over. We have to practice."

"You'll keep an eye on Zach."

"Of course."

My parents drove off with Lucy and Willy in the back of the Plymouth and me promising to be good.

Three minutes later a flat-topped wrestler in the 168-pound weight class named Joel appeared, greeting me with a simple, "You tell your parents, you're dead meat." When I tried to follow them down to the basement rec room where a phonograph and a stack of 45s were waiting to cover the sounds of heavy petting and dry humping on the squeaky-springed old couch by the furnace, the door was slammed in my face. Fiona giggled as the lock slid home, the 45 dropped, and Chubby Checker told me, "It's pony time, boogety boogety booogety shoo." The couch began to squeak. Usually my sister danced to that song. I thought it odd she and Joel would be so secretive about moving furniture and stopped listening.

Fifteen minutes later I was so bored, I wished I'd gone to the beach. The air was still and oppressive, the house unairconditioned. What to do? A bowl full of lemons on the pink Formica kitchen counter gave me an idea: *I'll set up a lemonade stand, charge five cents a cup . . .* I counted the Dixie cups stacked in cellophane—there were twenty-five—and did the math. If I sold them all, I'd make more than a dollar.

When my father saw my siblings watching TV after school or on a Saturday, he'd always say, "Why do you rot your brain when you could be reading, learning a foreign language, or getting some exercise? Christ—anything. When I was your age, I had a job. And the nickel I earned made a difference in the Depression." The truth was, I would have happily spent that Saturday watching TV if Dad hadn't put a padlock on the doors of the TV cabinet.

Convinced a display of enterprise, get up and go—i.e., a lemonade stand—might atone for my failure to swim, I took out a large knife and began to halve lemons, careful not to add one of my thumbs to the recipe—four lemons, a gallon of water, most of a pound bag of cane sugar, and ice. I made a sign with a red crayon on cardboard: ICE COLD LEMONADE, 5¢.

It was lukewarm sugar water at best, but I set up a card table on the sidewalk in front of our house, and much to my amazement, cars began to stop. I had made thirty-five cents when a Cadillac pulled up to the curb. The man who got out wore a clean white lab coat, just like the ones the doctor friends of my father wore at Needmore, a state mental hospital. Sometimes my father would bring us along when he went to see patients they were testing drugs on. It had a lawn bigger than a football field. And after my father did his business, he'd take us fly-fishing in a river too shallow to attempt a swimming lesson.

The man who got out of the Cadillac had a stethoscope in his pocket. When he first looked at me, he seemed more lost than interested in lemonade. After a puzzled silence, he said: "You can't be who I think you are."

"I'm Zach Friedrich, Dr. Friedrich's son."

"Of course." He fished a dollar bill out of his pocket and handed it to me. He didn't drink the lemonade, but he told me, "Keep the change."

"My mom and dad are at the beach with Willy and Lucy." Gray was on the porch, eyeing us as he pried the last kernels of corn off last night's cob. Mouth full, Gray ruffled his feathers and called for the dogs.

"Spot! Thistle!" Inside the house the pointers jumped up on the couch, noses to the window, and barked ferociously.

"You here all alone?" He had a slow, calm voice, like the one my father used when he talked to you after a bad dream, or to explain why you needed "quiet time," i.e., solitary confinement in your room.

"My sister's babysitting me." The man in the lab coat stepped into the shadow of the maple tree. "She's in the basement with her boyfriend, Joel, but . . ."

"But what, Zach?"

"Joel said I'd be dead meat if I told."

"I'm good with secrets."

"Are you a friend of my dad's?"

"Old friend. I know your whole family. Even Gray." Unlike most grown-ups, with the exception of Lazlo, he seemed to be actually interested in what I had to say. "So then why didn't you go to the beach?"

"I can't swim."

He smiled and put his hand on my shoulder. He had fingers like my mom's, long and thin and pink. "Want to learn?"

"I tried. I can't. I'm hopeless."

"That's what they said about me." He had a nice smile.

"No fooling?"

"No fooling. Everybody made fun of me. Wrote me off. It's hard when you can't do something that's so easy for other people."

"How'd you learn to swim?"

"Scientific technique. It always works. But it's a secret. If I show you, you can't tell anybody."

"I promise. Cross my heart and hope to die."

He looked at his watch, only there wasn't one on his wrist. I guess he forgot to put it on. My father was absentminded like that. The dogs were still barking, Gray whistled. "I guess I can squeeze you in." It was just what my father said when he talked to his patients on the phone. "Get in the car."

"We better tell my sister."

"Then they'll know I know about Joel and we'll both be dead meat." We shared a laugh and I skipped toward the Cadillac. He opened the driver's door.

I started to get in, then froze. "What about my bathing suit?"

"You won't need it. It's part of the secret technique." Just before we drove away, he told me, "Put on your seat belt."

We drove south on Route 1 with the radio tuned to a ballgame. The Yankees were playing the Dodgers. He knew more about different players' batting averages and time on base versus at bats than the announcers. When I asked him how come, he said, "When I was in the hospital I listened to a lot of radio with the other patients."

"You were sick?"

"Very. That's where I learned how to swim." When I said I was hungry he stopped and bought us foot-long hot dogs and orange pop.

After a while we turned off the highway and headed down a long dirt road. Yellow dust billowed up around us and the air smelled like Christmas trees on account of we were in the middle of a forest of stunted pine, and just when I was thinking we were an awful long way from home, he stopped the car. When the dust settled, up ahead, through a break in the trees, there was a stretch of water blue and glassy and smooth as a marble.

"What's this place called?"

"It doesn't have a name, Zach." I liked that idea.

The small lake was deserted. I was relieved that there were no children to shout "Chicken! What are you scared of?" No grown-ups to offer encouragement. It was just the man in the white coat and me and a crow being chased away from a nest full of eggs by a songbird who had been sitting on them.

We walked around the edge of the pond and paused to sample wild blueberries. At the far end of the lake there was a long concrete dam, mossy and green with water flowing over the top.

"When are you going to teach me to swim?"

"When we get to the other side." I thought it odd that he didn't take off his shoes before he started across the spillway. From where I stood, it looked like he was walking on water.

He was halfway across when he turned and looked back at me standing on the bank. There was a six-foot drop on the other side of the dam. The water was dark, the concrete slimed slick with algae.

"Are you scared?" His voice echoed across the emptiness.

"A little bit." I was following him out onto the spillway now. It was less than a yard wide. The pond's overflow rippled over the tops of my sneakers, then cascaded down into a deep pool. From there, a fast-moving river disappeared into a scrub forest I did not know was called the Pine Barrens.

Suddenly struck by the emptiness of the place and the sky overhead, I stopped and called out, "I think I want to go home now."

"It'll all be over soon." I heard him tell me that twice on account of the echo. "Once you make friends with what you're scared of, it's not scary. Letting go's half the secret . . . of swimming." The lesson had begun.

"What's the other part?" I was hurrying to catch up. I kept my eyes on his back to keep myself from looking down. I was halfway across the dam and feeling brave.

"Of what?"

"Your secret." The crow cawed and swooped low and close over my head. There was a tiny speckled egg in its beak. I waved my hands thinking it was going to fly right into me. The crow lost its grip on the egg. As I watched it fall, I made the mistake of looking down.

My sneakers skidded on the slime. There was nothing to grab hold of. Gravity did the rest. As I toppled back off the dam, I caught a glimpse of my swimming instructor staring at me, eyes wide and blank like he was watching a commercial on TV.

I hit the water with a quiet, relaxed splash. Gasping for air, yanking my head from side to side, I looked up at the spillway—my instructor was nowhere to be seen. My head was underwater now. My eyes were open. The water was freckled with sediment. The pool was deep. I was sinking, and the bottom was a terrible darkness that wanted me. Even though I was underwater, all my mind could tell me to do was, "Run away!"

Sinking deeper and deeper, feeling the chill of the water, panic setting in as my bloodstream ran low on oxygen, no one to listen to but myself, I began to run, run as if I were on dry land. Arms pumping, legs stretching out with nothing to push off but fear, I gagged on pond scum and brown water as I broke back to the surface. My instructor was kneeling on the spillway, smiling down at me. When I screamed, "Help," all he said was, "You're swimming."

Arms flailing, legs pedaling, still running—I was swimming. Sort of.

I closed my eyes and swam/ran faster. I made a few feet of headway. But when I got near the dam and tried to grab hold of the concrete lip, the overflow pounded down on me. The current was pulling me back. I was tired, I couldn't hold on. At the last minute his hand reached down and grabbed hold and pulled me up next to him.

He took off the lab coat and wrapped it around my shoulders. The sun was hot on my face. I forgot I was ever scared, which seemed the same thing as being brave to me. Without any warning I shrugged his white coat off my shoulders and slipped off the edge of the dam into the pond, and gleefully swam/ran/doggie paddled in a small circle.

"You really taught me how to swim," I shouted with pride and disbelief.

"I did . . . didn't I?" Cleaning his glasses on his necktie, he looked as full of wonderment as I felt.

It was just after six when we got back to Greenwood. The sunset torched the horizon a happy shade of pink, as warm and soft as a stuffed animal. My father's friend let me off two blocks from our house. He said he had "things to do." He shook my hand quickly, then told me, "Thank you for today, Zach."

It seemed odd, him thanking me. I was the one who learned how to swim. As he put the car in gear, I called out, "When are we going to go swimming again?"

"Don't worry, I'll be around." As he drove off, he shouted out the window, "Tell your father I'll be in touch."

I cut through two yards and jumped a hedge to get home as fast as I could. It was getting dark. Just as the chimney of our house came into view, I saw our neighbors combing their bushes with the beams of their flashlights and calling out my name. I ran in the backdoor, eager to tell my father the good news.

I found my family huddled around the dining room table. My mother was crying. Fiona wailed like Homer, "I'm sorry." Lucy was praying, Willy was eating a Mars bar. My father was on the phone. I didn't know a police car was parked outside. They didn't hear me enter.

"Dad, Mom, you're never going to believe it." It was the best moment of my life.

"Thank God," my mother shot out of her chair and grabbed hold of me so hard it hurt.

"The boy's here. I'll let you know what I find out." My father hung up the phone.

My mother was kissing me and my father was madder than I'd ever seen him. "Where the hell have you been?"

"We went swimming." I thought he'd be as excited as I was.

"You don't know how to swim. This is serious, I want to know the truth, goddamn it!"

"It is the truth. I *can* swim."

"You're scaring him, Will." I was scared, my father was terrified.

"Why are you so mad at me?"

"I'll stop being mad if you tell me exactly what happened."

"Your friend taught me how to swim in a gigantic pond."

"What was his name?"

"Casper."

"What?" my mother shouted in my face and pulled back in horror.

"His name was Casper. You know, like the friendly ghost." I was more than disappointed that my father didn't congratulate me on my victory over fear.

"What did this Casper look like?"

"Like a doctor. He had a white coat and a stethoscope."

"What did he say to you exactly?"

"He said, 'Thank you.' "

My father crouched down next to me, his face inches from mine. His voice was calm but his hands trembled. "For what?"

"For letting him teach me how to swim."

My mother shot my father a look. "What's that mean?"

My father held up his hand for silence. "Did Casper say anything else?"

"He said to tell you he'll be in touch."

Dinner was cold cuts and potato salad. As I ate, my father asked me questions. His manner was casual and friendly. He wore the same smiley face he put on for my birthdays. He worked hard to make it clear to me he wasn't mad. I knew he was something because when my mother interrupted his warm, fuzzy debriefing to ask me if I wanted more chocolate milk, he slammed his hand on the table and shouted, "Nora, for God's sake, will you shut up and let me talk to the boy?"

He started off asking questions about the swimming lesson. Did Casper help me take off my clothes? Did he try to touch my penis? Did he ask me to touch his penis? Between mouthfuls of potato salad I explained how I had swum in my shorts and T-shirt because I had fallen in.

Satisfied I wasn't sexually molested, he focused in on how I'd come to fall off the spillway. When I told him about the crow almost flying into my head and slipping, he acted like he didn't believe me. He kept asking me, "Are you sure Casper didn't push you?" He made me repeat the part about Casper's pulling me up out of the water three times.

Finally I protested, "You act like you think I'm making it up."

"I'm just trying to make sense of it all."

I remember my father made notes on a yellow legal pad as we talked, while I spooned my way through two scoops of butter pecan ice cream. He asked me questions about the car ride. From my description of the hot dog stand's green awning and cheese fries, he knew that Casper had taken Route 1 south. He drew our route on a map in a black wax pencil. When I told him about the dust and the Christmas trees, he circled the Pine Barrens.

A little after eight he told my mother to put us to bed and got up to go outside to talk to the state police. When Fiona complained that she wasn't sleepy, my father cocked his right hand back as if he were going to slap her. My mother called out, "Will, don't make it worse."

My father put his arm round Fiona's shoulder, as if he'd forgiven her. "If you're not sleepy, I suggest you lie down and think about what your afternoon of mutual masturbation almost cost this family."

My mother tucked me in after she read me a story and kissed me good night. She fixed her gaze on me and told me with strange, dry-eyed determination, "I'm not going to permit anything bad to ever happen to you, Zach."

Tired of explaining that nothing bad had happened to me I yawned and said, "I love you."

She whispered, "I love you more," and went back downstairs to my father and the police.

My night-light glowed in the darkness. Lucy tiptoed into my room first. Fiona followed, then Willy. That's when my sisters and brother whispered their version of what had happened to our family. I heard about Dad's being on the top of Casper's death list, how he came to kill us on a stolen motorcycle but drove off and murdered Dr. Winton instead.

When I asked, "Who's Dr. Winton?" Lucy said, "She was Mom and Dad's best friend."

Fiona insisted Jens was their best friend and Dr. Winton was somebody "Daddy worked with who Mom was jealous of." They all agreed that the Wintons were rich and that Casper shot her in the throat. There was disagreement over how many bullets were fired, but they all concurred that Mr. Winton was left paralyzed, and Willy said Dad said he had to wear diapers. They talked about people I'd never met or even heard of, a street I never played on, a home, a life I knew only from snapshots. It was hard for me to fill in the blanks, especially when it came to Jack.

Willy said, "Casper killed Jack, too."

Fiona, a stickler for accuracy, corrected him. "We don't know that."

"Why not?"

"No proof except for what Lucy thinks she saw."

"I don't think, I know. I saw a man's shadow in the pricker bushes."

"That doesn't mean that it was Casper's shadow, or that he killed Jack." Fiona was always accusing Lucy of jumping to conclusions. They knew Jack, I didn't. It made me sad that they could talk about him without crying, which is what I started to do.

Willy told me, "Don't be a baby."

Fiona reminded me, "You said you wanted to know everything." It was what I couldn't know that had me crying.

Lucy was crying now, too. "I don't want to think Casper killed Jack. Maybe Jack just bumped his head on his own and . . ."

"He's a killer. Killers kill people." Willy had no doubts.

"I told Mom and Dad he was creepy. Riding up to the house on a girl's bicycle. He had pimples and he didn't wash his hair."

"Yeah, but he got handsome."

"But why did he shoot the lady doctor?"

"Moron, have you been listening? He's *crazy*." Willy began to flick my night-light on and off to scare me.

"He's a paranoid schizophrenic. That's why they didn't send him to the electric chair." Fiona was using words I didn't understand.

"Killers deserve to be killed." Willy was still flicking my night-light.

"Daddy promised us he'd never get out of the mental hospital. He said there'd be bars and guards and it'd be impossible for him to get out." At least Lucy was upset.

"How did he escape?" I asked.

"Probably killed a guard or strangled a nurse." Willy was convinced.

"It's not Dad's fault he escaped." Fiona felt so guilty about Joel she stuck up for my father, even though she would stay angry about the mutual masturbation crack for the rest of her life.

"You're lucky Casper didn't drown you. That was probably his plan." I didn't believe that.

"Shut up, Willy, you're scaring him." I was crying harder now.

Fiona put on her grown-up voice. "Mom and Dad have told you a thousand times not to talk to strangers." I felt like a stranger as I stared out my window at the darkness.

"What were you thinking, getting into that car with him?"

"I thought he was a friend of Dad's."

"Dad hates him."

"I don't."

"What are you talking about?"

"He taught me how to swim."

Fiona said that when I was older I'd understand. Lucy said if I got scared, I could come into her room. Willy told me, "You're as crazy as Casper."

It was hard to sleep after that. Every few hours, the phone would ring. When I got up to pee, I heard my parents talking downstairs. I heard my father say, half pleading, half shouting, "Nora, I have done everything I can."

My mother answered softly, "No, you haven't."

When I got back in bed I heard the metal chains of the swings in the backyard creak in the wind. When I looked out the window, I saw a man sitting on the swing seat, looking up at me in the dark. Sure it was Casper, I opened my window to warn him. "Run away!" was what I was going to shout. But before I could, the shadow lit a cigarette. The glow of the lighter revealed a policeman with a pump shotgun cradled in his lap.

Willy was wrong, at least about Casper's escape from the Connecticut State Hospital for the Criminally Insane. No one was strangled, no one was shot. At 6:30 A.M. the Pep Boys woke Casper and the twenty-three other men in Ward B. They slept on thin mattresses in wrought-iron beds with eyehooks at their heads and feet for those occasions when restraints were prescribed. Three rows of eight in a green room the size of a basketball court. As always, the room smelled of urine and spunk. As always, Manny, the most gregarious of the Pep Boys, woke them with his usual greeting, "Rise and shine, girls."

Casper was in his bed. The bars were still on the windows, and everything was as it had been on the ward since Casper had first woken up there over nine years earlier. After breakfast—oatmeal, powdered skim milk, and a slice of stale toast spread thin with margarine—Casper and his ward mates received their meds. In Casper's case, 40 mg of reserpine.

Casper had a spotless record of good behavior, a model patient willing to discuss his problems and shortcomings in group therapy. "I use big words and try to impress people with how much I know and that I went to Yale because deep down inside, I know I'm weak and frightened. I want to change, I have to change; I know I'm kidding myself when I say I'm trying my best." But it was the remarkable progress he showed in his weekly fifty-five-minute therapy sessions with Dr. Shanley that turned the key for Casper.

Week by week, year by year, Casper dazzled and titillated Shanley with a slow, psychic striptease, revealing in installments a life history of sexual shame, repressed homosexuality, Oedipal rage (Shanley was particularly pleased when he got Casper to remember his mother slapping him when he got an erection during one of the cold cream enemas she gave him to cure his chronic constipation), adolescent rage, cruelty to animals that took the form of setting cats on fire. None of which ever happened.

Casper would never have been able to concoct such a seductive case history for himself if he had not had the help of a red-tailed hawk. Casper found its wing feather on the ground just a few feet from where he had helped himself to the locoweed. It was eight inches long and marbled in shades of butterscotch and cream.

A memory from another life, an art history lecture he had attended back in Yale, a professor with a fruity voice describing the wonders of Nero's vomitorium, how the Romans feasted, gorged, and then inserted a feather down their throats, tickled their glottis, and then vomited so they could gorge again, gave Casper the idea of taking that feather the hawk had dropped from heaven into the toilets just after meds were handed out and dutifully swallowed in front of the nurse. Regurgitating his breakfast and the 40 mg of reserpine before it had a chance to dull the razor's edge of his thoughts allowed Casper's feelings for Dr. Friedrich to evolve.

Armed with a feather, no longer having to fight the daily battle against the poison they pumped into him, the thought of revenge distilled into a far more intoxicating and noble idea. That feather gave Casper's rage wings, enabled it to soar to a lofty place and perch on the righteous thought that by killing Friedrich, he would be preventing Friedrich from contaminating anyone else's mind with hope.

Now that Casper could think clearly, his mission was sanctified. If he could save just one soul from his own fate, all that he had suffered would have meaning.

Casper was careful to let Shanley feel he was peeling Casper's onion, rather than the other way around. He was never too forthcoming. He'd clam up for months at a time before treating Shanley to a breakthrough. Casper made himself into a perfect case study, a textbook case worthy of publication.

Seventeen months prior to his escape Casper had in fact caught sight of a letter from a publisher on Shanley's desk. Casper read it upside down and began to turn the key. He didn't say anything about the letter. He just planted the idea. "You know, sometimes, after we finish, I remember things I should have told you."

"What sort of things?"

"Embarrassing stuff, mostly."

"That's the stuff we need to talk about in order for me to help you."

"I know. It might be easier for me to tell you everything, go into detail, if I wrote it down instead of saying it out loud."

And so it was that Casper earned the privilege of spending two hours each morning in the hospital library with a yellow legal pad just like the ones my father had used and a thick, child's blunted pencil. Shanley was aware Casper was still a danger to himself and others. He was vigilant in keeping implements of menace far removed from Casper Gedsic's grasp. Sharp objects were stowed out of reach. Metal spoons that could be ground down into shivs on concrete were counted after each meal. Strings, shoelaces, old rags, torn bedsheets, anything that could be braided into a garrote or a hangman's noose was kept under lock and key. His psychiatrist wasn't stupid. It was simply that Dr. Shanley and everyone else at the Connecticut State Hospital for the Criminally Insane had an IQ forty points lower than Casper's.

The implement of menace Casper constructed was inside his head. That was no man's land but Casper's. Shanley was no match for him there. The boy who had drawn up plans for an atom bomb at seventeen grew into a man who turned himself into a different kind of secret weapon. Working slowly, patiently, outside of time, while Casper constructed one persona to distract and disarm Dr. Shanley, he reconfigured himself from within, rewired his heart to wreak havoc on Dr. Friedrich.

At first his motivation had been revenge, old-fashioned, biblical, eye-for-an-eye revenge. *Friedrich has made me miserable, so shall I make him.* Casper had nothing but contempt for the nineteen-year-old sophomore who had gotten back on the motorcycle and let Dr. Friedrich go on planting his tulips that afternoon back in Hamden. A different Casper, one he did not recognize, had followed that impulse. Yes, Friedrich had lost a son, but Casper had lost himself.

After he'd gotten his medication lowered with the help of jimson weed, this was how Casper had thought about it. At night, when Socrates came calling and penetrated him with his madness, revenge was a pleasant distraction. He could forgive Socrates. He was crazy. He couldn't help himself. But Friedrich . . .

For the first month or so Casper's two-hour morning visit to the library was supervised by Shanley himself. The yellow pad, the blunt-tipped pencil, the quiet of the library were all so Casper could put down on paper the history of his madness. Dr. Shanley believed the act of writing would be therapeutic for Casper and a boon to the book he was working on: Shanley's insights plus first-person remembrances of a genius turned homicidal maniac. It was not long before Shanley was entertaining the possibility that his tome on Casper Gedsic might reach a larger readership than usually afforded scientific publications. Doctor and patient were both trying to write their way out of that grim, nineteenth-century insane asylum.

From day one of this experiment in mutual self-promotion Shanley was in awe of Casper's ability to commit his life to sentence and word. Casper did not need to compose himself before putting his thoughts down on paper. No outline or daydreaming, no hesitation, no doubt. As soon as Casper sat down, the pencil began to fly across the page. Dr. Shanley was not the first mental hygienist to envy Casper's brain. By the end of their initial two-hour session of longhand therapy Casper had filled twenty-seven single-spaced pages, all neatly printed and perfectly spelled.

> Though the degree to which heredity predetermines an individual's psychological propensities and emotional predilections from birth onward has yet to be fully studied, and is therefore open to scientific debate, I feel in my case it is worthy of examination.
>
> My father joined the Nazi party at the age of 16. At the age of 24, a Captain in the SS, he took part in the assassination of Ernst Röhm.

Casper's father was no such thing. He was in fact a Latvian fisherman. But he had Shanley hooked from page one. Casper wrote over a hundred pages before he got to the imaginary cases of epilepsy, incest, and rape on his mother's side of the family. Casper's output was so prolific, so rife with guilt and shame and phobias, whether or not insanity was hereditary, madness was his birthright. Shanley could barely keep up; there weren't enough hours in the day to study them as carefully as he would have liked. When Casper asked permission to consult the works of Doctors James, Freud, Jung, and, most especially, Emil Kraepelin's 1899 classic, *Psychiatrie: Ein Lehrbuch für Studierende und Ärzte,* to acquire psychological language, the technical terminology necessary to make himself clearer to the psychiatrist, Shanley saw no reason not to oblige—less work for him. It was in those volumes that Casper hid the pages of his real history, the one that started the day he made the mistake of bicycling out to take pictures of Friedrich and his parrots.

He worked on the truth far more slowly and painstakingly

than the fiction he confabulated to distract Dr. Shanley. It was a strange paradox; the more he lied, the more the truth mattered. It was not long, three to four weeks at most, before Shanley tired of watching Casper write. One of the Pep Boys was assigned to accompany Casper to the library. They quickly tired of paying close attention to Casper's industry, especially Manny. "You're not going to climb up on that bookcase and jump off on your head and kill yourself while I go out and have a smoke, are you, Casper?"

Two months after that, Casper's request for a typewriter was granted. Shanley loaned him the old black Underwood portable he had used as an undergraduate. It was while Manny was sneaking a smoke that Casper removed the Underwood's least used key, @/¢. He replaced it after he took out the typebar, which in turn he sharpened and bent, then used to pick the lock of the coat closet, where he obtained the lab coat I saw him wearing when he pulled up in front of my lemonade stand.

The second-floor windows of the library were secured with painted metal grills bolted to the outside of the building. A problem until Casper scraped away the paint and discovered they were made of bronze. The window in the northwest corner of the library near the shelf that contained works on behavior modification was only partially visible from the armchair where the Pep Boys lounged while he labored. Casper cut through the bars of the bronze metal grill slowly, micromillimeter by micromillimeter, using the conveniently serrated strip of steel that backed the Underwood's ribbon guide, speeding the process with the acid of his own urine.

He could have escaped long before he finally did. He had the lab coat for more than a year. Shortly thereafter, on a rainy afternoon he acquired a slightly rumpled blue oxford cloth shirt and gravy-stained necktie. They were still warm. Dr. Shanley had just taken them off to put on a fresh shirt and new tie—he was going to New York to meet his publisher. He was hurrying out of the office, worrying that the rain would make the trains late, when Pep Boy Moe brought Casper to his door, asking for a new typewriter ribbon. Moe leaned out the doorway to eyeball the gluteus maximus of the new nurse pushing a trolley of evening meds down the corridor; Casper snatched shirt and tie off the back of Shanley's chair and deftly hid them inside the loose top of his ill-fitting, state-issued green pajamas while Shanley turned his back and unlocked his desk drawer.

It was a few weeks after that that Casper found himself staring out the library window at 8:55 on a Saturday morning and noticing a green-and-white Townsend taxicab pull up to the front gate. The backdoor opened slowly; the suspension heaved as a man as big around as the Michelin Man in a brown topcoat unloaded his girth onto the sidewalk. He carried a briefcase and wore a gray fedora.

Casper didn't know that he was a certified public accountant who came in to do the books. But from the way the guards greeted him Casper could tell that the fat man was a regular, an expected visitor. Casper looked for him every morning after that. When he failed to appear for the next six days, Casper was disappointed. But on the seventh day, the same green-and-white taxi reappeared at exactly 8:57 A.M., and the fat man was off-loaded. Rain or shine, even when it snowed, the taxi with the fat man in the back pulled up every Saturday morning a few minutes before nine. Casper didn't know or care when he went home.

The pair of navy blue gabardine trousers Casper had worn on the day I saw him came into his possession by pure serendipity just before Christmas. Rufus, the black cook in the institution's kitchen, had lost his grip on a cauldron of boiling turnips. The pants were removed to treat second-degree burns covering his thighs and groin. Rufus's trousers were put in a brown paper bag and handed to Manny on the way to the library with instructions to hand them over to Rufus's wife on his way home from work. Manny, not knowing there was a five-dollar bill in the pants' pocket, forgot all about them. Casper didn't.

By the time the metal grate on the window to Dr. Friedrich's world was ready to give way, Casper's disguise was neatly folded behind the twelve-volume collected works of Dr. Cotton.

Casper lingered in hell six months longer than he had to. The bomb was assembled, the fuse was set, what was he waiting for? He had to finish his case against Dr. Friedrich, 732 pages in all. At 11:30 on the morning of July 4, Casper wrote the last word and went to sleep that night, sure of the fact that he would have it out with my father the next day.

Manny took him to the library that morning. As always, they arrived just after 8:30. As usual, fifteen minutes later, Manny inquired, "You're not going to break my heart and kill yourself if I go for a smoke?"

They both laughed when Casper said, "One day I'll be gone and you'll miss me."

Manny locked him in. Casper waited until he could no longer hear the Pep Boy's half-soled shoes echoing down the hallway before he wedged a chair against the oak door and changed his clothes. Dr. Shanley's blue shirt was a perfect fit. It took Casper several minutes to remember how to tie a necktie. The scalded cook's trousers were too big, but there was no time to worry about that. He used the heft of Wilhelm Reich's classic *The Mass Psychology of Fascism* to knock out the corroded grate.

The drop from the second-floor library to the ground was more intimidating once his head was out the window. He had fallen so far, what difference would another fifteen feet make? Clutching a pair of oversized manila envelopes bulging with his 732 pages of the truth tight to his chest, Casper jumped—the long awaited leap from thought to deed had finally begun.

Casper landed in a bed of blue hydrangeas. The flowers were wet with dew. Angry bumblebees buzzed round his head. As he tumbled forward, he lost his grip on his secret life. He had forgotten to close the metal clasp on one of the envelopes. Pages—two, three, no more than that—fluttered across the lawn. Scrambling to his feet, snatching up the envelopes, Casper watched the wind steal the opening of his prologue. Fighting the urge to run after them, Casper walked slowly to the concrete path that snaked its way across the lawn and out the front gate.

A guard was waving an ambulance through the gates. The nurse whose ass had distracted Moe was walking toward Casper.

As she approached, her eyes squinted in recognition, her mouth opened, he waited for her to shout to the guard, not sure what he would do then. But as the gap between them narrowed, her mouth closed. Pulling lipstick and a compact out of her pocket, she pursed her lips as if she were kissing him good-bye.

He was close now, less than thirty feet. Ten, fifteen steps at most. Casper straightened his tie and thought of how surprised Dr. Friedrich would be when . . .

"Hey, you." A voice Casper recognized shouted at him from behind. Casper looked down at the ground; the voice must have spotted the hospital slippers on his feet. He was just about to run when a hand, as meaty and firm and hairy as Socrates's, clamped down on his right shoulder. No running now. It was Fred, the red-haired guard who worked the recreation area when one of the Pep Boys was sick or had to straitjacket a patient who didn't want to go to shock therapy.

Casper turned round slowly. He wondered what it would take to finally accept the inevitability of disappointment. The bomb was armed. If he had to detonate it before he reached his target, so be it. Murder can be an act of suicide, after all. That is, if you believe in justice—he had cultivated his rage for too long not to reach some semblance of that. Casper fingered the ballpoint pen in the breast pocket of his lab coat. Where would he puncture Fred's face first?

The eye would be the easiest point of entry. If I got lucky, I might be able to . . . Casper corrected himself. *I'm not lucky, but there's a possibility I might penetrate the lacrimal gland . . . a lobotomy performed with a pen would make a point.* Casper almost smiled at his joke.

"Is there a problem?" Casper gripped the pen in his clenched fist.

"I found this on the walk. Is it yours?"

The red-haired guard handed him a stethoscope, unaware of just how close he'd come to being turned into a vegetable.

"Thanks. I knew I was missing something."

Stethoscope in hand, lab coat billowing behind him, Casper

walked tall out the front gate of the Connecticut State Hospital for the Criminally Insane without incident. It was 8:54 A.M. The green-and-white taxi was just pulling up. Casper opened the door for the fat man with the briefcase. One man got out, another man got in.

As the taxi pulled away, Casper considered the possibility that he might be lucky after all.

The pages Casper lost when he hit the ground read as follows:

THE CONNECTICUT STATE HOSPITAL FOR THE CRIMINALLY INSANE

GODDARD STREET. P.O. BOX 264.

TOWNSEND, CONNECTICUT

1951 wasn't a good year to be crazy. Mental hospitals were overbooked with deranged World War II vets and the wives, sweethearts, and children they infected and depressed with their patriotic gore. Doctor Egas Moniz had recently been awarded the Nobel Prize for calming an agitated Portuguese woman by severing the front of her brain from the rest of her gray matter. She later stabbed him. Doctor Freeman, the goateed, Nembutal-addicted president of the American Board of Psychiatry and Neurology, had been crisscrossing the United States in a snow-white Lincoln convertible, curing thousands of every variety of mental misfortune—schizophrenia, anxiety, depression, paranoia, from the barking-dog mad to the front-porch masturbator—simply by lifting up an eyelid, inserting a sterilized, gold-plated ice pick through the tear duct two inches into the brain, and giving it a sharp twist. The procedure was performed under local anaesthesia. Patients left Freeman's office with blackened eyes and a pair of dark glasses. Zombified into silence, they were cured because they no longer had the mental faculties to know they weren't. They ate, they talked, they slept; they were as easy to care for as a household pet. His lobotomies were performed before live audiences, lauded in the *New York Times* and the *Ladies Home Journal,* and, on one occasion, broadcast on national television.

In these enlightened days, the argument is often made that it used to be worse for those with troublesome minds. The great naturalist Charles Darwin's grandfather, Erasmus Darwin, had invented a mechanical antidepressant called the "spinning chair." Not surprisingly, it spun one. Once a patient was strapped into the chair, patient and chair were rotated on both north-south and east-west axes, until the patient vomited, bowels were voided, hair stood on end, and patient swears he or she is well. About that same time, the French had an equally ingenious nautical remedy, the "drowning machine," a metal cabinet they'd lock the patient in and then drop into the water. Those who stayed with the treatment long enough were cured of life, if not schizophrenia.

The spinning chair, the drowning cabinet are positively humane compared to what I have seen and heard. There's a doctor down in Baltimore who's working on cyanide treatments. And there's a professor at Harvard who's become famous for strapping you down to refrigerator coils that cool you out to eighty degrees Fahrenheit—coma therapy. If you don't trust me to be impartial, look it up for yourself.

Physicians who shared Freeman's ambitions but were too squeamish to pick up his bloody pick armed themselves with hypodermics. It is tempting to try your hand at greatness when patients are more plentiful than guinea pigs, consent forms unnecessary, and malpractice suits impossible to lose when the person testifying against you has already been diagnosed as crazy. Up at the Verdun Hospital in Montreal, Dr. Lehmann's lust for a cure inspired him to inject the lost souls in his care with a hellishly painful concoction of sulfur suspended in oil in the hope that the fever it induced might make them less crazy. When that didn't work, he tried shooting them up with typhoid antitoxin. Still no improvement? The hypo-happy doctor administered hot shots of turpentine straight into the abdominal muscles, postulating that the huge sterile abscesses these injections produced in their stomach muscles might raise the white blood cell count. Which just might possibly make them feel less crazy for reasons other than that he stopped. It wasn't just in Canada but here in the States.

No question, madness was in the air.

In 1939, there were a half million Americans being treated for mental health problems. By 1951, by my calculations, the number had more than tripled. Anxiety of the atomic age? Failure of religion? Photographs of the ovens at Auschwitz published in *Life* magazine (I, for one, found those particularly disturbing)? The corrupting influence of comic books whose heroes wore tights and shared domiciles with devoted younger male acolytes, also in tights? Negro rhythms? Too much sex? Not enough sex? Was there something toxic in the atmosphere? In the milk? Radioactive fallout? Television, fluoride, UFOs? Prosperity? Or was it simply that we finally had enough leisure time to realize just how miserable we always were? Whatever, the problem was epidemic. Something had to be done, and whoever did it first, found a magic bullet for schizophrenia or depression, or better yet, just plain old-fashioned inconvenient eccentricity was going to be as famous as Pasteur.

Dr. William T. Friedrich's ambitions were more modest. He just wanted to find a way to prescribe happiness.

Fuck him fuck him fuck him fuck him fuck him fuck him fuck him fuck him fuck him fuck him fuck him fuck him fuck him fuck him fuck him fuck him fuck him fuck him fuckhimfuckhimfuckhimfuckhimfuckhimfuckhimfuckhim fuckhimfuckhimfuckhimfuckhimfuckhimfuckhimfuckhim fuckhimfuckhimfuckhimfuckhimfuckhimfuckhimfuckhim fuckhimfuckhimfuckhimfuckhimfuckhimfuckhimfuckhim fuckhimfuckhimfuckhimfuckhimfuckhimfuckhimfuckhim fuckhimfuckhimfuckhimfuckhimfuckhimfuckhimfuckhim fuckhimfuckhimfuckhimfuck

The cover page bore the title of Casper's opus: *PHARMAKON,* a Greek word that can be used to mean both the cure and the poison.

I slept late the morning after my swimming lesson. When I finally woke up and looked out my bedroom window, the policeman with the shotgun had vanished from our backyard. Rubbing the seeds of sleep from the corners of my eyes, I took in all that was familiar, unchanged, my small bedroom, my little world—the night-light that looked like a pink elephant, the watercolor of the ugly duckling, the teddy bear missing a glass eye, and thought for a yawning moment that yesterday was just a bad dream.

Then I saw the shorts and the T-shirt I had been wearing when Casper taught me how to swim. My mother, distracted with worry, had left them draped wet over the footboard of my bed. They were still damp and smelled of pond water and the promise of mildew. They had already left a ghostly white stain on the varnished wood of the footboard. With time and polish it faded, but the mark Casper left on me was indelible.

When I got downstairs, my mother was scrambling eggs. My sisters were setting the breakfast table. Willy was talking to a policeman I hadn't seen before who was sitting on the back steps.

I thought the fact that he wasn't holding a shotgun in his lap meant that things had gotten less scary. Strange but true, learning to swim had made an optimist out of me.

My parents had showered and changed clothes, but they had not gone to bed. My father was on the phone to Neutch, the police sergeant from Hamden, who had driven up to Townsend at my father's request. Neutch was a lieutenant now. The opening pages of Casper's prologue, stolen by the wind when he leapt from the library window, had just been found. Neutch didn't have them in front of him; he promised to send them on and paraphrased. "He made up all this B.S. about stuff you do to patients, and then he ends, if you'll pardon my French, by writing 'fuck him' about fifty times."

"I see," was what my father said to Neutch. But he didn't. What was frighteningly unclear was why Casper had not begun his revenge with me. My father and mother both knew Casper had reason, opportunity, and motive. They had traded insights and accusations all night, trying to make sense of it. Sometime between 3:00 and 4:00 A.M. my father put forth the theory that Casper had intended to drown me but had changed his mind, returned me unharmed, to send a message: "You are my prisoner now. I can hurt you any time I want to."

In my father's mind, there was no question. As the night's second pot of coffee boiled over, he announced, "Casper's demonstrating his power over me, prolonging his euphoric delusions of omnipotence that we are at his mercy, that we are . . ."

My mother interrupted him. "We *are* at his mercy."

"Nora, they'll catch him."

"What happens the next time he escapes? He'll never forgive you."

"Goddamnit, I've done nothing that needs forgiving." He knew that wasn't true. And having to face that fact across the kitchen table made him at that moment hate her. "I tried to help him."

"I believe that."

"But you blame me."

"It's my fault, too. If I had let him kill himself that day at

Sleeping Giant, Jack wouldn't be dead. And we wouldn't be . . . what we have become." She did not want to put that into words.

What was resolved between them in whispers as the sun rose over Greenwood was not shared with any of us. Likewise, my parents did not discuss the details of Casper's escape from Townsend and subsequent arrival at my lemonade stand. That was so mysterious, it bordered on the impossible.

The cab driver who'd picked Casper up at the front gate at nine said they made two stops. The first was at the Townsend Theological Seminary Library. Casper was inside for about ten minutes. After that they went directly to the Townsend train station. Casper had paid with a crisp twenty-dollar bill; a New York–bound train had arrived approximately five minutes later. Logic would indicate that Casper had boarded. But the conductors could not remember taking a ticket from anyone matching Casper's photograph. And, more important, if he had traveled to New Jersey by train, he wouldn't have arrived until 4:20 in the afternoon; Casper had appeared in front of my lemonade stand just after noon.

Though no black Cadillac or any other dark-colored sedan had been reported stolen in the Townsend area, even if he had hot-wired a car whose owner might not have reported it missing for what was now over forty-eight hours, if Casper had driven south, at the very earliest he would have arrived three hours after he had. The only explanation was that he flew. Prop plane, helicopter, broom . . . New Jersey and Connecticut police were at that moment checking local airports and charter services.

A mental patient who could walk out the front gate of a hospital for the criminally insane, hail a cab, stop at a library, hop a plane, and acquire a late-model Cadillac was not omnipotent, but he was a force to be reckoned with and frightened by.

All of which in hindsight makes my parents' behavior that morning doubly strange. When I came back from swimming the night before, my father's phone calls to the men who were trying to help him were spiked with threats and obscenities. He told my mother to shut up and promised a state policeman, "If you don't find this creep, I will make it my life's work fucking your life up." I had never heard him say the F word before. And even though he used his soft, warm, patient voice on me, I felt burned by the rage that boiled beneath his self-control. Overnight, something had changed. And that morning he was full of "thank-yous" and "I appreciate it" and small talk about Lieutenant Neutch's wife and children.

Most surprising of all, when we sat down to breakfast, my father took my mother's hand and announced, "I am not going to let a man I tried to help deny my life. We are not going to let him defeat us."

"What if they don't catch him? He'll wait a year or two years and come back and . . ." Lucy blubbered what Willy and Fiona were thinking.

"Even if they catch him, he's smart, he went to Yale, he can escape again, you're not God." Fiona gave my father a look that told him she was talking about Joel as well as Casper.

"I'm not God, but by God I'm not powerless. Casper Gedsic is going to be dealt with. I'm not promising, I'm telling you." The others didn't believe him, but I did. I was the only one at the table who wasn't scared of Casper. It was my father who frightened me now. He made me think of a movie Willy had taken me to called *The Vikings*. My father wasn't wearing a helmet or carrying a battle-ax, but he was making a blood oath.

He wasn't finished surprising us. "We are not only going to continue with our lives, we are going to make the most of them. Your mother and I are going to Philadelphia to attend a psychological conference where I'm scheduled to read a paper."

"You're going to leave us here alone?" Willy spit egg out of his mouth in my father's direction.

My mother took over. "Of course not. You children are going to stay with Lazlo for a few days in New York."

"What if he follows us to New York?"

"He won't, Lucy."

"But what if he does?"

"Slavo will shoot him." Lazlo stood in the kitchen door. "Which will cost extra, but my pleasure." Slavo was one of two Yugoslavian licensed bodyguards Lazlo had hired.

Six foot six and three hundred pounds of muscled fat, Slavo hunkered behind Lazlo, casting a shadow across the breakfast table. When he bent down to shake my father's hand, I saw a revolver in a shoulder holster. Later, I'd notice he had another pistol, so small it didn't look real, strapped to his ankle.

Willy must have seen the guns, because he stopped being scared and started to complain. "What are we going to do in New York?" Willy didn't like Lazlo, mostly because I did.

"You'll see the sights, go to museums." My mother pushed Willy's hair out of his eyes.

"I hate museums."

"Do you like television?" Slavo lit Lazlo's cigarette. "I have three sets. One color."

Willy was happy. Fiona was thrilled. Lazlo lived in Greenwich Village. Joel the wrestler and she had been planning on sneaking in to see the Kingston Trio at the Bitter End. Lucy cheered up when she looked out the window and saw the other bodyguard leaning up against the side of the limousine Lazlo had rented for our rescue. He looked like Bill Holden in the movie *Picnic,* only with better cheekbones. Lucy, at fifteen still a sucker for fairy tales, had fantasized what it would be like to ride away from Greenwood in a limousine.

Suddenly, suitcases were being pulled out from under beds. We were packing clothes and toiletries and changes of underwear as if we were going on a holiday, not running away from the shadow in the pricker bushes.

All of Greenwood knew about Casper now. The police had circulated a photograph of him sent by teletype, told our neighbors to be on the lookout, cautioned them to remember to lock their doors and bolt their windows. When I had first disappeared from my lemonade stand the day before, the Lutzes and the

Murphys and the Goodmans had organized search parties and yelled themselves hoarse calling my name into the evening. But when I showed up unharmed and they found out what my father's ex-patient had done to Dr. Winton back in Hamden, their goodwill evaporated into outrage.

How dare my father not tell them, warn them he had a homicidal maniac on his trail? How dare he bring a killer to Harrison Street? And most galling and inexcusable of all, how could my parents send us off to New York in a limousine and take off to Philadelphia so my father could play the big shot at a medical convention, leaving them to face our nightmare?

Now that they knew why we were so weird, they thought even less of us. What if Casper came back and, finding us not at home, kidnapped one of their children for a swimming lesson? Put a bullet hole in their necks? Gave them a beating with a field hockey stick that left them wearing diapers in a wheelchair?

They stood on the porches and peered over their hedges as we carried our bags to Lazlo's rented limousine. Their eyes narrowed at our gall, their jaws set with contempt. Children darted into the road, eager to try out the backseat of the limousine and ask me questions about my maniac. But before they got to our side of the street, their parents called them back and ordered them inside, like what we had was catchable.

What did they expect my father to do? Would they have respected him more if he took his revolver out of the bedside table and patrolled the yard, waiting for Casper to return? I didn't want my father to hurt Casper, but at the same time, I did not want Dad to run away. It was okay for me to do that to keep from drowning, but not my father. He didn't sound like a coward over breakfast, but I couldn't shake the feeling that we were doing something that wasn't right.

My father was oblivious to the neighbors' disdain. My mother lined us up and they kissed and hugged us, one by one, and put us in the limousine. The policeman said, "Don't worry, everything'll be back to normal in a couple days." I didn't believe him.

As we drove away, I looked back for one last wave. My parents had already turned their backs on us.

I had been to New York before, the Museum of Natural History, the Bronx Zoo, the Metropolitan Museum of Art, Grand Central Station. It was a place where it wasn't safe to go to the men's room without my father, a place where my mother embarrassed me by insisting on holding my hand and constantly warning us, "Don't wander off or you'll get lost." In short, it was the last place in the world you'd go to be safe.

None of it made any sense to me. If they waited until I was four and a half to tell me I had a brother who'd drowned in a birdbath, waited until I was seven to let me know there was a killer after us, what else hadn't they told me? If I couldn't trust my parents or Fiona or Willy or even Lucy (who liked me enough to share her last Tootsie Roll with me, even when she had to take it out of her mouth to do it) to tell me the truth, who could I trust? Lazlo? Sure, he came to my birthdays, gave me cool presents, but he hadn't warned me. If I knew someone wanted to hurt Lazlo, if his name was on a death list, I'd have told him. My seven-year-old mind boggled at the deception of life.

As Willy and Lucy fought over command of the electric windows, I turned around in the backseat and stared out the rear window, looking for Casper.

We got to New York just in time to see the city get out of work: 5:05 P.M., and suddenly they scurried and ran and tripped and bolted out of office buildings and skyscrapers, hitting the summer streets in a frenzy, as if they had just been sprung from a giant trap. I don't know how the others saw it that day, but it made me think of a nature show on TV called *Wild Kingdom,* hosted by Marlin Perkins. Anyway, he was always catching wild animals in the wilderness only to put metal bracelets on their paws or radio collars around their necks, so that when they were set free, they'd think they were free, but really weren't.

The sidewalks were a grim, haphazard migration. I'd never known there were so many different kinds of people in the world. Only when I looked at them all at once, they didn't seem like people. The way they pushed and jostled each other, some running for cabs, others charging, heads bowed, toward the subway, some thundering east, others stampeding west, all anxious in their hurrying, as if they were being stalked by a predator they could smell but not identify.

It made me lonely to think of people like wildebeests. So I tried to concentrate on faces, pick out individuals to focus on who were heading in our direction as the limousine inched its way east, crosstown on Forty-second Street. The trouble was, when I looked at them one at a time, people looked even more like animals. A little woman in a blue-and-white polka-dotted suit clutched her pocketbook to her breast with both hands and darted through the crowd like a mouse who feared she might be mistaken for a piece of cheese. A tall woman made taller by a blond beehive and high heels bounded into traffic to escape in a taxi like an albino gazelle. A lion with a briefcase, a jackal sipping a paper-bagged beer waited for his moment in the cool shadow of a marquee.

Not wanting to be any more scared of the migration we were on than I already was, I made myself stop thinking of a wild kingdom and concentrated on the familiar—a businessman whose seersucker suit rumpled just like my dad's, a mother with four children had the same distracted smile my mother wore when she couldn't hold everyone's hand in a crowd—yes, they looked normal, safe and human. But so had Casper.

The scariest thing of all about this first inkling of the wild wideness of the world around me was that none of the people I was watching had any idea I was thinking about them. And because they didn't know I was alive, they would not know I was dead. Unless they read about it in the papers. Which made me think of Casper again.

I'd been quiet for a long time. Lazlo asked me to push in the lighter and inquired, not unlike my father would have, "What are you thinking about, Zach?"

"Our dogs." Fiona was reading *The Scarlet Letter*. Lucy sat in the jump seat and leaned through the divider and made small talk about Yugoslavia with the bodyguard who looked like Bill Holden. Willy was eating Oreos.

"What about them?"

"Who's taking care of them?"

"Your father checked them into a pet motel . . . what do you call it . . . ?" Lazlo inhaled a filterless Lucky and searched for the word "kennel." Suddenly his nostrils flared so wide you could see the hairs in his nose. "*Scheisse,* what is that stink?"

Lucy interrupted her conversation with Stane (that was the Yugo Bill Holden's name) long enough to bellow, "Jeez Louise, Willy, put your sneakers back on."

"I can't help it, I have athlete's foot."

Fiona punctuated the command by smacking Willy on the back of the head with the flat of her book.

Lazlo sniffed the air and grimaced. "No athlete's foot smells that foul. Is like the shit of a dog that eats cat shit." Everybody thought that was a scream. It had been a long drive.

"What's *scheisse* mean?" I asked.

"How you say 'shit' in German."

"How do you say 'shit' in Yugoslavian, Stane?" If my parents had been in the car, they would have stopped the limousine to wash Lucy's mouth out with soap.

"No such language. In Serb, 'shit' is *govno*." Suddenly, even though we were being chased, we felt free.

"Or *sranje,* which is a dirtier kind of shit." The way Slavo said it, you could almost smell it.

"In French, it's *merde*." Fiona thought it was juvenile to talk about shit, but she couldn't resist an opportunity to flex her French.

"What's it in Czech, Lazlo?"

"*Hovno*. The Hungarians have a wonderful word for it: *székés*."

Willy rolled down the window. "Hey *hovno*-head! Go eat *székés*!" It actually was funny the way he said it. Everybody laughed. Willy could be a real card. And so, as we made our way downtown through the canyons of the city, Lazlo taught us how to say "shit" in every language of the free world.

Home for Lazlo was a townhouse on Horatio Street in the heart of Greenwich Village. He had four floors all to himself. From the outside, I expected something ye olde, but when Lazlo opened the door, it was like stepping into the Jetsons' living room.

The staircase was just boards sticking out of a wall. And all the furniture was curvy and backless and shaped like amoebas, and there was a see-through, kidney-shaped bar that made the bottles and glasses look like they were floating in midair. And everything was white, even the floors. And instead of rugs, there were zebra skins. And coolest of all to a seven-year-old who had no idea Lazlo had stolen the aesthetic from Hugh Hefner, there was a remote-control panel built into the coffee table that, at the push of a button, lowered the shades, dimmed the lights, and made the stereo play Frank Sinatra, "Life's a wonderful thing, as long as I hold the string."

In short, it was the most ill-designed house possible for children. Without my parents there, I was free to spin myself around on the bar stools and run up and down the railingless stairs without my mother tripping up my enthusiasm by shouting, "Stop that before you fall and break your neck." Which was always the surest way to make me fall.

"Does everybody in New York live like this?" I was trying out a chair that looked like a giant egg.

"Just short, ugly men who want girls to like them." Lazlo ordered Slavo to stand guard on the front steps. Stane took a bottle of Coca-Cola and his revolver out behind the house. We hadn't forgotten about Casper; we just weren't talking about him.

"Why do you want them to like you?" I asked.

"So they'll . . ."—Lazlo was distracted. Willy had commandeered the control panel and was raising and lowering the shades in time to the music—". . . do things for me."

"Where's your powder room, Lazlo?" Lucy was trying to sound grown-up for Stane, who winked at her as he took off his shirt.

"What sort of things?" I persisted.

Lazlo was regretting babysitting us even before Willy broke the remote control. "Make goulash."

Stane thought that was hilarious. The lights were dimmed, the shades down, the ambience stuck on cocktail lounge.

"You're not going to tell my dad I broke it, are you?"

"I am many things, but not a squealer."

"What's so funny about goulash?" I asked.

Fiona closed *The Scarlet Letter.* "It's a metaphor for sex, Zach. Lazlo means that he does all this to get women to sleep with him."

"A good goulash is much harder to obtain than sex. Twenty-seven kinds of paprika."

I opened the bathroom door. Lucy held up her finger to her lips. She was stuffing toilet paper in her brassiere. "Sorry, Luce." My sisters were acting very strangely.

Having broken the control panel, Willy announced he was hungry. Lazlo had more kinds of ice cream than Howard Johnson's. A quart of chocolate chocolate chip in one hand, a fresh bag of Oreos in the other, Willy called out, "I got dibs on the color TV." Lazlo pointed to the den at the top of the stairs, relieved to have made one of us happy.

Lucy emerged from the bathroom two cup sizes larger and joined Stane in the garden. "How many tattoos do you have?"

"Four that you can see." Stane shrugged off the look Lazlo gave him.

Fiona had her own agenda. "I think I'll go up to Bleecker Street and check out the guitar store." She'd learned the expression from Maynard G. Krebs on *Dobie Gillis.* Fiona reached for her purse.

Lazlo took it out of her hand.

"What are you doing?"

"Tomorrow, maybe."

"My parents said we could see the sights."

"They meant you can see them later. Maybe, it depends."

"My parents don't lie."

Lazlo was running out of patience. "Everybody lies."

"My mother and father are not liars." Suddenly, Fiona was crying.

"Fiona, give me break. You know why we're here. You know what has to happen before we can go outside and have fun. Once they call me, I don't give a shit what you do. As long as you don't rat me out."

Lucy called out from the garden, "Lazlo doesn't mean they lie about important stuff." Fiona was crying harder than ever. I'd never seen her cry like that. When she fell on her chin skating, she'd had to get eight stitches. She hadn't shed a tear. But now she was bawling about Lazlo saying the obvious. I liked her more for crying, and yet I wanted to make her stop.

Fiona grabbed the telephone on a long cord and locked herself in the bathroom. I listened at the door. She called the hotel my parents were staying at in Philadelphia. They hadn't checked in yet. Fiona left a message anyway. "Please tell them that one of their children has a problem."

I waited until she'd hung up to tap on the door. "Fiona, let me in."

"Use another bathroom."

"I don't need to pee, I need to tell you something." She let me in. "It's going to be okay."

"That's what you came in here to tell me?"

"Yeah."

"You're seven years old, what do you know about anything?"

There was only one thing I knew more about than any of them. "Casper told me so."

"What did he say?"

"He said he's not going to hurt anyone ever again." He'd said nothing of the kind.

"Why didn't you tell Dad that?"

"Casper said Mom and Dad would never believe him. He just escaped to check on us, to find out if we were happy." Saying it out loud made me feel almost like it was true.

"What'd you tell him?"

"I said everything was great."

Fiona blew her nose and put her arm around my shoulder. "So you lied."

It was at that moment I began a lifelong bad habit of laughing at things that made me want to cry.

By the time Fiona and I came out of the bathroom, Lazlo had already sent Slavo out to the guitar shop, where he'd bought a Gibson six-string and a songbook that showed her all the chords, and she said "thank you" about a hundred times and began to practice "Wimoweh." Already being able to play the piano, by the time Lazlo ordered in Chinese, she was strumming and changing chords and singing "In the jungle, the mighty jungle, the lion sleeps tonight" over and over again. And instead of chanting "Wimoweh," we all chanted in unison, "Please shut up, please shut up, please shut up. Please shut up . . ."

Lucy was jealous of Fiona's guitar and would have shown it if she hadn't had Stane to play with. I watched them from the kitchen window after dinner. In broad daylight, Lucy looked older than fifteen. But with her brassiere stuffed with toilet paper, hair teased up, and face painted with the lipstick, eye shadow, and mascara my mother forbade her to wear back in Greenwood because my father said it made her look cheap, Lucy, in the moonlight of the city, suddenly looked to my seven-year-old eyes grown-up and expensive next to Stane, with his tattoos and broken English.

I got the idea that Lucy was trying to look older, but I didn't understand why, if that was how she wanted to misrepresent herself, she was leaning close and talking to Stane in a breathless, little girl voice. "I've always wanted to go to Yugoslavia," she proclaimed with childlike innocence.

"Why is that?"

"Because I'm a communist." The only two places Lucy had told Lazlo she wanted to see in New York City were Saks Fifth Avenue and the Plaza Hotel.

"You don't look like a communist."

"My whole family are communists. Did you ever get to meet Marshal Tito?"

"How do you know about Tito?"

"Being a communist, I find him very attractive."

"No, I have not met the bastard, but if I had, I would have shot him."

"I'm sorry to hear that."

"What's it to you?"

"When I thought you were a communist, I wanted to kiss you." Her lips were two inches away from his.

"Just 'cause I don't like Tito doesn't mean I don't believe in the ideals of communism."

"I think you're just saying that so you can kiss me."

"No, it's true, I swear."

"Wish I could believe you."

"Believe me." He leaned forward, she leaned back.

"I suppose part of the reason I'm so passionate"—Lucy flared her nostrils and shook her head as she said the word "passionate," and liked the effect so much, she did it again—"terribly passionate about communism is due to the fact that I was adopted. My real parents were famous Russian spies. You've probably heard of them—the Rosenbergs?"

"The bastards they put in the electric chair?"

Lucy nodded sadly as she lit the wrong end of one of Stane's cigarette's. Two lungfuls of burning filter and she didn't cough.

"That's a sad story."

"Not really."

"What do you mean?"

"I just said that."

"Why?"

"To see if I could get you to believe it, silly."

Me making up lies to make Fiona feel better, Lucy telling lies so she could see if Stane wanted to kiss her without having to kiss him: I agreed with Stane when he looked at her in lustful disgust. "You're all crazy."

Fiona had moved on to "Kumbaya." Lazlo was on the phone trying to explain to one of his girlfriends why he'd stood her up. "I have to babysit. Family emergency." He held the phone away from his ear as she yelled at him, and made a face that cracked me up, even though I was feeling sad. "Yes, I know my family is dead. This is the emergency of another family."

Lazlo sighed as he put down the receiver. "The only time I ever told her the truth, and she doesn't believe me."

Desperate to find something normal to hold onto, I went upstairs to the den to see what Willy was watching on TV. When I opened the door, he yelled, "Get out, dog breath!" Which in fact did cheer me up, because that's what Willy always called me. But when I pushed the door open all the way, I wasn't treated to the comforting sight of Willy noshing his way through *Bonanza*. The TV wasn't even on. The Oreos and ice cream were untouched.

His pants were down around his ankles, a copy of *Playboy* open to the centerfold. He was breathing hard, and his right hand had a stranglehold on his dick. "What are you doing to yourself?"

"Beating my meat. Wanna try?"

"No, thanks."

I went to bed early. It was the first night in my life I had not slept under the same roof as my parents. I missed my mom. Not like how she was, but how she would have been if she'd been a mom in a storybook, like *Charlotte's Web*.

Lazlo came in to check on me. "Will you read me a story, Lazlo?" He was smoking a cigar.

"Sure, as long as it's not the *Little Red Hen*. What books did you bring?"

"I didn't bring any."

"I'll read you one of mine." Lazlo eyed the bookshelf and pulled down a cracked volume and began to read. " 'It was the best of times, it was the worst of times.' "

"Like now, you mean?"

"Like always."

I fell asleep before he got to the part about chopping people's heads off.

In the morning, Lazlo let us have ice cream for breakfast.

When Fiona came downstairs, she hugged me and gave me two kisses. I could tell she appreciated the lie I had told her about Casper. I only wished there was some way to make up a story that would make me feel better.

"What's that for?"

"First one's from Mom, the second one's from me." My parents had called after I fell asleep.

Between bites of fudge ripple, Willy announced, "Dad says he's going to buy me a microscope to make up for Fiona getting a guitar." I imagined Willy peering at a centerfold magnified to the hundredth power.

Two new bodyguards had taken the place of Slavo and Stane. Lucy already had one of them convinced that our grandfather was Albert Schweitzer. Fiona had moved on to a new page in her songbook: "If I had a hammer, I'd hammer in the morning, I'd hammer in the . . ."

"If I had a hammer, I'd break your damn guitar." Lazlo laughed at Willy's quip as he stuffed his briefcase with papers and got ready to go to work.

"What am I going to do all day?" I asked.

"Play with Willy."

"Willy likes to play with himself." Lazlo thought that was funnier than I did. He was the one who had told Willy about the *Playboys.*

"You can play with Zuza."

"Is she my age?"

"Sometimes." Lazlo motioned for me to follow him. English being his fourth language, he didn't try to explain everything.

He opened a door in the kitchen and we descended a dark narrow staircase. At the bottom, there was a metal door covered in cork.

"Foot thick, lead-lined so I don't hear her pounding." Even though I didn't like playing with girls, I was curious.

When Lazlo opened the door, I was greeted by a family of marble statues that looked just like naked people, except that they had eyes carved into their stone flesh in places that eyes don't belong, eyes on the back of their heads and on the inside of their thighs and on their stomachs and feet and the palms of their hands. Some were squinting. Some were surprised, others seemed stunned by what they didn't see. No matter where you looked, they were watching.

There was marble dust everywhere, even in the air. And the light that poured in through a pair of sidewalk-level windows at the end of the room drenched the figures in a pearly haze. I was so busy looking back at the eyes, I didn't even realize the chalky white figure standing in their midst holding a hammer up over her head was alive until Lazlo said, "Zuza, what are you doing?"

"They're all *székés*." I knew from yesterday's lesson that that was Hungarian for shit.

Lazlo took the hammer out of her hand. "This is Zach."

I didn't exist for her. "Sod off and give me back my hammer, Lazlo." She had an English accent, but I could tell she was from somewhere else. She was taller than Lazlo, and even though she had hair shorter than mine and wore dirty men's overalls and was covered in dust, she was pretty. The powdered stone that caked Zuza's face made her eyes look like they belonged to a cat, and now that she'd wiped the dust from them, her lips showed purpler than red, like she'd been eating mulberries.

She bent back Lazlo's fingers, trying to pry the hammer from his grip. When that didn't work, she leaned over, openmouthed, and bent down to bite his hand. Lazlo laughed. She looked like a feral doll. "Get out of my studio. I made them, I can do what I want."

"First, since you haven't paid me rent in over two years and I pay your fucking marble bill, it is my studio and they are my naked eyeball people. Second, the last time you smashed everything up, you felt even worse afterward." It was only then that I realized what she was going to do with the hammer.

"You were gonna wreck 'em?"

"Just her." The statue that offended her eye was pregnant.

"What don't you like about her?"

"Too pretty."

"What's wrong with pretty?"

"Ask Lazlo." Lazlo was rummaging through her purse. "What are you doing?"

"Whenever you get like this, it means you haven't been taking your pills."

"They make me dumb."

Still holding onto the hammer, Lazlo was trying to pop the lid off of her pill bottle with his teeth and talk at the same time. "Someone who'd rather break than fix is smart?" The cap popped off and the pills scattered.

Zuza gave Lazlo a surly glare as I squatted down to pick up the pills off the floor. They were lavender, and when I blew the dust off them and saw they were stamped with the letter L, I realized I'd seen them before. "My dad has a giant one of these inside a glass paperweight on his desk." A drug company had given it to him to celebrate the sale of their millionth pill.

"Your father must be very depressed." Lazlo thought that was funny.

I offered Zuza the handful of pills. She took one, swallowed it dry, flopped onto an old sofa, and retreated into a cloud of dust.

Lazlo handed me the hammer. "You can give it back to her in an hour." He bent down to kiss her good-bye on the forehead, like she was the child and he was the parent. Then, at the last second, she looked up at him, scared and angry, and kissed him on the mouth. Then she pushed him away and snarled something that sounded less friendly than shit in Hungarian. He left by the little door that opened up under the front steps. Zuza waited until it slammed shut and he couldn't hear her to call after him, "Sorry."

Zuza chain-smoked a fresh pack of Kent cigarettes, tilting her head first to the right, then to the left, she ashed on the floor and stared at her stone-eyed statues, as if she were waiting for them to tell her what they saw. I sat across from her and waited for her to say something. After ten minutes of silence, I started to get restless. "Can I look around?"

When she didn't answer, I began to explore. At the other end of the studio there were other things that didn't make sense, sculpted in clay and chiseled from tree trunks. A giant terra-cotta egg that sprouted a dozen arms, all giving it a hug; and clay hands with wings draped in damp swaths of cheesecloths; and on the wall there was a poster of a medieval drawing that showed a castle and towns and mountains drawn as if the world was flat, and the ground they rose from rested upon the back of a giant rhinoceros that stood on the back of an elephant that rode on the shell of a gigantic turtle that swam in an underground sea filled with tiny mermaids and monsters.

Pinned up next to it was a drawing that she had made based on her vision of the universe, only her flat world had skyscrapers and cars, but instead of the ground's being supported by giant beasts, it teetered on a huge bomb that was held aloft by an even bigger baby that was being held up in the air by a man who stood on the shoulders of a woman who was trying to swim, but looked like she was drowning.

I looked at that drawing a long time before I asked Zuza, "Do you make goulash for Lazlo?"

Zuza smiled and lit the last cigarette in her pack. "Once upon a time, I did."

"Did you know him when you were little?" I gave her back the hammer.

"Since I was sixteen. My mother was Hungarian, my father Czech. We met in Prague."

"Why do you have an English accent then?"

"After the war, I attended art school in London. Lazlo sent me."

"Do you sleep down here?" I saw a hot plate and a little refrigerator.

"Sometimes." She put a sheet over the statue she had almost smashed, and turned on the record player. A minuet played, and she began to move among the statues as if she were dancing with a hammer.

I didn't know exactly what my father had to do with the pill

Zuza had taken, but I knew he had something to do with it. And the way it cheered up Zuza made me feel proud of my dad.

"Where do you live?"

"In a tiny apartment."

"By yourself?"

"With a man."

"Is he your husband?"

She laughed. "Yes. We are married. I'm more old-fashioned than I look."

"Lazlo isn't old-fashioned."

"In some ways, that's true." She stopped dancing and tossed her partner, the hammer, onto the couch.

"Did Lazlo tell you why we're staying with him?"

"Yes."

It took five minutes of silence for me to well up the courage to ask, "Do you think they'll catch him?"

"I don't know." She was the first grown-up who didn't tell me everything was going to be okay, that I was safe, and that there was nothing to worry about. Knowing she might actually tell me the truth, I didn't want to ask any more questions.

"You want to touch something that will make you feel better about what you don't know?"

"Sure."

She took my hand, pulled it inside her overalls, and placed it on the smooth melon of her stomach. My father had warned me about strange men touching me, not strange women. Her overalls were so big, I hadn't realized she was pregnant. "Feel it."

My eyes widened, and embarrassment turned to wonder as her belly moved beneath my touch. "It's kicking!" I shouted. She was right; it did make me feel better.

After we talked about whether she thought it was a boy or a girl, and debated names, Zuza gave me a piece of emery cloth and put me to work polishing the rear end of a marble fat woman. When I was done with that, we split her liverwurst sandwich, which tasted much better than I expected. She thought it was funny when I told her I thought they called it "wurst" because it was the worst part of liver. Best of all, when my sisters and brother came downstairs to see if I was having more fun than they were, after saying nice to meet you and shaking their hands, Zuza ordered them upstairs. "Only one studio visitor at a time."

After lunch I helped her mix clay in a garbage can, and we were up to our arms in clean mud, and I was thinking that there was no place else on earth, regardless of if it were flat or round or balanced on a beast, that I would rather be. Then my brother bellowed down the stairs, "Mom's on the phone."

Knowing I didn't want to talk to her, that I'd feel worse no matter what my mother said, that I wanted to stay and talk to a stranger because there was no history to come between us, the cozy feeling I had found in that basement flew out the window. "Go on, talk to your mother; she misses you." Zuza patted her stomach. "We're not going anywhere." She made it seem like she and her baby were one person.

My mother and I were separated by more than a few hundred miles of long-distance static. She did miss me. I could hear her sniffle and imagined the tears running down her cheeks as she told me, "It's going to be okay, Zach. We know where he is now."

How? I wondered. I overheard my sisters talking about how weird it was that my parents went to a medical conference. Were they tracking Casper down?

As my mother reassured me, I began to worry that they were going to do something bad. "He'll be caught in a day or two, and then we'll be home, and everything will be good again." When I didn't say anything, she asked, "You believe me, don't you?"

I said nothing and handed the phone to Lucy.

Zuza was waiting for me. She put me to work, helping to knead all the air bubbles out of the clay. But it wasn't the same. I felt guilty for not wanting to talk to my mother, and, worse, angry at her for asking me a question I had to answer with a lie.

I tried to imagine my mother happy to have me in her stomach the way Zuza was. But all I could think of was the way she cried at my birthdays, and how she got sad when she looked at me because she didn't see Jack, which seemed doubly unfair, because I was part of her, too. Struggling to find a way to shape all these thoughts that seemed wrong into something that would feel right, I asked Zuza, "Can you show me how to make something for my mom?"

And so I learned how to make a bowl. Her hands on mine, Zuza taught me to roll the clay into long snakes, then coil them around a circular base. Each one slightly longer than the last, to give it shape. She made one for herself along with me, so she could show me each step but not take over and end up making it herself, the way my father would have. And when the curve of my bowl suddenly turned wobbly, and I hit it with the mallet and shouted "Shit!" in English, she laughed.

"Now you know how hard it is."

"What?"

"To make something out of nothing."

And so I started at the bottom again and again and again, and by the next afternoon, I had a bowl my mother and I could both be proud of. And the day after that, she showed me how to paint it with glazes that all looked like shades of gray, but which Zuza promised would come alive with color once it was fired.

Around the outside of the bowl I painted my family holding hands. Stick figures, but I knew who they were. And Zuza kissed the top of my head and called me *drágám* when I included her stomach and Lazlo in the chain of my life. And as she fired up the kiln, I added one more person, and then I was ready to hand it over.

"Who's that one?"

"Jack."

When Lazlo came home from work that night, he called Zuza and me upstairs and announced, "Tonight, we all go out to dinner and celebrate."

We all knew what that meant. Fiona and Lucy and Willy cheered and jumped up and down like the home team had just won a football game. "Did they hurt Casper?" I asked.

"No more than they had to."

The next day, Lazlo took off from work and drove us home in his convertible Mercedes Benz. Top down, radio blaring, Fiona and her guitar squeezed in the front. I sat in the narrow backseat between Willy and Lucy, clutching the bowl I'd made for my mother with both hands as if it might blow away in the excitement of our return. Zuza had wrapped it in blue tissue paper. It was my mom's favorite color.

My parents were sitting on the front steps holding hands when we drove up. My mother was resting her head on my father's shoulder. They looked nervous when they saw us and jumped up, like we'd caught them doing something they didn't want us to see.

Willy leaped out of the convertible first, shouting, "Did you get me a microscope?"

Fiona held her guitar aloft and announced, "I wrote a song."

Lucy laid claim to newfound sophistication. "Lazlo took us to the Plaza for dinner. And I drank champagne."

They were all hugging and kissing as I walked toward them with the bowl. My mother pulled herself away from the reunion and ran down the walk to greet me. "It's all over, Zachy." I was glad because she was glad. Mostly, I was looking forward to surprising her with the bowl.

She missed me so much, she didn't hear me when I said, "You'll never guess what I made," as she pulled me into her arms. Hugging me to her chest, I shouted, "Don't!"

It was too late. I was the only one who heard the crack. My mother pulled back from me when instead of "I love you," I shouted, "stop!"

"Aren't you glad to see me?"

The bowl fell from my hands onto the sidewalk and shattered inside the blue tissue paper. I wept as she unwrapped the disaster and collected the pieces. "It's beautiful. We can put it together again. We'll get glue. We can fix it."

"No, we can't."

We had supper early in the dining room. Normally, we only ate there on Christmas, Easter, and Thanksgiving. My mother said this was a kind of Thanksgiving. She prepared our favorite meal: roast beef, mashed potatoes, fresh corn on the cob, and apple brown betty, a feast to welcome us home from our time in the wilderness and celebrate the incarceration of our oppressor.

The typewriter that usually sat at the head of the table had been excused, and the papers and manuscripts and abstracts and stacks of computer printout that normally monopolized the tabletop and sat in the chairs had been hidden out of sight and mind. As my mother and Lucy billowed out a tablecloth that had been embroidered by her great-aunt Minnie, Fiona and Willy and I set the table with china and silverware that were traditionally only brought out to impress strangers.

And just as we were about to dig in, my mother did something else she didn't normally do. She said, "I want us all to say a prayer."

From the expression on my father's face, you would have thought she'd requested a blood sacrifice. He gave us a look that begged us to do whatever she asked. Then she made everyone hold hands. There was a long moment of silence. I wasn't sure whether she had forgotten how to pray or was uncertain what she had to say to God. "Dear Lord, thank you for giving our family this chance." Everybody closed their eyes, except for me and Lazlo. "And forgive us if we have offended you."

"Amen" was followed by a serious silence.

Then Lazlo solemnly raised his martini glass and toasted, "*L'chaim,*" adding sarcastically, "Whatever the hell that means." Which made my father laugh. Then he lit up a Lucky and announced, "I hope you don't mind, I taught all your children to smoke this week." He even began to pass out cigarettes, which my mother thought was funny until Lucy lit hers up.

"You're lucky I'm in a good mood, young lady." My mother snatched the cigarette from her hands and smoked it herself.

Willy spooned a crater into his mashed potatoes, then reached across Fiona for the gravy. "Dad, why didn't the police just shoot Casper?"

My father had already told us how the police had tracked Casper to Baltimore and arrested him in a medical library in Johns Hopkins. "He surrendered, Willy."

"If you were there, would you have shot him?" Willy emptied the gravy boat, turning his crater into a greasy brown lake.

"Hey, Willy, thanks for saving some gravy for the rest of us." Fiona was big on manners.

"We'll talk about it after dessert. Right now, I'd like to enjoy my meal and not have to think about anything having to do with Casper." My father pushed his hair off his forehead and asked me for the salt.

"What happened to your head?" There was a crescent-shaped scab just at his hairline. Still unconvinced they ever really went to Philadelphia, I imagined Casper and my father fighting on the edge of a cliff, like they were in a cowboy movie and one of them was a bad guy and had to die.

"I hit it on the door of the medicine cabinet getting some Pepto-Bismol for your mother in the middle of the night."

"You had diarrhea?" Willy was always getting diarrhea.

"Yes, if you must know. Now can we change the subject?"

"I had diarrhea for six months after the war."

"Lazlo, don't encourage them."

"What'd you do?" I asked.

"I found an apartment with a bathroom that had the most beautiful view in Prague. Sometimes I'd eat my dinner there, invite my friends over, play cards . . ."

"Gross."

"Once, I won thirty thousand ducks on that toilet."

"What'd you want ducks for?"

"*Ducks* is Czech for how you say bucks. Greenbacks, dollars. Only by the time I tried to spend them, they were worth like three cents." Lazlo worked hard to keep us from thinking about Casper.

After Lazlo left for New York, and the plates were cleared and the leftovers were divided between the fridge and the dogs, my mother got out a tube of Duco cement and put newspaper down on the table, and we began to try to piece the wreckage of the broken bowl back together. My mother did most of the gluing. Her fingers weren't as clever as Zuza's, but there was a grace in her determination to make things whole.

And as I watched her struggle to figure out how the pieces fit together, I listened to my father in the adjoining living room reassuring my sisters and brother that Casper would never bother us again: "Casper Gedsic is in a place he can never escape from." My father's voice was tired. He sounded like he was reading from a script.

"That's what you said back in Hamden." Fiona looked up as she tuned her guitar."

"He's not in Townsend anymore."

"Where is he?" I asked.

"In a high-security facility at Needmore Mental Hospital."

Lucy stopped studying her split ends. "He's in New Jersey? That's just great."

Then Willy chimed in, "Whose dumb idea was that?"

"Mine. He's in a special new kind of cell. Monitored twenty-three hours a day by TV cameras."

"Why not twenty-four?" Willy didn't feel sorry for Casper.

"He gets an hour of exercise in a yard enclosed with a twelve-foot chain-link fence topped with razor wire."

"What's razor wire?"

"It cuts you if you touch it."

"Cool." That was Willy.

"On the way to and from his exercise session, his ankles and wrists will be shackled."

"What's he going to do all day?" I asked.

"He'll have a television he can watch, radio, books to read."

"He doesn't get to see or talk to anybody?" I could tell Lucy felt sorry for him, too.

"Outside of the psychiatric staff? No."

"He'll go crazy," Fiona said matter-of-factly.

"He is crazy, stupid."

"I would rather be dead than locked up like that." Lucy began to pick ticks off the dogs.

"If he can't get out, why watch him with the TV cameras?" That was Fiona.

"There are new drugs we're going to try on him, and we need to watch to see if they work."

"You think you can cure him?"

"No, I don't. But I think we can learn from him." Not knowing anything about GKD, we were spared the irony of the life my father had sentenced him to. "My hope is that we can use the tragedy of his life to discover something that might possibly help others lead productive lives." My father chose his words carefully. My mother never looked up from the broken bowl.

"So even if you cured him, you wouldn't let him free?" Lucy burned a bloated tick. Its skin popped and dog blood fizzled.

"They'll never find a cure for what's wrong with Casper."

"But what if they did?" I protested. "What if the medicine you gave him worked and he got well and he wasn't crazy and he promised not to hurt anyone?" Fiona fretted a minor chord and glanced at me, and then my father.

"Would you want me to take that risk, Zach?"

I fell asleep that night wondering what my father would do if one of us got crazy like Casper. Would he lock us up in a room with books and TV for company? Have us watched over by cameras and strangers? Try out medicine on us, knowing that even if we said it worked and weren't crazy anymore, he would never believe us?

When I woke up in the morning, the questions bothered me even more than they had the night before. Overnight, my unanswered and unasked queries raised more and more questions; so many it seemed as if I could feel them pressing against the inside of my skull. But when I ran downstairs in search of my father and the answers I hoped he'd give me, I found his seat at the breakfast table empty. "I need to talk to Dad."

"He's upstairs. And tell him his eggs are getting cold."

When I went back up to his bedroom, I found him sitting on the edge of the bed. "What would you do if one of us got crazy?" I waited for him to say something that would make me feel better. But he said nothing. He had one shoe on and a sock in his hand.

"Dad?" He looked right through me. Again, I waited for an answer that would reduce the unknowns that were crowding my brain. Unable to stand it a second more, I finally shook him. "Dad, answer me."

He blinked twice and looked at the sock he was holding as if it belonged to someone else. "What's going on, Zach?"

"What would you do if one of us went crazy?"

"We don't have to worry about that."

I did, though.

My father's first Sock Moment was a harbinger of other changes that Casper's capture wrought on our family life. Not all of them were as spooky as Dad's shoeless catatonia. In fact, some of them gave me hope that the low-grade fever of unacknowledged melancholia that afflicted my family might have finally broken.

Later that day, my mother asked me to help her move her things out of the little room under the stairs where she had slept since my birth back into my father's bedroom. I never knew how lonely I felt, knowing they slept alone, until I experienced the joy of having a bad dream and being able to snuggle into the soft darkness that lay between them even in sleep. My mother said she came back to Dad's bed because he'd stopped snoring. I knew it wasn't true, because when I snuck into their newly conjugal bed, I was surprised to discover they both snored. But I liked the idea that they were in love.

That was the biggest change of all. I didn't fully understand what had been done with Casper. But whatever it was, it had an immediate, startling, and profound effect on how my parents interacted. If they weren't holding hands, my mother was sitting on his lap. And I heard her tell him he was handsome, and my father answer, "That's because I have a beautiful wife," and he'd kiss her on the mouth right in front of us; they'd wrap their arms around each other when my father left for work in the morning like people did in movies when they were saying goodbye forever.

Their public displays of affection made Willy stick his finger down his throat and make barfing noises.

Fiona's explanation for the sudden onslaught of intimacy was more clinical. "Mother obviously wants to have another baby."

Like all youngest children, though I did not like being referred to as the baby of the family, I enjoyed being a baby. The thought of being replaced would have caused me more anxiety if Lucy hadn't set the record straight: "Don't worry, Mom's taking the Pill."

Thinking of the giant antidepressant that kept the papers on my father's desk from blowing away, I thought of the mood change I had witnessed in Zuza. "Mom's taking medicine to make her like Dad again?"

"No, silly. She's taking *the* Pill. It lets you have sex without having to worry about getting pregnant." In 1962, in twenty-two states it was still against the law to take G. D. Searle & Co.'s synthetic progesterone for contraceptive purposes, but not to imbibe it for "menstrual disorders."

"Why does Mom want to have sex if she doesn't want to have a baby?"

"Because sex is the most beautiful thing in the world." Lucy's voice was solemn.

"You've had sex?"

"Sort of."

Before I could ask her what that meant, Lucy announced dreamily, "Mom's having her second spring with Dad. I'm happy for them."

"Me, too." I was, at first.

Unlike the rest of us, my mother did not wonder if Casper, with his demonic genius, might still, like Spiderman's nemesis,

Green Goblin, have enough superpowers in hidden reserve to short-circuit the TV cameras, trick his psychiatrists, kill his guards, and break the grip of the cure that could not be trusted, even if it worked. She believed my father when he told her Casper could never touch us again.

My mother was, in fact, so sure in this belief that in this second spring she flowered overnight in exotic and unexpected ways, intent on making up for lost seasons. She went to a beauty parlor, a first, according to Fiona, and had her hair cut almost as short as Zuza's. She gave away all her old clothes and bought new ones. My mother looked like someone else when she called the Salvation Army and had them come by and pick up Jack's old crib.

My mother's days of going back to bed after my father left for work and we were off to school were over. The same new reenergized ardor she displayed for my father was manifest in the most mundane minutiae of daily life. Dust bunnies were no longer allowed to breed beneath sofas and beds. Bookcases were rearranged according to subject matter and alphabetized by author. The jumble of closets was sorted out and the mess of life was labeled and organized into plastic bins.

My mother, who once took pride in her lack of domestic aptitude, began to clip recipes and arrange flowers and invite my father's graduate students over for casseroles flavored with wine. She even invited our neighbors, who didn't like us to begin with, and who still hadn't forgiven us for Casper and trusted us even less when she served them bœuf bourguignonne.

My father liked her new haircut, the colorful clothes, and the newfound tidiness of our household, and enjoyed being sucked up to by the graduates who suddenly invaded our home in search of an A. He was even able to take a certain perverse pleasure in using his skills both as a bartender and a psychologist to get our neighbors tipsy enough to admit things he knew they'd regret telling him when they woke up with a hangover the next morning. Who would have thought Dr. Goodman and his wife once went to a nudist camp? Or that Mrs. Lutz, head of the PTA, had met her husband at the party his parents had thrown to announce her engagement to his twin brother. Or that Mr. Murphy's father and grandfather had both shot themselves with the same shotgun that, weirder still, they hadn't thrown away.

When neighbors were embarrassed or ashamed of what they'd revealed under the truth serum of alcohol and unexpected conviviality, my father would tell them "we're all complicated creatures," and then throw them for a double loop with the kind of facts he loved to shock people with. "George Washington suffered from Klinefelter's syndrome."

"What's that mean," they would ask.

"He had breasts and atrophied genitalia." No question, my father knew things the rest of the world didn't. When I was little, I was impressed. But as I got older, he could never resist the opportunity to demythologize anyone more famous than himself.

Gandhi drank his own urine, JFK had a ghostwriter, Winston Churchill was a drunk. Eleanor Roosevelt chewed with her mouth open and was a lesbian. (He'd actually had lunch with her once. He and Mom had met the former first lady at the medical conference I still wasn't quite convinced they'd actually ever gone to in Philadelphia.) Unable to believe in his own greatness, he couldn't allow himself to believe in the greatness of anyone else.

My father not only welcomed but made the most of all the innovations my mother instigated in the weeks and months after Casper's capture. Except for one.

Just after Halloween, my mother woke us all up early Sunday morning announcing, "You're going to church today."

"What for?" Except for a second cousin's wedding, Willy and I had never set foot in a house of God. She handed us neckties and freshly ironed shirts.

"Because faith is an important part of life."

"Don't you think it's a little hypocritical making us go to church while you and Dad stay home?" Fiona had graduated from "Kumbaya" to "We Shall Overcome." She slept in black tights and a turtleneck, hoping to wake up in the morning a real beatnik.

"We're all going to church." My sisters groaned when Mom told them to put on dresses and hats.

"Why?" I still didn't get it.

"Because I said so, and because sometime in your life, you'll need to believe God loves you."

"Nora, I'm not going to be part of this." My father was still in his pajamas. He was willing to make peace with the next-door neighbors, but not with God.

"I'm staying home with Dad." Fiona was still in turtleneck and tights.

"It won't hurt you to go once." My mother was tying my necktie.

"Will it hurt you?" my father called out from the other room.

"Mother, can I borrow your pearls?" Lucy was all for any excuse for getting dressed up, even for church.

"No."

"Can we go to a Catholic church?"

"We're not Catholic." My mother slid a Windsor knot tight to my neck.

"We're not anything," Fiona protested.

My father was curious. "Why Catholic, Lucy?"

"I've always thought that when I'm old and been married and my third husband's dead, it'd be nice to become a nun and marry God."

My mother had her pilgrimage already worked out. "We're going to go to Christ Church." It was an elegant eighteenth-century Episcopalian Church in what had now become the Negro section of New Brunswick.

"Why there?" my father asked.

My mother smiled. "They have the prettiest graveyard."

My father stayed home and cleaned out his closet.

The choir sang, the minister gave a sermon, Fiona sulked, Lucy made eyes at the altar boy, and Willy read a classic comic of *Moby-Dick* until my mother took it away from him. I was pleased to see several kids I knew from school sitting with their brothers and sisters and parents. I held my mother's hand and craned my neck stiff looking at the light shafting through stained-glass windows of water turning into wine and Jesus walking on water and getting nailed to the cross and coming back from the dead, and compared them to the miracles I'd experienced. A psycho killer teaches me to swim instead of killing me, my parents sleep in the same room, and now, most unbelievable of all, I was sitting in church.

We went back the following Sunday. And the Sunday after that I went to Sunday school with Willy, and Fiona and Lucy sat in on a youth fellowship meeting where Fiona got to play the guitar and sing "Michael, Row the Boat Ashore" while Lucy, I learned several decades later, was paddling to second base with the altar boy in the coat closet. After our third visit, there was even talk of getting us baptized. We were all just getting used to getting up early on Sundays when we heard a sermon titled "What God Expects of Us," in which the minister referenced the story of Abraham's hearing God's voice telling him to kill his child as a metaphor for the hard choices in life.

My mother came out of church with a distracted look on her face. She was in such a hurry to get away from the service that she walked across a grave. And when she got home, the first thing she said to my father was, "Do you think Abraham could have been depressed?"

"Abraham who?"

"The man who said God told him to kill his son." My father looked worried. His mother had left him for theosophy. Did he think my mother was going to leave him for Jesus?

"Sounds more like a schizophrenic."

As my mother climbed the stairs, she unpinned her hat. "Maybe depression's God's way of testing us, of seeing what we're capable of. I mean, how weak we are."

My father was right behind her, and I behind him. "Let's talk about this another time." They were in their bedroom now. He knew I was eavesdropping.

My mother didn't seem to hear him. "Maybe you're right."

"How's that?"

"Maybe we are Druids after all." I didn't get it. But when my father closed the bedroom door and turned the latch, I knew a "lie-down" was being prescribed.

The box spring squeaked. My mother giggled. My father growled like a bear who had just been woken up, and then she began to sob. "What's wrong?" My father's voice was husky.

"That sermon about Abraham made me think of Jack."

"Don't."

"It was my fault."

"No, it wasn't."

"I should have done something to stop it."

"We've done everything we can do."

"You don't understand. Sometimes, when I close my eyes, I see it happening, but I don't stop it."

"The past doesn't exist." Friedrich told himself that in the hopes that one day, when he recalled the chain of events that made up his life, they'd be different.

"Do you forgive me?"

"For what?" My father's voice was impatient. "You haven't done anything wrong."

"You don't understand." Neither did I.

There were whispers then that I couldn't make out. Then I heard my father talk to her the way he spoke to our dog when there was thunder and she didn't want to come out from under the bed. "All we need is this."

I heard my mother sigh a groan of painful pleasure. My father gasped. No one had told me sex sounded so sad. I felt creepy for listening. But since all the popular kids in my class bragged about listening to their parents doing it, I thought I, like my mother, was finally figuring out how to be normal.

We were doing it together: She was keeping the house clean, sleeping in the same bed with Dad, I was going to Sunday school . . . I figured Little League would be next. But my mother came out of their bedroom that day with a new resolve. She dropped her infatuations with God and being the perfect suburban mom as quickly as she had picked them up and committed a heresy that made her more suspect than ever in Greenwood—she got a job.

Officially, she worked for the university. Her employment category was "research assistant"—my father's research assistant. She had always helped him with his work, typing out manuscripts, proofreading galleys, but being paid, having a job title, gave her an excuse to fill up every free moment of her days and her nights, of her life, with his life. The job wasn't just full time, it was all the time. And that was the point. She went to the office with him in the morning and worked with him into the night. At the time, it seemed like she was sacrificing her life for his. But as I think back on it, I see that she didn't want time for herself. By embracing my father's career so completely, she found a way to escape her own nightmare. The circle of their partnership closed into a knot that held us fast—but didn't include us.

Except for when they went to the bathroom, they were joined as tightly as Siamese twins. They took turns between being parent, child, and lover to one another. My mother didn't mind that my father got all the credit, that his name was on the book jackets, that the checks were made out to him. My mother didn't relinquish her ego; she merged it with his. Weaving herself so tightly into the fabric of his being was her way of keeping herself from picking at the past and unraveling her hope for a future.

And because they worked so many nights and weekends, I got to watch them without their knowing I was watching. I'd stand in the doorway and stare at the backs of their heads, wondering how long it would take for them to feel my presence. They didn't feel it. But when I got tired of waiting, I'd interrupt them, even if I didn't need anything, ask them to help me with my homework, even when I didn't need it. How to spell M-i-s-s-i-s-s-i-p-p-i, help me build a papier-mâché Statue of Liberty, and later a plaster of Paris imitation of the Hoover Dam for an imaginary cross-country trip my class was taking.

Both believing now that work was going to set them free, they would always stop what they were doing if my interruption was connected with school. My mother would do all the helping, my father would tilt back in a chair and impatiently call out every few minutes, "If you do his work for him, he's never going to learn." Or, if he was feeling funny, "Nora, you're not being paid to do his homework, you're being paid to do mine."

My mother knew all the tricks of being a good student. But as my father waited impatiently for her to get back to his work, their work, I sensed I was stretching the invisible membrane of interdependence, gossamer and slightly spooky, that connected them. Like a spiderweb against your face, even though you knew you couldn't see what connected them, you knew you were caught in it, and it would be rewoven as soon as you left the room.

Amazingly, the friction of living and working together twenty-four hours a day, seven days a week, fifty-two weeks a year didn't diminish their post-Casper ardor. Their flirtation was at times by nature of their research unfathomably academic. Late at night, for fear of waking us, they'd whisper words like "meprobamate," "diazepam," "chlorpromazine," as if they were speaking a secret language of love. As I got older, watching them go at it day after day, fertilizing each other's minds with ideas beyond my interest and understanding, I realized they were having intercourse even when they weren't.

The closest I ever came to hearing them argue over work occurred when my father was dictating to my mother at the typewriter. Like most scientists, he had a weakness for the run-on sentence. Adding commas on top of colons on top of parentheticals, and mixing in both dependent and independent clauses, my father would have to take three breaths and seventy-five words before he finally got to the end of a sentence. My mother, meanwhile, would listen without bothering to strike a single key; then when he finally said "period" she'd nod appreciatively and think for a moment, before quickly typing fifteen, rather than seventy-five, words. My father, eventually tiring of waiting for her to put down the other sixty-odd words on paper, would come around to her side of the table to see what was holding her up, and, seeing what she had written, would protest, "Nora, that's not what I said."

She'd look up at him innocently and reply, "I know. It's better."

It was, for them. With my mother sitting beside him, serving alternately as audience, critic, and groupie, my father's career experienced a second spring. With my mother's help, twice as many articles were written; Dad cranked out a new book in six months. With her sharing the load, he took on more consulting jobs. Invitations to give speeches and attend conventions and colloquiums and conferences suddenly began to pour in from all over the world. And with no Casper to fear, there was no reason for them not to attend.

Or as my father put it to my mother one evening when I was eight, "Nora, it's time for us to start making the most of our lives." It was just after dinner on a Saturday. As usual, they and their work were at the dining room table. We ate in the kitchen. Lucy, Fiona, Willy, and I were having dessert.

"I didn't know I wasn't making the most of my life." My mother had spent the previous half hour scurrying back and forth between our dinner and my father and his deadline. She was back at the typewriter now.

"Nora, don't be obtuse, you know what I'm talking about." My father had been invited to read a paper in France and then fly on to Geneva and give a speech. He'd been trying to talk her into going with him for days. My siblings had urged her to go; two unchaperoned weeks was their idea of heaven. Willy, thirteen, wouldn't have to do his dreaded French homework, and Fiona, age eighteen, and Lucy, now sixteen, would have a brief respite from the shame of my father telling the teenage boys who mustered up the nerve to ask them out on a date, "I want you to enjoy yourselves, but I also want you to know I expect you to return my daughters on time, and, more important, in the exact same pristine condition in which you found them."

We listened in the kitchen as my father hammered away at my mother in the other room about the trip. "Your tickets are paid for. There's nothing to keep you here."

"Nothing but our four children." I alone was relieved to hear my mother say that.

The kettle on the stove whistled and my mother hurried back into the kitchen to make herself a cup of tea.

"Nora, it will be good for them," my father called after her. "The girls can look after the boys."

Dad stood in the doorway and looked at us with the same exasperation that surfaced on his face when he was stuck in traffic behind a stalled car. "Fiona in particular might benefit from looking after a household, caring for children. See what she's turning up her nose at by insisting on going to college in New York City."

Fiona had passed on Vassar to go to art school at NYU. Worse, she had thwarted him by winning a scholarship so he couldn't accuse her of making him pay for her mistakes.

Fiona took offense. "What is that supposed to mean?"

"Simply that in New York City, you'll never find a husband interested in providing you a home like the one you grew up in." My father had a farm boy's mistrust of the big city. He also felt cheated that she chose to go to a school he couldn't brag about.

"That's why I'm going there, Dad." Fiona knew how to give as good as she got.

My father was momentarily relieved when he glanced over and saw Lucy's head buried in the SAT study book. When he looked closer, she closed the study book quickly. The copy of *Confidential* that she'd hidden in its pages slipped out onto the floor. She'd been reading an article about Chuck Berry's getting arrested for taking a fourteen-year-old Mexican girl across state lines for immoral purposes. All my father said as he handed it back to her was, "Planning for your future?" Lucy's cheeks flushed like she'd just been slapped.

Willy laughed. That was a mistake when my father was in one of his moods. He picked up one of the six Oreos Willy had stacked next to his ice cream. "Willy, do you know how many calories are in each one of these belly builders?"

Willy split one of the Oreos and licked the creamy center before he answered, "Fifty-five." Willy was smart.

My father threw up his hands and went back to work. "I give up."

But he didn't. Not ever. As soon as my mother sat back down at the typewriter he started in. "Nora, just give me one reason why you're fighting me on this trip."

When you didn't agree with my father, you were fighting him. And if you fought him, he knew how to make you feel like you had lost even if you won. Part of my mother's job was to jolly him out of these moods.

"Zach's too young. In a few years, I'll go with you." She smiled at him, fingers poised over the keyboard.

"I don't want to wait a few years. I've waited too goddamn long for this as it is."

I sat with my siblings, trying to figure out what "this" was that made my father slam his fist on the table so hard her tea sloshed over the lip of the cup and a stack of computer printouts toppled onto the floor. As my mother cleaned up the mess, she said, "For God's sake, I'm not saying you can't go. Go on without me."

"If I wanted to go on without my wife, I wouldn't have married you." The way my father said it, it wasn't clear if it was a compliment or a threat.

Fiona heard it the same way. "Does that mean you're going to divorce Mom if she doesn't go to Europe?"

"This is a private conversation."

It was Lucy's turn to give it to him. "If it's private, why don't you close the door? Or go to the bedroom?" Lucy smiled innocently. "Or go out to the car like you used to do back in Hamden."

My sisters giggled conspiratorially. Willy and I didn't get it.

"This happens to be my house, and I'll say what I like in it." My father was not a shouter, it was when he lowered his voice and cut the emotion out of it that told us it was time to shut up.

Having silenced the peanut gallery, he softened his tone, reached out, and took hold of my mother's hand. "Nora, this trip, this kind of opportunity, this is what we've been working for all these years."

"This is what *you've* been working for."

"Well, if it's all for me, why do I want you there?"

"I'm not sure." My mother had never been to Europe.

"Christ, most wives would jump at the chance to go to Paris. Why would you want to be here when you could . . . ?" My father shook his head in genuine bafflement. "What aren't you sure of?"

My mother raised an eyebrow. "A great many things. But we'll leave that for another time. What I am certain of is, I don't want to miss Zach's play." Struggling to decipher the code they spoke in, I had completely forgotten I was to be the Pied Piper of Hamelin.

"You are going to pass up an all-expenses paid trip to Europe with your husband to attend a third-grade play?"

"Yes." My mother hadn't had time to help me with my costume or rehearse my lines. I felt guilty for thinking she didn't care.

My father thought for a moment, then clapped his hands. "Well, since it's Zach's play, why don't we let Zach decide if he thinks it's a good idea."

"Fine, but you're not going to like his answer."

I was summoned out of the kitchen. My mother smiled at me as I stood between them. My father was suddenly positively cheerful; he loved a test. There was not a touch of intimidation in his tone when he said, "Now, Zach, I want you to answer us honestly. Speak from your heart." My brother and sisters crowded in the doorway to hear my judgment. "Would you rather your mother go to your play or go to Europe and see all the things she's always wanted to see but never had the chance? And help me with my work, which, by the way, is what pays the bills around here?"

My mother knew what I wanted. I'd been pestering her to help me learn my part for days. There was no question my heart was set on her being front and center as I charmed the rats and led the children into the mountain after the townspeople had cheated me. Just as I was about to say "Stay, don't go, I need you," my father smiled at me with a warmth as real as a heat lamp. Knowing and fearful that that smile could be replaced by a look so cold and withering you felt like the sun had excluded you from the privilege of its warmth, I answered, "I think you should go with Dad."

My mother was shocked. "You don't really mean that." I didn't. I missed her already, in fact. But more than anything, I missed that look that was now on my father's face. When I added, "Dad's right, you should listen to him," my father chuckled and winked at me.

"Smart boy." His hand was on my shoulder, but I was in the palm of his hand. My father always called me his friend; now I was his accomplice. We had our own spiderweb of connection.

My brothers and sister cheered the same way they had when Casper was captured. My mother was puzzled and relieved. The last battle was over. "You know you can change your mind about this if you want to, Zach."

"I don't want to." I had disappointed her; I was her last excuse from complete immersion. I had also disappointed myself, and yet I was happy. To please my father was a rare and wondrous thing, like an eclipse.

And so Willy and I were left in the care of my sisters, which was not unlike being suckled by benevolent wolves. My mother had left the kitchen so heavily stocked you would have thought she was anticipating a natural disaster.

Breakfast for me was a candy bar, dinner, pizza ordered in. The casseroles my mother had precooked were never served. Willy surprised us; as soon as my parents left for the airport, he took all his Oreos and flushed them down the toilet. Stranger still, he then ran to the supermarket (Willy was not a big runner) and bought chicken breasts and heads of broccoli. Back home, he weighed out four-hundred-calorie portions, and every day for the next two weeks, that was all he ate.

Freedom from my parents meant different things to each of us. I fell asleep in front of the TV and stopped bathing. Every night was date night for my sisters. Boys roamed our house as if it were a Boy Scout jamboree, and Chubby Checker records were played at full volume.

Curiously, the one area where responsibility was not shirked was my third-grade class play. Lucy helped me memorize my lines, Fiona made me a costume of green-and-yellow satin. Gray the parrot supplied the feather for my cap. Together they taught me how to play a four-note tune on the recorder. They all got dressed up and sat in the front row. Everybody clapped, even Willy. And afterward I heard my teacher say I was the best Pied Piper they'd ever had, and then add with a sigh, "It's a shame how his parents suit themselves."

It was strange how much better we all got along without my parents there. Thirteen days later we spent the whole day vacuuming and Windexing and gluing together the stuff we had broken. And that night, after we watched *77 Sunset Strip* on TV, Fiona and Lucy said good-bye to their short-lived freedom by having a beer and smoking the last of their cigarettes. Lucy blew smoke rings. "We have to get our stories straight."

"What do you mean?" I said.

"Well, we can't tell Mom we missed her."

"We didn't miss her." Willy volunteered.

"Exactly, but if Mom thinks that, she'll get upset, and she won't go away again."

Lucy chugged the last of her beer and belched. "I got it. Just tell Mom, it's not the same when you're not here."

"What do we tell Dad?" I asked.

Fiona thought for a minute. "That you learned a lot about yourself."

They all thought that was really funny. After that they began to trade anecdotes about, as Lucy put it, "how totally bonkers Dad is." The TV glowing before us like a campfire, Willy, Lucy, and Fiona shared stories in the darkened room about their childhood. Some I'd heard but never really listened to, others happened before I was born or too little to remember. I listened as they tried to top each other about who Dad had done the most twisted thing to.

Fiona started out recalling the bowl Dad had filled with tadpoles caught in the shadow of Sleeping Giant. "He put it right by my bed and told me, 'If you look at them every morning when you wake up, one day you'll get a surprise.' And sure enough, one day I wake up and look over, and they were all dead. And when I ran to Dad and told him, 'The tadpoles are dead,' he said, 'I told you you'd get a surprise.' "

"So what?" I didn't get it.

"He wanted me to look at them every morning so I'd see them turn into frogs. Like a science class experiment. And when they died, he acted like that was what he had wanted me to see." What I could see was that it bothered Fiona.

It was Willy's turn now. "When I was three, Dad told me I could have anything in the world if I peed standing up."

"If you were three, Willy, you wouldn't remember," I interjected. Their stories were scaring me.

"This happened," Lucy assured me.

"And after I peed standing up, I asked for a broom so I could be just like Mommy. Then you want to know what Dad did?" Willy was practically shouting.

"No."

"He bought me a pair of boxing gloves and told me I was going to need them if I was going to act just like Mommy."

But Lucy won the prize. "Remember the dead mouse in the orange juice bottle?"

"It was a milk carton," Fiona reminded her.

"Whatever. When you were little, Zach, Mom was an unbelievable slob."

"What do you mean?"

"I don't know, she just seemed tired all the time, and took naps, and let the dishes pile up, and left food out. Used to drive Dad crazy. One day—"

Fiona interrupted, "Don't tell this one, Lucy."

"It's not that scary. One day, he's making us dinner—"

"Dad made you dinner?" I'd never seen my father cook.

"He used to do stuff like that when Mom was depressed."

"Mom was depressed?"

"Let me finish my story. So, he's making us peanut butter and jelly sandwiches—"

"They were ham and cheese," Willy corrected her.

"Okay, ham and cheese sandwiches, and he sees a mouse running along the counter. And Dad takes the knife and throws it."

Willy, smiling, nodded "yes" to the story. "Amazing shot. Stabs it from like three feet away."

Lucy continued. "And then he picks it up and holds it up in the air. Its legs are still wiggling. And then he opens the refrigerator door . . ."—Lucy leaned close to tell this part of the story—". . . and he puts it in a milk carton. He tells us, 'A little surprise for your mother in the morning.' "

"Then what happened?"

"Mom never noticed it."

"Why did Dad want to do that to Mom?"

Fiona took a deep drag from her cigarette, then exhaled through her nose like a dragon. "I think it was a crude attempt at shock therapy."

I decided it was safer not to ask what shock therapy was.

When my parents came home the next day, they had hugs and kisses and presents for us. Eventually, my father took a long, hard look at my brother and said, "Willy, have you lost weight?"

Willy said, "No," even though he'd shed ten pounds.

Every few months after that, my mother and father would leave for a week or two, sometimes three, on a pharmaceutical junket. Strangely, I missed them most when they came back home.

Casper didn't trick the surveillance cameras or knock out the guards or send us ominous, creepy warnings. He never escaped from Needmore. But there was no escaping him. Even in his impregnable isolation, he had always been, and still was, the force that drove our lives.

If it had not been for Casper, we would never have made our forced march south to the pharmaceutical wilderness in New Jersey, settled on the PCB-polluted Raritan, or tried to call a place like Greenwood home. I think my father, during all those years of hiding out on Harrison Street, knew that Casper would one day catch up to him. The gun in his bedside table, the dogs that were encouraged to bark at strangers, losing the street number from the front of our house, my father had been so busy looking over his shoulder, he couldn't enjoy what he had. He had spent so many years waiting for the past that haunted him to take corporeal form for a final reckoning that when the thing he feared most did happen, and he and we, much to his amazement, survived, my father had forgotten how to relax.

It was clear my father and mother both believed there was no longer any physical threat from Casper. The front door was now left unlocked. The dogs were defanged with leather muzzles that left them prey to the bullying of neighborhood cats. The revolver was taken out of the bedside table and hidden in the top drawer of his dresser in the closet. Not even my father's reach was that long. And had they had the slightest fear Casper could escape the life sentence my father had given him, they never would have left us alone for weeks at a time.

But still my father could not shake the idea that catastrophe was just around the corner. Though Casper had been recaptured, simply by existing Casper was a constant reminder that bad things can, do, and probably will happen if your name's Friedrich. Part of my father's lingering paranoia stemmed from growing up on a farm. He was full of stories of boys and girls who had been strangled by scarves caught in the gears of farm machinery or mutilated by thresher blades and runaway tractors, and of entire families murdered overnight by a hidden army of bacilli in a mason jar of stewed tomatoes that should not have been brought up from the cold cellar. Coming of age in the Great Depression, he knew money couldn't be trusted. But it was Casper who made him think life was out to get him.

No matter how hard my mother tried to distract him with herself and work, my father had a way of steering the conversation, especially at dinner, around to the subject of calamities and how to avoid them. Willy gagging on too large a bite of steak prompted a lecture on how to perform a tracheotomy. I still remember his guiding my fingers on his throat to demonstrate the ribbed ridges of the windpipe that we were instructed to slice open with a steak knife, as opposed to the jugular, which would cause you to bleed to death, even if you happened to have needle and catgut on hand. The menu of hypothetical disasters in the restaurant of life was long and varied. Petting a neighbor's pet rabbit was an invitation to tularemia. Eating from a slightly dented can of tuna fish was a death wish via botulism. No question, if there were game show called *Worst Possible Scenarios,* we would win: poisonous snakes, spiders with necrotic venom, tics that could kill you with Rocky Mountain spotted fever. Willy maintained that my father warned us about everything so that they wouldn't have to feel guilty if one of us died while they were gone.

Who knows? Perhaps my father's warnings, reminders, and cautionary tales saved our lives many times over. My father tried to protect us with knowledge. But contrary to what he and I believed, he didn't know everything.

Not all Casper's magic was bad. In the logic of my mind, if it had not been for Casper, my mother never would have fallen back in love with my father. And just as his initial imprisonment at Townsend had sent us retreating south to Greenwood, his brief escape and convenient entombment at Needmore prompted us to make our next move.

There had never been any love lost between us and Greenwood. My father had always hated suburban life—houses built eight to an acre, neighbors looking over hedges and peering into windows, observing our life the way my father observed patients through Needmore two-way mirror. The Illinois acres my father grew up on had been hardscrabble, but there were three hundred of them. He was suspicious of sidewalks that told you where to walk, and homes that lacked a barn.

Before Casper obliged us by his timely capture in the medical library of Johns Hopkins, the thought of living in the country, of not having neighbors who could hear our screams for help, was out of the question. But now, as the new decade of the swinging sixties unfolded before us, my parents could no longer use him as an excuse for not going after the life my father had told himself would make him happy back in the days when he drove past the big houses of Hamden in the White Whale.

And so it was Casper Gedsic's recapture that gave my father permission to begin his search for a house that would provide a suitable and conducive home for his dreams. He traded in the Plymouth that had carried us south for a gaudy new red 1962 Buick Skylark station wagon, equipped with air-conditioning, to make the quest more comfortable.

Every Sunday my parents would pack the Friedrich tribe into their new wagon and set off in search of a new homestead. North, south, east, west, my father did not have a specific location or destination in mind, just so long as it was within an hour's drive of work and conducive to a change in his state of mind.

Getting lost, turning left when we should have gone right, rolling countless miles down country lanes and gravel roads, choking on the dust of the realtors who led the way up ahead, bickering about what radio station to listen to, where to stop for lunch, why Willy insisted on taking off his shoes if he knew his feet stunk, could Lucy have a horse? (yes, if you get a summer job and pay for it yourself), could I finally ride the minibike Lazlo had given me? (maybe), could Willy have a rifle and get a hunting license? (no), could Fiona *please* stop playing her goddamn guitar? can we join a country club? (why not?), can I go to the bathroom? (you should have thought about that when we stopped for gas), if Lucy can have a horse, why can't I have a rifle? (because you'll shoot it). At first it was fun, in a kind of hellish way.

But finding a place where he could feel at home was not easy for Dad. My mother told us and whoever else was listening that all she wanted was for her husband to find something that would make him happy. My father slowly and torturously made it clear that happiness was something he knew nothing about. He would tell the realtors in no uncertain terms that he was interested in an old house, a house with character, i.e., a house that had a sense of a past he had not known but sensed he would have liked to have had.

When he was shown charming colonials with Revolutionary War provenance or elegant country homes with white pillars built to last in the 1920s, Dad would at first get all excited and imagine the antiques he would collect to fill them—a sideboard we didn't have against the dining room wall we had not bought; imaginary wing chairs like the ones he had sat on at the Wintons' placed on either side of a fireplace we did not own.

But after he had gotten us all revved up about the peace and joy and harmony of the good life that was waiting to be had within those walls that were for sale, he'd start to see cracks in the foundation, gaps around the windows. Soot that said the furnace would have to be replaced, and then he'd turn to the realtor and sigh, "I don't know. It's an old house."

"Isn't that what you wanted?"

Careful to avoid answering that one, he would answer, "I don't know, it's the kind of place that would take a lot of upkeep. Just keeping the lawn mowed would be a full-time job for somebody."

"If you'd like to see something less expensive . . ."

"It's not the money. It's the time I'd have to waste thinking about it."

"Could you be more specific, Mr. Friedrich?"

"Well, now that I've looked at it, it just doesn't seem that much better than what I have now."

At which point we'd all groan and say, "You've got to be kidding," and "Harrison Street's a dump compared to this."

Which would embarrass my father into asking the realtor,

"Do you have anything better to show me?" Invariably, they would say yes. And after seeing what another ten or twenty thousand dollars would get us, Dad would decide to "keep looking." Which really meant, wait until he had another ten or twenty thousand to spend. And we'd drive back to Greenwood feeling tricked, and he'd go to work and make more money.

The trouble was, when he'd saved the additional ten or twenty K he'd needed to buy the house that had seemed perfect six months earlier but out of his budget, and we'd go back to look at it, even if it had been repainted, in his eyes it would have lost its luster. Even if it had a tennis court or a pool, my father would find a way to convince himself that it was a fundamentally unsound and shabby investment compared to what we could have, if we just waited for him to make another thirty or forty thousand, in his fantasy of the good life.

After a year or so of looking at lifestyles we were longing to live but my father refused to buy into, Lucy, Fiona, and Willy went on strike. Fiona and her guitar were in college by then. Lucy had a boyfriend who had a house and a pool and a tennis court of his own. And Willy had stayed off the Oreos, lost thirty pounds, and grown four inches and was on the high school cross-country team. Lucy and Fiona refused to get into the Skylark; Willy ran from it. I was happy to have my parents to myself.

I was as sick of looking at houses Dad wasn't going to buy as they were, but without my sisters and brother to complain, it was easier to cajole my father into stopping the car at a likely-looking stream or brook or river and go fly-fishing. I'd turned ten by then. I wasn't very good at fly-fishing, and hooked far more innocent branches and defenseless shrubs than I ever did fish with my casts.

But I loved it all the same. Partly because my father loved it, but mostly because Dad was different knee-deep in a brook with a fly rod in his hand. On dry land, anger could spark out of him, as though an invisible squall had knocked down a high-tension wire inside his head. He was grounded in such a way that he was unaware of the voltage he unleashed at those closest to him. He'd say things that were bothersome, scary, and sometimes mean, oblivious to the effect they had on others. And after ten or fifteen minutes had passed, most of his brain would forget he had ever said them, and he'd be left wondering why his children stayed away.

But out on the water, standing against a current that could be gauged, thinking only about how to think like a fish, my father could relax and stop thinking about what would make him happy and actually be happy.

Though I wasn't cognizant of it at the time, I can see now that what I also loved about fly-fishing on those phantom house-hunting trips was, when we were on moving water, I didn't have to compete with anyone but the trout for his attention. The only part of my father's life my mother did not feel the need to share, the single passion she did not claim and invade with heart and soul, was fishing. In the solitary arena of gurgling brook and rock-strewn streams, with their deep pools riffled with shadows cast by the low overhang of woodland hemlock and beech, my mother was content to sit on the bank and read secondhand paperback mysteries and be an innocent bystander to his life.

I did not mind if the mosquitoes bit and the fish didn't, because it was safe to be close to him on the river. Knowing that one of the catastrophes Dad imagined was buying hip boots for his youngest son only to have him slip and fall and the boots fill with water, drowning me in a trout-filled pool, I did not complain that while Dad was snug and warm in sure-footed, felt-soled, chest-high rubber waders, I was shivering bare-legged in icy brooks, wearing only shorts and sodden sneakers.

In the summer of '65, we got lost on the way to look at an old house down near Chester. A colonel in the Union Army had ordered it constructed in the shape of a heptagon, so that when he came back from the war, he and his bride could have a different view for every day of the week. It was unclear whether it was the fact that the house had seven sides, or that the colonel didn't live long enough to ever sleep in it, but my father thought that this unseen mansion might just be strange enough for him to feel at home there.

Each time we made a wrong turn, my father would mutter, "I have a good feeling about this place."

My mother smiled as she flipped the pages of her mystery. "That's what you always say."

"What if it's haunted?" I was just making conversation while I studied the map, looking for a place to fish.

My father laughed. "You don't believe in ghosts, do you, Zach?"

My mother looked up from her book. "I believe in ghosts."

My father gave her a look. "No, you don't."

"Have you ever seen one, Mom?"

Before my mother could answer, my father announced, "I think it's time we go fishing."

I don't remember the name of the river he found to distract us, but it was narrow and deep and walled on either side by chestnut and dogwoods all tangled up in wild grapevines as thick as my wrist.

We followed our usual routine, rods were assembled, flies chosen, and a fresh hatch of damselflies darting and hovering over the river told us which feathered hook to pick. My mother spread out an old army blanket and retreated into her mystery as I waded out after my father into the undertow. Sometimes, fishing made my father talkative. He would become generous with stories of his youth and random thoughts in his head. But that day he was quiet. My mother's saying she believed in ghosts bothered him. I waited for the white noise of water moving over rocks rounded by the Ice Age and tree trunks felled by lightning we had not witnessed to drown out his thoughts of all that could still go wrong.

But that nameless, crooked tributary we had chanced upon was hard fishing for a boy not yet twelve. Even my father was challenged. The leafy overhang that jungled up and out over both sides of the stream made it hard for me to cast my line where I wanted it to go. My hook snagged branches and vines. Each time I tried to free it, my line tangled. After losing three flies and dropping my rod in the water twice, I shouted to my father, "It's too hard for me."

"We're here."

"That doesn't mean we can't go somewhere else."

"What do you have in mind?"

"We're not too far from Needmore."

"What's that got to do with fishing?"

"Remember the river you used to take us to, before I knew how to swim? It was full of trout, and no trees."

My father took his eyes off the shadow of the fish he was trying to lure up off the bottom and stared at me. "I don't think that's a good idea." He began to walk toward me gently, as if I were a trout that might be spooked.

"Why?" I slapped at the greenhead that had bit the back of my calf.

"To get there, we'd have to park at the hospital."

"So? You know all the doctors there."

"I don't want to risk it."

"Risk what, dammit!"

The greenhead had just taken a bite out of my other leg.

"Casper might be looking out the window of his cell and see us. Might bring on a setback."

"What kind of setback?" My father didn't like talking about Casper.

"Cause him distress."

"Did he ever say why he didn't drown me?" The question rose up in me like a fish striking live bait.

"No."

"Why do you think he didn't?"

"I wish I knew."

"Do you think he'll ever tell us?"

My father shook his head no, then put his hands on my shoulders and brought me close to him as if to make sure I was seeing what he wanted me to see. "It's time to forget about Casper."

"What if I can't?"

"Sometimes, if you stop talking about something, you eventually stop thinking about it." They'd tried that with Jack.

"Does that mean I can't talk about him?"

"No, you and I can talk about him anytime." I was glad he said that. But then he had to add, "Of course, since it's not a subject I'm particularly fond of discussing, you might want to consider why you're so determined to bring it up." He took his hand off my shoulder.

"What do you mean?"

"Just don't bring it up in front of your mother."

"How come?" I knew why, but I wanted to hear what he'd say.

"It distresses her." I had suspected she and Casper had something in common.

Back then, it was easier for me to fish by my father's rules. Which is to say, it worked for a while. Not talking about Casper didn't make me forget about him. But I thought about him less and less often.

In 1966, much to my entire family's amazement, my father finally not only found but bought a house he could live in. It was a barn that had once been home to a herd of black-and-white dairy cows, built with beams of black walnut felled and squared by hand with double-bladed axes a hundred years earlier. Set into a hillside, it was four stories high and constructed upon a foundation of stones and rocks pulled from its fields by mules when that part of Hunterdon County was first being cleared of stumps of hardwood trees crosscut into eighteen-foot lengths with two-man handsaws to provide boards for the siding. It was a monument to sweat and backbreaking work. And my father loved the struggle that had gone into its construction even more than its unwalled cathedraled hayloft or its cozy stonewalled milking stalls.

In the course of a little less than a year, my father succeeded in paying for the installation of a kitchen, bathrooms, plumbing, and huge picture windows that made it hot in the summer and cold in the winter but allowed him to spy visitors half a mile before they knocked on our door.

The most exciting thing about the barn my father bought to

shelter the Friedrich herd was that the twelve pie-shaped acres that came with it had a river, well, a stream, really, running along its longest border. It was fifteen feet wide in places, and had a waterfall that dropped four feet into a pool that was over-your-head deep and home to native brook trout, savage and shadowy. No matter that it was called Cold Creek; it was a major tributary in my mind, the place where my father and I would bond not just for a few hours on weekends, but for forever.

When Dad committed to the purchase, I was in heaven. At the age of twelve, I had become almost as good as he was at losing myself and my worries in the certain sound of water falling downhill from the heartland to the unseen sea. But in the year it took to construct his sanctuary, I gave in to a different kind of gravity.

By then Fiona was in a graduate school MFA program that allowed her to keep painting and still live in New York City. Her paintings were big, six, sometimes eight feet across. She'd start out painting a family, mother, father, couple of kids, then she'd cover the whole thing over with a thick glop of pigment mixed with beeswax, and then smear off just enough with a spatula to make you wonder what she'd covered up.

My mother said Fiona had found her style. My father thought he was being funny when he'd say "I just wish she'd find a husband who could pay for her to keep painting paintings that nobody but me and Lazlo buy."

Lucy was looking for her style, too. She was the only senior in her college who had had two engagement parties and was secretly contemplating a third. Willy and I had fulfilled our father's upwardly mobile dreams by being accepted by a private boy's school older and more snobbish than Hamden Hall, called St. Luke's.

My parents, especially my father, had made a big deal about how important it was that we get into St. Luke's. He didn't come out and say we'd grow up to be losers if that prep school of choice turned us down; he just made it clear we'd be "perceived" as losers. In spite of it being such a big deal, my father's career, coupled with his anxiety about rejection, prompted my parents to procrastinate in mailing in our applications until after they returned from eight weeks spent in South America testing antidepressants on people who, he came home saying, wouldn't need mood elevation if they had better plumbing. Perhaps he wanted to be able to blame himself if we didn't get in. Whatever, after several nervous-making months, our letters of acceptance finally showed up in the mailbox midsummer.

I was too crazy about fishing to get revved up about going into eighth grade at St. Luke's in September. School was school for me. But Willy was even more excited than Dad. He jumped up and down, clapped his hands, and shouted, "Yes!" The St. Luke's cross-country team had won state championships four years running.

He felt differently about things when my father announced, "Willy, after giving it some thought, I decided that it might be best if you repeated your junior year." Willy stopped jumping up and down. I saw the betrayal he felt flush his cheeks. My brother was looking forward to being a senior—Willy was good at school, impatient to get away from us and go to college.

"Why?" Willy's voice was a whisper.

My father smiled like he was doing him a favor. "Well, a lot of boys, scholar athletes like yourself, take a postgraduate year when they make a change from public school to prep school."

"Kids who stay back are stupid—I'm smart."

"That you are. And because of your intelligence, you'll realize another year of high school competition will toughen you up for the big races you'll face in college." My father was doing a good job of pretending he cared about track. Dad liked the winning, but the race bored him.

Willy glared at my father and smiled. "What's the real reason?"

My father looked at my brother as if he saw something invisible that made him sad. Then he put one hand on each of our shoulders. "Well, it had occurred to me that if you repeated your junior year, when you'd be a senior, Zach would be out of junior high and a freshman. Maybe if you shared a year of high school, went to classes in the same building, ate in the same dining hall, went to the same dances, you two would find you have more in common than you now imagine."

Willy hated my guts before my father applied the brakes to his life for my benefit. Now, in a matter of moments, my father had cubed the distance between my brother and myself.

In fairness to Willy, I was not an easy younger brother to be burdened by. I started fights with him, and then when he won, made him out to be a bully, i.e., I fixed it so there was no way he could win. But part of what separated us was more fundamental than that. Our natures seemed to demand mutual disdain. Willy didn't care enough about what other people thought of him; I cared too much.

That night, after we found out about St. Luke's, Dad took us out to a restaurant called the Ryland Inn, and Lazlo drove out from New York to join us and ordered champagne and gave me a present from Zuza, a small bronze brain with wings on it. Between having my own river and getting into St. Luke's, the future looked like a sure thing. Until I got up from my shrimp cocktail to go to the bathroom, and Willy followed.

"You're lucky to have me for a brother." As Willy straddled the urinal next to me, he fingered the tie tack he had gotten for coming in second in the state cross-country championship.

"We're both lucky."

"I work for what I get. With you, it's just dumb luck."

"You're just jealous 'cause fish don't like you." If I hadn't been feeling so good, I would have said, *You're just jealous 'cause Dad likes me the best.*

"I don't think they have courses in fishing at St. Luke's."

"What's that supposed to mean?"

"You told me yourself you didn't know half the answers on the entrance exam."

"So?"

"So the only reason you got in was because the track coach

wanted me on the team, and Dad said we were a package deal, and told him you were psychologically scarred because of Casper."

"Dad told you that?"

"He tells everybody that before they meet you. That's why everybody's so nice to poor little Zach." He flushed the urinal and let me linger with that possibility.

The next morning, I greeted my father at the breakfast table with "Do I have to go to St. Luke's?"

"We paid for it." He meant that in more ways than one. "What's wrong?"

I told him what Willy had said. My father looked out the window. He could see Willy running down the hill, shorts over his long winter underwear. "Is it the truth, Dad?"

"It's Willy's truth."

"Was he lying?"

"You didn't flunk the entrance exam."

"You're just saying that because you don't want me to give up."

"I wasn't going to tell you this, but you scored higher than anyone else who was applying in your class."

"But I guessed." We both knew I wasn't very good at school.

"Maybe you know more than you think you do."

I liked that idea. And after I let it sink in, I asked, "Why'd you hold Willy back for me?"

"I did it for Willy, not for you. He needs more time to think about who he is."

Even though I didn't like Willy, I thought it was shitty of my father to stick him with an extra year of high school. And yet, I sensed my father wasn't trying to be shitty; he was trying to do something kind for his first-born son. But at that moment, what I wanted most was for Dad to stay focused on me, say something else that would make me feel better about myself.

"But Dad, what I don't get is, if I know more than I think I do, why don't I do better in school?"

My father was pleased I'd asked that question. "Maybe you're mad at me."

"Why would I be mad at you?"

"You tell me." Like I said, you had to be careful of my father on dry land.

My brother had his driver's license now. In a well-meaning attempt to bribe Willy into befriending me, my father gave our now old Pontiac Skylark wagon to my brother and bought himself a fuel-injected Volvo with leather upholstery. Perhaps if he had kept the Skylark for himself and given Willy the Volvo, my brother might have been more cooperative.

What I knew was, Willy liked to say no. And my father, like all fathers, liked to hear yes from his children. Willy said no to accompanying my father on his search for a house, and no to fly-fishing; even when he ate Oreos and cocooned himself in fat and beat off, he was telling my father no.

When you said yes to my father, he'd get close to you. At first, it'd make you feel special and safe. You'd tell him your problems. But once you told him, they became his problems, not yours. He swallowed you up.

I remember on Sunday night when Willy and I were fighting over what to watch on TV, my father changed the channel on us and made us watch a new show that had just come on the air called *60 Minutes*. There was a shrink on who he was friends with and who had been to our house, talking about antidepressants, and even mentioning my father's name. Which seemed impressive and cool to me, even though Dad put it down with a shrug. "It's not going to change my life."

But hearing my dad mentioned on TV got me thinking, *What could I ever do to get my name mentioned on television?* And that worried me, because I knew that's what he expected. At dinner that night, I asked my father, "What could I be great at?"

My mother was quick to answer for him, "There are lots of things you boys could be great at." But I wanted to hear from

Dad. Even Willy was interested. We looked at my father for a response.

He cleared his throat and sighed. "I could have been more successful, famous, if I didn't have children. But I enjoyed having them. It was important to me."

It wasn't what my mother wanted to hear. "Zach was asking about himself, not about you."

"I want them to learn from my mistakes."

Willy excused himself from dinner and went for a run. I was left at the table to digest it. My father never mentioned the fact that they'd interviewed him for that *60 Minutes* show, but in the end, he'd been cut out.

Every few months my parents would suddenly remember they were parents, and try to throw Willy and me together in what my mother called "outings for the boys," whether it was a trip to the Philadelphia Museum of Art with a bonus stop on the way to see medical oddities preserved in the Mütter Museum (Grover Cleveland's tumor, the skull of a man with a horn coming out of his forehead, midget skeletons, and my favorite, the world's largest colon), or a long weekend at the beach house Lazlo now owned but rarely used out on the tip of Long Island. Willy would say no by saying, "I have a race to get ready for." Saying no, like running 10K in 35:40, made Willy feel like he was in control. It gave him the last word and freed him from the tyranny of wanting and waiting to be loved.

I, at thirteen going on fourteen, was a people pleaser. Trouble was, I was better at pleasing adults than teenagers, and I was lonely now that my semiadult sisters were out of the house. It was not so much them I longed for; it was having somebody around who I could make laugh, for distracting others was my way of distracting myself. Adults were blind to my neediness. Kids my age could smell it a mile off. Worse, I was not content to be liked. I wanted to be loved by everyone, even my brother, Willy.

Willy and I had all sorts of reasons not to get along—the age difference; the explosive mix of teenage male testosterone; the years of jokes I'd made at his expense to feel the afterglow of making my sisters cackle cruelly; his being punished with another year in high school to keep his baby brother company. A psychologist once told me it was obvious that after Jack died, Willy enjoyed being the only son and resented my intrusion. Maybe. But when I look back on it now, it seems like saying no to me was just a new kind of no for my father.

If he had openly bullied me, flicked my ears, bruised my kidneys with rabbit punches, or called me "dickhead" or "maggot" or "dogbreath" like other kids' older brothers did at St. Luke's, I wouldn't have minded so much. But Willy knew the biggest torture of all for me, the one thing I could not bear, was to be ignored. Running marathons gave him the discipline to ignore me completely. I felt like I was being erased. Mostly by my father, but Willy did his share.

We rode to school in silence in the station wagon he did not want. If I asked him a question he didn't feel like answering, he'd turn on the radio. And as was my habit from day one, when we were halfway down the drive and I had realized I'd forgotten something I needed—homework, textbooks, term paper, note from a parent excusing me from gym because I had pinkeye, or a permission slip to attend the class trip to the Benjamin Franklin Institute and walk through its gigantic rubber heart—he would of course say no, and then give me a thin-lipped smile.

"Why?" I'd plead.

"My car, my rules."

"But it's important."

"Well, maybe this will teach you to grow up."

Once we arrived at St. Luke's, I existed even less. In the halls he'd walk right past me without so much as a nod. When I'd say something about it over dinner to my parents, Willy would swear he hadn't seen me. Then I'd shout, "BS," and Willy would give my father the grimace that passed for a smile and say, "Dad, what other possible reason could I have for not saying hello to my own brother?"

Calling him a liar only made it worse. "He's being paranoid,"

Willy would say. And my father, knowing something about paranoia himself, would look at me with sympathetic suspicion. Might he have passed that on to his younger son, along with the cowlick and high arches?

Because of track, Willy had instant friends. When I'd see him loitering with them, naked in the locker room or shower, flexing their muscles and soaping their hairy chests, and I'd approach, skinny and pimply, my towel hiding the few hairs I had on my balls, he'd say, "What's up, little brother?" Or, "How's it hanging, Tiger?" (That was the one I hated most.) I knew he was just pretending to be friendly because not to be so to his own brother would make him look strange, and my brother did not ever want to appear strange. But because of the discipline he applied to his normalcy, the total lack of irony in his voice when he addressed me in public as "Tiger" or "little brother," and because I remembered the way my father looked at me when Willy accused me of being paranoid, it was not long before I began to wonder, *Am I?*

My world suddenly seemed like such an unpleasant place, I found myself chewing at the edge of the possibility that I was imagining all this emotional static. Soon I was wondering full-time what was really going on inside both my own head and my classmates' craniums. *Was I hearing them right? Did they really mean what they said?* Before long, teachers were accusing me of daydreaming, of not concentrating on my work. It is difficult to think about two things at once, especially if one of the things you are thinking about is *"Am I crazy?"*

The more I worried about the realness of what I thought was real, the more forgetful I became. Lack of sleep and having an innate aversion to organization, I was unable to leave the house for school without forgetting something. And, of course, when I asked, begged, pleaded with my brother to stop the car and let me go back the answer was a friendly no.

A grade point was deducted for homework turned in a day late. When I'd forget it twice in a row, another grade point plus demerits, which meant I had to stay after school, which by the third day of forgetfulness meant coming in for Saturday morning detention and copying passages out of the King James Bible.

When my English teacher, Mr. Fagin, gave me an F for a paper on *Pride and Prejudice* that had started out life as an A, he asked me, "Is there something wrong at home?"

I shook my head no, only because I did not know where to begin. Homer was crazy, even though my father called him "special." Ida was a theosophist, which, according to my father, meant she was "certifiable," and then there was the matter of Dad's Sock Moments. What if what ailed me did run in my family? Mr. Fagin sensed I was holding back. "Maybe you'd feel better talking to the school psychologist about it?"

"My father's a psychologist."

"I see."

I considered sharing my fears with my father. I went into his shelf-lined bedroom/office and waited for him and my mother to get back from the university. Looking at the giant pill in the paperweight, I wondered what they could give me that would make me feel less crazy. Then I wondered back to Casper. About where my father had put him. Not wanting to risk being checked into a place like Needmore, I borrowed the thickest medical textbooks I could find on his shelf and retreated to my bedroom.

An old copy of the *DSM* didn't give me a lot to choose from. In fact, there were only four basic choices; imbecilic, depressive, schizophrenic, or psychopath—aka, criminally insane. I ruled out imbecilic, not out of arrogance or because I had gotten into St. Luke's, but merely because my brother would have been nicer to me if I was a retard. I tried reading a chapter on adolescent schizophrenia in a much-thumbed tome from the 1940s by somebody named Dr. Gunderfeldt—"ambivalence," "apathy," "cries for reasons known only to self." It sure sounded like Dr. G. was talking about me. But what sent me into a real panic was looking at Gunderfeldt's black-and-white photographs of mental patients, identities hidden by a black bar across their eyes. Even though they were masked, I still saw pieces of myself in their grimaced faces.

I was just getting around to the idea that the reason Casper hadn't drowned me was that he saw himself in me, sensed I was like him, smelled screwiness coming out of my eyes, ears, nose, and throat when my father opened the bedroom door.

"What are you reading?"

There was no time to hide Gunderfeldt between the boxspring and mattress with the beat-off magazines I had inherited from my brother. My father smiled and picked up his old copy of the *DSM*. "Like father, like son." Dad didn't get it. The fact that he was proud of me made it worse. "So, what do you think, Zach?"

"It's no fun being crazy."

Though I could not find anything in the indexes of either Gunderfeldt or the *DSM-I* on "eavesdropping, teenage," I knew my predilection for putting my ear to locked doors and lingering in the hall outside my parents' bedroom-cum-office wasn't healthy. These and the other reference works concerning the norm and deviations from it that sagged my father's shelves made it clear paranoids go nuts because they can't stop thinking people are saying bad stuff about them. But I could find nothing about the mental disorders that arise when you think people are thinking worrisome things about you and you find out you were right. Once you've thought it, you're already sick.

Two or three months into the unhappiness of my first year at St. Luke's, my parents were, as usual, working late in their office bedroom upstairs in the hayloft. The barn, with its cracks and open spaces and uninsulated walls, made it easy to listen in on what transpired between them, especially when you did your homework at the kitchen table directly below their room.

My mother's typing upstairs provided a staccato backbeat to the Cream album I was listening to on headphones. My parents didn't like me playing rock 'n' roll while I did my homework. I always kept one earphone off so I could stash the headphones if I heard them coming downstairs.

I was playing a track called "Sunshine of Your Love." My father was dictating his run-on thoughts on the effectiveness of niacin on mood. Eric Clapton was singing into my left ear "I've been waiting so long/To be where I'm going"—my mother stopped typing.

From above I heard, "Nora, for the love of God, just type what I say."

"I'm worried about Zach." Her voice sounded a lot farther away than just upstairs.

"I was absent-minded when I was his age. It's hormonal." Jack Bruce's six-string bass thundered into the left side of my brain. *Da*-nanh-*nah-nah-nahn Duh-nuh-nuh-da*-nuhn-*nuh*.

"I'm worried he's getting like me."

"If he was like you, he'd be on honor roll." My father was trying to joke her out of wherever she was going.

"I mean, like the way I was. He's drifting away from himself."

"Our son is not suffering from postpartum depression. It's a physiological impossibility."

"You think that's what I suffered from after all these years?"

"Yes, I do. I think recovery takes longer than anyone realizes."

"My God," my mother was almost shouting. "For an intelligent man, you sometimes say stupid things."

"We both suffer."

"I'm talking about Zach!" My mother was yelling at him.

"Zach is fine."

"That's what you said about me."

After a long silence, my father sighed like he was surrendering. "I love you."

"I know that." She sounded as helpless as I felt.

"What are you thinking?"

"You don't want to know." I wanted to know. But instead of pressing my mother for a less oblique answer, my father came downstairs and prescribed himself a shot of Scotch.

Even though my father didn't say it, he must have been worried about me, too, because he didn't protest when my mother announced she was going to stay home instead of attending the American College of Neuropsycopharmacologists (ACNP) annual meeting in Puerto Rico with him in December. And a month later, she passed when they were invited to give a paper they had been working on at an international psychiatric convention in Tokyo. That winter, my mother threw herself into my life with the same ardor she had invested in Dad.

Instead of sitting up late at might making him smarter, she focused her skills on my dim bulb, correcting grammar, sentence structure, punctuation, crossing out words with a red pen; she laughingly accused me of inheriting my father's weakness for the run-on and taught me to share her appreciation for the beauty of a declarative sentence. She did not teach me to love math, but at least she got me to write my numbers neatly enough, so that if I lucked out with the right answer, my teacher would be able to read it.

To combat the driftiness, she moored me to what would become a lifelong habit of making lists; she stood over my shoulder and watched as I wrote out everything I needed to remember each day before I went to bed on those same long legal pads she used to keep herself sane. And in the morning, she observed me closely as I checked my lists against reality to make sure I didn't stumble upon a new way to mess up as I loaded books, papers, homework, clean gym shorts, etc, etc., etc., into the leather briefcase with my initials embossed with gold on it that she had given me for Christmas. As my mother put it, she was teaching me how to "keep your head screwed on right."

Yes, my grades improved, but I was still flunking making friends. When I first started at St. Luke's in the beginning of eighth grade, I was the new boy who forgot everything, i.e., loser on my way to being kicked out. But after my mother screwed my head on straight and my grades rose and teachers singled me out as a sterling example of what hard work could do, I became something even less worthy of friendship. I was now a list-making grind, a suck-up with an old fart briefcase who forces the whole class to learn how to make footnotes, because his mother makes him do it. And then, of course, there was my brother: lean, muscly, older, and cool, with a beard worthy of a five o'clock shadow and track trophies presented and held aloft to thunderous applause in the chapel. To my classmates, it was obvious: "If his own brother won't say hello to the dork, why should we?"

I tried to convince myself that I didn't care what the kids at St. Luke's thought. But I knew that really wasn't true after April 4. That's when Martin Luther King was assassinated. When the headmaster told everybody in chapel that school would be closed for a day of mourning, everybody clapped and cheered. I told myself they weren't happy he was dead, they were just stupid, white, and happy to have the day off. But even so, just the fact that they clapped seemed so creepy and crazy, I went home feeling like I must have made it all up.

My days were hell, and my nights feverish. After the last list was made, I would pull Gunderfeldt from beneath my bed and ogle the snapshots of looniness with the same look I saw on my brother's face when I had caught him beating his meat: repulsed, and yet attracted. By now my readings had extended beyond Gunderfeldt and the *DSM*. But I still could not decide which particular from of mental disorder I suffered from, since the symptoms of all the bad ones included phrases that applied to me: "has difficulty making friends"; "spends inordinate amounts of time doing repetitive and pointless actions" (casting, fly-fishing); "obsessive and compulsive behavior" (my mother had passed that one on to me); "violent fantasies of inflicting harm to himself and others" (every time my brother smirked a no on the drive to school, I thought about grabbing the steering wheel and driving us both into a ditch, just to wipe the smile off his face).

By the spring of eighth grade I didn't know what ailed me, but I knew I was not well. Desperate to lose at least one of these symptoms, I sought out the friendship of the two most unpopular boys in my class—the Ortley twins. This pair of massive eighth-graders had already had to stay back, and would have been kicked out of school on numerous occasions if their mother had not been related to an aspirin fortune. Flakey with eczema, aggressively fearful due to lethal peanut allergies, I had nothing in common with the identically unpleasant brothers Chas and Peter except that I had a river and they liked to fish.

They had all the right gear: Orvis fly rods, Medalist reels, waders perfect for drowning. I wanted it to go well. Recognizing that I needed to make an effort if I wanted to feel less crazy, I even pretended I thought it was okay that they fished with live bait: eight-inch worms, live grasshoppers attached to hooks with model airplane glue. They even told me a story about plugging for bass with live mice. Still, I could not help but admire their results.

I watched in horror as their bloodworms pulled more trout from that creek than I had seen, much less caught, all year, with my father's sportsmanship and wet flies. With each Ortley outing I grew sulkier and more resentful of the ungentlemanly tactics they used to spell success. Frustrated and embarrassed that my inability to fit in at St. Luke's had reduced me to this level of low, I did not tell my father that I, too, had resorted to fishing with live bait.

On the second to last weekend of the school year, as the Ortleys and I stood midstream in adolescence, Chas suddenly asked, "Wanna see something wicked cool?"

Lacking my brother's strength of character, I said, "Yeah, I guess." Before I knew what I had agreed to, Chas's twin, Peter, pulled a Zippo lighter and a bright red cherry bomb out of his pocket.

Firecrackers in general, and cherry bombs in particular, in my father's cautionary dinner table tales were "invitations to losing a few fingers or an eye." The excitement of the forbidden distracted me. The cherry bomb was being tied to a rock. I didn't know what was happening until it was too late. Rock, with cherry bomb attached, was heaved into the pool I had been fishing. A moment later, a soggy "boom" erupted from the spring-fed depths, followed by a whoosh of muddy water and smoke-filled bubbles, followed by dead trout. The only symptom the *Diagnostic and Statistical Manual: Mental Disorders* said I lacked, I had now acquired: "tortures animals."

"Stop!" I shouted, but these friends I no longer wanted to have didn't hear me. "I fucking mean it."

"Don't be a wuss." Two cherry bombs were now being strung to a second rock.

"Put it down." The lighter was aflame. What lit my fuse was that when I started to cry, they laughed. Feeling sorry for myself and the fish, mad at myself, angry about the fish, I swung wild. My new Shakespeare fly rod snapped clean just above the cork handle and broke across the bridge of Chas's pug nose.

I didn't see the blood. The bomb was lit. Peter Ortley was running toward my father's favorite trout pool. The twin fuses sparkled in midair. It was a mistake to kick him in the balls. Rock and cherry-bombs bola'ed toward my head. I held up my hand to keep it from hitting me in the face. Reflex action kept it from blowing out my eye. I felt the heat of the explosion spread up my arm as the blast deafened me to the white noise of the river and Peter Ortley's cries for help.

My hand was bloody and numb. His waders were filled with water. Both things happened just the way my father had said they would. Peter nearly drowned, and I lost the tip of my left index finger.

All three of us had to go to the hospital. I told my father everything that had happened. I was surprised he wasn't more angry with me. I knew he hadn't really listened to what I said when I overheard him tell my mother, "If nothing else, it shows he has a strong sense of self." My father stuck up for his children just often enough to make it seem like it was your fault when he didn't.

The Ortleys were expelled. The headmaster, being a fly-fisherman and a member of the American Society for the Prevention of Cruelty to Animals, let me off with a warning. Now, in addition to all the other things I still wasn't at St. Luke's, I was now the new boy suck-up crazy enough to lose the end of a finger trying to save the lives of a bunch of fish he spent every weekend trying to kill.

I wasn't the only one who was out of his mind. The night after

I had my stitches taken out, we stayed up late watching TV. We cheered as Bobby Kennedy won the California primary. He'd just finished his acceptance speech, promised to see everybody in Chicago, and then he was dead.

By the start of my freshman year in high school, I was so desperate to be well, I resolved to be more like my brother, to say no to craziness. As we drove off down the drive for the first day of my second year at St. Luke's in September 1968, I asked Willy, "What do you think my biggest flaw is?" I knew I was taking a risk.

"You're not me." Willy smirked, but at least he didn't turn on the radio.

"I know, I'm me. But what I mean is, what could someone who's in the position of being me do to make you, for instance, like me . . . more . . . a little."

"Did Dad tell you to ask me this?"

"No." He looked at me suspiciously, like he thought I had a tape recorder hidden in my briefcase.

"Because, Zach, I don't dislike you, I feel sorry for you."

"Why?" It was like getting someone else to pick my scab.

"Because you think Mom and Dad know everything."

"No, I don't."

"Then why do you say yes to everything they ask you?"

"It's easier." I felt stupid saying I wanted them to be happy.

"You've got to think for yourself. You're almost fourteen years old. Grow up. Your problem is basically . . ."—Willy thought for a moment—". . . a fundamental lack of character."

"How do I get that?"

"You don't get it, you earn it."

"What would you do if I said I was ready to earn it, to work for it."

"I'd say, as usual, you're just telling somebody what they want to hear."

"Hypothetically . . ."—I did my best imitation of my father—

"theoretically, for the sake of argument, what could I do that would make you want me to sit down and hang out with you and your friends at lunch. And not just so one of them could pull the chair out from under me."

Willy laughed and squeezed the hard, dirty rubber ball he kept in the front seat to strengthen his finger muscles while he was driving. "Get me a date with Constance Murdoch."

"Who's she?"

"A girl."

"I figured that much." I never heard my brother mention her before. Willy kept his interests in that department to himself. "What's so special about her?"

"All the guys on the track team say she's the best-looking girl in town. Shot every one of them down. If she's the best, then why settle for less?" He was talking to himself. Still, it was the longest conversation we'd had in a number of years.

"Why don't you ask her out yourself?"

"She goes to boarding school in Rhode Island." My brother was still squeezing the rubber ball.

"Look, how am I going to introduce you to someone who doesn't even go to school here? Give me something I have a chance at."

"Do five miles under thirty."

"What?"

"Run five miles in under half an hour."

My brother was surprised when he saw me that afternoon at the tail end of a line of twenty-odd freshmen and sophomore boys signing up for the junior varsity cross-country team. He was even more surprised when I put on my sneakers and followed in his footsteps and began to run. We started out with a three-mile jog. I walked the second mile and limped the third.

That night, every muscle in my body screamed in protest. I felt like I had been disassembled and put back together incorrectly. After my mother helped me rub Ben-Gay on my legs, I got into bed stinking of menthol and reexamined what the *DSM* had to say about sadomasochism.

Much to my amazement, after two weeks of cross-country, my lungs ceased to burn, my legs stopped feeling like they were being flayed, and I was finally able to complete the three-mile course Coach Wyler called a "stroll" without becoming separated from my lunch. My father was so hopeful of a long-distance rapprochement between his sons, he bought me a pair of the same expensive kangaroo-hide running shoes Willy wore in his victories. They made me feel like I was running faster, even though I still came in last.

Mind, body, or heart. I'm still not sure which part of me was most ill suited to long-distance running. If the sun was shining and the sky blue and there was the slightest breeze at my back, I could not resist the urge to start off faster than was wise. And when it was cold and drizzly, I lagged behind right from the start, as if I were waiting for a change in the weather to inspire me.

On those rare occasions when I found myself in the lead and actually had a chance to beat someone, I would suddenly feel so unfamiliarly good about myself, my mind would wander off course. The sight of a pond, its surface glimmery with thin ice, would make me wonder how many snapping turtles were sleeping in the mud of its bottom. The vapor trail of a jet passing overhead at thirty thousand feet would prompt fantasies of myself not as I was but as the first-class passenger I would become once I had character.

Once I let one kid pass me in a track meet, I'd be so busy convincing myself that coming in second wouldn't be so bad, my pace would slow even further, and then another boy would overtake me. And then as I struggled to lower my sights to third, another one would pass me. The worst thing was seeing my father clap when I came in last.

The final meet of the fall, I made my best showing, thirteenth out of twenty-six, the middle of the pack. Coach Wyler said, "Nice try."

My mother said, "You're getting better."

My father waited until I caught my breath to ask me, "What are you thinking about out there?"

"Running." I wasn't about to tell my father the truth, and he knew it.

"You're soft. Soft mentally and physically."

"What?"

All the other dads were patting their sons on the back, giving them cups of cocoa. "I could take you right now. In street shoes. And I'm fifty years old." He was fifty-one.

"No, you couldn't." Willy's voice was cold and matter-of-fact. He didn't like either one of us, but if he had to choose . . .

When I went out to put my book bag in the back of my parents' Volvo, I heard my parents talking in the parking lot. My mother was mad at my father. "You shouldn't have said that to Zach."

"I said it so Willy could stick up for him. I wanted to give the boys something to bond over."

My seemingly lackadaisical disinterest in winning had a strange way of devaluing the prize, the ribbon, or cup Willy invariably won. My brother was the state champion now. Photographs appeared in newspapers of his breaking the tape at the finish line, arms raised, body pitched forward, eyes already looking ahead to the next race.

By the spring of 1969, I was less than four minutes away from running five miles in thirty minutes. My parents knew about Willy's challenge by now, and it had become something of a family joke about what would transpire between us when and if I ever met his challenge.

It was around this time, I think, that my father suggested we go on a double date. Having been sent to an all-boys' school while still in puberty, my experience with girls my own age was nonexistent. Having never gone on a date with a girl, the idea of stepping out in virgin territory with my brother watching was a nightmare.

Willy wasn't much of a dater, either. Girls were always paying attention to him, but he was so busy running, he only asked girls out when his star status at St. Luke's demanded his attendance at a school dance and he needed someone on his arm to impress his teammates. On those rare occasions, he would double-date with his best friend, Emory Nicholas, a two hundred and forty pounder with a strangely high-pitched voice who threw the hammer, javelin, and shot put. I found it interesting that they both went for the same type—blonde, overeager, and big boobed. As Emory put it in his near castrato tenor, "Sure things."

It was Emory who had told Willy about Constance Murdock. From our limited conversations about the mythic beauty, I inferred Constance wasn't easy. This, coupled with the fact that she was the New England girls' champion in the mile, prompted me to imagine her as a female mirror image of Willy. I could imagine Willy making love to himself.

They had met the year before at a winter track meet outside of Boston that Willy had attended with my parents. I wasn't there. My mother said she was pretty. My father called her "unusual." Which pissed Willy off. I tried on more than one occasion to get Willy to talk about Constance, but at the mere mention of her name, he'd smile and say, "No."

Willy wasn't amused by the prospect of a double date, but I could see he was looking forward to having me as a friend, now that it was clear to one and all that he had set the terms of our bond.

One morning in the last week of March, as I was checking my list against the contents of my briefcase, my father took me aside and told me, "It's time for you to quit dawdling." Willy was outside waiting behind the wheel of the Skylark. I thought my father was talking about being late to school.

"I'm not dawdling."

"You and I both know that you could run five miles in thirty minutes if you really wanted to." Willy honked the horn for me to hurry up.

"He'll do it when he's ready." My mother still watched to make sure my head was screwed on straight.

"You're putting it off because you're ambivalent."

"About what?" My mother and I said the words simultaneously.

"About having a friendship with his brother." Of course, he was right.

I didn't like it when my father talked about me in the third person, like I was one of his patients. For so many months, running had seemed the cure. Now, suddenly, a few words from my father and a brain that needed a smooth combing had turned the cure into a symptom.

Overdosed with family, a delicate balance within myself was shifting. The need to say yes versus the need to say no versus the need not to feel crazy anymore. My feelings were further complicated when I passed my brother in the hall that day after lunch, and he not only talked to me, he stopped to inquire, "What's wrong?"

"I'm nervous."

"About what?"

"I'm going for it. Five miles, thirty minutes, today's the day." I tried to sound more Clint Eastwood than John Wayne.

"I understand." He didn't. But he filled Coach Wyler in on the time trial. At three o'clock, my brother unstrapped his chronograph and buckled it onto my wrist. The whole track team, JV and varsity, were assembled behind the field house. They all knew of the challenge now.

Coach Wyler drew out the course I would run in the dirt with a stick from the popsicle he had just finished. "Gentlemen, since no hills were specified in your challenge, I suggest up through the sanctuary, twice around town, then back down through the goalposts."

I shook my head no. "Too many distractions. I want to run on the road." My brother nodded in agreement. "Five miles is five miles." A new course was imposed by Coach Wyler. "Fair enough. Zach'll go out the back, turn right on 512, left onto Mill Road, then take Long Lane, then back through town and in the front gate." I pulled off my sweats. Coach Wyler mounted his bicycle. My brother shook his head no.

"You don't need to go with him, Coach."

"I don't mean to impugn your little brother's character, but how are we gonna know he's run the full five miles?" Everyone laughed except me and Willy.

"I trust him." Suddenly, in that moment, we really were friends.

I ran as I had never run before. I forgot about my father and my mother and the warmth of my brother's handshake and listened only to the beat of my heart. Matching its rhythm to my stride, I kept my eyes down to avoid getting caught in the vapor trails of jets or the dreams of sleeping turtles. I knew I was going to be okay, even before Willy's chronometer told me I'd covered the first mile in five minutes and twenty-two seconds. Breathing easy, muscles relaxed, not a thought in my mind except covering ground with as little emotional involvement as humanly possible, I did the second mile in five seventeen.

As I turned onto the rutted macadam of Mill Road and passed the red silo that marked the halfway point to victory, I had character. I wasn't just a fourteen-and-a half-year-old, I was my own man. I had out-distanced all my doubts and ambivalence, and outrun even my family.

Heading down Long Lane now, the wind at my back, anything was possible. The road narrowed, potholes topped up by the morning rain reflected the grace of my velocity. Fields turned over but not yet planted, and hedgerows flecked with forsythia sweetened the air I breathed. I was so much better than fine that when a pickup piled high with baled hay barreled by me, blasting its horn as it showered me with a spray of pothole water, I did not lose stride or concentration.

I was fine until I took my eyes off the blur of ground beneath my feet to wipe the muddy water off my face . . . that's when I saw her.

She stood atop a five-foot-high stone wall postered with signs that read "No Trespassing." From a quarter-mile away, her body was so quiet, she looked almost like a statue. Curious, I quickened my pace to get a better look. Her hair was long and the color of butterscotch. Though the day was hot for the last of March, she was dressed for the summer to come, not for the spring that was. She had taken off her flannel shirt. At first I thought she was standing up there in just her bra. But now I was close enough to see the bra was the top to a bathing suit—which must have been a bikini, because it was skimpier than any of the bras my sisters or mother wore. Her jeans rode so low on her hips, I wasn't imagining she wasn't wearing any underwear. They were bell-bottomed and frayed, and secured with a macramé sash. My knowledge of hippies in the spring of '69 was limited to what I'd seen on the pages of *Rolling Stone* magazine and read in an issue of *Time* with a cover with the words TUNE IN, TURN ON, DROP OUT. But that's what I knew her instinctively to be. She was barefoot, her feet and her hands were dirty, her eyes were closed, and her arms outstretched. She stood as still and primeval as a lizard warming itself in the sun.

It is difficult to run with an erection, but it and I pressed on. I was almost upon her now. She must have heard me panting, but she showed no sign of it. She looked old to me . . . seventeen?

As I ran by her, I could see the blonde down of her unshaved armpits. For a heartbeat I was close enough to imagine what it would be like to count the freckles that dappled the hollow of her belly just below her right hip. Before I had time to ponder the weight of that fantasy, my legs had carried me past her. Now there was nothing but the empty road and the race ahead.

Of course, I had to look back. I was still running, but instead of looking where I was going, I was reexamining what I had passed by. She was looking at me now, then she waved. If it had been a friendly, up-in-the-air wave, a "hello, see you around" wave, it would have been easier to resist. But it was a low-armed, lazy wiggle of the fingers. Subtext: Don't even think about it.

Still, I kept running. It wasn't until I heard her laugh that I stumbled. At first, she laughed because I was out there on a beautiful day busting my ass running. After I lost my footing she laughed because I was lying facedown in a mud puddle.

When I got to my feet and turned to demand "What's the joke?" she had disappeared.

My brother's chronometer weighed on my wrist. I checked my time. I'd lost less than three minutes. I still had a chance to show my character. I did when I ran back to the stretch of the wall where I'd seen/imagined her standing. There was no sign of her. I was disappointed and yet relieved to know that, once and for all, I did have a screw loose.

I was just about to start running when I heard her voice echo up from a grassy berm on the other side of the wall. She was singing "Sunshine of Your Love."

First her head, then her body, surfaced on the far side of the berm. She walked in time to Cream as she crossed a stretch of lawn, as flat and green and chancy as the felt on a poker table. Unlike me, she didn't look back. My eyes stayed on her even after she disappeared amid the ornamental shrubbery in the distance.

My thirty minutes were up by then. The race wasn't over, it was lost. Mind, body, and heart too weak to stay the course; I retraced my steps and headed back to school. When I got to the field house, my brother was the only one still waiting.

"What happened?" he called out.

I feigned a limp as I answered, "I sprained my ankle." I had no intention of telling Willy what had really happened, in part because I was embarrassed, but mostly because I did not want to share her.

"You'll do better next time."

"I hope so."

The sprained ankle I didn't have got me out of track practice. The next day, as soon as my brother and the rest of the team took off after Coach Wyler on his bike, I slipped out of the school grounds and took off down 512 toward the stretch of road where I had first seen the sunshine of my love.

She wasn't there. I ran my hands over the stones where she had stood, barefoot and life changing, and reimagined it. When it began to rain, I still waited for her to appear. She didn't, but I was glad I had made the pilgrimage. For if I hadn't, I would have been convinced she was waiting for me and that I'd blown yet another challenge.

The next day, I continued my deception. Struggling to remember which ankle I supposedly had sprained, I limped through my classes. At three o'clock, I again waved good-bye to my brother and teammates, then immediately snuck off. Changing into my track shorts in the woods so as not to sweat through my school clothes and give myself away, I ran my own race back to the wall.

This time, I was in luck, or so I thought. After fifteen, twenty minutes of peering over her wall, scanning the horizon, as nervous and anxious as the teenage Green Beret sniper I saw Dan Rather interview on last night's news from Vietnam, I caught sight of her. I heard her calling for somebody named "Bill." I was jealous until I realized Bill was a dog that looked to be a golden Lab. She wasn't wearing her bikini top, but it was still nice to see her. I have a distinct memory of envying Bill as she bent down to rub his stomach.

Not knowing what I could or should say to her, I ducked down behind the wall and hid. Knowing I was there, she punished me with a song. "In-a-gadda-da-vida, baby/Don't you know that I love you?" She was singing Iron Butterfly. But she was still the sunshine of my love.

Low as the sideswiped animal I was, I crawled the whole length of that wall on my hands and knees. I could not face her. I knew I was in love by then, not with her, but with the possibility of a world beyond the web of family. A realm of the senses that would make me feel less alone with the strain of being human.

After three days of limping, my ankle in fact began to swell. The *DSM* told me my symptoms were hysterical. It wasn't funny to me. On Saturday, my mother took me to the local hospital to see if I had a hairline fracture. Needless to say, what ailed me didn't show up on X-rays. The doctor told me to keep it elevated. As we drove down Main Street, I had my ankle up on the Volvo's dashboard. We were just pulling into the parking lot of the supermarket when I saw her coming out of the drugstore carrying the new issue of *Rolling Stone*.

She walked the pavement barefoot and had a wreath of daisies in her hair. Her leashless dog followed at her side, sporting a bandanna instead of a collar. She drew stares from the passersby, and not just because she wasn't wearing a bra beneath her Grateful Dead T-shirt. Even my mother would have given the sunshine of my love a sideways look if she weren't so worried about my ankle.

When the subject of hippies came up, Mom always made a face like she'd just found a hair in her tuna fish. It wasn't their politics that bothered her. My mother was against the war, and all for peace and love. But having grown up in the Depression, she could not get her head around the idea of anyone wanting to look poor.

When Mom asked me what I wanted for dinner, I answered, "I don't care." she thought I was depressed about my ankle, and tried to cheer me up with the promise of roast beef. I shrugged ungratefully, pointed to my imaginary injury, and told her I'd wait in the car and keep it elevated. As soon as the electric doors of the supermarket opened for Mom, I gave chase to my fantasy.

Cutting across the street, keeping low behind parked cars, I stalked her as she and her dog proceeded down the opposite sidewalk. I had made up my mind. This time I was not only going to see her, I was going to open my mouth. For it seemed to me, in the hysteria of my neediness, if I blew it again, chickened out one more time, I would be trapped in the cellar of loserdom for the rest of my life.

She turned down a side street. The sidewalks there were empty. Better for me, I knew I was not at my best with an audience of more than one. I sprinted to catch up to her. Silent in sneakers, just as I was close enough to touch a strand of the warm ginger of her hair, her dog caught sight of a squirrel and gave chase. Not wanting to be interrupted by the competition, I waited until she had gotten him on the short leash she kept in the back pocket of her jeans. She tethered him to a bike rack. Just as I was finally welling up the courage to speak, she darted into the hardware store. Standing outside looking in, I hid behind the chain saws on sale in the window and watched her shop for dog toys. Five minutes, ten, when she disappeared into the back of the shop, I made up my mind to go in and blurt out the truth: "I need to talk to you."

Then, just as I swear I was about to make my move, the scent of patchouli filled the air and goose bumps rose on the back of my arms. And even before I felt the whip of her hair on my skin, I knew she was behind me. Her eyes were lidded in a blue-gray squint, like she was looking at something small, alive, and annoying. I hadn't realized she had a chipped tooth. Before I could remember how to speak, she hit me between the eyes with a loud, "What do you want?"

I wasn't sure, except she was part of it. When I gave no response, she took a step closer, wrinkling her nose as she inquired loudly, "What is your problem?" I didn't know where to begin. But I wanted to tell her something that was true, not just a pickup line. All I could do was stare. She spoke slowly now, so I'd be sure to understand. "Why . . . are . . . you . . . such . . . a . . . freak?"

A gray-haired lady across the street looked over at me like I'd exposed myself. I hadn't, but I was about to. The only thing I could think to say was, "Casper Gedsic." My voice broke as I said his name.

"What the fuck is that?"

I shared my secret in a burst of adrenaline and honesty. I don't know exactly when it was, but some time in the course of the story, we shifted positions. Before I was finished, we were sitting shoulder to shoulder on the curb, our feet in the gutter. I forgot how frightened I was of the mystery of her girlishness and was reminded how scared I was of Casper. I jumped back and forth in time, from the drowning that turned into a swimming lesson, the murder of Doctor Winton, the death of Jack, the accident that wasn't, the Yugo bodyguards that took us to hide in Greenwich Village, the TV'd cell at Needmore, and the drugs he was being fed as we spoke.

She was still and silent and interrupted me only to offer condolences, "That's heavy . . . far fucking out . . . what a mind fuck." That was my favorite.

When I was finished, it was as if Casper was sitting right there with us. She took a deep breath, then exhaled with a whistle at all that I had unloaded on her. Studying me for a moment, without warning she wrapped her arms around me with a hug that flattened her breasts against my hollow chest. "Poor you."

"Not really."

"What do you mean?"

"Poor Casper." I suddenly felt bad for him being so alone while I was feeling so unbelievably close to her.

Then she stood up. "I gotta go. My mother'll kill me if I'm late."

"My mom's waiting, too."

"Wanna hang out?"

"Sure."

"Meet me at the wall, tomorrow morning. One thirty."

"That's not morning."

"It is for me." She and the dog were running down the street now.

"Hey, what's your name?" I called out after her.

"Sunshine." It was too good to be true.

"I'm Zach."

She stopped and looked back at me. "See you, Z."

A girl, a nickname—I didn't know what was next, but whatever it was, I wanted it.

The next day, I told my parents I was going fishing and rode my bike toward the wall. Down our hill, along the river that no longer beckoned me, through the town—I pedaled with a secret beating inside of me that made me feel for the first time in my life that there was no one else in the world I would rather be than me.

I felt a little less that way when I arrived and she wasn't there. Then it began to rain. Was there some part of our conversation that I hadn't understood? Had I gotten the time wrong? Had she remembered I was the jerky kid who had hidden behind the wall and stalked her through town, and decided I was unworthy of a rendezvous, much less the nickname Z?

It was raining hard now. Cars and pickup trucks towing horse trailers honked and splashed me as they drove past. The secret I harbored still beat within me. But now I felt stupid for holding onto it, for not being able to let it go and ride back home. Slumped against the wall, knee-deep in weeds, my head resting against the "No Trespassing" sign, I was so lost in self-pity, I did not see the convertible Mustang skidding toward me down the mud-slicked lane with its brakes locked until it came to a stop a foot from my head with a metallic crunch. Its right front tire had flattened my bike lying next to me.

The window on the passenger side of the Mustang rolled down with an electric whirr. "Sorry."

"It's okay." It was better than that—it was her.

She put the Mustang in reverse, then pushed a button that folded back the roof. The rain was coming down in sheets, "What are you putting the top down for?" It was a brand-new Mustang.

"I lost the key to the trunk. You can put your bike in the backseat."

"What about the rain?" I was putting the bike in now. "It's leather upholstery."

"It's my mother's car, fuck it." She said it with a laugh that made me laugh; though I didn't know many girls, I knew this was my kind of girl.

Rain pouring, soggy cigarette in her mouth, Led Zeppelin blaring on the eight-track, "Been dazed and confused for so long it's not true/Wanted a woman, never bargained for you," the interior of her mother's Mustang filling with water, we fishtailed through the gates of her world.

"My parents are home." I saw two cars parked in front of a house so white and tidy, it looked like an ad for Sherwin-Williams paint. She drove around back to the pool house and screeched on her brakes. "You can't stay that long."

"You want me to leave now?"

"No. I'm not ditching you. I just mean this guy's coming over this afternoon."

Not wanting the Mustang to feel as neglected as I did, I raised its roof. "Is he your boyfriend?"

"He'd like to be."

"Maybe I'd better go home."

"Want to get high first?"

"Sure." I'd never seen pot, much less smoked it. We were in the pool house now. The shades were drawn, it smelled of mildew, and was dark. When she flicked the lights on, it seemed even darker because all the bulbs were ultraviolet, and the posters on the wall Day-Glo. A lava lamp bubbled voluptuously as she pulled out a knee-high Plexiglas bong.

My father, being a psychopharmacologist, had warned me about marijuana, cocaine, heroin, amphetamines, and the brain damage they were guaranteed to inflict. He had warned me about so many things that attacked the brain: mosquitoes bearing encephalitis; dementia due to syphilis; snake venoms that tell the brain not to breathe . . . when you're conditioned to be frightened of everything, you end up being scared of nothing.

When the first toke of cannabis hit my lungs, I gasped, sputtered, and gagged. "I thought you said you did this before."

"I lied." She thought that was hysterical. "So who's your boyfriend?"

"Some jock. And he's not my boyfriend, Z."

"Why do you call me that?"

"Sounds cooler."

"Why not *el Magnífico?*" We both thought that was a scream.

"You're not that cool." It was good pot.

"How'd you get the name Sunshine?" We were trading hits.

"The first time I took acid, it was all groovy. And then I started really bumming on myself, and who I was—I mean, I was sooooooo square, you wouldn't have recognized me: sports, honor society. And then on acid, it just seemed so bullshit. I decided, if I wanted to be a different person, I should come up with a new identity." She held her toke on that word, then exhaled. "So, like, I was standing there in the sun, and it was warm and felt good, and I knew that's what I wanted to be, like the sun. Sunshine."

"Wow. Where'd you get the acid?"

"I was visiting my roommate in Boston. Her older brother knew this dealer guy who hung out in Harvard Square. He turned us on for free." Her eyes were lit like sparklers as she twirled a band around her third finger that spelled L-O-V-E. "He gave me this ring that night."

"Is he your boyfriend?"

"He was. Sort of. Until he got busted and gave my real name to the police. That's how I got kicked out of boarding school." She said it with pride and stood up, turned her back to me, pulled off her wet T-shirt, and reached for a sweater. "It's okay, you can look." My mouth felt like someone had stolen my saliva. "Tell me some more about your friend." She flopped back down on the couch next to me.

"What friend?" The pot made me feel as if I were adrift in a fog bank.

"Casper." I hadn't thought of him as a friend until I met Sunshine.

"What do you want to know?"

"Like, could you tell he was crazy?" She lit a fresh stick of incense. A Moody Blues album was playing.

"No . . . well, he seemed a little weird. Even though he wasn't wearing a watch, he looked at his wrist to check the time." I hadn't thought about that for a long while.

"Did he tell you why he wanted to kill your father?"

"No."

"Ever wonder if your dad gave him acid? Doctors did stuff like that." Timothy Leary was all over the news that spring.

"My father doesn't work with drugs like that." But she had me wondering. Until that moment, the thought had never occurred to me that my father had done something to Casper to make him crazy. What if my father had made it happen? What if it was his fault? Questions beamed through the cloud of THC in my brain like searchlights piercing through the fog, looking for wreckage of a ship lost at sea.

Too high to grasp what had been momentarily illuminated, I let go of my father and the past when she took my hands in hers and peered at my flattened palm. "You have a cool life line."

"How come?"

"It's really short." When she finished predicting the future, she didn't let go of my hand. "Once I had this bad trip where I was suddenly sure I killed my parents but had forgotten about it. And then remembered it, like it was just, 'Oh gee, I killed my parents.' You know, like I'd left my purse in your car."

"I don't have a car." As I said, I was high.

"That's not the point of my bad trip. The point is, it really, really freaked me out that I killed them and forgot it and left them in the kitchen, like leftovers." She started off like she was telling a funny story. Now she was crying.

"Everyone has crazy thoughts." At that moment I was thinking about what it would be like to get naked with her in the shower.

"I think I'm having one now."

"You mean, like an acid flashback?"

"No, just a crazy thought."

"What is it?"

"That you tell girls about Casper just to get into their pants." She smiled with tears on her cheeks. Then she pushed me back on the couch and began to tickle my stomach.

"You're the first girl I ever told." She liked hearing that. Pinning my arms back behind my head, she kissed me on the mouth, her tongue licking unseen wounds.

As she took my hands and guided them up under her sweater, I knew it was Casper who made it possible for me to touch her nipple with the fingertip I'd lost to a cherry bomb. It was Casper's gravity that drew her close.

As we pulled off each other's clothes, I saw him on the small screen in the back of my brain. I heard him say, "Don't worry. I'll be around."

I was down to my underpants—she didn't wear any—when we heard a knock on the door. "Constance, are you in there?"

I was so high, I didn't recognize the voice until the door opened and I saw my brother standing there.

That night, my brother and Emory drove into New York City and got so blind drunk on the way home, the Skylark jumped the divider on Route 22. Emory ended up with a concussion. My brother broke his leg in two places—compound fracture. The police said they were lucky to be alive. When my father asked my brother why he did it, all Willy had to say was, "I wanted to see what I was missing."

My brother never said a word to me about Constance. My father thought I quit the track team because Willy couldn't run that spring. My mother thought it was for the best. "Zach likes to play games with other people" was how she put it.

Once word reached St. Luke's that I was going out with Constance, aka Sunshine, my status rose. More titillating to my classmates than her lack of underwear or the fact that she had gotten kicked out of boarding school for drugs was the story that had won her heart (Sunshine even told her mother about it). Over hand-rolled joints and purloined beers, kids would ask me to tell them about my bogeyman. Having Casper in my life gave me far more character in the eyes of my peers than all my brother's track trophies combined. I got good at telling the story, dropping it into conversations, using it to answer questions before they were asked. I kept Casper alive, for he had given me an identity and made me cool.

My popularity was a relief to my parents. Now that my head was screwed on straight, they felt it was safe to leave me home alone. They were wrong.

Teddy Kennedy gets so bombed he drives off a bridge on Martha's Vineyard and leaves his date to drown. The Manson family dines on acid, then eviscerates a pregnant movie star in the Hollywood Hills. A man takes a walk on the bright side of the moon, then a couple hundred thousand kids, stoned on peace, love, and (most of all) each other shut down the New York Thruway on the way to Woodstock. And then we find out about this army lieutenant who herded three hundred women and children into a ditch in a place called My Lai and shot 'em all. He said he was acting under orders. They say everybody in Vietnam smokes dope. It's the only way they can get through it. If they weren't high before they pulled the trigger, they were afterward. It seemed like everybody was operating under the influence of something in 1969.

Sunshine called it a contact high. She swore that if you're just near someone who was really fucked up, you'd get fucked up on whatever they were fucked up on.

I never ran five miles in thirty minutes, and though I failed to earn my brother's friendship in high school, I was compensated by the loss of my virginity—a fair bargain. I was sure as only a teenager can be that I had found something that would last forever. At night we would sneak out and meet at our river and slip into the water naked as the trout I no longer tried to catch.

Halfway through the summer, Sunshine stopped answering my calls. I figured she'd found someone older and cooler to swim with. Hoping I was wrong, needing to hear something that would make me understand, make me feel less guilty for bragging about our intimacy, I pounded on her parents' door.

They told me Sunshine had been arrested for buying two

pounds of Acapulco gold from an undercover agent in Washington Square Park. My father's inquiries on the subject revealed that her parents had kept her out of jail by committing her to a private mental hospital called Payne Whitney. Dad told me it'd probably be six months before they let her write me a letter. I was surprised at how sorry he felt—for both of us.

Late at night, sleepless and hungry for dreams, I would think about how sometimes, after we'd gone skinny-dipping, we'd lie naked on flat river rocks warmed by the sun, and she'd take the damp end of her braid in her hand like it was a paintbrush and write messages down the length of my spine. I could never tell what she was spelling out. But sometimes, in the darkness just before sleep, when I'd be thinking of her, my brain would suddenly change channels, and I'd see Casper looking out at me from the video monitor of a security system that watched him sleep.

You might have thought that Sunshine's fate would have scared me straight. My brain didn't work that way. It seemed to me that drugs, like being sent to the loony bin, were part of the risk one took in being young.

If drugs weren't part of your problem, they were part of your answer. At least, that's how it was at St. Luke's. Pot, mescaline, vodka: Rarely did I imbibe all three at the same time, but at least one figured in the equation of my idea of weekend fun. I knew I was burning brain cells, but thanks to my father, I knew I had over a hundred billion to blow. Like the Stones sang, time was on my side.

My dad helped make drugs, I took them. In the stoned logic of my teenage mind, my self-medication seemed like I was carrying on his work. Like the starship *Enterprise,* I was determined to go where, if not no man had, at least my father had not gone before.

By 1970, my hair was down to my shoulders, and I did my homework with my head between hundred-watt speakers that blasted the joys of sex and drugs. Since my father was, according to *Who's Who,* one of the world's leading authorities on memory, learning, and drugs, one might be tempted to criticize Dad for not suspecting I was conducting a drug study of my own. But in all fairness, my parents were not entirely to blame for not noticing my chemical drift.

Besides being a first-rate people pleaser, I was also an excellent liar. I loved my parents, but, like all children, I had reached that point where I no longer believed in them. My questions were varied, my suspicions vague. Had my father dosed Casper with something that had done him irreparable harm? Had Casper killed Jack? And if my father was responsible for Casper, and Casper was responsible for Jack, did that mean my father had a hand in Jack's death? Was that why my mother had stopped sleeping in his bed? Why did Casper's recapture make everything right again between them?

And was this nagging sense that I was not being told the whole truth the reason I felt free to keep them misinformed about my own state of mind? It wasn't that my parents didn't deserve the truth; it was just that in my heart, I did not believe they wanted it, at least not when it involved drugs. Mine or theirs.

The compulsive list-making my mother had taught me kept my head on straight enough for me to keep my grades up, but at night I had to write more and more reminders to myself. It wasn't just schoolbooks and papers I had to remember; my lists now included notations such as "Find new hiding place for pot, buy air fresheners, remember to bring breath mints, use eyedrops, flush all roaches."

By Christmas of '70, five kids at St. Luke's had been kicked out of school for drugs. The headmaster had a list, and I was on it. Whether I was a hypocrite or just a foot soldier in the assault on ethics, I realized that drugs weren't a problem unless you got caught doing them. Since I was on the headmaster's list, the only way to avoid getting caught, disappointing my parents, and still be able to get high was to tell a lie so large and preemptive, no one would suspect I had the balls to be so shameless.

When I told my father I wanted him to help me write an article for the school newspaper about the dangers of recreational drugs (working title: "What Comes Up Must Come Down"), he got that same dreamy smile that had appeared on his face when he caught me consulting the *DSM* to find out how crazy I was.

As it turned out, the research part of the article was fun for both of us. He took me to the headquarters of one of the big pharmaceutical companies, and we watched a 16 mm film of lab monkeys getting addicted to cocaine. They were hooked up to a drip, and all they had to do to get another hit of coke was push a button. After a couple of weeks they got so high that they began to eat their own fingers. Having not yet done cocaine, I was glad I wasn't a lab monkey in a drug test.

I guess it was the animals being locked up alone in the cages with nothing to keep them company but the whirr of the camera and the buzz of cocaine that made me think of Casper. On the drive home, we stopped at a Stewart's and had root-beer floats. My father said that that had been his and my mother's idea of a big treat when they first met over the Bunsen burner. When I asked my father if I could look over any of the videos they took of drugs being tested on Casper, he winced and rubbed his forehead.

"That would be impossible."

"Why?"

"Because it's unethical."

My antidrug article appeared on the front page of the school newspaper. Letters an inch high: WHAT COMES UP MUST COME DOWN, subheading: "The Hidden Menace of Recreational Drugs."

Everybody I smoked pot with at school thought I was a complete asshole, phonier than phony, right up there with Richard Nixon. One kid actually spit on me. Since I didn't like to get high alone, I probably would have quit drugs now that I didn't have anyone to do them with, if only the headmaster hadn't decided to read the article out loud in chapel. When he got to the last paragraph, his voice cracked as he quoted me. "Why has our generation turned to drugs? Why do we want an imitation of life, rather than the real thing? I don't have the answer to these questions, but St. Luke's has taught me this much: If you don't like your world, change it. Don't run away from it."

When he'd finished, the headmaster took out his handkerchief. Some say he blew his nose; others swear he wiped away a tear. Whatever, he announced, "Thank you, Zach Friedrich." Slowly, he began to clap and motioned for me to stand up. Two by two, other hands began to join in. The applause built. Those who didn't know me clapped because they thought I was someone else, someone even worthier than my brother had been, and those I had gotten high with, even the kid who spit on me, smirked as they mistook my hypocrisy for high irony. They thought I had deliberately made the headmaster look like a fool; they believed they were privy to another one of my secrets. Casper, drugs, school . . . I inadvertently turned them all into one huge joke.

The stoners joined the jocks, the applause echoed as they began to stamp their feet, whistle, and hiss "Zeeeeeeeeee." Everyone believed what they wanted to believe, including me.

The headmaster entered "What Goes Up Must Come Down" in the state high school journalism contest. Worse, it won first prize. My self-loathing peaked when my father put the trophy I received on the same mantle that held all the cups and bowls Willy had won for running. My father, being an academic, took more pride in mine than he did in all Willy's combined. For I had won not with heart or body but with mind.

A psychiatrist I went to once years later told me that writing that article was an incredibly hostile act. And though she pretended not to judge, I could tell she loathed me. As she pulled cat hairs off her skirt and dropped them in an ashtray one by one, she told me it was hostile to my father, and to my friends, and to the headmaster who had given me a break and not expelled me for the cherry bomb incident, and, most of all, it was an act of aggression toward, and showed profound disrespect for, myself.

I told her, "You're missing the point. I wanted to get caught."

"Did you think you needed to be punished?"

"No. I just wanted to start fresh. Confess."

"Did you make any attempt to tell your father the truth about your drug problems?"

"Once."

"What happened?"

I didn't mind her sitting in judgment of me, but I could not bear to have her pass psychological sentence on my father. "Dad was preoccupied."

"You sound angry."

"That's the sort of thing my dad used to say."

"What was your father preoccupied with?"

"Let's get into that next session." Our time actually was almost up. She gave me a prescription for Paxil, even though I didn't ask for it.

After a week or so, my journalism trophy began to mock me from its sterling position of honor on my parents' mantle. I could almost hear it whisper to me as my breath tarnished its glow, "None of it's true."

I was high that Saturday morning when it all became too much, and I suddenly willed up enough shame and courage to shout out, "Mom, Dad, I've got to tell you something you're not going to want to hear." My parents knew I only used that expression when I had fucked up big time.

I braced myself to be echoed back with shouts of "what's wrong, what have you done now?" Until I realized there was nobody home but me.

Looking beyond the trophy through the big picture window that faced west, I could see them in the distance, walking with Alfie. Alfie was a giant poodle with caramel-colored hair and a long, undocked tail that curled up behind him. My sister said my mother got him because she missed Willy now that he'd left home to go to Princeton.

I knew if I waited for them to finish their walk, I wouldn't go through with my confession. The lie had me feeling sick to my stomach. I felt like it was poisoning me.

It was May outside, the sky was a surreal blue like a Magritte, except the clouds were as big and white and airy as loaves of Wonder Bread. Morning hadn't yet burned off the dew, and my sneakers were soaked through before I had crossed the lawn. I followed the path my parents had taken with Alfie through our old apple orchard in bloom, with the song of golden finches and the buzz of worker bees.

Mother, father, and dog were on their way to the river as I cut across a field fallow with lavender and did not stop to pick the wild strawberries that passed beneath my feet. My father had put down his fly rod and stopped to fix a gate that wouldn't stay closed. He grimaced as he struggled to bend a length of barbed wire into a latch. My mother was up ahead of him, walking the edge of three acres thigh-high with feed corn, throwing a red rubber ball for the dog. The corn was just high enough so that the poodle's head appeared and then disappeared with each stride he took after the ball.

I called out to my father, "I need to tell you something."

"I'm here."

"I need to say it to both of you."

My tone distracted him. The barb of the wire cut his knuckle. He cursed softly, licked away the blood. "Well, then, I guess you'd better go get your mother."

She was a hundred yards away, holding the ball up over her head. The poodle was balanced on his hind legs, tongue lolling, jaws snapping, as she held the ball just out of reach. She talked to Alfie with the same voice she had used when I was a little kid. "How's my big boy . . . ? Oh, yes, you are a ferocious thing."

"Mom," I shouted, "I need you."

She waved and threw the ball back toward us, and Alfie sprang after it like the beast he was. My father and I were walking toward her and she toward us. She was looking at me and smiling, pushing her hair out of her eyes with the back of her hand because her fingers were muddy from holding the ball. She was about to say something when her expression suddenly changed. She saw something that jerked her head around and drained the color from her face. As the wind gusted across the feed corn, rippling its surface like water, we saw it, too.

There, standing at the edge of the field, still as stone, was a deer. Tan, sleek, and female, its nose and eyes and hooves dark as the shadows cast from the overhang of dogwood that grew up out of the stone hedgerow, it was hard to see her. Life was so cleverly camouflaged, it was a long moment before our retinas could sort out the puzzle enough to see that a few feet away was her fawn, dappled with white and flecks of darker brown, two days old at most.

The dog was running straight toward them, cutting diagonally across the rows of corn like a shark. My mother shouted his name, "Alfie! Come here! Alfie!" The dog did not listen. The fawn was oblivious to the danger. Its mother was paralyzed by it.

My own mother was running now. She had her leash out and was angling into the field, trying to distract Alfie, shouting and waving her arms. "Alfie, don't you dare!"

Alfie was downwind from the pair. His head disappeared in the corn. He growled and shook something. I thought the worst until he came up with the ball, wet and red in his jaws. He was running back to my mother. I looked over at my father. He raised his eyebrows and shook his head with relief. We'd lucked out, it was going to be okay.

But just as my mother was reaching out to grab hold of our family beast, the wind changed, the poodle's head turned back, and his eyes rolled. Nostrils flaring, the ball fell from his mouth as he spun away from her. The deer and her fawn thought the danger had passed, that they were safe if they just stood still. But my mother knew that didn't work.

As Alfie ran, so did my mother. Reaching out, she grabbed hold of the fur on his back as if she wanted to rip his hide from the bone. Alfie felt the sharpness of her nails, felt attacked. He did not understand. The princes of France had bred poodles to run down deer in fields on clear May mornings. The dog had his own chemical memories to listen to.

Feeling my mother clawing at his withers, Alfie yelped, arched his head back, and snapped at her with a growl. My mother called him a bastard as his teeth bit into the flesh of her right hand. My father and I were running to help.

"Stop him!" she shouted.

We were too far away. She was the only one close enough to catch the dog before it reached them. Alfie had lost sight of the deer for a moment. My mother was running right behind him. It all happened within a matter of seconds. And yet, the trajectory of animal instincts that were about to collide were so hopelessly out of our hands, close at hand and yet beyond our reach, it felt like time slowed, like God put it in slo-mo, as if there was a lesson to be learned from what we were watching.

My mother's hand was just closing on Alfie's collar when the fawn moved. She was still holding on as Alfie's jaws bit down on the baby's neck. Dog, fawn, and my mother tumbled through the grass. Teeth flashed, and tiny hooves flailed between the sounds of growls and screams.

I had to hit the dog in the head with a rock to get him to let go. The fawn's throat was ripped open. Except for the blood, it still looked as perfect as a Steiff toy.

My mother was sobbing so hard she couldn't catch her breath. As my father helped her up off the ground, she screamed, "You bastard!" When she kicked the poodle in the ribs, my father shook her.

"It's not the dog's fault."

Her shirt was torn and splattered with blood. "Whose fault is it, then?" She wailed.

"Christ, Nora, are you crazy? You're lucky the damn dog didn't go for your throat."

My mother didn't hear him. The mother deer was at the far end of the field now. She had saved herself. She disappeared without ever looking back. My mother looked at the fawn like she was waiting for it to say something. "I couldn't let it happen again."

"Alfie's done this before?" At the mention of his name, the

poodle licked my hand and wagged his tail. He was over it, but my mother wasn't.

My mother looked at my father. "Tell him." She was both begging and daring him.

"Tell me what?"

"I think your mother's in shock. She might have hit her head as well. Put the dog in the house, bring the car down."

I knew my father was worried about her, because even though I didn't have a driver's license, he had me drive us to the emergency room so he could sit in the back of the car with her. I watched them in the rearview mirror. He cradled her head in his lap and kept talking to her so she wouldn't fall asleep.

The doctor said my mother had a slight concussion. That night my father made her soup. I stood in the doorway of their bedroom/office and watched him watch her eat it. After a few spoonfuls, she took a bite of a saltine. "I'm sorry I got so hysterical."

We both told her not to worry about it. When she finished with the soup she looked at me thoughtfully. "Your father said there was something you needed to talk to us about."

"It was nothing important." The trophy on the mantle suddenly seemed like the least of our worries.

"It didn't sound like nothing when you brought it up." My father eyed me carefully.

I didn't like to look him in the eye when I lied. I stared at the floor and saw a magazine with Pelé on the cover. "I was thinking about going out for soccer next year."

"But you've never played soccer." Even with a concussion, my mother could be counted on to be practical.

Where I was concerned, my father's optimism was blind. "That doesn't mean he wouldn't be good at it. What position did you have in mind?"

"Goalie."

"Why do you want to be a goalie, Zach?" I couldn't tell if my mother was being genuinely curious or just being polite.

"I think I'd like the feeling the game was in my hands."

Eventually, I did get caught, but not for drugs.

I went out for soccer fall of my senior year in the hopes that I could find a way to make at least one of the lies told in our house feel like the truth. I didn't want to spend my fall afternoons getting high and thinking about what made my mother fight a dog to save a fawn. No matter how much dope I smoked, I could still hear her pleading and taunting my father, "Tell him." There was no escaping the fact that they had a secret bond. Weighted down with my own deceptions, I did not want to be burdened with theirs. For what I had witnessed the morning of the dead fawn could not be blamed on Casper Gedsic.

When the soccer season began, I was the fourth-string goalie, so limited in ball-handling skills, my presence in the net was only slightly preferable to having no goalie at all. Normally, the coach only carried three goalies. The only reason he allowed me to join the team was because of my public stand against drugs. He had the scrambled thought that I would keep the team straight.

Soccer was a distraction. Except for having to cut off the shoulder-length hair I'd spent the last two years growing, I liked being a goalie. Within the confines of the net, there are no mysteries. Happiness for a goalie is simply keeping the ball out of the net. And a fourth-string goalie, who knows he is never going to get in the game, doesn't even have to worry about that.

But as seemed to be my fate, a series of catastrophes changed the course of my life in the week prior to the first game of the season. The starting goalie broke his collarbone. The day after that, the number-two man came down with mono. On Thursday, the third-stringer got kicked out of St. Luke's for cheating on a French test. Which left them with me.

The opening match was the next day at 3:30. It was a home game. After lunch, there was a pep rally in the cafeteria. The soccer coach and the captain of the team gave speeches. Then I ran out with the starting lineup as five hundred–odd boys screamed and shouted, *"Beat Lawrenceville!"* Even though I liked the boisterous teenage camaraderie of it all, relished the wholesome normalcy of the moment, as I stood, hands clasped behind my back, macho prep, I felt as if it were not happening to me, but rather, to someone who looked like me but I knew was an impostor.

If I had been high, I would have thought of team spirit as an out-of-body experience—sober, I just felt like a fake. The feeling persisted and grew as game time approached. As I suited up in the locker room with the rest of the team, stepped into my steel-cup jock, pulled on my red-and-white shorts and jersey, adjusted my knee pads, it felt as if I were dressing somebody else for the game.

My mind was disconnected from my body and the moment in my life it occupied. So much so that looking down to lace my cleats gave me a stomach-churning rush of vertigo. The locker room and my teammates began to spin around me. And even though I was sitting down, I felt like I was falling within myself from a great height. I wasn't just dizzy; it was F-16-dropping-from-the-sky-about-to-crash-and-burn-in-enemy-territory falling.

I bolted out of the locker room and ran to a lavatory at the end of the hall. I was in a cold, bilious sweat, pulling toilet paper from the roll by my head to wipe the vomit from the white letters that spelled "St." on my chest, and an echoey voice told me, "You're gonna get creamed." I looked up. Chas Ortley was staring down at me in the neighboring stall. If his hair had been straight, it would have been down to his shoulders. But red and kinky, it formed a Celtic afro worthy of the Jackson 5.

"Creamed? He's gonna get killed." Peter Ortley peered over the other wall of my stall. "Lawrenceville has this kid from Gambia, who's like six foot six, kicks the ball ninety-three miles an hour."

"He killed a goalie in Botswana."

"I thought he was from Gambia."

"Whatever, you're dead meat."

"Fuck you." The worst part was, I knew Lawrenceville did in fact have a forward who had played on the Gambian junior national team. And though I doubted he had killed an opponent with his shot, I believed he had the power to break ribs.

"You figured out your strategy?"

"Survival." I flushed the toilet and got up off my knees.

A gift of a field house had gotten the Ortleys a second chance at St. Luke's. They had made the most of it, and become the school's drug dealers. We'd renewed our friendship. The Ortleys spoke to me in stereo: "You're a slow, uncoordinated white kid; he's a fast, shifty Zulu."

"Zulus aren't from Gambia."

"You've got to level the playing field. Speed up your reflexes."

The game hadn't even begun. My hands and feet felt leaden. "How the fuck am I going to do that?" Chas opened his hand. There were a hundred tiny, multicolored beads of chemistry in his palm.

"Speed: pharmaceutical."

"Just like the East Germans take in the Olympics. We stole it from our mom." I had to take the offer seriously. Mrs. Ortley's family owned a pharmaceutical company.

"Each color goes off at a different time. Next two hours, you're rocket man."

"It'll give you the reflexes of a cat." He poured a tiny mountain of granules into my hand.

Knowing we were going to lose the game, I thought I had nothing to lose. I licked the beads of medication off my palm with the tip of my tongue.

By the time we hit the field, I was as fidgety and twitchy as a dog with distemper. The bleachers were packed. My parents had brought Alfie. My mouth was dry and spitless, and my socks refused to stay up. Even in the half speed of warm-up drills, the soccer ball was a blur. The Gambian dribbled it like a yo-yo, with his lethal feet. He wasn't six foot six, he was six foot four. He kept it popping in the air in front of him. First kicking the ball with his left, then twice with his right, then kneeing it up high in the air, he bounced it off his head, then cartwheeled his legs backward and nailed it with a bicycle kick over his right shoulder. You would have thought it was shot from a cannon.

When the whistle blew, something strange happened to my neurotransmitters. Though I felt like I was moving in slow motion, as I positioned myself to cut off the angle of the shot that was a few strides away, the speed combusted with the adrenaline of my pounding heart, and the force of the silent explosion within me spread out across the field in shock waves I could almost see. Suddenly, the Gambian and the ball and everyone and everything else on the field seemed to slow down as well. It was my time.

As the ball left the Gambian's foot, I could see the black-and-white hexagons that made up its surface not as the usual gray swish sailing past me, but as a sphere, moving as slowly and spacey as a blob in a lava lamp. I could see the seams of the ball, and I had all the time in the world to reach out and grab it. And best of all, when my arms closed round it and brought it to my chest, my ribs did not crack. My heart did not stop.

Though I didn't do a very good job of booting back to my teammates (my kick barely reached the midfield line), I had made a save. Having made one, I was able to make another, and another. And suddenly, playing goalie seemed as simple as playing catch with someone who doesn't want you to catch the ball.

I wondered why they called it speed. For the next ninety minutes, the soccer ball and the action on the field and the very spin of the planet slowed down enough for me to step back into the body that had seemed to belong to a clumsy stranger when I was suiting up.

When the final whistle blew, the score was 0-0. Though it went down in the record book as a tie, it was a victory. My teammates hugged me. The coach patted me on the back so hard it hurt, and told me, "Whatever the hell got into you today, Z, I want you to bottle it and bring it to the next game."

As I looked over his shoulder, the Ortley twins were giving me the thumbs-up sign. I ran to the red-haired pharmacists. "The speed's fantastic."

"We got you good, didn't we?"

"I'll buy as much as you can steal from your mother." The

twins staggered with laughter. Chas pulled a packet of capsules out of his pocket. “Not here,” I whispered. My parents were walking over; Alfie was barking.

He tossed me the packet right in front of everyone. As I grabbed it, I saw it was Contac. The cold medicine.

Now, if my life were a Disney movie, the idea that I had done it without drugs, on my own, would have made it all the sweeter. But I was depressed. For ninety minutes I’d actually thought I had found a cure for being me.

We lost the next game 5-0. But we won the following two. The coach said I had potential. I wasn’t sure for what, but by the time the season was half over I was getting used to being the person I felt myself becoming. I was not sure who he was. But I had stopped reading the *DSM* and no longer looked for myself in the faces of the crazies Gunderfeldt had photographed.

St. Luke’s had a sister school, the Essex Academy for Girls. On the second Saturday of October, they held a fair with booths and carnival games of chance and skill, ring throws, and guessing the number of jelly beans in a five-gallon water bottle, all to raise money for the scholarship fund. And because it was for a good cause, the seniors on the St. Luke’s sports teams were encouraged to lend a hand.

It wasn’t my idea to spike a bowl of punch solely reserved for Essex girls with grain alcohol. But I knew about it. The prospect of getting bombed with a bunch of girls on the sly in front of everyone appealed to me. Since the Contac incident, I hadn’t stopped smoking pot, but at least I had realized that toking up the night before the game wasn’t going to help me keep the ball out of the net.

You could say I was on the road to recovery. And most definitely, we would have gotten away with it if one of the girls hadn’t started the rumor that the punch was laced with acid. Which prompted another girl who was merely three glasses tipsy to convince herself the headmistress had horns, and to shriek, “I’m having a bad trip!”

To get out of being arrested we had to show them the bottle of grain alcohol, which in fact is as colorless and tasteless as acid. And though the police weren't called in, we were in the kind of trouble that gets you kicked out of a school like St. Luke's.

The honor society was convened. Our parents were told. If the entire starting lineup hadn't been involved, we would have all been kicked out, tuition not refunded. To avoid the embarrassment of having to cancel the rest of the soccer season, and thereby advertise our collective lack of character to the other prep schools in the state, it was decided that we would be allowed to stay in school and, if we kept our noses clean, graduate.

The punishment was nonetheless severe. In addition to losing all senior privileges and having to wait on the underclassmen's tables at lunch, each and every college and university we were applying to would be informed, in detail, of our shameless behavior, i.e., none of us had a snowball's chance in hell of getting into any college that was any good. Or that our grades and ambitions had been pointing us toward.

My father, displaying the snobbery of a person who has been excluded from a club he both loathes and envies, had only been half joking when he told me on one occasion, "If you don't get into an Ivy League college, you might as well go to Vietnam." But he was dead serious about wanting me to go to Yale.

What had been a long shot, even with my bogus trophy for antidrug journalism, had become an impossibility, now that my résumé was rounded out with varsity goalie who spiked the punch with grain alcohol. In my father's narcissism, he was convinced I had done it to spite him. Willy had said no to my father for years. But my no came as a shock and a personal insult.

He picked me up after school the day the headmaster had passed judgment (my driving privileges had already been revoked). Dad was alone. He never went anywhere without my mother.

As soon as I closed the car door, he tore in. "What in God's name were you thinking?"

"I wasn't thinking, I was just trying to have fun."

"Fun . . . Do you know what your fun has cost you? Do you realize what you have done to yourself?"

"I'll still get in somewhere."

"I didn't bust my ass to get to this point in life for you to end up 'somewhere.'"

"I'm the one who has to go to a shit college, not you."

"I've had to pay for it in more goddamn ways than you can imagine, sonny boy." My dad took it as an insult when his mother called him "sonny boy." So did I.

"I've had to pay, too."

My father's head slumped forward and swiveled toward me, like a water buffalo who's just been shot. "Is that what this is all about?"

"You're the psychologist. You tell me."

His tone of voice changed. "I just don't want you to look at yourself in the mirror at forty and say, 'You bastard, you. Look what you've done to me.'" I wasn't sure whether the antecedent of "me" was my father or myself. He said it like our fate had already been prescribed.

"I did it to me, not you."

"You're my son." I liked hearing that. "You're an extension of me . . . of my DNA."

"Jesus Christ, Dad, why'd you even have me?"

"What?"

"I know how it happened. Jack died, Mom was depressed, you just wanted to have another kid to take his place, get her back."

My father looked at me as if I had just hit him. A car honked as he swerved over to the side of the road. "That's what you think?"

"I've known it forever."

"We didn't have you to take Jack's place. I wanted another child because I was lonely. And somebody I tried to help wanted me dead. Me and my whole family, erased. And I thought to myself, you bastard, you want to deny my life. And I'm by God not gonna let you do it. I was not going to be denied. I was alive. And I was going to have another child to prove it. Having you kept me going, made it all right. Better than all right."

My father sat in silence, looking out at the horizon, nodding every so often as if he were carrying on the rest of the conversation inside his head. As if I could read his mind, I watched him look back at the dark days of Casper. Finally, my father sighed, like he'd made everything perfectly clear by osmosis. "Do you understand?"

"What?"

"I love you."

I owed that to Casper, too.

That night, I stayed up until the sun rose, rewriting the essays I had been working on for my college applications. I didn't understand my father, but he had given me an idea. It wasn't the one he had been trying to convey.

After a few days, my father mellowed on the subject of my disgrace. But not much. As he watched me send off my college applications, I heard him tell my mother, "Well, now that he's blown his chances at Yale and the Ivies, he'll have to start off where we did. Some second-rate state school."

"It's not the end of the world, Will." My mother tried to give him a hug; he shrugged it off.

"No. There are worse things that could have happened to Zach . . . I guess."

My father did not like to be ambushed by life. He had kept us from being done in by dented cans of tuna fish, drowned by hip boots. He had taught us how to perform tracheotomies and, in spite of his farm boy prudery, had made sure his daughters knew enough about birth control and the horrors of sexually transmitted diseases to get them through high school and college without getting knocked up—no small feat in those days. He had even protected us from Casper Gedsic. But the fact that he could not protect us from ourselves made him feel defeated and depressed.

I was not the only one who disappointed my father during the course of my last year at high school. For six months now, Fiona had come up with a good reason to refuse every invitation to come out to the country. At the age of twenty-seven, my oldest sister lived alone with paintings that could not find a gallery and a cat her last roommate had left behind along with a foldout bed when she had gotten married.

Shortly after my fall from grace, my father called Fiona and invited himself to dinner at her place. He wanted to see his daughter by himself. Fiona agreed, then promptly outflanked him by immediately calling my mother and insisting she and I come, too.

She lived seven floors up on the top floor of an old pickle warehouse on Spring Street that smelled of brine. There was no elevator. We arrived two hours early and climbed the stairs quickly; Fiona wasn't ready. T-shirt, ripped shorts, dirty hair, and, even for a warehouse, it was a mess. Dad apologized for getting the time mixed up, but I could tell he had wanted to catch her off guard. If my father had wanted to catch her with a man, he was disappointed.

None of us had ever been to her loft, or any loft. It had fourteen-foot ceilings and a pull toilet and a bathtub that used to be a pickle barrel. A mattress on the floor at one end, a ratty old couch by the dirty windows at the other, it seemed like she was camping out rather than really living there. My father noted that any agile sex offender could climb up her fire escape, and my mother wished there were bars on her windows and worried aloud about who would hear her daughter if she called out for help. Fiona nailed her canvasses right to the walls, and there was paint splattered on everything, including Fiona.

When we arrived, Fiona was just about to go out and shop for our dinner. My father stayed behind while my mother and I descended the six flights we had just climbed and went out on the street to help her buy groceries. Fiona got everything you couldn't get in the country and she knew my father liked: smoked whitefish from Canal Street and oxtail from a butcher on Mulberry, and she insisted on not letting my mother pay for anything, even though she was broke.

When we climbed back up the stairs with the bags, Fiona started to sing "Wimoweh." Mom asked us what was so funny. It was good to see her until we walked in the door. Dad was standing in front of a large, unfinished canvas of a family bunched together, as if posed for a snapshot, and obliterated by an opaque patina of beeswax and brown pigment that was just the color of shit. My father was holding a paintbrush as long as a yardstick in his hand.

"What are you doing?" Fiona's voice was as sad as it was angry.

"The eye wasn't quite right."

"My God, Will." My mother wanted to say worse than that to him.

"Don't ever touch one of my paintings again, please." Fiona dropped the groceries on the counter and opened a bottle of wine.

My father held out his hands and gave me a "What? Me?" look. I was embarrassed for him and got on Fiona's bicycle and rode to the other end of the loft.

"I was just trying to help." He waited for Fiona to say something. When she didn't, he pushed on. "Do you think you have something special to say as an artist?"

"What do you mean?"

"Well, you know, like Picasso or Matisse or Jasper Johns or Rauschenberg? They show you something you haven't seen before."

"You mean 'original'?"

"Yes. Do you think you have something original to say?"

"Do you, father?"

My mother stopped washing the dishes. I pedaled back to watch.

"Yes, I think I've broken some ground."

"But not like Freud or Jung or Skinner or Wilhelm Reich."

"Reich believed in flying saucers."

"Let's stay on the subject."

"You're mad I touched your picture."

"Yeah, I am."

"Well, I'm not mad that the father in all these pictures is me. I just thought I'd give one of them the right color eyes." It was a decidedly awkward dinner.

When we climbed back down the stairs an hour and a half later and got into the Volvo, my father turned to my mother and said, "I just want what's best for my children."

Dad was still digesting the punch bowl and the Fiona dinner when a certified letter arrived from Lucy. She was twenty-five by then, in the start of her second year in Columbia's PhD program in psychology. My father had had to pull strings with more than a few old colleagues to get her admitted. But once there, she had done him proud, dean's list, in fact. It still amused Lucy to tell people she was adopted. And thrice engaged, she continued to go through men like toilet paper. And as of late, she had developed the habit of dyeing her hair a different color every other week. She looked best as a redhead.

It was my father's idea that she become a psychologist. Lucy wasn't really interested in psychology, but she knew enough about psychology to realize that by staying in my father's shadow, she avoided becoming a target for him. Her favorite part was arguing with Dad in shrink talk about the collateral damage his madness had inflicted on us as kids. Which, now that I think about it, drove my father crazy. But all in all, he was proud of her, proud that she was joining the guild of his dark art. He talked about the research they would one day conduct together, and genuinely thought she was on the road to his idea of happiness until he opened that certified letter.

He wouldn't let me read it, but from the argument that erupted between him and my mother after she had read it, the salient points conveyed on that single sheet of onion skin were, not necessarily in this order: A) She loved them. B) She didn't want to become a psychologist, because it was depressing. C) She had quit graduate school and was on her way to Morocco to work in an orphanage. D) She was sorry, "but I need to establish an emotional boundary between my life and yours." My father read that part aloud. Twice.

The letter also included a check for $12,153, the amount my parents had spent on room and board and tuition for grad school.

A) through D) upset him on so many different levels, he chose to focus on the most superficial part of the kiss-off, the check. "She thinks sending me a check makes this all right?"

"I think it's Lucy's way of trying to take responsibility for her actions." My mother's lips trembled as she handed the letter back to my father. Her eyes watered up, but no tears fell.

"Dropping out of the graduate school I had to beg to get her into in the first place is responsible? And running away to an African orphanage is taking responsibility? She should have at least had the decency, the backbone, to tell this to my face. Putting it in a letter is cowardly."

"Will, she said she was sorry. She knew you'd try to talk her out of it, and you would have."

"You think this is a good idea?"

"No, but she's twenty-five years old. And what we think doesn't really matter."

"And what's this horseshit about emotional boundaries?"

"I can suspect what she might be referring to." My mother glanced in my direction. Whatever she thought Lucy meant, she didn't want it discussed in front of me. "But since I didn't write the goddamn letter, I suggest you ask your daughter that question yourself."

"I would, but as you seemed to have failed to notice, she was careful not to include her phone number or the name of this orphanage. Did you notice the return address on the envelope is the American Express office, Tangier?"

My mother gave in to her tears. "I should have known she was up to something when she asked me to mail her her bathing suit."

"Why didn't you tell me?"

"It was just a bathing suit!"

"She's going to wear a bikini at the orphanage?" At first, it was a relief to have their disappointment directed at someone other than me. The check fell out of the envelope.

"Where do you think she got the twelve thousand bucks?"

"Please stay out of this, Zach."

"Her brother's raised a valid question. How does a girl who's trained for absolutely nothing, whose only previous job experience was being a camp counselor, get someone to give her twelve thousand dollars?" I didn't like where my father's paranoia was taking him.

Gray squawked on the sill. My father slammed the window, just missing the old parrot's claws. "She always wanted to marry an African prince. Remember the Christmas she insisted we get her a black doll?" My father was showing his own colors as he free-associated a pattern to Lucy's betrayal.

"Dad, you can't honestly think Lucy's getting money for sleeping with a black prince?" In truth, I thought it was kind of a cool idea.

"Anything is possible. She got the money from somebody. Her marketable skills are limited. She's pretty, agreeable, not too particular . . ."

My mother slammed down her coffee cup so hard against the table it shattered. "I won't stand for you talking about your own daughter that way!"

"When a daughter of mine carries on like she's a cross between Baby Jesus Christ, Marilyn Monroe, and Job, what am I damn well supposed to think?" I didn't like the way he said it. It made me wonder what he said about me behind my back.

"I think it's great she's going to work in an orphanage."

"Sadly, Zach, that doesn't surprise me."

The next body blow to my father's fantasy of his family was delivered by Willy. He, like Lucy, chose not to deliver it in person. He didn't even hand in his resignation in writing. He called and talked to my mother, and asked her to relay the bad news to Dad. Willy had decided to give up premed at Princeton to study art history. What's more, he was going to spend the next semester studying art in Florence.

My mother didn't think she'd heard him correctly, and made him repeat it. I was listening in on the other line. "I thought you wanted to be a neurologist."

"It doesn't suit my sensibilities any longer." His voice had gotten *Masterpiece Theatre*-ish since he went to Princeton. "My aesthetics have changed."

"Willy, there's nothing wrong with art history, but you don't even like museums." That's what I was thinking.

"I do now."

"But it's such a drastic change."

"I've been thinking of making a run in this direction for a while." Still the long-distance runner.

"I'm not sure your father will pay for Florence." My mother said it like the city was a girl.

"He doesn't have to. Professor de la Rosa has fixed it for me to get a fellowship."

"Who's this professor de la what's-it?"

"Visiting lecturer. He's a curator at the Tate. He says I have a great eye."

"You're going to have to tell your father this yourself." My mother handed the phone to Dad.

My father listened patiently as Willy laid out his plan. He did not interrupt. He listened carefully, then inquired politely, "Are you finished?"

"It's not the word I'd use for it."

"Willy, being your father, I've known you for a long time, and I'm for you in the long and the short run. And I think you will regret this decision."

"I think you think you know me."

As my father hung up the phone, my mother said, "At least he's not dropping out of Princeton."

"You're right, Nora, it could get worse." My father went to the liquor cabinet, and with careful deliberation, mixed himself a Manhattan with a fresh slice of orange. He waited until his cocktail was finished to explode. "Christ almighty! Companies pay me tens of thousands of dollars to tell them what to do.

Governments hire me to think about their goddamn problems. You'd think one of my children would listen to me when I give them advice."

"I listen to you, Dad."

"You try."

In the weeks that followed, every day began and ended with a Sock Moment. Sometimes my father would become becalmed in the middle of the day. My mother would leave him at their desk to Xerox something or make a cup of tea and come back and find him holding the glass paperweight with the giant antidepressant entombed within its sharp-edged clarity. He'd stare down at it with a grimace, as if it were a splinter that he could not see well enough to remove from his flesh. She would pull him back from wherever it was he'd drifted with the weight of her hand on his shoulder and the gentle reminder, "We still have work to do."

After the mixed bag of tribulations his children had hit him with, my father was on his guard. My grandmother Ida said that bad news comes in threes. Dad knew better. He was on the lookout now. He didn't say it out loud, but I could tell he thought it was his fault we had strayed from the trajectory he had plotted for our lives. He had become complacent, self-satisfied, bourgeois in his gentrified barn. Worse, middle-aged—that is, if he were going to live to be a hundred and six.

At the age of fifty-three, my father bought a slim volume titled *Royal Canadian Air Force Exercise Plans for Physical Fitness* and a set of barbells. Dad began to do push-ups, sit-ups, squat thrusts, and curls while he dictated breathlessly to my mother about the latest final solution for troublesome thought: Zimelidine, the first of the fabled SSRIs to hit your local drugstore. If you'd taken it, you might know it as Normud, later banned due to side effects that included Guillain-Barré syndrome, exanthema, arthralgias, and, according to some, suicidal ideation.

Lazlo had been in Europe most of that fall. He no longer dealt in garbage. He bought and sold companies. "Garbage that doesn't know it's garbage" was how he put it. My father called him about Lucy. Lazlo got somebody who worked in Tangier to check on her. She was indeed working at an orphanage.

My mother placed a call to Lazlo as well. Not about Lucy; she was worried about my father. When Lazlo heard about the barbells, he called me. "How mad is he?" Lazlo was in Zurich.

"He's pretty pissed off."

"No, I mean, how nuts is he?"

When I told Lazlo about how my father was convinced that Lucy was being kept by an African prince, Lazlo exhaled a laugh. He always laughed at sad stories.

Lazlo invited himself for Thanksgiving that year. It was his way of checking up on my father. He arrived early in the day, long before the bird had gone into the oven. It had been cold the week before, the ground frozen solid, the river laced with ice, but overnight a warm air mass mugged New Jersey. The mercury was in the sixties. Steam rose up off the frozen fields as Lazlo pulled into our drive, top down, in a brand-new fire-engine red 4.5-liter six-passenger Mercedes-Benz convertible.

My mother wasn't amused when my father called out, "Lazlo, in my next life, I want to be you!" Lazlo, now forty-eight, a bald spot, a shag, and a Fu Manchu mustache, had a twenty-four-year-old blonde cuddled up next to him, who wore a tube top, cowboy boots, and a fringed leather jacket.

When Lazlo announced in a stage whisper, "I think she's too old for me," my mother laughed, mostly because my father thought it was funny, and it had been a month since she'd seen him smile.

The blonde's name was Ula. And Lazlo swore she had an MBA, even though they had met while she was a first-class stewardess for Scandinavian Airlines. She looked at my mother, my father, me, and the barn, pronounced us all, "Fantástico" in a Swedish accent.

I thought my father was just pretending to like the red Mercedes so as not to make my mother jealous of Ula. But when

Lazlo and his Swedish babe went inside, Dad stayed out on the lawn, staring at Lazlo's red lacquered ride. After a while, he opened the door and sat on the cream hide and gripped the wooden steering wheel, and smiled at himself in the rearview mirror.

Fifteen minutes later my father was still sitting in the Mercedes, going nowhere. Lazlo went out to check on him. I followed.

"I've always wondered how the world looks from a car like this."

"If you weren't such a cheap bastard, you'd buy yourself one." Lazlo put a finger to his nose and gave himself a blast of Dristan in each nostril.

"Even if I could feel comfortable wasting this kind of money on a car that becomes secondhand as soon as you pay for it, I'm too old to pull it off."

Lazlo tossed him the keys. "Take it for a spin."

My father shook his head no.

"He's scared he'd like it."

"Come on, Zach." In that moment, my father had not just forgotten about the punch bowl, he had forgotten I was his son. Stepping on the accelerator, popping the car into low, he fishtailed onto the lawn. When he saw the double Ss he'd just gouged in the sod he put down last summer, he laughed.

We stayed on the back roads. My father asked me to find a station. We tuned in on Pink Floyd. Dad seemed to like "Dark Side of the Moon." The sun was in his eyes. He reached into the glove compartment, found a pair of shades in Lazlo's hat. He put on Lazlo's dark glasses and beret. He looked like a white Miles Davis. All the while, the speedometer was creeping up on him. The Mercedes was a red tank. We were doing sixty down gravel roads, cutting corners with a drift. Then we turned onto the interstate. Pedal to the metal, our differences blurred.

We were doing a hundred and thirty-three miles an hour when we heard the siren. A cop car pulled us over. My father smiled as he handed over his driver's license.

When the cop asked for the registration, and I couldn't find it, my father laughed.

The cop looked at him. "What do you think you're doing?"

My father still had on Lazlo's dark glasses. "I'm a doctor returning a patient to the mental hospital."

The cop eyeballed me. "What's wrong with the kid?"

"Nothing. I'm the patient."

My father seemed disappointed that the cop let him go with a warning. We laughed as we turned back toward home. As we headed up our road, my father announced, "I'll never have a car like this."

"Someday, I'll get you one, Dad."

"From you, I'd accept it."

Thanksgiving dinner was at 6:30. Willy was in Florence, Lucy orphaning in Morocco. Not knowing Lazlo was bringing Ula, and to make the table seem less empty, my father had invited a German ethnobotanist and a French chemist who worked for a drug company. He'd met both of them the week before at a symposium.

My mother warmed toward Ula when the ex-stew changed out of her tube top and put on an ankle-length peasant dress that revealed nothing but a desire to please. And when Ula volunteered to mash the potatoes and make the gravy, my mother decided she rather liked the bombshell. The two of them made jokes about Lazlo's nose hairs and his Hugh Hefner–esque bachelor pad, and they laughed together about men's snoring. All of which gave me an unexpected glimmer of what my mother must have been like before she was my mom, or anyone's mom. It was a glimpse of her, not unlike the one the ride in that red Mercedes had afforded me of my father—I was happy they were not always the people they'd had to become.

My mother and Ula uncorked a bottle of white wine and were smoking Ula's cigarettes. By now Ula was doing all the cooking and my mother was sitting on the counter having a good time.

"How did you get your man?" Ula's accent was singsong.

"Organic chemistry. He asked to borrow my Bunsen burner."

My mother said it like the punch line to a dirty joke. Ula laughed, likewise.

"Hot stuff."

"Yes, he was . . . still is."

My father was in the hayloft that had been turned into a living room with an eighteen-foot ceiling. Logs crackled in the fireplace they had made of river rock picked out by hand.

My father was having a good time, enjoying listening to the French drughouse guy telling the ethnobotanist how brilliant Dad was. "You know, Will was the first to see the potential of the inhibitors in the reuptake of the neurotransmitter serotonin."

Usually, I tuned out when my father and his friends talked shop. But after the ride in the Mercedes, and being startled by the way my father had talked to the cop, and surprised by how my mom talked about sex with Ula like part of her was still a twenty-four-year-old babe, it occurred to me that I was missing something.

And so I listened as my father shrugged off the compliment. "Back in the sixties I was intrigued by diphenhydramine, and even before that with the synthesis of the first SSRI, zimelidine, from chlorpheniramine, also an antihistamine, but then and now the side effects worry me."

The French chemist tried to include me in the conversation. "Your father always worries about the side effects."

"Not that they listened to me."

The German was listening carefully. "Professor Friedrich, have you ever worked with natural drugs?"

"No," my mother answered for him.

The German looked confused. "But I was led to believe you worked with Dr. Winton."

"How did you come to hear that?"

"A professor of mine, Dr. Honner, had a correspondence many years ago with Dr. Winton that led him to understand that the two of you had worked together on a psychoactive plant native to . . . where was it?"

"Cool. Dad, why didn't you ever tell me about that?"

"Dr. Winton and I were colleagues at Yale, but I wasn't aware of any correspondence. You'll have to ask your professor about that."

"Unfortunately, my professor is no longer with us." There was a look of relief on my father's face. "Perhaps you know how I can get in touch with Dr. Winton?"

My father shook his head no. The conversation moved on like nothing had ever happened. I had to say something. "She was murdered."

High beams arced across the lawn and into the window. Fiona had driven out from New York with "a friend," i.e., a boyfriend. It had been years since Fiona had brought a boy home, and after the dinner in her loft, I was surprised to hear she was coming.

When I think back on it, I can see that Fiona kept men at arm's length for the same reason Lucy toyed with them. The smothering intimacy of my parents' union scared them. Back then I simply thought Fiona wasn't that into sex. I wasn't entirely wrong.

We were all in the living room looking out the floor-to-ceiling windows as Fiona and her new friend pulled up. They parked directly beneath us. The garden lights illuminated them. We all kibitzed as Fiona's "new friend" (that's what my mother called him) got out of his white BMW. He wore a houndstooth tweed suit, a mauve shirt, and a floppy bow tie. He looked to be thirty or thirty-one. "*Ja,* cute, but not my type," was what Ula had to say.

"What do Americans have against American cars?" was the German ethnobotanist's take.

The French chemist poured himself another glass of wine. "What is the name of your daughter's fiancé?"

My mother corrected him. "He's not her fiancé."

"Not yet, at least." My father watched the new friend pull a bouquet of flowers and a small gift-wrapped square out of the backseat.

My mother stood, craning her neck to get a better look. "I think he's called Michael Charles."

"I do not like people with two first names." Everybody laughed, and Lazlo lit a fresh cigarette.

"Well, if those flowers are for me, I think he's very nice." Everybody laughed again, except for my father. Dad chewed a dry cracker and observed Michael take a silk pocket square from his jacket and wipe away three specks of mud from his fender. He was about five six or seven, with very good posture, so he seemed taller. He had wavy brown hair and the profile of an Indian head nickel.

As he stood there bearing gifts, waiting for Fiona to finish reapplying her makeup and get out of the car, he looked up at the barn, which at night looked bigger and more impressive than it was, then over at the red Mercedes, then down toward the trout stream, visible through the barren branches of our wood, and smiled, not like it was pretty, but grinned and nodded as if to say, "This will do."

My father watched him just the way he watched groundhogs steal the peaches from his trees before he shot them.

When Fiona's new friend walked around to the passenger side of his BMW and opened the door for her, my mother called out, "Two points for gallantry."

When my sister stood up, Michael Charles slowly brushed the hair out of her face, took hold of her chin like it was a jewelry box, turned her head slightly to the side, and kissed her on the lips. I was the only one that noticed he had to stand on tiptoes to do it.

The Frenchman and the German clapped, and my father said to no one in particular, "He's good with an audience."

My mother didn't like that he said that. "What is that supposed to mean?"

"He knows we're watching. It's for our benefit, not hers."

The bouquet was indeed for my mother. Two dozen calla lilies. The gift was for my father's benefit. It was a framed black-and-white photograph Michael Charles had taken of Fiona over the summer. She had clearly known him longer than they realized.

Fiona was the kind of pretty woman who didn't photograph well. As soon as someone pulled out a camera, the smile would slide from her face. Her expression would change, her eyes would narrow, she'd stick her chin out and tilt her head back and look down her nose at the person who'd dared to try to capture her likeness. When you looked at snapshots of Fiona over the years in our family photo album, you can almost see her thinking *This isn't me. You'll never get me.*

But in that photo Michael took, posed in a shade garden, her face half hidden by ferns, he had captured a side of Fiona that was softly voluptuous, mysteriously exotic, and as fiercely intelligent as one of those plants that eats insects.

I could tell Fiona liked how Michael saw her more than my father did. My father said thank you and smiled as Michael pulled a Leica camera out of his pocket and photographed Dad putting his image of Fiona up on the mantle next to my bogus journalism trophy.

As my father carved up the bird, five minutes of small talk revealed that Michael Charles had grown up in St. Paul, Minnesota, attended Stanford Law School, and come to New York to practice corporate law at what he called a "white-shoe law firm." But he quickly added, "I realized it wasn't for me."

"White meat or dark meat?" my father inquired.

"I'm easy."

"That's good to hear. What *is* for you, Michael?"

"I started my own firm. We specialize in entertainment law. Actors, directors, producers, a few writers. Not many. They're pains in the ass, and they don't make enough money." His voice was casual and cocky, so matter-of-fact his candor came across as honesty.

"My son Zach's a writer." My head spun around.

Michael looked at me curiously. "You don't say."

"He won the state journalism contest." My father pointed toward the mantle with the carving knife. "But I think his real talent lies in fiction." From the way he said it, it was hard to tell whether my father was implying that he knew my prize-winning reportage about the dangers of drugs was not heartfelt, or that I simply was comfortable with something other than the truth.

"What was your article about?"

"It's too lame to go into."

Michael looked at me and smiled, not like I was the kid brother, but like winning the trophy made me worth getting to know. I liked the feeling. "Send me something you've written."

When I put down the peas I was carrying in, he handed me his business card. Fiona chimed in, "He's *my* little brother; I get ten percent." She gave me her usual kind of hug, more headlock than pat on the back. "When did this happen?"

There was no "this" to tell. Like most teenagers who aren't good at math or science, I daydreamed about the life of a writer—not the sitting down at the typewriter part, but the making sense of all the bad stuff after it's too late to do anything about it except write it down. Holding Michael's card made the fantasy take root.

Fiona whispered in my ear, "Do it. Michael knows everybody."

"Why entertainment, Michael?" My father had already rearranged the place cards. He put Michael across from himself, and sat Fiona and me at the other end of the table.

"On a personal level, I like working with creative people, helping them bring their dreams to life. And from a business point of view, entertainment's the future."

"How so?" My father gestured for him to sit down.

"Entertainment's what America knows how to make best. Dreams, fantasies, movies, television . . ."

"Everybody in Germany loves *Bonanza*."

"In France, too. Every channel, *Columbo!*"

The news cheered Michael. "Exactly. And I don't know what your politics are, Dr. Friedrich, but it seems a more honorable way for America to make a profit than exporting wars like Vietnam and making crap cars."

"That's an interesting way of looking at things. But what if we're exporting our anxieties?"

The French chemist poured a bottle of St. Emilion that he had brought. "That is why we are in the drug business."

My father laughed and focused on a more immediate concern.

"So, Michael, tell me about yourself." Dad asked him so many questions over the next three courses, you would have thought he was interviewing a guy for a job. Which, of course, in a way he was.

My father kept refilling Michael's wineglass, all the while making inquiries that seemed casual, offhand, unrelated, but I knew were designed to lull Fiona's new friend into revealing more about himself than he realized he was revealing.

"How did you feel about that?" "What did your family think about that?" "That's an interesting choice of words."

Most cunning of all, my father told embarrassing stories about his own youth to prompt Michael to treat him to anecdotes that he would not have otherwise shared with a girlfriend's father. My dad knew how to pretend he was a nice guy.

I was on my way for seconds of turkey when I overheard Michael tell Dad about the Halloween he collected $147 for UNICEF by dressing up as a nun. The joke being that at thirteen, he had made such an unattractive nun, people in the neighborhood contributed more than they would have normally. My father ate that one up.

When I got back to my seat, Fiona was telling Lazlo and Ula about a line of clothes she was designing. When I asked her, "What about your painting?" she answered with a sneer, "There's this thing the Friedrichs never talk about. It's called making money." Everybody got it but me.

"So you make dresses and stuff?"

Fiona, unlike my mother, was always good at sewing. "Menswear." Before I could ask any more, she called out, "Michael, darling, stand up and show everybody how fabulous I am."

On command, Michael stood up and showed off his houndstooth suit. Everyone oohed and aahed, and my father smiled and said, "I was about to ask him where he got that."

Then Lazlo asked, "Do you have clothes that would make me look less bald, fat, and old?"

Ula called out, "Lazlo, you are the kind of man who is more beautiful naked than dressed."

"Ula, how much did Lazlo have to pay you to say that?" Everybody roared when my mother said that, not so much because it was so funny, but because they'd drunk most of a case of wine and it was Thanksgiving, and it felt like there was more fun to be had at our table than any other table in the world. *Gemütlich* was the word the German ethnobotanist used to assess the day as he and the Frenchman said good-bye.

I walked Fiona out to the car when they left. Michael was already behind the wheel. As she got in next to him, I heard him whisper in her ear, "I told you your father would like me."

When I went back inside, Lazlo and my mother and Ula were doing the dishes. As I looked at the business card I had been given, I listened as the three of them concurred—Fiona and Michael were, as my mother put it, "serious." And as for Michael, Lazlo put it best. "What's not to like?"

My father sat alone at the dining table looking into the sad eyes of the poodle that had ripped out Bambi's throat. My mother waited for him to give his opinion. When it didn't come, she said, "Well, Will, what do you think of her new friend?"

"I think Michael's intelligent, very well educated, ambitious, and, in general, I like him."

"Thank God."

"I just don't like him for Fiona."

"Why not?" I was mystified, but not surprised.

My father spoke slowly, as if he were a spy sending a coded message. "Some . . . women . . . might be . . . comfortable . . . in a marriage with a man like Michael Charles. I just . . . don't think . . . Fiona is one of them."

"Why not?" That was my mother.

"She's not that sophisticated."

My mother took exception, "Fiona has an MFA. She's very sophisticated. Why do you underestimate your children?"

"I don't underestimate my children, and I certainly don't underestimate Fiona or goddamn Michael Charles. I just expressed my opinion based on observation."

"Well, can you be more specific?" There was an edge to my

mother's voice. Ula and Lazlo were wondering if they'd made a mistake asking if they could spend the night.

"I will have this discussion with Fiona when and if I think the time is right."

"They're already engaged."

"Christ." My father picked up a meatless bone from the turkey carcass, took it outside, and gave it to Gray. Mother followed him out onto the deck. When they saw I was eavesdropping, they moved away from the house so I couldn't hear. The parrot waddled after them, calling out the names of the departed. "Fiona, Lucy, Willy . . . Jack . . ."

Lazlo glared at the parrot. "When is that damn bird going to die?"

"Parrots can live sixty years. Longer in captivity." I'd done a report on African grays in the eighth grade. "There's a gray in Los Angeles that has a vocabulary of seven hundred words."

"Well, this bird is going to bed." Ula headed upstairs. Lazlo, out of cigarettes, scrounged a half-smoked Lucky from the ashtray.

"Lazlo, what's going on? Why's Dad hate him?"

"Gray?"

"No, Michael."

"Your father doesn't like being a bastard; he just can't help himself." Lazlo took two more hits of Dristan. At dinner, he'd told everybody he'd developed a dust allergy.

"What do you mean, he can't help himself?"

"People ask him questions, he assumes they want to hear what he really thinks."

"He's not always right about people."

"Not always. But when he says something that seems crazy, especially if he pisses you off, it has a way of turning out to be true. Truer than he wished it was."

"You're just sticking up for him because he likes you."

"Once, I owned a company, part of a company. Sold scrap steel to the Japanese. We needed a president, good businessman. I find six, seem good to me. I ask your father if he'll meet with them, tell me what he thinks."

"And he told you which guy was the best and you hired him and he turned out to be great and you made a lot of money."

"No, wiseass. Your father tells me this guy named Slaussen, he's the best one, but I shouldn't hire him, I should hire the second best. I forget his name. And I tell your father, 'You're crazy, why should I not hire the best, the smartest?' And your father looks me in the eye, and I'm quoting now, and tells me, 'Slaussen's too tightly wound. In six months he'll either have a heart attack or shoot himself.' I laugh, I say, 'Thank you for nothing,' and I hire the best, Slaussen. First six months great, seven months, jumps in front of a subway."

"How'd my father know?"

"He told me there was something about the way the guy ate his steak that told him he was off."

"How'd he cut his steak?"

"Ask your father."

My father would not tell me why he was so sure Fiona wasn't "sophisticated enough" to marry Michael Charles. He said his concerns were no one's business but Fiona's. Michael called my father at work a week after Thanksgiving to invite him and my mother to lunch at a restaurant called La Grenouille. He said, "Fiona and I have something important to ask you."

Dad agreed to meet them, providing Fiona came to the country to talk to him first. Three hours later, she was on our doorstep. Clearly, she was eager to close the deal.

An ice storm had made the world slick and glassy. I was just being dropped off from school as she stomped out of the house; she'd been there less than fifteen minutes. My mother stood in the doorway, looking sad as she watched her daughter slip and fall in her hurry to get away from our father.

Struggling to help her in the failing light of that cold December afternoon, it looked like Dad was wrestling with his shadow.

When he reached down to help her up, she shouted, "Get away from me!"

"If I didn't love you, I wouldn't have said anything."

"I feel sorry for you." Fiona had skinned her knee and torn her tights. Her high heels sank into the snow as she teetered toward the BMW she'd borrowed from Michael. "No, I feel sorry for Mom and Zach, because they have to live with you." She couldn't find the right key to open the car door. "You can never believe anybody is just what they seem to be." If she hadn't locked the car, she wouldn't have gone on to say, "You're so busy psychoanalyzing the world, you can't see how nuts and paranoid Casper Gedsic's made you."

My father took her best shot without blinking. In the cold, his breath looked like steam. "Being right about me doesn't mean I'm wrong about your new friend."

Fiona slammed the car door, started the engine, and began to back out.

My father shouted after her, "Ask him yourself."

Fiona stopped the car and rolled down the window. "I already did."

My father wasn't prepared for that. "What did he say?"

"He's not gay."

I was stunned. Of all the things I suspected my father might suspect, that was not one of them.

"How do you know he's telling the truth?"

"I've had sex with him. Lots of sex."

"That doesn't prove anything."

"You'd rather be right than have me be happy."

My father looked like he was going to cry. I followed him back into the house, suddenly convinced he was even crazier than I was. My mother distracted herself by apologizing for burning the chicken. My father told her, "That's the least of our worries."

I was a high school senior; it was 1971. "Dad, if Fiona slept with him, he can't be gay."

"That shows how little you know about the world, Zach."

"You could be wrong, Will." My mother had scraped off the burned parts of the chicken.

"I wish I was, but I fear I'm not. She's setting herself up to fail. He'll need something she can't give him, and it will break her heart."

"You're not a prophet."

"If he likes to have sex with guys, why would he want to get married?"

"All sorts of reasons. Shame, guilt, fantasies that a wife will change his inclinations, a genuine desire for children. If he had the balls to be honest, I'd have respect for him. But to deceive her . . ." The more my father thought about it, the angrier it made him. "Christ, a hustler like him? He probably thinks being married will be a business asset. She's the perfect beard; she loves him."

"Why do you make everything so ugly?" My mother pushed her plate away.

"I'm answering Zach's question. Lots of homosexual men get married, Zach. The vast majority of them make themselves and their wives miserable by doing so."

It was as if he'd told me dogs walked on their ears. I had seen nothing in the world to lead to such conclusions. "Like who?"

My father rattled off a list of names, two of whom were shrinks who had come to our house with their wives and kids.

"How do you know they're gay?"

"Because they told me so."

"Why did they come to you?"

"Because strangers, unlike my family, think I'm an understanding man."

"What did you tell them to do?"

"Don't live a lie."

My mother picked up her plate and headed toward the sink. "That's easier said than done."

"I am not ashamed that I have done what I had to to protect my children." They weren't talking about whether or not Michael Charles was gay.

"I think you're jealous." It was the meanest thing my mother could think of to say to him.

"Of a chickenshit lawyer who doesn't have the testosterone to admit what he is?"

"You're jealous because he's ambitious, just like you were. And he's successful and young, and your daughter's in love with him, and most of all, because the world's still ahead of him."

"How could you think so little of me?"

"Because I think you're human."

"Yes, I am guilty of that."

I was not included in the Grenouille lunch. According to my mother, Michael Charles asked my father for permission to marry his daughter over a lobster salad, and my father grimly gave his blessings. Michael gave her a diamond-and-ruby engagement ring that my father told me he suspected was "as phony as he is."

Surprisingly, Michael and Fiona visited us often in the months leading up to the wedding. I couldn't tell whether Fiona had told him or not. My father believed she had, and Michael pretended everything was okay just to piss Dad off.

To Michael, he was reserved but polite. To Fiona, overly affectionate. In the photos Michael continued to snap as the wedding drew near, Dad always has his arm around her shoulders. And in more than a few, she's not looking at the camera but at my father's hand, with an expression that made it clear she no longer thought it belonged there.

He never discussed the question of Michael's sexuality or the reasons for his suspicions, at least not in my presence. But when Fiona and her fiancé weren't around or out of earshot, my father could not bear to mention his name without adding the word "chickenshit."

I liked Michael. He let me drive his BMW, he invited me to the movie set of *The Godfather*. Told Marlon Brando I was a writer. I liked him even more when I sent him my antidrug article, "What

Goes Up Must Come Down," and he called me and said it was "interesting."

I could tell he wasn't impressed until I nervously volunteered, "I made it all up. I wrote it stoned."

"Love it. You had me totally fooled. It's much better, knowing that." I also liked Michael because he had great pot.

I was surprised that my father not only wouldn't let Michael help pay for the wedding, but insisted on sparing no expense on this party he wished he was not throwing. A marquee tent, sit-down dinner for 150 people, eight-piece orchestra, open bar, and Veuve Clicquot champagne on tap from start to finish.

The wedding was scheduled for Saturday, April 17, the same week college acceptance letters went out. Knowing I wasn't going to get in anywhere I wanted to go, I had my mother check the mailbox for me. The Friday before the wedding, I was still waiting for the bad news.

Willy flew in from Rome that afternoon. Lucy was scheduled to arrive then, too, but she missed her plane out of Tangier and now was supposed to get in the morning of the wedding. Fiona said she did it on purpose. Lucy had written Mom announcing she was inviting her "new friend." We didn't know his name.

When my mother wondered aloud what she should write on his place card, Dad told her, "black prince." At this point, he was beyond caring. Just as long as Lucy didn't bring another chickenshit.

When I got home from school that Friday, the tent was just going up. A catering van and a party rental truck blocked the drive. Chairs and tables were being unloaded and set up. A dance floor that sloped downhill was laid flat across the lawn. The house was crawling with florists and workmen. A pair of handymen were repainting the front steps, fixing doors that didn't close properly and windows that refused to open. All the little stuff that my father had complained about for years but never got around to having fixed for himself was made right for the wedding Dad wished weren't taking place. At first I thought Dad wanted to make it look perfect because it wasn't. But as that weekend progressed, I began to suspect that he was doing it all just so Fiona couldn't accuse him of setting them off on the wrong foot when the marriage turned to shit.

Most surprising of all, as soon as I stepped in the door, the brother who had acknowledged me with a surly smirk or, at best, a "hello" that had sounded like a snarl since the Sunshine incident, called out to me, "*Ciao,* Z!" Willy, just back from Florence, called me by my nickname, a first, and actually sounded like he'd missed me. "Come up here and fill me in on what's happening in the asylum."

Willy was in his old bedroom. He was getting dressed. We had to be at the church down at the village for the rehearsal by five. Willy and I were ushers. After that, there was a rehearsal dinner. Michael had taken over the Ryland Inn so their New York friends could make a weekend of it.

In the hour or so he'd been home, Willy had taken down all the photos of himself straining across finish lines and winning races. The track medals that had hung from doorknobs and necklaced lampshades had been put away. Willy hadn't simply reclaimed his old room, he'd made it his own. His walls were barren, except for an old drawing of a guy tied to a stake with two dozen arrows sticking through him. The weird part was, from the expression on the guy's face, he didn't seem to mind.

"Good to see you, brother." Willy gave me a hug.

"Cool picture." I was so taken aback by Willy's friendliness, I didn't know what else to say.

"It's a sketch by Jan Mabuse, sixteenth century. I bought it in a flea market in Milan. Five bucks. It's Saint Sebastian."

"Patron saint of archery."

I was in shock: Willy actually laughed at my joke. "So what's the family been up to?"

"Didn't Mom tell you?" They'd talked over the phone.

"She said Dad had mixed feelings about Michael." Willy hadn't met him yet.

"He fucking hates his guts."

"What'd he do?"

"Nothing. Except Dad thinks he's a homo." Willy laughed, but I could tell he didn't think it was funny.

"Why did Dad say that?"

"He has homophobia." I'd read about it one of my father's psychology books; I was diagnosing the whole family now.

Willy tied his necktie thoughtfully. "Dad has a lot of things going against him, but not that." Usually Willy was the first one to say no to our father's pronouncements.

"Fiona told him he was crazy right to his face." It wasn't gossiping so much as stirring the pot. "She told him the thing with Casper made him nuts."

"Fiona is bold."

"You think he's crazy?"

"I'll tell you that after I meet Michael."

The run-through at the church went smoothly. Michael's best man was this actor who had won a Tony for a play on Broadway. He seemed nice, had dyed hair, and even though I hadn't heard of the play, everybody made a big deal over him. And he definitely wasn't gay, because he hit on Fiona's bridesmaids right in front of their boyfriends. Lucy was going to be maid of honor if she didn't miss her plane again.

The minister acted like he was an old friend of the family, and after he rambled on about how important love and home and honesty had always been to Fiona, even though he had just met her, Dad slipped him a check.

The rehearsal dinner was more fun. Michael's best friends from New York were interesting once they stopped talking about people I didn't know and places I had never heard of. St. Bart's, Todi, some restaurant called Elaine's—the biggest yawn was all the talk about the price of real estate. But they gave really good toasts, and some made up songs and poems about how Michael and Fiona met that were funny, and just dirty enough to make the minister blush and laugh at the same time.

The only person from Michael's family who showed was his mother, a doll-like little woman who wore a mink stole and a lot of jewelry my father told me was as fake as the engagement ring. Trying to make small talk, she announced, "They are going to give us beautiful grandchildren, aren't they, Doctor Friedrich?"

My father made a face like he'd just broken a tooth and whispered in my mother's ear, "Michael probably left the rest of his family home because they all have harelips and webbed fingers."

Michael's mother was seated next to Ida, who still hennaed her hair and still smoked Chesterfields through a cigarette holder. Time and cigarettes had turned her face as dry and wrinkly as an old alligator purse. Ida told the mother, "I had a dream they had twins. One dark, one light. Write it down, be sure to put the date, so you can see that I'm right. They're going to be the biggest, fattest babies you ever laid eyes on."

Michael's mother, unaware that Ida believed herself to have second sight, exclaimed, "Oh, Lord, I hope not!"

Ida didn't mince words. "The future doesn't care what you hope."

Homer wore the same suit he had had on that first day I tore the page, or at least it looked to be the same. His hair was the dull gray of an aluminum pan, but his beard was still black and as lustrous as licorice, except for a stripe of white that headed south from his lower lip that made him look like a very intelligent badger.

Taking in the spectacle of the rehearsal dinner, Homer rocked himself back and forth, and repeated the obvious in a cautionary tone, "When you're married, you're married."

After about the tenth time he said it, Michael's mother asked, "Is he going to be alright?"

Ida tuned to Homer. "Are you going to be alright, son?"

Homer thought about it for a long time before he answered, "No."

As dessert was served, Michael surprised everybody with a trio of guitar-strumming Mexican mariachi singers sombrero'd in costume. Fiona acted like she was surprised, but she must have known, and then they did a dance you could tell they had rehearsed. And when it was over, everybody clapped as he bent my oldest sister back over his knee and, just as her hair touched the floor, he kissed her neck like a vampire.

After dinner, Willy got up and mingled with Michael's and Fiona's friends. When he told them he was studying art in Florence, they were all friendly. The best part for me was getting so loaded I forgot I was worried about not getting into college, which required some serious inebriation, since all night long everybody kept asking me where I was going to college. Willy reappeared just in time to hear me announce "I'm giving serious thought about doing my undergraduate work in Saigon."

He whispered something in my ear. I couldn't hear what he said. Old R & B was blaring, and Fiona and Michael were getting down with their bad selves. No question, I had never seen her so happy. Or, at least, looking so victorious.

When I shouted to Willy, "What'd you say?" my brother pulled me into a corner and whispered, "Definitely gay."

"You're kidding."

Willy shook his head no. Michael waved for us to come over and join him. They were line dancing now.

"How can you be so sure?"

Willy looked at me quizzically for a long moment, made the same face my father did when he sized up a stranger, and told me matter-of-factly, "Because I'm gay."

I was staggered, and not just because I was drunk. "Seriously?"

"It's not a medical condition."

"No, no, that's not what I meant." Bombed as I was, in my mind I began to connect the dots I had never gotten about my brother. "I mean, that's great. If it's good for you, it's good for me." I meant it. He was the same person, only now he was so much happier, he could even be friends with me. I had missed him, even when he was living at home and didn't like me.

"Shit, are you gonna tell Dad?" My father was sitting at a table, smoking a Cuban cigar and talking to Lazlo and Ula.

"Dad's known I liked men for years."

"How many years?"

"I told him after I wrecked the Skylark coming back from New York that night."

I suddenly felt like I knew less than nothing about my family. Drunk, I wondered if they'd all have to turn gay for me to stop being strangers with them. "Wow, what did Dad say?"

Willy mimicked my father's slow, thoughtful voice, "That's why I kept you that extra year at St. Luke's. I wanted you to resolve your sexuality before you went to college."

"That's it?"

"He told me all he cared about was that I find somebody I loved." We watched as my mother took the cigar from my father's hand, tossed it out the window, and sat on his lap.

I didn't care about Michael Charles, but what did bother me was that I had so misjudged and so misunderstood my father. Suddenly, I felt like crying. "What happened then?"

"Dad spoiled it."

"How?"

"He told me the only thing I could do that he would have difficulty forgiving was if I let my sexual appetites distract me from a career in medicine."

It rained on their wedding day. Lucy called from the airport. Her plane from Tangier was late. She missed her flight in Paris. She had to drive straight from JFK to the church, and change in the backseat of the rent-a-car while her friend drove.

The church was packed. The organist played "Ode to Joy" twice to stall for time. Willy and I waited outside with the best man and the bridesmaids. Lucy's friend screeched to a stop in front of the church just as my father and Fiona the bride pulled up in the limo.

Lucy greeted us in Arabic, *"Assalamu alaikum,"* then added, "Nigel, where are my shoes?" That was her friend's name.

"I believe they're in the boot, darling." Nigel was tall, English, tieless, and rumpled. He wore sandals and drawstring trousers, and had a mustache and goatee worthy of the three musketeers, and hair like the lead singer of Led Zeppelin. Nigel pulled on a formal morning coat and popped a top hat on his head as he scurried back to the boot, i.e., the trunk. I guess he found her shoes. I was trying to figure out why he had a surfboard sticking out of his trunk.

"Daddy!" Lucy raced toward my father.

"Daddy!" That was Fiona. Her train was caught on the limo door.

My father stopped worrying about Fiona when Lucy got close enough for him to see she was six months pregnant. Dad glared at Nigel. Clearly he would have preferred a black prince. My father refused to shake Nigel's hand, turned his back on Lucy without so much as a hello, and walked Fiona to the altar.

My mother wept; my father ground his teeth through the ceremony. When it got to the part where the minister asks, "If anyone here has knowledge or reason why these two should not be lawfully wed, speak now or forever hold your peace," Willy and I were sure Dad was going to say something. He didn't.

My father didn't just ignore Lucy and her English surfer, he treated them like they were invisible. Which was hard to do, given the size of Lucy's stomach and the fact that Nigel was wearing pajamas, a morning coat, and a top hat.

Dad put on the same strained smile he had worn at my birthday parties when I was little. I felt bad for him. I wanted to do something for my father. I knew I couldn't make it right for him, just more bearable. Dad's new son-in-law made it worse when he gestured toward Lucy and the surfer, "Would you like me to ask them to leave?"

When Lucy heard my father whisper to my mother, "Keep that English bastard away from me," she began to weep.

"I hate it here."

"No, you don't, darling, it's a lovely party." While the rest of us gagged on the awkwardness of the situation, Nigel sailed above it.

"The hors d'oeuvres are wonderful . . . Yes, please . . . Thank you so much . . . How very kind." He had impeccable manners, dirty fingernails, and a la-di-da voice. But he wasn't snobby at all.

"I want to go back to Morocco."

"I think you're being unfair to your father."

"The bastard didn't even shake your hand."

"He knows I'm British. We don't shake hands." Nigel cracked me up. "If you ask me, I think your old man's being very cool about the whole scene. I mean, given you are preggers, and the baby already looks like me, and he hasn't produced a shotgun or let loose the hounds on my nether regions, I'd say he's shown admirable reserve. Definitely a cool cat."

Nigel told me that he had gone to Morocco to surf the break just south of Cádiz. "Wind off the desert holds the waves up." He had met Lucy on the beach and had gone to work at the orphanage "to get into your sister's knickers."

Lucy smiled. "You see why I love him?"

I began to get it when one of Michael's friends from New York asked, "What do you do, Nigel?"

Nigel answered with conviction, "As little as possible." Then he pulled a block of hash the size of a cigarette pack out of his pocket that he'd smuggled through customs and inquired innocently, "You don't suppose anyone would mind if I smoked a hash joint inside the marquee?"

Nigel and I lit up behind the portable toilets. Lucy abstained on account of the baby. Lazlo walked up just as we were lighting up. It was the first, but not the last, time I got high with him.

"Are you guys gonna get married?" I asked Nigel with a cough.

"Weddings are a drag."

I couldn't argue that point. "What about your kid?"

Lazlo giggled, then cleared his sinuses with a double blast of his ever-present Dristan bottle. "He couldn't be more fucked up than you."

"He/she/it will be fine."

"How do you know?"

"Lucy's magic." We watched as she danced with her stomach on the sloping floor.

When we went back in the tent, my father was sitting alone with my mother. Everyone was dancing but them—my father had never learned. My mother waved me over. I concentrated on not acting stoned. My father was too busy feeling sorry for himself to have noticed my condition. We were exchanging a look of misunderstood concern when my mother said, "There's something I have to tell you both."

My father rolled his eyes. "Nigel's gay?"

My mother didn't think that was funny. "I was going to wait until tomorrow but, well, maybe this will cheer you up." My mother opened her purse, pulled out a fat envelope, and handed it to me. The hash had me a beat behind the action.

"Congratulations, Zach. I'm happy for you and proud of you." My mother was in the midst of kissing me when I realized the letter was from Yale. I got in. They wanted me. I was staggered.

My father threw his head back and laughed. Sheer joy flooded his face with color. He took my hand and led me up to the bandstand and motioned for them to stop playing. My father held our hands up over his head like we'd won a prizefight and cleared his throat into the microphone. "Ladies and gentleman, the Friedrichs have yet another reason to celebrate today. Life has not only given me a son-in-law and a daughter with a grandchild on the way, but I have just found out that my youngest, Zach Friedrich, has been accepted at Yale University. It's the one in New Haven, in case you haven't heard of it."

I was stunned, stunned that I had gotten in, stunned that I had made my father so happy. Everybody clapped and patted me on my back. I had finally done something for my father he couldn't accomplish by himself. I had made his life more bearable; I had fixed the day after all.

After I'd basked in his and everyone else's compliments and good cheer, Dad asked, "How did you do it?"

High on hash and the possibility of happiness, I answered, "It must have been the new essay I wrote."

"What was it about?" My father was still grinning.

"Growing up with Casper."

My father stepped back from me like I had just stabbed him. "What in God's name did you tell them?"

My mother could tell something had gone wrong from the expression on my father's face. When he told her what I'd done, she looked at me like she wished I'd gone to Vietnam and gasped, "What have you done?"

BOOK III

NOVEMBER 1992

W*hat have you done?*

Twenty-one years later, Z was still trying to figure that out. At the moment, he lay sleeping on his stomach, face stuck to the mattress tag of his unsheeted bed. Z's snore was loud and strangely melodious. The hole his addiction had burned in his septum had turned his head into a pipe organ.

The room he was confined in was small and barren and smelled of chlorine. Just a bed and a footlocker. Sheets and a towel were brought in once a week; he used the towel but did not bother to make his bed. He had done that a long time ago. He accepted his punishment, and at the moment was attempting to sleep through it.

A TV, supported by chains from the ceiling in the corner, had been on all night. Sometimes, when he left it glowing, his dreams would be interrupted by voices from his past. He'd open his eyes and see old friends on chat shows promoting their latest movie, book, or noble cause. Before his lockup, the sight of them used to make him feel envious and lonely, and prompted him to call their unlisted numbers in the middle of the night "to catch up."

The awkward and prolonged silences that passed for conversation were far more embarrassing than the quick snub. Even if Z's confinement for these last months had included a phone, he knew there was no catching up. Two nights ago he heard his old friend and fellow drug fiend Belushi yelling at him. When he opened his eyes, he saw it was just *The Blues Brothers* on Channel 4. He did not think of his friends as dead so much as "missing in action."

This morning he had heard a novelist he'd been engaged to in another life tell *Good Morning America,* "Z and I were never that close. But I do hope he's getting help with his demons."

Z was awake now. He tried to begin each day with a positive thought. He said it out loud, "If you like superficial people, you can't blame them when they're superficial to you." He sounded like Homer. Lying on his back, belly-up in his boxer shorts, his skin was the color of a frog who had slept in formaldehyde. Even though he'd lost most of the weight he'd gained from the sugar in the one (usually two) bottles of white wine he used to consume each night to come down from the cocaine, Z was still as bloated as two-day-old roadkill.

Sitting up, examining himself in the mirror, he thought, *What has happened to you?* The easy answer was cocaine. The hard one he'd yet to figure out. As he ate breakfast—Kit Kat bar, Diet Coke, and a Marlboro Light—he remembered the day his father had told him, "I just don't want you to look in the mirror one day when you're forty and say, 'You bastard, you. Look what you've done to me'." At age thirty-eight, Z was two years ahead of his father's schedule.

Once, not so many years ago, Zach Friedrich had been, in the parlance of the eighties, "happening." He owned a loft in Tribeca—paid for with the screenplay he had written of his first novel, which he never got over not being produced, and did studio rewrites that allowed him a room at the Chateau Marmont and a leased BMW. Now all his possessions fit into the footlocker at the end of the mattress. It was empty except for some old clothes and a laptop crowded with megabytes of the cliché he had become: pitches and scripts no one wanted to read, and first paragraphs of novels he'd been too high to write.

As Z finished the last of his Kit Kat, he reached for a pen and crossed off yesterday on his calendar. Not being overly optimistic with regard to his cure, Z waited till the day was over before he credited himself with making it through another twenty-four hours without fucking up. There were fifty-seven Xs preceding the one he had just made: 1,392 hours without cocaine. The first few hundred were Spanish Inquisition hard. He had felt like he had poison ivy on the surface of his brain, a fiery rash of anxiety he could not balm and thereby control with a numbing, cooling snort of powdered distraction.

It was the feeling of control, the mastery of feeling, an on-off switch you could trust to turn on the lights inside you that he was addicted to. He knew now why the lab monkeys he'd watched with his dad bit into their own flesh when the alkaloid anaesthetic had ceased to flow—the sharpness of your own teeth, the pain you inflicted on yourself, was preferable to the helplessness of life in a cage.

At the beginning of his withdrawal, Z railed at the world and its hypocrisy, damned his friends who had traded lines with him at parties he was no longer invited to, and cursed lovers who made small talk about his being "such a waste of potential" while they continued to get wasted.

A few weeks earlier, day twenty-nine of his incarceration to be exact, he had had his second epiphany in the long-drawn-out end of his romance with cocaine. After 697 hours without his lover, Z was able to see that the intimate strangers of his life had not turned on him because he was a drug fiend. They understood addictions. He now saw it was pure narcissism that had inspired him to imagine that he had been spurned because of his contempt for the money and success. What his world wouldn't accept was that he ceased to be able to laugh at it *with* them. Worse, he had felt superior for burning the bridge while he was still standing on it. No question, a drug addict who wants the world at moral attention is a boring thing.

Now, on the morning of day fifty-eight, Z's brain no longer itched. It had been over a week since the urge to distract himself from his longing with a blast of dopamine had made him bite his knuckle and imagine eating one of his hands, i.e., he no longer wanted to trade his cage for that of the lab monkey with unlimited access to cocaine.

Which is not to say Z was entirely comfortable feeling human.

It took all his energy to pull on sweatpants and a T-shirt. He was wondering if a second Diet Coke would give him enough of a caffeine boost to get moving when his mind treated him to a third epiphany—the hardest part of giving up drugs, of escaping the alternate/synthetic universe of addiction, is not the cold turkey, the physical withdrawal from the drugs and the people he shared them with. The hardest and scariest part was figuring out how he was going to reenter and navigate life without the certainty that comes when you are misguided enough to believe that all you have to do to feel your lover's embrace is to reach into your pocket for a gram. How do you replace longing once that, too, has deserted you?

Z felt old. Back when his brain was still itching, he had had panic attacks, shortness of breath that made him hyperventilate till the numbness moved up his arms, and his brain told him he was having a heart attack. He reminded himself of his father, checking his pulse two and three times a day to see if he was still alive.

He was checking it now. His heartbeat seemed irregular, or was that just his imagination? He knew he had damaged himself. The only question was how much was permanent. Except for getting tested for AIDS—negative—Z had not been to a doctor in seven years. Z smiled at the thought that at thirty-eight, he was old enough to remember that once upon a time sex was safe and cocaine wasn't addictive. He wondered how he would go forth alone into the brave new world of the 1990s.

The prison Z had chosen to detox himself in was a thatched-roof pool house on an estate that had once belonged to the Ortleys. The bars on the windows had been installed to break the townies of the habit of breaking in and stealing the TV when the twins and their family went south for Christmas break. Lucy owned the place now. She'd moved in a few months after the car accident that had killed Nigel and their baby.

The "good news," as he heard his father once say, was that Lucy was alive and Nigel had turned out to be a surf bum with a very large trust fund. Lucy was seriously rich, and she used her money to help her escape the sadness of her stillborn life by adopting children no one wanted.

She had five. Eleven-year-old Leila, an Afghani with blue eyes and the nose of Alexander the Great was four when she lost her leg, six when Lucy adopted her. Annabel, twelve, was born in Colombia with a harelip. Lulu, fifteen, was the child of a Cambodian sex worker. Alistair was a blond nine-year-old whose parents were Swiss heroin addicts. William, sixteen, named after Friedrich, was tall, black, handsome, and almost totally deaf. His parents were killed in the Soweto riots by the South African police. Lucy had always had a fondness for damaged creatures, starting with Z.

Z heard the key turning in his lock—exercise time. He looked up through the bars of his windows as he tied his left sneaker and cursed. The sun was shining and the sky was as cloudless and unweathered and blue as a computer screen. It was easier to muster his lethargy into a run if it were cold, or rainy, or better yet, both. Z liked the feeling that he was being punished, even if he had to do it himself.

The door swung open with a creak. Usually, Lucy unlocked the door for her brother, but today his jailer was Leila. "Mom says I'm supposed to take you for your run this morning."

She stood in the doorway, backlit by the morning sun. Tall, slim, and sharp as a spear, she'd never worn a skirt because a land mine had blessed her with a plastic leg. Leila eyed her uncle with curiosity and mistrust. After a moment, the girl added with a backward glance, "I brought my bike so I could keep up with you." It was a girl's mountain bike that she'd just gotten for her birthday.

"I think the question is, can I keep up with you?"

"I'll go slow." Of all Lucy's children, Leila was Z's favorite, perhaps because she didn't trust him, perhaps because she was the most obviously damaged. Whatever, the sight of her made him feel ashamed for feeling sorry for himself. It was Z's idea to be locked in. When he had first shown up on his sister's palatial doorstep fifty-seven days earlier, he had been rightfully fearful that his craving for powdered companionship would torch his resolve, drive him to borrow, aka steal, a car. Or, if the keys were hidden, hitch a ride into the city in search of a line of relief.

His parents had no idea Z was less than three miles down the road. They hadn't talked on the phone in almost a year, and it had been longer than that since they'd stood in the same room. Their last conversation dealt with a check for a thousand dollars Friedrich had cashed for their son. It was still bouncing.

Z had arrived on Lucy's doorstep in September. The pool had just been drained. Hidden behind the stables, shielded from the main house by a stand of pines and a tennis court, Lucy and her children were the only ones who knew Z had come home to put himself under house arrest.

Z's sneakers were laced now, his stocking cap pulled low over his ears and unwashed hair. Leila stood in the doorway and watched him as he stretched out his hamstrings by perching his toes on the back of a dictionary.

"Mom thinks now that you're better, you should have this." The girl limped toward him and offered the key on the flat of her hand, fingers pressed tight together, the way you would offer a carrot to an animal that bites. If his sister had handed him the key, he would have said he wasn't ready. Embarrassed to be so fearful in front of a child who had been told she was lucky to have a stump below the knee, Z took the key.

He tried to distract himself from shame with polite conversation. "How's Alistair doing?" Alistair was born addicted to heroin. He was now getting over the measles.

"He thinks you're a werewolf."

Z growled and made a scary face. Leila didn't laugh. "What do you think?"

"Mom says you have a substance abuse problem."

"Your mother's being polite. I was, I am, I always will be a drug addict." Z remembered hearing at a Narcotics Anonymous meeting he had attended a few years back that admitting you were powerless over what you longed for was the first step to recovery. The reality that need was a life sentence was so depressing he had left the meeting halfway through to cop an eighth. He still had money then.

Z was remembering that the drug dealer he'd gone to lived on Mulberry Street, and he used to feed live mice to his pet snake. Z had stopped stretching to recall the dealer's name when Leila asked, "Why did you take drugs in the first place?"

"Cocaine made me think I was smart and brave and . . . funny." Curiously, he had never taken any of the drugs his father'd worked on. No pharmaceuticals, likewise no heroin, no methamphetamine, just cocaine (snorted, never booted or freebased). He used to joke that he used cocaine homeopathically. It didn't seem so funny now.

"Why did you stop?"

"It stopped making me feel good." Z didn't feel like having this conversation with an eleven-year-old. He wanted to start his run.

But Leila had sat down on the edge of the bed and pulled up her pant leg to readjust her prosthetic shin and foot. The scars on her stump looked red and angry. "How'd it make you feel?" She took a small bottle of baby powder out of her pocket and dusted her stump.

"Sick."

"If it made you feel sick, why didn't you stop sooner?"

It was the obvious question, the one neither Lucy nor the psychiatrist she took him to see once a week at the outpatient drug clinic in Summit had thought to ask. As long as his blood test showed no sign of the demon, they thought he was making progress. Even if they had asked him, he would have lied. Leila's stump merited the truth. "The truth is, I didn't realize how sick I was until I got a postcard from an old friend."

"What was on the postcard?"

" 'I am worried about you.' " Z had stopped at his ex-agent's office to pick up a residual check. The postcard was a tourist shot of a man and a boy in the surf. "Welcome to the Jersey Shore" was printed on it.

"That's all it said?"

"It resonated. You know what that means?"

"Hits a note inside you that means something." Leila was a smart girl. "Who sent it to you?"

"The man who taught me how to swim." The postcard was signed "CG." If Casper was worried about him, he knew he was in trouble.

Instead of taking a cab to cop in Los Feliz, Z cashed the check, hopped a bus to LAX, and called Lucy. He made no mention of the postcard, just said he needed to come home to get well.

"Did you thank your friend?"

"Not yet." He didn't know where Casper had gotten the postcard. It was postmarked about a week after a picture of Z getting busted had appeared in the tabloids, and was addressed care of the William Morris agency. He guessed Casper had gotten a guard to mail it. Z had written a letter to him, care of the Needmore Mental Hospital.

A few days ago, he had received a letter from the mental hospital informing him that patients committed by the court cannot receive correspondence from nonfamily members without written approval by their legal guardian or their physician. The letter he had written to Casper was returned unopened.

His niece had her leg back on now. "I'm ready, are you?"

Leila mounted her bicycle and started to pedal, pant leg rolled down, sneaker on her plastic foot. She worked the bike effortlessly. Z began to run after her. If you saw them, you would have thought them both whole.

He followed his niece down a bridle path and across a pasture. She deftly guided the knobby tires of her pink mountain bike over ruts and through puddles. Out of breath already, Z felt his fat shake and regretted having a Kit Kat and a smoke for breakfast. Pedaling standing up, absorbing the bumps with her knees, Leila built up speed as she turned up the hill. Z bellowed after her, "It's too steep for me! Let's stay on the flat and circle back by the house."

"You don't want to go there."

"Why not?"

"They'll see you."

"Who's 'they'?"

"Aunt Fiona, Uncle Mike, Willy, Grandma . . . they're all coming to our house this morning to talk about Grandpa's birthday party." His father was months away from turning seventy-five. Lucy had told him that the old man had not only made it clear he didn't want a party, but had threatened to check into a hotel the morning of his birthday if he heard a celebration was being planned. Friedrich wasn't always wrong when he said they didn't listen.

"I'm not ready for that."

"That's what Mom and I figured." And so Z pushed his body and began his slow assault on the hill. After all these years, he was still running after his character. When he got to the top, he held his hands up over his head in victory, and vomited.

Fiona and Lucy had been politely bickering back and forth for weeks about whether the big birthday bash they refused to believe their father did not want should be held at Fiona's apartment in New York or Lucy's place in the country. Fiona had argued that because she and Michael lived in the city, as did a great many of their father's friends, it would be easier for the city people to stay late if the party were at her home on Central Park West. Lucy countered that most of their father's drug company friends lived in New Jersey and were old and might not come if they had to go to the expense and inconvenience of booking hotel rooms in New York.

Both sisters thought, but didn't say, *If it's at your house, you'll get all the credit.* And though, like a pair of tag-team wrestlers, they never missed an opportunity to browbeat their father with the gone but not forgotten slights, unfairnesses, and disappointments inflicted by Daddy on their childhoods, each was determined to use the occasion of his seventy-fifth to convince herself, if not Daddy, that she loved him best and therefore was entitled to feel most shortchanged of his love.

Lucy, being so much richer than her big sister, could afford to be more passively aggressive in her competition. "My house has tons of extra bedrooms. You and Michael and your kids and everybody from New York can stay over with me. I'll get rooms for anybody who wants at the Ryland Inn."

Fiona thought, but didn't say, *I want to show off my apartment.* It was sleek and white and modern and had recently been featured in *New York* magazine. *Michael and I had to work our asses off to get eight rooms with a view of the park. We didn't get left seventeen million pounds.* Michael had left entertainment law and was now one of the three producers of the eleventh highest rated TV show in America.

Fiona tried to put her sister in her place with a casual blow. "Lucy, it doesn't matter to me, but we'll get a more interesting crowd if we do it at our place in the city. You know how Dad likes talking to people who are doing things out in the world."

Which made Lucy rise to the bait with her trump card. "We could let Mom decide, but if we have it here, I'll pay for the whole thing."

Fiona was furious when her husband called Lucy to say, "I think it's a great idea to have the party out at your farm." Lucy's "farm" was in fact a faux Georgian manor house with formal gardens. "I'll talk your sister into it, but I wouldn't feel right you paying the whole thing. At least let me get the band." Fiona was rich, but not as rich as Lucy; that was one of the crosses she had to bear. The other was the fact that Michael's gap-toothed blond assistant, Ben, was her husband's lover. Willy dubbed him "Ben the Bottom."

What infuriated Fiona more than Ben was that Michael wouldn't just get a band, he'd get somebody semifamous to play, somebody that would have cost Michael ten or fifteen thousand dollars, but because he was a hot producer, he'd get them to play for free, only Michael would make it seem to Lucy and her parents like he'd paid out-of-pocket. And most infuriating of all, she'd corroborate the deception. For Fiona, at the age of forty-eight, was still standing on tiptoes trying to cast a shadow that made her seem bigger than she felt.

As Z crested the hill, Fiona and Michael were trying to make up for lost time in the fast lane of Route 78. He still drove a BMW, only now it was a 7 Series. He was doing eighty, and the radar detector was on. Black car, black interior, black clothes. Life was shades of gray, but they, like most New Yorkers, dressed like every day was a casually chic funeral.

Michael was on the car phone to the assistant/lover for most of the ride out to the country. Fiona had not had sex with Michael since the Carter presidency. She wore her Walkman. Having forgotten her cassettes, she just pretended to be enjoying the music. She knew Ben the Bottom was not her husband's only "friend."

They hadn't argued about Michael's homosexuality (he was bisexual only regarding her) since that afternoon six months into their marriage when she had walked in on him and the interior designer he had encouraged her to hire to make his apartment feel more like it was hers. He said all there was to say when he told her, "Nobody wants to eat the same thing every night for dinner if they're not in prison."

The couples therapist they had gone to said that there were no rules about marriage as long as both partners are in agreement. Fiona's self-esteem improved after she started having an affair with the star of Michael's TV show.

Fiona was like the boiler in their co-op. Once a year, she'd boil over and break down and demand a divorce. Then they'd meet with their accountant and decide it didn't make sense to divide their assets until their twins, now teenagers, were in college. No question, Fiona was more sophisticated than either she or her father had imagined her to be.

Her siblings believed that the only reason she stayed with Michael was that she couldn't bear to admit Daddy was right. Contrary to what people thought and how she acted, she still loved Michael, not because he was faithful or true, but because she believed him when he told her she was the only woman he ever wanted.

Lucy and Willy and their mother had been talking about the party for almost an hour by the time Michael and Fiona joined them in the dining room. Nora sat at the head of the table, her back supported by a petit point cushion that read "Life isn't a rehearsal."

The look of Lucy's home was the then trendy Shabby Chic. Her money had come at the cost of such sadness, she delighted in encouraging her children to do their best to deconstruct the formality of the old Ortley mansion. Rollerblading, badminton, hockey in the ballroom were not only allowed, but encouraged. School projects were painted and glued and slopped on Aubusson carpets. Lucy wanted everybody to have fun—her way.

Lucy began to run through some of the ideas they'd been throwing around. Fiona cut her off with the expression she disliked most out of her own seventeen-year-old daughter's mouth: "Whatever . . . it's yours and Dad's party anyway."

Nora looked at her daughters. None of her children's lives had turned out as she had expected, as she would have wanted. Willy had changed for the better, Zach for the worse. But the girls remained unaltered. Fiona, in her Prada suit, accessorized with calm and the numbness that passes for sophistication, was still trying to be more grown-up than she was. And Lucy, a blouse purchased in Kazakhstan, a sarong acquired in Madagascar, arms bangled from wrist to elbow with bracelets bought in the stalls and flea markets of the second and third worlds, was still playing dress-up, masquerading as a college student at the age of forty-seven.

"Fiona, if it's going to make you miserable, we'll have the party at your apartment."

"It's not my party, it's Dad's."

Michael got up from the table. "I left something in the car."

"You're implying I'm giving this party for myself."

Willy watched his mother nervously spinning her wedding ring with her thumb. "Why don't you two grow up?"

The sisters turned their heads toward him. Lucy fired first. "I'm raising five children by myself. I think that qualifies me as more of a grown-up than you."

Fiona joined in on the attack. "If you don't like the way we're doing it, Willy, why don't you take over? You and your boyfriend can throw the party for Dad."

"Henry and I have a one-bedroom apartment. If you want to have a party for twenty instead of two hundred of your friends who Dad couldn't give a *shit* about, I'll be happy to . . ."

"Stop it, the three of you, this instant, or there won't be a party." Nora rapped her knuckles on the table. The siblings grew silent and looked at their feet. It unnerved and charmed her to see her three middle-aged children swirl back to the family dynamic of 1952.

Lucy broke the ice. "Are you gonna pull the car over, Mom? Or send us to bed without our dinner?"

Willy joined in. "Remember that time I hit you in the head with the fishing rod and you locked us in the Whale?"

Nora started to laugh. "I never locked you in the car."

Fiona liked this game more than the other one they'd been playing. "Yes, you did. They arrest mothers for doing that now."

Michael came back into the room, opened his briefcase, took out copies of the guest list his assistant had drawn up, and started handing out CDs. "Now, about the band . . ."

Nora held up her hand for him to stop. "No band, no dancing."

"Why?" Fiona protested.

"Your father doesn't like to dance."

"You mean he doesn't know how."

"I mean I have made up my mind there'll be no dancing, and the party will be at our house. That way, no one will feel short-changed."

"Mom, no one feels shortchanged. We like to fight."

"It will be a picnic lunch. I'll leave the food to you all, but I'll make the cake."

Lucy was looking at the guest list Michael had handed out. "Why isn't Zach's name on the list?"

Everyone looked at Michael. "I didn't have an address for him, and wasn't sure you wanted him."

"Of course we want him. He's our brother." Lucy was adamant.

"The last time he came to our apartment, he was so fucked up he spent half the time in the bathroom and the other half embarrassing our friends, pestering them for work."

"He's better." Lucy tried to sound convinced.

Willy was curious. He had sent his younger brother a long letter volunteering to pay for rehab but had received no answer. "When did you see him?"

Lucy lied. "A few days ago."

"Christ, why didn't you tell us? Where is he?" Whenever Fiona felt low about her own life, the thought of Z cheered her up.

"He doesn't want anybody to know where he is until he's well."

"That means he's still getting high."

"He isn't. He's been clean for fifty-seven days."

Fiona rolled her eyes. "Of course he's going to say that, Zach's an addict. Addicts are liars."

"He's not lying this time." Lucy was on the edge of tears.

"Lucy, I love Zach, too, but the way he's ruined himself is so pathetic and depressing, I just don't want to inflict that on Dad on his birthday. I mean, Jesus, remember the Halloween party we had? He came dressed as Casper." The table went silent. Fiona wasn't finished. "Our children still have nightmares about it."

"So does Zach, for Chrissake." Willy stood up. "After the shit he went through as a kid, it's no wonder he's a drug addict."

"We've all been fucked up by that."

"If you don't stop saying 'fuck,' I'm going home." Nora's voice quavered. Hearing Casper's name said out loud had rattled her.

Fiona hammered the point. "I'm not a drug addict. You haven't blown hundreds of thousands of dollars on cocaine."

"I've taken it, and so have you, Fiona." The sibling rivalry had slipped from Lucy versus Fiona to Willy versus Fiona.

"I've never taken cocaine in my life."

"Liar." Lucy, not wanting to feel left out, threw herself in on Willy's side.

Tears were streaming down their mother's face. Lucy handed her a napkin. "Congratulations, Fiona, you succeeded in making Mom cry."

"Zach is making Mom cry, not me."

Nora slowly shook her head no. "You like to think you did the best you could for your children. But you know that's never true."

"So does that mean you want Zach or not?"

Their mother said nothing. Pushing back her chair, she got up and hurried to the door. Fumbling with the lock, she cursed herself—"Damnation!"—then, slamming it behind her, walked out onto the lawn.

No one said anything until Michael's cell phone rang—he excused himself to talk business in the library. Willy shot his sisters a reproachful look as he collected his mother's purse and sweater and ran outside after her. The girls watched the wind swirl dead leaves up around their mother. One caught and crumbled in her white hair as their brother tried to button the sweater around her shoulders.

Fiona and Lucy couldn't hear what was being said outside. All they knew was that their mother was shaking her head no to something. As Willy guided her toward the car, she looked older and smaller and frailer than she had when she first sat down at the head of the table an hour ago.

Fiona spoke first. "What do you think's going to happen to Mom when Dad dies?"

Lucy answered solemnly, "You can't kill the undead." Their laughter reminded them that they were once and still friends. "Mom's tougher than Dad, if that's what you mean."

"What I guess I mean is, what's going to happen to us?" Fiona stared out the window.

"You mean after Dad dies or when we're old?"

"We are old. I'm worried about where I'm going right now. Christ, I'm forty-eight, and I pick a fight so I can have Dad's party at my apartment simply because I think you want it at your house?"

"I don't want to give him a party either."

"You're kidding?"

"Whatever we do end up doing won't be right with him. But if we don't do anything, we'll wake up depressed and tell ourselves we would have felt better if we had tried."

"You know what's the worst part of having our father for a father? You can't even take antidepressants without thinking about him."

"You, too?" Lucy slapped the table. The sisters howled with laughter, and then, after a quiet moment, began to weep.

Z woke up the next day hurting. The hill he had climbed to avoid seeing his family left his calves feeling flayed. Before opening his eyes he stretched out and absorbed the ache. His body felt the same way the last time he had made a run in search of character. Unable to find it at fourteen, it seemed unrealistic to think he'd have it in him to grab hold of at thirty-eight. But then again, no one had ever accused Zach of being realistic.

The bed of his pool house prison felt cozy. He opened his eyes and saw that he had bothered to put the sheets on the night before. It was the first time he'd done that since he arrived. A good sign? Or an indication that his subconscious had no intention of leaving the isolation ward Lucy had provided? Remembering his mantra of beginning each day with a positive thought, he cleared his mind by staring at the ceiling and waited for one to come. *I miss my parents.*

He was not at all sure that that was a positive thought. Z got up and tried to open the pool house door and found that he had locked himself in. The key Leila had given him was on the floor next to the bed. Where did he think he was going? Why did he not think he should go there? Z thought he felt no longing for the drug. Trouble was, he couldn't be sure he wasn't conning himself. He was expert at that.

Zach picked up the key and turned it in the lock. The hollow place he still felt inside him was not about a lack of dopamine, or a chemical imbalance in his bloodstream; at least, that was not the source of his denial.

He pushed the door open and cautiously inspected the day that faced him. The last leaves of fall were being blown from the trees. The woods looked threadbare. A November wind pushed the clouds across the blue, seamless sky at a pace that made him feel like his life was suddenly on fast-forward.

Z turned and looked at himself in the mirror. It was not a pretty sight. Opening a drawer, he took out the Swiss Army knife he had found on yesterday's run. He had offered it to Leila. She had refused. "Mom doesn't let us play with things that can hurt us."

Unfolding its four-inch stainless steel blade, he tested its edge with the ball of his thumb, then reconsidered and unfolded the scissors on the other end, and began to cut his hair. After that he showered, and nicked himself twice shaving.

Throwing the jogging suit he usually wore into the laundry hamper, Z pulled on the cashmere sweater Lucy had given him but he had not bothered to take out of the box. Then he opened the footlocker and pulled on the rumpled jacket and jeans he'd arrived in. His clothes smelled like the bar of a nightclub after last call: alcohol and chemical sweat. His jeans were two sizes too large for him. He found a rolled-up twenty in his pocket, both ends caked with snot and a hefty white residue of blow. If he had found it a month ago, he would have licked it clean. Z washed the bill with a bar of soap in the sink and pocketed his net worth. After he laced up his sneakers, he checked himself out in the mirror one last time. "You're not perfect, but at least you're human."

It was only after he was out the door and had walked past the piney curtain that smelled of Christmas and was halfway across the lawn, ankle-deep with a red and orange rustle of leaves, that it occurred to him that he had left the key in the lock. He guessed it was safe. It occurred to him to wonder, had he been locking the werewolf in, or the werewolves out?

Lucy's house was deserted, save for an illegal alien from Guatemala who cooked and didn't speak English. He guessed his sister was taking the kids to school. Lucy paid for the cook's daughter to go to St. Luke's with her children. It was coed now. Lucy did her part to change things. It was his turn now.

He had wanted to borrow Lucy's bicycle. When he discovered it had a flat tire, he climbed on Leila's. Knees hitting the handle bars, he pedaled the girl's bike out into what had once been his world.

Z told himself he had not yet made up his mind where he was going that morning, that he was on a bike because he needed exercise and his muscles were too sore to tackle a run. But his body knew his intention, even if he did not. His arms turned the handlebars left and right and left again. Pedaling with a sense of urgency, he was jockey and beast in one, riding himself to a place he was not sure he wanted to go—home.

He would have liked to have pedaled all the way to Greenwood, to walk through the house on Harrison Street, the place where he'd first been introduced to his family's ghosts. But Lucy's house was twenty miles as the crow flies from the banks of the Raritan. Besides, the dead don't stop haunting you just because you move on.

Turning into his parents' driveway, he told himself he was there in search of reconciliation. But the werewolf in Z knew that he had come to conduct a séance.

His parents' last three Volvos were parked side by side in the drive. They could bear to part with less and less as time went by. Z propped the bike against the trunk of a hickory tree, and took in the changes he'd missed during the years he'd been high. Two of the twelve pear trees he had planted with his father twenty years ago had died. One was twice as large as the rest, its branches reaching just short of the second story of the barn. His parents had finally gotten around to adding the balcony they had always wanted off their bedroom/office. A new retaining wall now tidied up the front walk, and his father had finally fulfilled his promise to the groundhogs and built a chain-link rectangle over his vegetable garden—a long trench was cut down the center so he didn't have to bend to pick the tomatoes and squash he no longer shared with the groundhogs. Z shook his head in marvel and disdain at the idea of his father reaping his harvest in a cage.

Z had hoped, as a child hopes, for things to be as they are in a storybook, for his parents to look up from their work, catch sight of him, run to the door, and greet the prodigal son of the drug age with open arms. It didn't happen that way.

He knocked on the door and waited. Gray squawked and flew to the rail of the balcony above and called out the names of dogs that had been dead for nearly thirty years. "Thistle, Spot."

Z knocked again. Still no answer. He told himself he would come back. He started to leave. But knowing that if he walked out on this, he would have run out on more than himself, he turned and tried the door. It was unlocked.

Stepping inside, he called out, "Mom . . . Dad." His voice was as tentative as it had been when he had come home from seventh grade with an F in math, or with that note from the headmaster recommending he see the school psychologist.

"Father . . . Mother." It deepened and became more formal, as he considered the possibility that something was wrong. He was in the kitchen now. He tripped over a dog dish with the word "Fred" written on it. He guessed Alfie, the Bambi killer, had passed on. The hook where they kept the dog leash was empty. Maybe Fred was taking his parents for a walk.

Relaxing, Z stepped into the living room. The slipcovers were new, but the furniture was the same. Willy's track trophies still lined the mantel, and there, in their midst, was the cup he had won for "What Goes Up Must Come Down." It wasn't so bogus after all. There was much to explain, and more to be ashamed of.

Dazed by the rush of memory, he went through the fortress of his youth like a sleepwalking thief. Opening doors and closets and cupboards, he was not sure what he was looking for or expecting to find. His bedroom had been turned into a guest room, his bed replaced by a foldout couch. From the scraps of cloth on the Hepplewhite table in front of the window that overlooked the valley, he surmised his mother had taken up quilting.

Z drifted slowly up through the floors of the house that used to be a barn like a plume of smoke from a fire that had been left smoldering for a long time. His parents' bedroom/office was untouched by time. He had never noticed their massive desk was exactly the same size as their bed. Work and sex, life's tasks. He had not had sex for—five? six?—months. He felt like he had slept alone for years. His parents' intimacy had always been enviable and suspicious. He imagined them working at their desk, naked.

His mother's old manual Underwood typewriter with its extra-wide carriage to accommodate a computer printout sat squarely in the middle of her side of the desk. The vowels of her keyboard were worn faint and ghostly with use. Drafts, rough and polished, were stacked like bricks and secured with rubber bands and identified with Post-its. Correspondence waited to be answered in folders filed in an antique wooden dish dryer, bought while attending a symposium in Oslo.

Halfway across the desk, just past the wall of framed photographs of her children, there was an irregular battle line, demarcating where her organizational skills gave way to chaos and his father's penchant for multitasked thought.

Her side of the desk and his father's were as different and clearly defined as halves of the same brain. Ideas for books and articles and research projects scrawled out late at night in red pen on yellow legal pads were shuffled in with the pages of texts—the half-done, the finished, and the forgotten. A note to himself written on the back of an envelope that contained his American Express bill read:

1. Change snow tires.
2. Buy potting soil.

3. Get Foundation to establish Prize for first scientist to replicate photosynthesis in lab—solves all problems, food, energy, environment.

Z wondered if his old man suffered from ADD as he pushed open the door to his father's closet. Minus the round window, it was the same as it had been on Harrison Street. It still smelled of cedar and shoe polish and dust. The stone ax heads and flint arrow points his father had collected with his father still lived in a wooden crate that bore the seal of Château d'Yquem. The split bamboo fly rods too fine to fish with were stacked in the corner. The mahogany chest of drawers no longer seemed so massive.

Still unable to resist the pull of the forbidden, Z opened the top drawer and looked for the loaded Smith & Wesson revolver nestled on a stack of clean handkerchiefs. It wasn't there—he wondered where it had gone. He guessed his father finally felt safe from ambush.

Wishing he could still say the same for himself, Z recalled the morning he had considered waking his father from that Sock Moment with the missing pistol. Remembering all that was secret and forbidden in their home, Z got down on his knees, pulled aside the suits and sport coats that hung neatly on hangers, and reached into the darkness for the old steamer trunk that had been such a mystery to him. He could still hear his father growl, "There's nothing in there that pertains to you." But it, like the revolver, had vanished. What else was not as he remembered it?

Back out in the hall, a narrow set of rough-hewn steps, bowed with wear from farmers' hobnailed boots, climbed steep as a ladder to a long, narrow loft that lay under the barn's slate roof. There was a skylight in the middle. Climbing the steps, Z followed the memory of an afternoon when he and Sunshine had lain naked on their backs, sharing a joint as thunder cracked lightning overhead.

The loft was just storage space now. Boxes stacked on boxes. His mother had written the contents on the side of each, but an old leak had rendered her neat script illegible, save for the word "fragile." A pane of glass had fallen out of the square window that wasn't designed to be opened at the far end. A swallow darted from shadow to light, alarmed at his intrusion. A rattrap, cocked but missing its cheese, lay unsprung by his old headboard. Mice had eaten holes in his mattress.

He picked up the grown-up briefcase his mother had bought him to bring order to his life. He opened it. Nothing, except for a single piece of bubblegum. He put it in his mouth and began to chew. Dust and mold and bat droppings made the mystery of the past palpable.

In the corner, squirrels had clawed a nest out of a cardboard box full of snapshots he presumed to be of his mother's side of the family. He recognized a five-by-seven of Great-aunt Minnie standing next to his mother at her high school graduation. When he tried to pick up the box, the bottom fell out.

There, amid the squirrel's nest of snapshots of the dead, he found an envelope, thick and long, with his mother's name typed out above their address in Hamden. The words "Deliver by hand" were written on the outside and underlined twice. Inside was a one-way unused steamship ticket to France on the Holland-America line. Z studied the ticket. His mother had purchased it with cash when she was pregnant with Fiona. She had paid for a single berth. She had intended to travel alone.

Z slipped his mother's unused ticket into his back pocket. Squatting down, collecting the snapshots of relatives he could not name but felt should be saved, Z caught sight of that old trunk his father had told him he could not open because he'd lost the key. It was hidden behind a thicket of broken furniture and cardboard boxes. The treasure chest of his youth had been moved, but it was still there.

Because he had been told it did not pertain to him, he knew it must. Was it his mother's trunk? Was she packed and ready to sail off from all of them on the Holland-America line? Was there another man? His father was not there to pull him back by the feet from the secret this time.

Cardboard boxes ripped and packing tape snapped as he pulled and pushed aside cartons stuffed with snowsuits he had hated and toys he had forgotten getting for Christmas. A broken chair he recognized from photographs of Hamden lost a second leg as he tossed it over his shoulder and clawed his way into the past.

The heat rose. In spite of the broken window, the attic was hot. He was sweaty and breathless from pulling away the domestic debris his family could not part with. Z picked up a screwdriver someone had used to stir a can of green paint. *Fuck the key,* Z thought, *I'm going to pry it open.*

As Z slipped the screwdriver under the latch, it popped free on its own. It had never been locked. Z opened the trunk slowly. The adrenaline rush of taboo denied accompanied the lifting of the lid. He did not know what he expected to find, but when he pulled the open trunk out into the light and saw its contents, he was disappointed. The mystery was nothing but old papers. Four stacks of the Friedrich Psychiatric Rating Scale, evaluations of patients made in 1952, all neatly tied up with butcher's twine.

When he was eight or nine, his father had tried to explain how his scale worked. He hadn't understood it then any more than he understood it now. But he could see that this diagnostic tool that his father had devised reduced happiness to a number. Was an 8.3 good or bad?

The people his father had tried to help back in '52 were faded initials: MV, RS, BT, their sex a circled M or W. Age was a blank filled in with a number 2 pencil. The youngest was eighteen, the oldest fifty-seven. His father's judgment was always clinical.

Stacked up and tied tight as a month of old newspapers waiting to be recycled, they were heavier than they looked. If that was all there was, he would have closed the lid of the trunk and left it there. But beneath the rating scale that had kick-started his father's career were forty marbleized-black-and-white composition books.

The initials became human as Z read the words used to describe the feelings his father had treated them to over those twelve weeks. SV was a nurse who wrote in loopy script on the twenty-first of

May: "Woke up. Took sugar cube with black coffee. Was hungry, but didn't eat. Surprised everybody at cafeteria by passing up dessert. After putting kids to bed, let my husband fool with me, even though I was having my monthly. Which isn't like me." Four weeks later she had written, "Lost 17 pounds!!! Hooray for me!!!"

The diary that got to Z the most began with an entry printed neatly in block letters with a black fountain pen: "May 13th, 1:30 PM. No Change. Hopelessness^2 = pointlessness^3. Being alive feels like an embarrassment." Z knew the feeling. He flipped to the last page. The final entry read:

> Dear Dr. Friedrich,
>
> I hope that someday I will be in a position to repay you for what you have given me. I am still me, but because of you, that no longer feels like such a bad thing to be.
>
> Yours respectfully,
> Casper Gedsic

Wrapped in a moth-eaten army blanket, he found the two-faced ironwood demon with bone and coral eyes. He did not know it was a fermenting vessel, but he wanted to know more. Untying the knots in the butcher's twine, he shuffled through the tests like a loser looking for the marked cards that had tricked him. He found the psychiatric rating scale initialed CG. The first evaluation was administered on the twelfth of May, the second and last in the second week of September '52.

Even though Z had failed his own introduction to psychology class his freshman year at Yale, he could see that Casper had the lowest score at the start and the highest score by two points at the finish. Born two years to the day after Jack and Winton had died, Z knew that just ten days after scoring off the charts and thanking Dr. Friedrich for changing his life, Casper had repaid him with one and possibly two murders.

What had happened? What had gone wrong? If he was mad,

why didn't he kill the whole family when they were planting tulips?

Z put the notebook in his book bag and returned the rest of the disaster to its box. He was just closing the lid when he saw the manila envelope stuffed inside the sleeve built into the interior of the trunk. It contained tape recordings, spooled on six-inch reels. The only two he cared about were labeled CG sessions. They pertained to him.

Hurrying now, knowing he was running out of time, Z pushed the trunk back into the dark corner where he had found it and carefully reburied it beneath the rubble and discarded furnishings of their lives. Z was not the only one who had some explaining to do. The questions were obvious. Z was not yet sure whether he wanted his father to know how many answers he already had before he asked them.

Z was back downstairs in his parents' den staring at his father's old reel-to-reel tape deck, wondering if he had time to play the tapes back, when a dog barked. Looking out the window, he saw that Fred was a Rhodesian Ridgeback. His parents had taken him for a walk in a four-wheel-drive golf cart Lucy had bought them for Christmas. They were getting out of the cart now, and Fred was pissing on the chrysanthemums.

Z was stuffing the tapes back into his old briefcase when the dog bounded through the front door, snapping and barking. The dog circled him. Z turned his back to the door and kicked at Fred. Friedrich shielded his wife with his body and raised an umbrella as if it were a club. "What the hell are you doing?"

"It's me. I should have called, but—"

"Heel, Fred!" The dog obeyed.

Nora disarmed her husband of the umbrella. "What are you doing here, Zach?"

"There are some things we need to talk about."

His father didn't look at him. His eyes were on the clutter of the dining room table.

"Such as?"

"How about let's start with 'Glad to see you'?"

"What's so important that gives you the right to barge into our home?" His mother spoke for his father.

"The door was open. This is my home. This is where I grew up."

"Zach, you always were good at avoiding answering questions you don't want to answer. But we're old, and I'm sorry you're a drug addict, but it's not our fault. I want an explanation—what do you think we have to talk about?"

His father had put on his glasses and was sorting through the books and stacks of mail on the table. It was then Z noticed the winged bronze brain Zuza had given him so long ago.

"We can start with this." Zach handed her the steamship ticket.

"What did he give you?" Lucy had told him his father's eyesight was failing.

"Nothing." Nora folded the ticket neatly and slipped it into the waistband of her skirt.

"Is there anything else?"

Z winced and cocked his head like a dog that doesn't know why it's just been kicked by its master. Before he could retaliate, his father pointed his finger at the table. "There was three hundred dollars for the gardener on that table when we left."

Z reeled back. His mother wiped away a tear. "How can you do this to us?"

"You think I came here to steal from you?"

"Besides the fact that writing someone a bad check is a form of thievery, I think you're a drug addict who won't get treatment."

Z pointed to his father's feet. "Open your eyes." Three one hundred dollar bills were on the floor. "You owe me more than an apology."

Friedrich stepped back as Z reached for the table. Son and father were frightened of one another. Z picked up the bronze. "What are you doing?" For an instant Friedrich thought the boy was going to strike him.

"Taking what's mine."

Z was out the door when his mother called after him, "Are you coming to the party?"

"I wouldn't miss it for the world."

Z called Lucy from the train station down in the village. He apologized for borrowing Leila's bike without permission and told her where he had parked it. His sister had been worried, coming home from school, finding him gone. "You haven't had a slip, have you?"

"Not the kind you mean. I went to see Mom and Dad. It felt good, actually. Angry, but good."

"How'd it go?"

"As well as could be expected."

"That bad?"

"Let's just say it was a mixed message." He leafed through Casper's diary as he talked to her from the phone booth.

"You sound sad."

"Thoughtful." He knew what he had to do, but had no idea how he could do it.

"What are you doing, Z?"

"I'm not sure, but it feels right." The New York train was pulling into the station. "I've gotta go."

Lazlo had an office. He had several, in fact. New York, London, L.A., Tokyo. But over the last few years, since he'd turned sixty, he saw less and less reason to go to them; like the Friedrichs, he preferred the desk in the bedroom. He was there now, 4:07 in the afternoon, and still in his Sulka pajamas. He had just put on an overcoat over his robe. The sun was shining, but he felt cold.

Computer screens glowed on his desktop. The New York Stock Exchange was closed for the day. It was already tomorrow in Japan, but the markets weren't open yet. Lazlo's success was due to the fact that he was uniquely comfortable assuming financial positions of great risk. Gambling was his antidote to the anxiety of success. Lazlo never worried except when things went well, for he knew that could not last.

He still lived in the house on Horatio Street in Greenwich Village. When he began his ascent, his life had been sex first, work a distant second. Over the years, more work and less sex. He still had girlfriends, but now instead of breaking it off when he began to fall in love and blaming the impossibly young women he courted for fulfilling his addiction to disappointment, he thanked them and said good-bye by sending them to college or graduate school, or giving them money to fly home and marry their high school sweethearts.

Lazlo still liked to gamble, but he had so much (or so little, depending on how you looked at it) that it was hard to tell if he was winning or losing. Lazlo lit a fresh cigarette off the one in his lips, called Chicago, and bought some futures.

Remembering it was Monday, he thought of *Monday Night Football,* hung up in the middle of the trade, and called his bookie. "Who is playing who?" His accent, like his stomach, had gotten larger over the years.

"Eagles, at home against the Giants." Lazlo never bothered to learn the rules of the game. It was more fun to watch that way.

"Give me two dimes on the Giants at plus seven and a nickel on the over."

"That's it?"

Lazlo wanted more action. "I want a dime on the coin toss. I say 'heads.'"

"We only take bets on the coin toss in the Super Bowl."

"Fuck you, let's bet."

"Against the rules, Lazlo." His bookie was just a phone number and a voice. They had never met.

"What rules? You're a bookie. Are the bookie police going to come and arrest you? Take my money on coin toss." Lazlo didn't like rules.

When the bookie answered, "Fuck you, too," and hung up, Lazlo was left unsure what he had wagered. Lazlo liked having somebody to root for.

The doorbell rang. The maid was out. He looked over at the small screen of his security system and saw Zach Friedrich standing on his doorstep. The fish-eye lens distorted his godson's face into a goblin's. He had not seen Z in over a year.

Lazlo pushed "speak" and laughed. "You look like shit." When he had had dinner with the Friedrichs two weeks ago, no mention had been made of Z.

"Thanks, Lazlo."

"I'll be right down." Lazlo put on a suit and tie. He did not want the world to know he was in the habit of loitering the day away in his jammies.

The door opened. Lazlo greeted Z with the hug he had hoped to get from his father. But their reunion wasn't out of a storybook. Lazlo broke the embrace quickly and let Z know where he stood. "I quit, you know."

The aging captain of industry had been a major blow fiend for years. He had diluted it and put it in the Dristan bottles he was always spraying up his nose. The last time he and Z had seen each other, they had snorted a few dry grams of blow while watching the ladies' finals of the U.S. Open on TV.

"Me, too." Lazlo smiled and gestured for him to come in. It was both a relief and a burden for Z to be taken at his word. Except for a couple of museum-quality paintings Willy had helped Lazlo buy at auction, the decor was still *Playboy After Dark*. The early Hugh Hefner look now seemed quaint rather than titillating.

Z put down his briefcase and perched nervously on a stool at the Lucite bar. The bottles still appeared to float in thin air, but he no longer felt the urge to spin himself around on the bar stool. He already felt dizzy.

Lazlo opened a glass door and took out a bottle of Montrachet Ramonet, chilled to thirteen degrees Celsius. "Drink?"

Z shook his head no, wondering if Lazlo was testing him.

Lazlo poured himself a glass. "So tell me, do you miss cocaine?"

"No."

"That's good . . . I do. People seem more interesting, likable, when you're high. The fucking is better now. I could never get it up, could you?"

"Sometimes."

"But the talk afterward is not so good." Lazlo stamped out his cigarette and rummaged through a drawer for a fresh pack. "Cigarettes taste better, too, when you're high."

Z came to the point. "I need help."

Lazlo's smile hid his disappointment. Money. If people didn't want to borrow it, they wanted to talk about it. "Cash or check?"

Lazlo pulled out his wallet. Friedrich had told him more than once, "If he comes to you, don't help him. He's got to touch bottom." Having spent a lifetime there, Lazlo did not agree.

Z shook his head no.

"Name something and it's yours."

Z reached into the briefcase of his youth and pulled out Casper's diary and the tapes. "I want you to tell me about Casper Gedsic."

"How much do you know?"

It had never occurred to Z that Lazlo might not tell him the truth.

Lazlo chain-smoked as he read the diary. When he got to the last page, he snorted like he'd just done a line of bad blow. "It would appear Casper, like your father, thought the drug worked."

"What was it?"

"Never told me. Probably thought I'd take it."

"Did you ever meet Casper?"

"No. Your father is, was, very discreet, very professional. He never said a word about it until the killings. Then we talked."

"What'd he say?"

"He blamed himself."

"Was it the drug?"

Lazlo shrugged. "Casper was fucking crazy before he took it.

Worst kind of crazy: smart crazy. Your mother still can't forgive herself for stopping him from jumping off that cliff."

There was no mention of that in the diaries. Lazlo filled him in on what had happened at Sleeping Giant, and then added, waving his cigarette in the air like a wand, "Crazy before he took the drug, crazy again after he stopped. Look what he did to you."

"All Casper did to me was teach me how to swim."

"If the bastard just shot Winton, I could say maybe, perhaps. He's a victim. He didn't like what the drug did to him so he killed one of the doctors that gave it to him. But killing the baby . . . for that the motherfucker does not deserve to live."

"I don't think he killed Jack."

"How come?"

"If he wanted to murder the children, he would have shot everybody on the front lawn before he went to the Wintons. It doesn't make sense."

"You know, the war, the Nazis, taught me one thing. Trying to make sense out of what crazy, sick motherfuckers do only makes you crazy."

Lazlo still had the old reel-to-reel tape deck that used to come on automatically and play Sinatra when he dimmed the lights. They ate Chinese takeout as they listened to the tape recordings of his father's weekly meetings with Casper.

As they played back those afternoons from the summer of '52, his father and Casper's disembodied voices came alive. Z closed his eyes and listened. It was as if Casper and Friedrich were in the room with them. His father sounded young, Casper even younger. Z was surprised how much his father knew about Casper, how much Casper felt comfortable revealing to him. Z was jealous.

It was after midnight when they heard the last of the tapes. He felt like he knew everything and nothing about the doctor-patient relationship that had spawned him. And yet, Casper and his father were more human than ever.

They sat in silence as the end of the tape clicked around the spool. Lazlo spoke first. "Is strange, one minute your father seems to like the son of a bitch, and the next minute—"

"That's the way it is with Dad."

"That's the way it is with all fathers."

Christmas came early for the Friedrichs. He was out walking Fred when the news came. It had snowed the night before, crystalline flakes that thawed and froze again.

Friedrich's wife was taking advantage of this rare moment of solitude to bring some order to her husband's side of the desk. The private chaos of his methodology was spilling over onto the floor, encroaching on the order she struggled to maintain in her half of the life they coinhabited. She had to be careful, tidy up in ways he wouldn't notice, or he'd blame her for what he could not find.

She smiled at the memory of all the times she'd heard him bellow, "Nora, for the love of God: Why can't you just leave things as I've left them?"

When the phone rang, she was looking for page twenty-seven of the appendix of the new version of his old book on depression. She was going to let it ring through to the answering machine when she heard, "Will, Stan Bender here. I've got a proposition for you, and I'm not going to take 'no' for an answer. We need you for this."

They'd known Stan for years. He'd been a graduate student of Friedrich's. Not the best student, but a go-getter. More important, he was vice president in charge of research and development at one of the pharmaceutical giants. "Stan, we were just thinking about you the other day." What she had been thinking was that it had been five years since they had needed her husband.

Stan didn't go into specifics. "I'll explain everything over lunch." Stan suggested the Four Seasons on the twentieth and volunteered to send a car. No question, they needed her husband. Nora checked the calendar and said yes for Friedrich, and asked after Stan's wife.

She greeted Friedrich at the door with a hug and a kiss and told him the good news. Friedrich took it with a grumpy shrug. "I wonder whose mess they want me to clean up."

Nora was impatient with him. "For God's sake, cheer up. How many men your age do you know who still get calls like that? The Four Seasons, a limousine?"

"It'll be a Town Car." Friedrich feigned indifference, but she could tell his batteries were recharged by the idea that he was still the only man for the job. "Let's knock off an hour or two of work before lunch."

Throwing Fred his plastic bone, Friedrich took her by the hand and they climbed the stairs together. She was just about to sit down at the typewriter when she felt his arms close around her and the fingers of his right hand on her breast.

"I thought we had work to do."

"We do." His eyesight was getting worse. He had trouble unsnapping her brassiere. They made them differently now. As she helped them undress, she looked into the clouded gray of his eyes and wondered how he saw her. It had been a long time since they had been like this. It still felt good to be alive.

"I told you so." Friedrich peered out the window on the morning of the twentieth. It was, in fact, a Town Car. "Come with me." He'd been trying to talk her into joining him for lunch since breakfast. "I'll take you Christmas shopping after lunch."

"I've done all my shopping." She had bought presents for everyone but Z. She neither knew what he needed, nor how to give it to him.

"We'll buy a present for you."

"It won't be a surprise, then." She was helping him on with his overcoat.

"Come on, Stan will be disappointed not to see you."

"Go on. They want the Lone Ranger, not Tonto." She pushed him gently out the door. The bells on their wreath tinkled.

The ride was uneventful. He read the newspaper with one eye closed. The doctor had diagnosed his problem as glaucoma. He had known the darkness was closing in for some time.

The right half of the Four Seasons was a blur. His narrowing vision detracted from the pleasure of being shown to a power table. Stan was waiting.

They started with littlenecks and small talk. "Did you hear they're doing a book on Dr. Petersen?"

Friedrich had not thought of the dead Freudian for years. Now that he did, he realized Petersen was seventy-two when a stroke pulled the plug on him. Friedrich was wondering how long he had left when he responded, "What an incredibly good idea for a boring book." Friedrich didn't care if they wrote a book about him when he was dead. He wanted it while he was alive.

Stan laughed. "One can always count on you for the milk of human kindness." Stan was squeezing the lemon now. "I agree about the book, but the graduate student who's writing it is my nephew, so I had to pretend I was interested."

A quiet rage rose up in Friedrich. Nora must have gotten it wrong. All he needs me for is a goddamn quote for his nephew's book on Petersen. Friedrich watched as the waiter took his fish off the bone. "I don't think I have much to contribute to your nephew's tome on Dr. Petersen."

"The book's not important. What I want to talk to you about is the study of yours he found going through Petersen's papers." Friedrich's appetite was replaced by a swell of nausea. He had no memory of turning in their results to Petersen. His write-up wasn't finished. He remembered handing Winton a rough draft. She was wearing gloves, and she had put it into a red leather briefcase that had an alligator snout for a clasp.

As his field of vision closed in on the past, he barely heard what the drug exec was saying. "I was stunned by the results."

"So was I."

"This degree of improvement in seventeen out of twenty subjects who were actually receiving the drug?" Stan had pulled out a copy of the study. "Granted, it was small study, but *gai kau dong* obviously has potential as an antidepressant."

"What?"

"We're interested in working with you on GKD."

Friedrich shook his head no. "The study doesn't give an accurate picture."

Stan sat back in his chair. "Are you trying to tell me the data isn't accurate? That's the reason you never published?"

Friedrich knew he should say yes, swear the results were falsified, blame it on Winton. After all this time, he was still caught between pride and shame. He could not betray that part of himself. "No, the results were as recorded." Stan was happy again. "But the study doesn't give you the whole story."

Stan was cutting into his steak. "It never does. But with you onboard, we can pick up where you left off . . . this could be incredibly beneficial to . . ."

Friedrich held up his hand as if fending off a blow. "Ten days after his last dose of GKD, one of the subjects suffered violent, paranoid delusions, which prompted him to attack Dr. Winton and her husband. She was killed; he lost the use of his legs."

Stan nodded as he chewed the undercooked meat. "I know about Casper Gedsic."

"No, you don't."

"Of course, what I mean is, I appreciate how you must have been shocked by the tragedy. I can understand why you decided to put it aside. But you're being too hard on yourself. According to your notes, Gedsic was a borderline to begin with."

"We didn't call them that then, but I would not have categorized him as such now. More important, he had no history of violence."

"He attempted suicide." Stan had done his homework. "If I recall correctly, you always told us that suicide is an act of aggression."

"It wasn't in his case."

"There are always treatment-resistant individuals with any antidepressant."

"There were other side effects not reflected in the study."

"Such as?"

"Diminished awareness of the feelings of others, narcissism, loss of empathy, delusions of grandeur, social aggression . . ." As Friedrich sounded his warning, he thought of the day Casper spoke pridefully of how he had mastered the applied physics of dishonesty involved in making people at the Wainscot Yacht Club like him, of the circumstances under which he had stolen his best friend's girl who happened to be the ex-governor's granddaughter, of the way he had looked in that tailored suit the day he had given Friedrich his formula for gold.

The smile was still on Stan's face. The man didn't hear what Friedrich was saying. "One of the subjects exhibited half of the characteristics the *DSM* uses to define a sociopath."

"The same could be said about every guy that graduates from Harvard Business School." Stan's smile was now tempered with pity for an old man who doesn't understand that the world has changed. "I think perhaps some of the side effects that may have seemed antisocial to you in 1952 are no longer considered negative qualities."

"The world hasn't changed that much."

"Your data indicates GKD helped make people feel better about themselves, it helped them make the most of their potential. The nurse loses weight and enjoys sex, what's-his-name, the one who was scared of heights, learns how to fly an airplane."

"His name was Bill Taylor, and the next year he was shot down in the Korean War."

"That's hardly the drug's fault. You came up with something that helps people self-realize, focus themselves, forget what they were and how they feel about it and think about what they *can* be, feel what they *want* to feel. I'm telling you, Will, this is a drug for the times we live in. It's not just an antidepressant, it's a prescription for achievement."

"You don't understand. There's a reason it was created by cannibals."

"Let's just explore it."

"I don't want it developed."

"I'm sorry you feel that way." Stan pushed his plate away from him. He'd only eaten the choicest parts of the steak. "I was looking forward to us doing great things together. But, and I wish there was a gentler way to put this, if you really felt that way, you should have patented it."

Stan shook Friedrich's hand on the sidewalk outside of the restaurant and wished him luck. Friedrich did not do the same. The chauffeur opened the car door for him. He got in wondering where he was going.

Holiday traffic blocked the cross streets to the Lincoln Tunnel. When the driver turned down Fifth to make his way to the Holland, Friedrich asked, "Is there time for me to stop?"

The driver double-parked on Horatio Street. Lazlo had told him Z was staying with him. Friedrich rang the bell. When he got no response, he pounded on the door so hard his knuckle split. Tilting his head back, he called, "Zach, open up, it's me."

No one answered his call for help. Friedrich got back in the car, blood dripping from the knuckles of his right hand. The drug he took for his heart had made his blood too thin to clot. Friedrich stared out the car window past his own reflection. The world was a blur. A shadow carrying a Christmas tree floated by him on the pavement. He did not see that it was Z.

BOOK IV

MARCH 1994

Friedrich survived the birthday party. In the end, there was even dancing. He was now four weeks from turning seventy-six, and there'd be another party he didn't want. Glaucoma continued to lower the curtain on his right eye. He still hadn't gone in for laser surgery. He'd read the literature. They said it was effective 98 percent of the time. As he told Nora, "I damn well guarantee you the 2 percent who wake up blind wish they still had glaucoma."

He was alone at his side of the big double desk in their hayloft bedroom/office. Nora was out running errands. He'd just gotten off the phone with a psychiatrist out at Washington University medical school in St. Louis. They'd spent thirty minutes talking about teenage suicides and Prozac. They discussed risk factors and statistical anomalies the way he imagined weathermen debated whether or not a circling air mass mandated a hurricane warning.

Though he had retired professor emeritus from the university, he still consulted for drug companies. As an elder statesman of pharmacology, a genuine trailblazer turned hired gun in the pioneer days of psychoactive drugs, Dr. Friedrich's seal of approval was invaluable. And even if he didn't approve, just having paid for his dissenting opinion made it appear as though due diligence had been done.

Friedrich looked out the window and waited for their new Volvo with Nora in it to round the bend of the road that curved out of town and snaked its way up their hill. The village had grown suburban. A new development of three-acre McMansions crowded his view. The tunnel vision of his glaucoma was a blessing in that regard. If he fixed his squint due west on the church steeple that peaked just over the pale green of the spring hillside where their river plunged into a gorge, he could pretend that his universe was all as it had been twenty-seven years ago when they first moved into the barn they called home.

But then he connected the steeple to the church beneath it, and he'd remember Fiona's marriage to the chickenshit, and Lucy flying in pregnant and beautiful, which he still regretted failing to tell her. There was much he regretted not telling Nigel as well.

Then he began to think of Zach. Yes, he should have told him more about Casper. He should have told them all. But once you weave the lie into the fabric of your life, how do you remove its tangle and still have anything to hold onto?

And then, lastly, he'd think about Willy, who he'd always felt he'd ignored, which in turn would lead Friedrich to ponder, *Perhaps that's why he's happiest of the bunch.*

Finally, on this spring morning, as was always the case when he looked out from his barn at the narrowing horizon and followed the chain of events that had led him to this point in time in regret, Friedrich cursed himself aloud. "Christ, Friedrich, you're thinking like an old man."

In fact, except for his eyes, Friedrich was in remarkable shape for a man who'd endured the planet over seventy years. Sunblock had kept his face free of age spots. His hair was silver and combed straight back, and he prided himself on still being able to wear suits that he'd bought thirty years ago, and never went anywhere without a tie. He looked polished rather than old.

The barbells and Royal Canadian Air Force exercises had kept his body lean enough to have a BMI of twenty-four. He could still bench-press 150 pounds. He checked his blood pressure twice daily with his own pressure cuff, breakfasted on a milkshake of brewer's yeast, seaweed, megavitamins, and powdered skim milk, and had not eaten ice cream in over a decade.

As long as he continued to thin his blood with rat poison (10 mg of Coumadin) daily and kept his heart rate regular with 5 mg of Lanoxin every morning, he could feel reasonably confident he wouldn't go brain dead from a stroke or heart attack for another ten years. Death did not frighten him half as much as stupidity.

Whenever a new intelligence test came out, he took it. Nora laughed at her husband for this, but it cheered him up that he still scored in the ninety-ninth percentile. He wasn't quite as quick with the answers, especially the math, as he once had been. But when Friedrich wasn't distracted he could still do a standard deviational analysis in his head.

Sometimes when he was feeling low, on days like this when Nora took longer than she'd said to come back from shopping, he'd work the numbers through his brain just to make sure it hadn't frozen up on him while he wasn't looking.

Though his hairline had retreated to the back of his skull, he still had his prostate. He could still perform. He still had work to do, and the possibility that his best work was yet to come filled him with a restless dissatisfaction that he still mistook for hope.

The pharmaceutical industry had boomed. His stockbroker, a young woman named Shirley, called him regularly to ask his opinion about new products that were in the pipeline, drugs that showed the promise of profit. He enjoyed talking to her because she had a Midwestern accent and a flat nasal voice that reminded him of the girl who'd sat next to him in fourth grade and died of spinal meningitis over Christmas vacation. He had a few million dollars worth of Sandoz and Merck and Hoffmann–La Roche and the like in his portfolio now. Back in the days when he was driving the White Whale through the streets of Hamden, he would have called himself rich.

But Friedrich did not feel rich this day. It didn't seem like he had much to show, not given the compromises and sacrifices and hours they had spent shackled to the desk whose veneer he was now picking at with a letter opener. And as he noted the need for getting it fixed, and all the trouble and time it would take to remove a lifetime of work from its drawers and file cabinets, the thought occurred to Friedrich that they had indeed been shackled, prisoners all these years, serving life sentences imposed on themselves, by themselves, with no chance of appeal or hope of pardon. It was then that Dr. Friedrich remembered that their new Volvo had a car phone, and that he could call his wife on it.

Unlike most of his generation, those that had come of age in the Great Depression, Friedrich was comfortable and adept with computers. He had worked with them since the fifties. His grandchildren came to him when programs malfunctioned, screens froze, and homework was eaten by hard drives. But mobile phones did not compute, and dated him.

He dialed Nora and got a recording. "Your service provider is not available in this area." He dialed again. Busy. The same hill that protected his view made it impossible to reach Nora when he needed to talk to her. He'd say he wanted to remind her to pick up a bottle of vermouth and a spare cartridge for the printer. But mostly he just needed to hear her voice to know he was not alone in the prison of the fortress they had constructed.

He was about to punch redial, another bit of nineties technology he'd forgotten he had, but then thought better of it as he fantasized Nora reaching for the car phone's ring while going round a corner and taking her eyes off the road to speak to him, cradling the receiver to the cheek he'd just kissed an hour ago, drifting lanes as she answered with "Yes, dear, I remembered the vermouth, and the toner," just before she ran head-on into a semi or a deer or a dump truck.

Friedrich mocked himself for clinging to the childish fantasy that imagining the worst would decrease the statistical probability of it actually happening. Life had taught him the world didn't work that way.

Friedrich was just checking his pillbox to make sure he had remembered to take his Coumadin and Dig that morning, as opposed to thinking he had remembered to take them, when he heard Nora's voice calling to him, "Will . . . Will."

He walked out onto the balcony and called out to her grumpily "What took you so long?"

Gray looked up at him. "Will?" The parrot mimicked Nora's voice perfectly. It was not the first time the aging African gray had tricked him that way.

The bird had seen it all. Except for the talons of his right foot being eaten by a fan, Gray looked just as he had when Friedrich had mistaken him for a hallucination perched in his mulberry tree. Then and now, Gray was an uncooperative witness. The thought that a bird would outlive him used to amuse Friedrich. Now it just pissed him off.

Friedrich slammed the balcony door as the parrot laughed at him. Friedrich opened the stereo and removed the CD titled *Learn to Dance at Home*. The numbered steps of a foxtrot were rolled out on a mat on the floor. After nearly a half century of marriage, Friedrich was finally so bored he was willing to learn how to dance.

He replaced the instruction CD with Billie Holiday. He preferred vinyl, missed the scratches on his old records. He tried not to think more old man thoughts, but it was impossible. Closing the door on Gray and turning up the volume of a stereo remix of Billie's sadness made it seem fresher than it had when he'd first heard her back in '39. But that didn't change the fact that in less than a month he'd be seventy-six years old.

He told his wife and children he did not, under any circumstances, want another party. He said he saw no reason to celebrate old age. He'd said the same thing last year, but they wouldn't listen . . . they never did.

Friedrich tried to change his perspective on this day by sitting in his wife's chair. But looking across the big desk they had shared, gazing on his empty seat, just made him think of the day when he'd vacate his place on the planet permanently.

He knew he was feeling sorry for himself. If Nora weren't dawdling on the way home from the office supply store, or hadn't turned back to get the vermouth, or worse, stopped in at

Lucy's down the road to talk about *my goddamn birthday,* she would have been there to pull him out of his spiraling funk, to say "Enough dillydallying, we've got work to do, a speech to write, a chapter to compose."

"Wiiiiiill?" He heard her calling now, stretching out his name into a shriek; he knew it sounded too much like her to be anything but the parrot he should have gotten rid of years ago. Friedrich reached for the remote and turned up Billie Holiday's call for emotional rescue.

The clutter of his desk was pinned down with a dozen paperweights, giant pills in Lucite, miracle drugs cast in Plexiglas to commemorate the millionth prescription, sales figures that made stocks split and dividends double. These trophies to his alchemy were lined up like chess pieces in a game played to a draw. Perhaps they had done some good, distanced a few hundred thousand unhappy souls far enough from their feelings to avoid getting fired from their jobs, or walking out on their children, or jumping into the paths of oncoming trains, and cars, and lives unlived. Yes, maybe he'd helped them feign a memory of happiness, kept them from being devoured by their guilt and shame. But then again, what were people to feel when they did things they should feel guilty or ashamed of? Synthetic joy?

There had been no miracle cures. Wonder drugs for the mind came and went out of style like the hemlines of ladies' skirts and the width of men's ties. Ultimately, they were remembered as ill advised as last year's fashions. Friedrich still read the latest literature; his advice and support were sought out and courted by young men and women with new pharmaceutical axes to take to market. Friedrich was tuned in, but had dropped out years ago.

MRIs, CAT scans, dye injections of radioactive tracers into the brain that showed thought mass and move across the mind like an advancing army were all promising. But sitting at his desk that morning, waiting for Nora to come home, listening to the parrot who had witnessed his fall from grace, calling out in the voice of his flesh and blood addiction, his ball and chain, his partner in crime, his wife, "Will . . . Will . . . ," Dr. Friedrich knew he and his kind were forty years away from having the hardware to understand how to rechannel thought to that uncharted beach in the brain called happiness.

If he were twenty-one in 2021, he would make a difference, he'd have a chance to be great then. Everything he touched and loved would have been better off if he just had more time. Friedrich knew these were old man thoughts, but he could not help himself. He *was* an old man.

The sun was behind a cloud now. He could see its shadow rolling up the hillside toward him. Rain was on its way. If the weather had been different, if Gray hadn't been calling up to him from the past, he would have gotten up, brought out the barbells, gone for a walk. This was not a Sock Moment, this was age-related depression. He knew how to fight it, raise the blood sugar, get the body moving, reach out to another human being. Instead, he stared straight ahead at the photos Nora kept on her side of the desk and made himself feel worse.

There was an eight by ten framed in malachite of Lucy surrounded by her five adopted children. No two were the same color. Black, brown, the color of unfired clay, the white of phosphorous—he called them Lucy's Rainbow Coalition. Friedrich wished Lucy had had children of her own, in part because he was soothed by the thought of his own DNA twirling into the future. But also for its therapeutic value.

Lucy had been in the eighth month of her pregnancy when she and Nigel went to surf the break in Rincón, Puerto Rico. The car they had rented at the airport was supposed to have a rack for his surfboard. It didn't. Nigel sat in the backseat and held the surfboard steady while she drove, nose end out one window of the car, fin end out the other. It wasn't Lucy's fault. She was driving carefully. A minibus passed her on the right, just clipping the nose of the board. The rental car plowed into a ditch. Nigel was basically decapitated by his surfboard at the third cervical vertebra, and the baby was stillborn while Lucy was trapped in the front seat.

Friedrich realized Nigel wasn't the bastard he had thought when his will was read and she had inherited all that money. That

Lucy had chosen not to tell him Nigel was rich, that she had let him think the father of her dead child was a worthless surf bum bastard right through the funeral was, in Dr. Friedrich's mind, cruel and unusual and deserved punishment. Yes, Nora was probably having coffee with Lucy right now, talking about the party he didn't deserve.

Billie was singing *Stormy Weather* now, and Friedrich was holding a small, tarnished silver frame with a photo of Homer and his mother back when they lived on Harrison Street. They died within three weeks of each other, in the summer of '84. Heart disease.

Softly touching Homer's cheek with his forefinger, Friedrich made a mental note to polish the frame. A glance at Nora's desktop pic of Fiona and Michael and the twins, a boy and a girl. Just as Ida had predicted, one was dark, one was fair, and both were born fat. The boy had red hair Ida would have envied, the girl had recently developed an eating disorder. The picture had been taken at last year's Emmy Awards.

The chickenshit lawyer was a big-shot producer now. His unwatchable TV show had won its third Emmy. It was a good photograph. The children were handsome, Fiona looked glamorous, and Michael held the Emmy with the disparaging grin of a man who thinks he deserves an Oscar. Just behind him and Fiona was the gap-toothed smile of Ben the Bottom.

Lucy had not forgiven her father for being wrong, and Fiona could not forgive him for being right. Friedrich did not feel like a man who was batting five hundred. His daughters invited him to his grandchildren's birthday parties, and school plays, and Christmas pageants, and soccer games. When he went, they treated him like a trespasser. And when he stayed away and let Nora carry the flag, they complained that he didn't care.

Friedrich cared. He loved them all, adopted and blood, but not alike, for he did not believe any two loves were the same. Yet when he looked at his grandchildren smiling back at him from the photographs on Nora's side of the desk, his own neurotransmitters did not send him the warm, fuzzy feelings he knew grandparents were supposed to be prone to.

Try as he might to well up pride or sentimental tears, the glaucoma of his clinical eye would only permit him to see side effects. Of his seven grandchildren, five were on Ritalin. His daughters said it helped them do well at school. One of them snorted it. Fiona's boy, who was diagnosed ADD, was on Ativan. And Lulu, sixteen now, who had the best brain of the bunch and had gotten a perfect score on her math PSAT and beat him in chess when she was ten, was on Haldol and had gained twenty pounds. Lucy had said puberty was "particularly hard" on her. Friedrich told himself they were strangers to him because they were strangers to themselves.

Friedrich muttered aloud to himself. "Christ, *life's* hard."

Friedrich wondered how his wife could bear to look at the snapshots of life gone wrong day after day. He wanted to sweep them off the desk, throw them in the garbage. But each was true. And as hard as they were to face, he could not look away.

After the disappointment his daughters reflected back at him, the photograph of Willy was a relief. It was taken last year. Willy's hair was almost as gray as his own. He's sitting somewhere—hotel? apartment? café?—pointing something out in the newspaper to his friend Henry. It makes them both smile, not so much because it's funny but because they see it the same way. Henry is a neurologist. Friedrich likes him, and would have liked him even if he were not his son's lover, but likes him more because of it.

Friedrich opened the drawer on his wife's side of the desk and took out her phone book. He would call Henry at the hospital. Willy was traveling. Talking to Henry was always a tonic. He was doing research on the temporal lobe, on that part of the brain where religious fanaticism and violence lived side by side. Fifteen minutes of listening to Henry's cerebral baritone complain about the bullshit of drumming up funds for research would pull him out of his malaise.

As he dialed Henry's number, it occurred to Friedrich that he used people to alter his mood, and he was turning the idea of people as drugs over in his brain, tilting it in the sunshine of his mind, looking for flaws and possibilities, the way a marooned sailor might examine a useful piece of driftwood washed up on the shore of his deserted island. But the recorded message he received did not provide the fix Friedrich was after. Friedrich, for all his years synthesizing emotion, had a profound misunderstanding of and a deep appreciation for the human factor. The recording told him that Henry was with Willy. He wished he were with them.

Friedrich was putting Nora's phone book back in her desk drawer when he caught sight of Zach's face torn from a magazine. *US? People?* He had not talked to the last of his children since he had accused Zach of stealing three hundred dollars off his dining room table. He had felt bad about that, less so in the few seconds that had passed since he had discovered this photograph Nora had hidden from him.

It showed Zach and a girl of about twenty or twenty-one with very long legs being handcuffed by the police. They're standing next to the Porsche Zach had been driving the wrong way down a one-way street in Los Angeles when he collided with a police car. The girl was the kind of actress they used to call a starlet. The Porsche had to be hers. If Zach had made that kind of money writing in the last year, Nora or Lucy would have told him.

Zach had not come to Friedrich's last birthday party, never called or wrote to explain his absence. Friedrich hadn't wanted the goddamn party, but if he had to suffer through turning seventy-five, the least his youngest son could have done was . . .

Friedrich checked his anger with clinical thought. *Probably the guilt and anxiety of seeing me and so many people who had had such high hopes for him prompted Zach's return to cocaine. That is, if he ever really gave it up in the first place.* He had told Nora she shouldn't get her hopes up about Zach's staying clean. Though the literature indicated 35 percent of cocaine addicts who undergo rehabilitation stay off it for life, Friedrich knew statistics were used mostly to give people false hope. *A case like Zach has at best a one in ten chance of making a life. Just because the truth is depressing doesn't mean it should be ignored.*

Friedrich rummaged the drawer for a magnifying glass to get a closer look at the wreckage. The article described Zach as a "screenwriter/novelist." He had been one once. The magazine said Z had 0.73 gm of cocaine in his possession. Misdemeanor? Friedrich reasoned it was a good thing his son hadn't rebuilt his career, made any more money writing. If he had, Zach probably would have been arrested for a quantity that would have netted him a felony.

Friedrich peered through the lens of the magnifier like a Victorian detective. The starlet looked scared and had one hand up to hide her face. Zach was smiling for the camera. His hair was greasy, he looked like he had needed a shave two days ago. He was twenty pounds overweight, but it didn't show. Cameras, at least, were kind to his youngest son.

Friedrich knew enough about showbiz to know the picture of his son's decline and fall would not have made the glossies if he had been arrested by himself. Zach was described as a "once promising writer." They misspelled "Friedrich."

Michael had written by hand across the page, "You better warn Dad." Nora had neither warned him nor told him, just buried it.

When Friedrich checked the date of the magazine and discovered it was over two years old, he felt tricked. He wondered what else his wife hadn't told him. Yes, he was wrong to jump to the conclusion that the article was recent, but that didn't mean he was wrong. Chances were, Zach had gone back to drugs. No question, the statistics supported Friedrich's lack of faith.

But the fact that he could not be certain about his son's fate, that he didn't know for sure why Zach hadn't come to his goddamn birthday, that he hadn't a clue where his boy was, both irked and bothered Friedrich. Whose pool house was he hiding in now? Was he alive? Dead? In jail? No, Nora wouldn't have kept that from him. The most troubling possibility of all was that Z was clean and sober and happy and denying his father the pleasure of knowing it.

Friedrich muttered aloud, "I could still help him, if only he'd . . ." Friedrich didn't like it when he talked to himself.

He put the clipping back where Nora had hidden it and slammed the drawer shut. An invitation for a psychiatric symposium in Iceland fell to the floor. It had been propped against a framed photo of Zach that was easier to look at. Michael had snapped it fourteen years ago at the publishing party for his first and only novel. Friedrich is standing next to Zach, his arm is around his son's shoulder. Friedrich fought the urge to dwell on how much better he looked at sixty-two than he did closing on seventy-six, and focused his magnified gaze on his son.

When that picture was taken, he and everybody else thought Zach was in the fast lane to something special. On his way to a success his father could both admire and envy, for he was not in a position to pull any strings to ease his son's way into the literary world. "Zach's done it all himself" was what he liked to say back then.

Now that he looked closely at the pretty picture, he could see the faint white alkaloid caked in his son's nostrils, the sweaty smile, the glassy mistrust in his son's eye, not just of his "success" but of himself. Friedrich wasn't wrong to think he should have known his son was self-medicating, anaesthetising himself for the surgery of life. Friedrich didn't know if Zach was a case of too much too soon, or not enough too late, but he was certain his boy was damaged long before the shutter clicked on that moment of their lives.

Billie Holiday had finished her last song. "Will . . . Will . . ." In the quiet of the room, the parrot haunted him with Nora's distant call for help.

The sky had cleared; the sun was shining now. Feeling misled and betrayed by life, Friedrich told himself he'd feel better if he ate something, and went downstairs to the kitchen.

Friedrich opened the refrigerator, intending to make an egg-white omelet. Gray stood outside the sliding glass door, hopping on his one good leg and ruffling his feathers. "Will . . ." He heard Nora call, but Gray's beak was preoccupied with a pumpkin seed. "Will . . . help!"

Nora lay sprawled facedown on the stone steps that led down

from the driveway. Her groceries were scattered around her. A roll of toilet paper on the lawn, a broken bottle of vermouth by her head, some frozen peas . . .

She had fallen more than an hour ago. When he ran to her side and tried to help her up, she screamed out in pain. "Don't!" she wailed.

Friedrich started to take inventory of the damage. Her nose was bloodied. She could move her left leg. At least she wasn't paralyzed.

"Did you faint?" He was thinking heart attack.

"Goddamnit, I slipped on a slug."

"What do you think's wrong?"

"Something's broken." His wife's diagnosis was correct, but incomplete.

Sirens wailed an anxiety-producing duet. Friedrich watched the flashing lights of a police car that led an ambulance up the hill and down his drive. As the first-aid squad lifted her onto the stretcher, Nora winced, then exhaled a long, brittle, staccato moan that made Friedrich think of the timbers of a ship getting ready to snap as it's driven up onto the rock by a storm.

Trying to concentrate on the wreck at hand, not the one his imagination was serving up inside his head to distract him, Friedrich focused on what was being done to his wife. A blanket was being tucked around her, the straps of the stretcher buckled tight: shrouded like that, she looked as fragile and old as a mummy he had once seen in a museum in Zagreb.

The cop was making notes in his logbook. "What happened?"

"She fell."

"How?" He said it like he thought somebody had pushed her, like he was responsible.

"She lost her footing." They were rolling Nora up the path toward the ambulance now. Friedrich watched the boots of the

EMS crew trample a row of tulips that would have blossomed pink in a day or two. The gnarled root of a sugar maple jostled the gurney.

Nora threw her head back and closed her eyes to the pain. "Christ."

Friedrich barked, "Give her two milligrams of morphine."

"Are you a doctor?"

"Yes."

Nora opened her eyes. "You're a psychologist, for God's sake."

"I can see you're in pain."

"Hold my hand; don't play doctor."

As he watched them lift her back into the ambulance, he suddenly felt as if he *had* pushed her. "As soon as the doc in the emergency room checks her out, they'll give her something."

Friedrich climbed into the back of the ambulance after the stretcher.

"I'm sorry, sir, you'll have to get out."

When Friedrich didn't move, the other EMS guy said, "It's the law; no one but the patient and medical staff are allowed in an ambulance."

"I'm not leaving her alone." Friedrich used his calm voice on them, but in the back of his brain, the panicky thought had taken hold that if they became separated, if he got out and let them close that door, she would die on him. Nora pulled her hand away when he finally tried to take it.

"He never listens. Just drive."

"Why are you angry at me?" The ambulance was moving now.

Pain and embarrassment reduced her voice to whisper. "I lay there an hour calling for you."

"I thought you were the parrot. It was an honest mistake."

Nora closed her eyes. "You don't know much about people."

An hour and a half later, Nora was in a hospital bed down the hall from the emergency room of Morristown Memorial. A hundred milligrams of Demerol had numbed her nervous system, but she still felt like she was in pain. She wondered where the hurt was coming from as Friedrich took out his reading glasses to peer at the X-ray the surgeon was holding up to the light. Was she imagining it? Was it a residue of the shock of her fall? Or was it simply, now that her body was numb, her mind was able to focus on what had always been there?

Her right femur was fractured. The surgeon wanted to operate before the swelling got any worse. "Get in and get out" was how he put it.

Nora could tell her husband didn't like the surgeon; he was young and had a ponytail. Worse, the young doctor gently pulled the X-rays out of Friedrich's hands. "Mrs. Friedrich, you have options. But in my opinion, you should take advantage of this opportunity and—"

Friedrich stepped between his wife and the surgeon. "Excuse me, if I could have a word alone with my wife."

The surgeon took a step back. When Friedrich saw he wasn't going to leave the room, he bent close to Nora's ear and whispered, "I've made arrangements for you to see a specialist in New York, Hospital for Special Surgery."

"I have a broken hip. How am I going to get to New York?"

"Helicopter."

"No. I like him."

"If he was any good, he'd be practicing in the city."

Nora peered out from behind her husband. "We're finished now. What were you saying about my options?"

"We could pin the bone together. But if you'll look here . . ."—he held up the X-rays and pointed at the ball in the socket of her hip with his forefinger. He had hands like Zach's—". . . you can see a narrowing of the joint space. There's erosion of the bearing surface of the ball of your femur."

"You mean I'm wearing out."

"Not all of you." Friedrich watched them jealously. "But if you're going to need a hip replacement in five or six years, why not just do it now?"

Friedrich volunteered, "Surgeons always like to cut." The doctor ignored him.

"Where's the consent form?"

Friedrich intercepted the consent form as the doctor was handing it to her.

"What are you doing?"

"I'm trying to fix things while they're still worth fixing. I've read the literature on artificial joints. They wear out in ten to twenty years."

Nora looked at her husband incredulously. "I'll be ninety-five then."

"You'll still be active."

"Unlike you, I don't want to live forever."

"You need another opinion."

"No, I don't."

"Why are you saying that?"

"Because it's my hip, not yours."

Two hours later, a nurse came in and said, "It's time." Friedrich stood in the corner of the room, holding onto his wife's wedding ring and watch, watching as the nurse put a Versad drip in Nora's arm. The nurse started to wheel her toward the operating room, then stopped. "Don't you two want to say good-bye?"

Nora reached out and took her husband's hand. "Lie down. You look tired." She was surprised when he kissed her on the lips. As they rolled her down the corridor, she watched him grow smaller and smaller. He gave her a little wave that made her think of a scared child. She was old, numb, broken, and every bit as scared of hospitals as she had been when her appendix burst at age eight. And yet, even as she felt the lights dimming in her consciousness, she was more worried about her husband than she was about herself. Was that love? Nora went under wondering how such an emotion ever evolved.

While his wife was in surgery, Friedrich fed quarters into a pay phone, trying to reach his children. He had forgotten to bring his address book. It rattled him that he could not remember their phone numbers—first sign of Alzheimer's? Fear? Guilt?

He called information. Fiona's number wasn't listed, Willy's answering machine was full, and Lucy's cook refused to speak English. Down to his last quarter, he called Lazlo. It felt strange and impotent, asking his friend to find his children.

Friedrich bought a Hershey bar from a vending machine with a dollar bill, hoping the lift in blood sugar would make him more optimistic. The chocolate was stale and waxy. He was wondering if it would have tasted sweeter if it still cost a nickel when the surgeon appeared in the waiting room. There was a drop of Nora's blood on the pocket of his scrubs. "The procedure couldn't have gone better. You're wife's doing fine."

A little after seven that evening, the nurse led him into the recovery room. His wife's heartbeat was a green spike on a monitor, her skin was as white and translucent as tracing paper. Her veins showed through purple-blue. "You're still here." The endotracheal tube that had been inserted down her throat had left her hoarse.

"Where else would I go?"

"Home." It hurt her to talk.

"I'll be lonely."

"There are worse things."

Lucy was there when he got back to the waiting room. Willy was landing at Newark Airport, Fiona was picking him up on her way out from the city. Lucy announced Zach was flying in tomorrow. Friedrich responded, "That's great," and got in a cab wondering, was that what he felt or just how he wanted to feel?

On the way home, he mused on the fact that it is hard to know what you think if you don't know what you feel. Or was it the other way around? All he could be sure of was confusion.

As Friedrich climbed into their bed, he realized it was the first time he had ever slept alone in the barn he called home. Having prescribed himself a Scotch, the emptiness was quickly filled by sleep.

Friedrich was in a forest now. He knew it was a dream because he was riding a pony that he had watched being put down when he was thirteen. Even though he had the feeling that something was sneaking up on him, he was enjoying the imagined sensation of riding bareback through the woods of his childhood. He was reining in the imaginary pony when he heard a sound that didn't belong in a forest, some thing, someone, was banging on a door. The sound of footsteps on hardwood floor echoed inside his head.

Friedrich's eyelids snapped open like sprung window shades. He turned on the light and cocked his head and listened to silence. Nothing. Then, just as his hand bumped the lampshade on its way to turn out the light, he heard it again. It was coming from downstairs.

Thinking it was one of his children coming to check on him, he called out their names. "Lucy, Fiona . . . Will." As he called out Zach's name into the darkness below, he considered the possibility that they had come to give him bad news. Had something gone wrong? Blood clot? Stroke? Wrong medication?

He called out, "Who's there?" but no one answered.

Halfway down the stairs, he heard it again. The noise was coming from the backdoor. Lucy had been broken into twice. She had pestered him to get an alarm system.

Quickly turning and heading back up the stairs, Friedrich told himself it was nothing. But then why was he walking on tiptoes? Why was he thinking about his revolver? Why was he now in the closet, opening the handkerchief drawer of his old bureau? He felt for the gun in the darkness. Then he remembered moving it, putting it somewhere the grandchildren wouldn't be able to reach it. Where? Shoebox, top shelf.

The adrenaline rush that accompanied thoughts of armed intrusion had him rummaging through boxes of high heels he'd never seen his wife wear. It took him several minutes, until he opened one where the revolver slept. Pistol in hand, he debated what to do next. He wasn't sure someone was out there, but he was certain it was possible. The worst could always happen. The day had reminded him of that. He felt foolish as he loaded the revolver, though not as foolish as he'd feel if the intruder wasn't a paranoid figment of his imagination and the bullets were still in his closet.

Friedrich slipped out the front door, gun in hand. The grass was wet and cold on his slipperless feet. The garden lights were off and the sky was starless, and even if he hadn't put off having his cataracts removed, he wouldn't have been able to penetrate the shadows that frightened him.

What was out there? He didn't think of Casper until the last moment of the charade. Had he escaped? Would he still come for him? How old was he now? Friedrich hadn't thought of his patient for so long he was almost disappointed to discover the intruder was a garbage can blown over by the wind.

If Nora had been there, Friedrich would have felt foolish. But alone and armed, he was able to laugh out loud.

Friedrich looked at his watch. It was almost three. As he carried the garbage can back to the shed, he heard songbirds overhead. Looking up at the moon, half curtained by clouds, he saw hundreds of them flying north with their song. He had read somewhere that they migrated at night to avoid being preyed on by hawks, navigating their way to safety with instinct and the help of the stars. He recalled being struck by an ornithologist's claim that when the stars that guided them were not visible, they relied on the lights of the world below.

Careful not to slip and fall or shoot himself in the foot, Friedrich went back inside. The revolver was unloaded, put back into the shoebox, and returned to the shelf. Opening the balcony door to the mildness of the night, he turned off his bedside lamp and crawled back into bed, quoting himself with a sigh. "We are complicated creatures."

Waiting for sleep, he looked into the darkness of his room. The doors opened wide to the fragrant damp of spring. Chlorophyll and rot freshening the air put Friedrich in touch with a scent from the past. The dark, earthy smell of the root cellar and of Homer. Closing his eyes to everything but the memory of his long-lost brother, breathing in the darkness of their childhood, Friedrich felt the overpowering urge to cry. He recognized its therapeutic values and was ready to give into it, but his eyes remained dry. Denied the reassurance that he could still weep, Friedrich wondered if there might be a way to prescribe tears.

ACKNOWLEDGMENTS

In the course of writing this book, a great many individuals were exceedingly generous with both their time and their knowledge. I would like to thank the following:

My mother, Sarah Wittenborn, for being so candid and generous with her memories of my father, as both a man and a psychologist.

Donald Klein, MD, for his insights into the pioneer days of psychopharmacology.

Andrew Scull, PhD, for sharing his encyclopedic knowledge of the history of the treatment of mental illness.

Phillip Bisco, PsyD, for his recollections of what it was like to have my father as a professor, and his help in locating out-of-print periodicals.

Gretchen and Jim Johnson, for their spiritual generosity, and the sheds, shacks, and spare rooms they have allowed me to write in over the years.

Angela Praesant, for her wisdom and encouragement.

Ephraim Rosenbaum, for reading countless drafts of this novel over the last two years.

Eric Schorr, for sharing his knowledge of New Haven and Yale.

Sebastian White, PhD, for correcting my physics.

Jennifer Duke, for letting me write in her boathouse.

Richard Wittenborn, MD, for shedding light on both neurological and family questions.

Carole DeSanti, my editor at Viking, for her calm and critical eye and unwavering support.

And most of all, I am indebted to my wife, Kirsten Stoldt Wittenborn, PsyD, for the education she has given me in the subtle sciences of psychology and the human heart.